P9-ELX-211

ROAR

ROAR

Cora Carmack

TOR
TEEN

A TOM DOHERTY ASSOCIATES BOOK

NEW YORK

ROAR

Copyright © 2017 by Cora Carmack

A Tor Teen Book
Published by Tom Doherty Associates
175 Fifth Avenue
New York, NY 10010

www.tor-forge.com

Tor® is a registered trademark of Macmillan Publishing Group, LLC.

The Library of Congress Cataloging-in-Publication Data is available upon request.

ISBN 978-0-7653-8631-1 (hardcover)
ISBN 978-0-7653-9705-8 (international, sold outside the U.S., subject to rights availability)
ISBN 978-0-7653-8633-5 (e-book)

Our books may be purchased in bulk for promotional, educational, or business use. Please contact your local bookseller or the Macmillan Corporate and Premium Sales Department at 1-800-221-7945, extension 5442, or by e-mail at MacmillanSpecialMarkets@macmillan.com.

First U.S. Edition: June 2017
First International Edition: June 2017

Printed in the United States of America

0 9 8 7 6 5 4 3 2 1

For my mother

I kept struggling to find the words to thank you, and the simplest ones seem to be this: I would be nothing without you. I love you.

And for Amy

You were the first to fan the flames of this dream, and it might have died out long ago without you.

PROLOGUE

He had waited for this day for so many years. It had been the thing that kept him alive when all the others had died, that had kept him sane when madness was his only friend. It drove him forward when his life had not seemed worth living.

Revenge, swift and sweet.

He'd turned the skies to fire and ocean waves into weapons. He'd blown winds strong enough to topple walls and dropped twisters from the sky like rain. He'd brought fury and ruin like Caelira had never known, but it was not enough. Revenge had slipped through his grasp this time, but he believed in second chances.

It was time again for tempests to reign, to purge those undeserving of their magic, and start again. This was a war only he could wage.

For the storms of his world were violent, hungry beasts intent on destruction and death and despair. And they called him master.

When the first tribes of Caelira forsook their ancestors in the stars, the goddess Rezna fashioned for herself new children. Children of light and air and water and fire, children whose wrath and sorrow matched her own. And from the heavens, she poured her progeny out upon the land. The skies went dark and the earth trembled, and all of man knew Rezna's rage.

—*The Origin Myths of Caelira*

1

You are lightning made flesh. Colder than falling snow. Unstoppable as the desert sands riding the wind. You are Stormling, Aurora Pavan. Believe it.

Believe it, and others will too.

It was a vow that her mother, Queen Aphra, made her swear on the day she reached twelve years. She had gripped her daughter's shoulders tight, and Rora could still remember the pinch of pain, the furious beat of her heart as she saw how afraid her mother was and learned to be afraid too.

Today that fear had led Aurora Pavan to sign her life away before she ever had the chance to really live it.

As she was primped and prettied like some kind of sacrificial offering, her mind remained stuck on her morning spent in the throne room. She recalled the rasping sound as the treaty was unrolled and the way her fingers suddenly felt too weak to hold a quill. Many days of her sheltered life had been spent writing out ideas and facts and figures for her tutors, yet in that moment, she had struggled to remember the letters of her name. Then she had met her mother's eyes, and those familiar words came to her again.

Colder than falling snow.

That was what Rora had to become as her shaking hand sealed her fate with a scratchy, bleeding line of ink. And now hours later a stranger peered back at her from the looking glass, powdered white so that none of her flaws would show.

Rora's white-blonde hair had been curled and bound up in an elaborate ceremonial headdress that was crowded with jewels, flowers, and four jagged crystals cut like bolts of lightning to mimic her mother's skyfire crown. Headdresses honoring a family's ancestors were an important part of the Pavanian tradition, from the upper echelons of nobility to the poor and working class. They were donned for birth and death and every major life event in between, including betrothals. But this headdress was larger than any Rora had ever seen. It had to be anchored to the thick metal necklace she wore about her collar with embellished fastenings, and it weighed on her nearly as much the events of the night still to come.

The shimmering white powder covering her already pale skin made her look like she'd just emerged from a blizzard. Her ribs were tightly bound in a corset that squeezed and squeezed until it felt like all her organs were in the wrong place. Over that was a heavy, beaded gown whose neckline dipped low, revealing far more cleavage than she had ever shown. The fabric clung to her frame until it fanned out at her knees into a long train, and the color of the dress changed from white to ash gray to glittering black.

Rora looked exactly as her mother had always told her to be— lightning made flesh: blinding white and bright against a dark sky, and the train that pooled around her was the ground, charred black by her impact.

It was stunning. Exquisite, really. Even Rora, who hated dresses of all kinds, could tell that. It was also a lie. Every jewel, every bead painted a picture of someone that wasn't her. But that was the goal for tonight's betrothal celebration . . . to be someone else, to be the perfect Stormling princess. Because if she failed, everything could fall apart.

A creak pierced the room, and every bustling body around her froze. Rora swore that the small sound moved through her bones the same way thunder did when it was close. Then the sinister tingle of storm magic spread over her like a second skin. Her gaze slid to the box her mother had just opened, to the jewels and stones inside that plagued her nightmares.

Stormhearts.

The hearts were not unlike the storms themselves—darkly beautiful but with an air of menace and deadly intent. It was an apt description of her future husband as well.

Slowly the room emptied of attendants and maids and seamstresses until only the queen and Aurora remained, ruler and heir. These Stormhearts had been passed down the Pavan family line for generations, the last remaining remnants of long-dead storms that her ancestors had defeated to gain their magic during the Time of Tempests. Back then, the continent of Caelira was ravaged beyond recognition, and people flocked to the Pavan family stronghold for sanctuary. They pledged service or goods or gold to live near those who had been blessed by the goddess with the ability to challenge the dangers of the sky, those that came to be called Stormlings.

Aurora's ancestors then passed along three things to their descendants—the crown of a newly formed kingdom, the hearts of the storms they had conquered, and the magic that ran through their blood as a result.

Without a Stormheart, a Stormling might have enough magic in their blood to influence small storms of their inherited affinities. But with one of those talismans amplifying their magic, one person could single-handedly bring down a tempest savage enough to wipe whole cities from existence. And tonight, as she and her betrothed were presented to the court, for the first time Aurora would wear the Stormhearts reserved for the heir.

Her mother lifted the first relic from the box, and the hair on Rora's arms stood on end. The air crackled, and she felt far more residual magic standing close to her mother than she ever felt holding the stones herself.

This Stormheart was a cloudy, pearlescent stone and represented skyfire, the strongest of her family's five affinities. When those jagged bolts of white fire streaked down from the sky, dozens all at once, it was her mother who protected the city of Pavan. And now that Aurora had turned eighteen, she would be expected to join in the fight the next time dark clouds rolled over their lands.

"Light in your blood, skyfire bows to you," her mother murmured before settling the stone into the hollow that had been left for it in the center of the ceremonial headdress. Rora shivered, and her mother's eyes darted quickly to hers. Queen Aphra interrupted the ritual to ask, "Did you—?"

There was such hope in her voice that Rora couldn't bring herself to meet the queen's eyes as she shook her head. Frowning, her mother bent to pick up the next Stormheart. This one was a deep ruby, thin and sharp like a shard of glass.

"Fire in your blood, firestorms bow to you."

Firestorms built quickly with little warning, and hot embers fell like hail. They could singe straight through skin; and in the flat, grassy kingdom of Pavan, they could set the land ablaze in a blink. It was said to be the rarest of all affinities. Carefully, the queen slotted the gem into an open space on Rora's necklace. It lay over her sternum with the sharp point coming to rest at the top of her cleavage. Several smaller versions of the crystalline lightning bolts that adorned her headdress fanned across her collarbone on each side of the bloodred Stormheart.

The queen added four more hearts to the ensemble, speaking the words that her father had once spoken to her. A flat blue stone set into a bracelet for thunderstorms. The heart of a windstorm, gray and cylindrical, slid into a socket on a thin silver belt around Rora's waist. A jagged slate-gray piece for fog adorned her other wrist. And last, her mother lifted a silver ring adorned with a small black jewel. It was the only Stormheart in the box that wasn't ancient.

No, this Stormheart was barely twelve years old. Rora's brother, Alaric, had stolen it from a twister that had touched down near the southwestern border of their territory. Stormling families were limited to the affinities they inherited from their original Stormling ancestors, but some believed it possible, though wildly dangerous, to gain a new affinity in the same way the first Stormlings were said to have done— by stealing the heart of a storm and absorbing its magic. At eighteen, Alaric believed he could take down a twister and gain the Pavan family another affinity.

He'd been wrong. He had thrust his hand into the heart of the storm to claim it as his own. And when the battle was almost won, the storm's winds returned the favor, thrusting a tree branch through the heart of the Pavan heir.

The few devout priests in the kingdom who still followed the old gods had claimed it a reminder from the skies not to reach above one's stars. Sometimes Aurora wondered if they weren't still being punished.

The ring did not rouse at the queen's touch, but remained a cold, dead gem as she slipped it onto Rora's finger. It only would have worked for Alaric or his offspring. Rora and her mother pretended it was just a normal ring. Just as Rora always pretended to be something she wasn't. And her mother pretended she wasn't disappointed with her daughter. And that they all wouldn't have been better off if Alaric had lived.

Rora would keep pretending, through the celebrations and the wedding after that. And then her entire life. She would pretend that she did not desperately wish she were better. Different. *More.*

Her mother took her shoulders in that familiar hard grip. "Remember, be confident and controlled. Do not let them intimidate you."

"I won't."

"Do not speak more than you must. Keep a tight rein on your temper lest you—"

"Lest I give myself away. I know, Mother."

The queen paused, the curve of her lips pushing into a frown. "I know this isn't ideal. I wish we had all the time you could want and could wait to find you a love match or at least someone of your choosing."

"But we don't. We are out of time. I understand."

Arranged marriages were rare in Pavanian royal history. Often, rulers chose for love, like her mother and father. Others held contests of skill for young nobles to prove themselves to the heir. But soon the skies would bruise and bleed and howl as the Rage season drew its first breath, and if Aurora was not married by then, her own little kingdom of lies would topple.

"Promise me you will try to find the good in this. To find some happiness," the queen said.

Rora nodded. She didn't have the heart to tell her mother how impossible she thought that was with a man as hard and cold as Cassius Locke, the second son of the Locke kingdom. The Lockes by reputation were cunning, smart, and as vicious as the storms that plagued their city by the sea. If she showed a weakness, she had no doubt they would exploit it. And if they learned exactly what all the jewels and powder and fine fabrics hid? Aurora's last hope to keep her kingdom would unravel.

"Are you ready?" her mother asked.

A small part of Aurora screamed in revolt; she wanted to ask for permission to leave, to disappear into the wildlands and find another life. But the queen had lost enough in this life. Her husband succumbed to a disease that her magic couldn't touch. And her son had captured a storm's heart at the expense of his own. And the only one she had left, her daughter . . . her daughter looked the part of the perfect Stormling princess—so impressive, so ethereal, that no one would ever dare to think the truth.

That she had no storm magic at all.

Aurora's muscles twitched involuntarily as she stood outside the throne room, as if her body might decide to run without her mind's consent. Two of her guards, Taven and Merrin, waited a few steps behind her. They followed her inside, and an eerie silence took hold after the heavy doors closed.

Moments later Cassius Locke melted out of the shadows, looking more like a villain than a prince—dressed all in black with dark hair and eyes to match. At twenty, he was a mere two years older than she. But the prince before her seemed bigger, older . . . much more a man than she had expected. He reminded her of those thunderstorms that stalled on the horizon—growing bigger and darker as they churned in on themselves.

Their gazes met, and she held his stare, shoulders square and back. Sweat dripped down her spine beneath the elaborate costume, and a headache knocked at her temples from the weight of the headdress, but she did not let it show. His eyes dropped, perusing her form. Rora's heart thumped a little faster. The longer he looked at her, the more uncomfortable she became. And she hated herself for it. For letting him get to her.

If her mother had taught her anything, it was that no one could make you feel small unless you allowed it. So she took a deep breath and let herself believe she was the fierce and powerful girl everyone thought she was. And she stared right back.

Maybe Rora didn't have magic, but Cassius didn't know that. She had spent her whole life preparing to be queen, and she'd be damned if she spared an instant of worry for what he thought of her. She evaluated him in return and spitefully hoped it made him uncomfortable. Starting with his neatly combed midnight hair, she assessed his looks—strong brows, straight nose, pointed chin. His face was almost too symmetrical, as if crafted by an architect. Rora frowned and swept her gaze down to his broad chest and large shoulders.

Instead of making him uncomfortable, *she* began to feel uneasy with her perusal. He was too attractive. Far more handsome than any of the local young men she might have chosen. But that beauty was tempered by an air of brutality—a hardness in his eyes and the precise, sharp movements of a man who was deadly and wanted everyone to know it.

He stood a handspan taller than she, a rarity for Rora's tall form. When she finally looked back at his face, he was quirking an eyebrow, one corner of his mouth lifted in a smirk.

"Don't stop on my account. Please, look your fill. See what you're getting, Princess." He did a slow spin, giving her a full view. She meant to scoff at his arrogance, but the sound was strangled beneath a gasp when she saw him in profile.

The folds of his black tunic left a gap down the middle of his back, revealing something that looked like armor beneath; and down the line of his spine were sharp, unnatural protrusions.

He angled his head toward her and smiled. It did not look as a smile should. It exaggerated the strong angles of his face, making him appear harsh . . . *dangerous*.

"Did you think you'd be the only one wearing hearts today?"

He turned fully and there, piercing the back of his tunic like monstrous vertebrae, were Stormhearts. Nearly a dozen. Some were familiar—the crystalline red of firestorms and pearlescent skyfire. Others were not like any she knew. And, unlike Rora, he even had duplicates.

"H-how?" Second sons never wore Stormhearts. Those remained with the ruler and the heir.

"These belong to me, not to the Locke kingdom." Suddenly her corset felt far more constricting, like a snake coiling about her middle tighter and tighter. A *dozen* hearts of his own? Even with Stormling powers, to take the heart from a tempest was to court death itself. Many more than just her brother had died in such an endeavor. The history books chronicled the stories, and even those few who succeeded were later plagued by tragedy and destruction, as if the storms somehow sought vengeance after their demise. Clearly Cassius did not fear the wrath of gods or storms. If he truly had taken those Stormhearts for himself, he was dangerous indeed.

"I enjoy the way it feels," Cassius said, his voice pitched deep. "To reach a hand into the dark depths of a storm and rip out its heart."

A shiver of unease ran down her spine. If she had magic, could she ever take that much joy in destruction? He was watching her, *reading* her, and she quickly pulled on a blank expression. Other than not having magic, that was her greatest weakness as a royal heir. She felt too much, *thought* too much; and even with years of tutoring, it was still an effort to keep the tempest inside her from showing on her face. "How was your journey?"

He lifted an eyebrow. "Long. The mountain passes were more *troublesome* than we had expected this time of year."

"Storms?" she asked.

"Blizzard."

Rora's jaw dropped. "But we're still in the Slumber season."

"The deluge of snow that nearly trapped us in the pass at Bone's Break cared little what season it was. The wildlands have been even more unpredictable of late."

As far as she knew, the Lockes had no snow blood in the family line. The snowstorms never ventured far enough south to matter in their kingdom. "Your father—was he able to control it?"

He shook his head. "None of us had ever seen a blizzard. And my father rarely faces storms these days. My brother and I battle most."

She supposed the same might have been true for her if she had magic. Instead, she and her mother had delayed the transfer of protection duties as long as possible. It was why she had to marry now. With the Rage season looming, they were out of time.

"How did you—"

Before the question was out of her mouth, he reached his free hand back to touch the Stormheart at the top of his spine. It was a glittering white, nearly silver, and almost perfectly round. "I did not have snow blood. But I do now."

Cold chased over her skin, and she shivered. He stepped into her space, taking both her hands between his and sliding his warm palms over the pebbled skin of her arms. "My apologies." His voice rumbled low in the scant space between them. "The newer hearts are . . . responsive." He used her elbows to tug her close, her palms falling flat against his hard chest. His hands kept skimming over her skin, slower now, rubbing away the cold. She told herself to pull away, screamed it inside her head, but the blood in her veins felt slow and thick like honey.

The storms in Caelira were dangerous not just for their destructive capabilities but for their magic. A potent storm could mesmerize a person, and even if you knew you should run or fight, you were too enthralled to care. All were trained to guard their minds as children, but sometimes it still was not enough. Whole Stormling armies had been slaughtered without raising a finger in their own defense, stunned into stillness even in the face of death. She wondered if Cassius had found a way to steal that skill from the storms along with their hearts. Because despite her unease, she could not seem to step out of his grasp. He leaned in close, until she could feel his breath tickling over her cheek. "You remind me of it."

She swallowed, and the skin that had pebbled from the cold grew blisteringly hot wherever his breath touched her. "Of what?"

"The blizzard. Fierce and beautiful and unlike anything my eyes have ever seen."

Her stomach tumbled at his words, and her mouth turned dry. She might have looked fierce in her skyfire-inspired attire, but she did not feel it. Not with him so close. He'd barely touched her, and she felt as if each of her walls was collapsing one by one.

The Pavanian princess stared at Cassius, her mouth open slightly. When she first walked into this room, Cassius had thought her stunning in her savagery, colder than the depths of winter. Her dress seduced and threatened in equal measure, clinging to her curves and adorned with carved skyfire crystals that jutted from her shoulders and head like the spikes of a warrior's armor. And yet for all that careful pageantry, it had only taken a compliment to rattle her. She looked very young in that moment, very *sweet*, which was never a good thing for a potential ruler to be.

She donned an unreadable expression before his curiosity was satisfied, and her lilting voice turned sharp. "Flattery is not necessary. The betrothal has already been set."

Another blast of that wintery gaze. She had unusual blue-gray eyes—wide and expressive and lovely enough to bring a lesser man to his knees. Her confident demeanor would likely have convinced most, but he had sharpened his instincts in a court little safer than a lion's den. Tension rode her—something between unease and fear. He gripped her wrist and had the inexplicable urge to drag her somewhere else, anywhere other than the betrothal celebration that waited upstairs with his family. She was a delicate songbird, and his father was a bird of prey. They all were, Cassius included. And he couldn't help but wonder how long it would be before this little bird had her wings clipped.

She tugged her arm out of his grasp, hard. He was tempted to take it back. That was part of his nature . . . to take. But she fixed him with a harsh glare, and he smiled in response. Perhaps his little bird had talons after all.

Enough. She was not *his* little bird. A jungle cat does not care for prey, even if he wants it with a hunger stronger than any he has ever known. He pushed his more ruthless instincts aside. That would be his greatest challenge here—fighting the need to seize, command, destroy. Those were the things he was good at. The things he'd been taught since he could walk. With Aurora he would have to coax and flatter and comfort—that was his path to control.

She said, "We should probably go. They'll be calling for us soon."

Cassius offered her his elbow, and her body was tense as she curled her hand around it. But before they even took a step, it became clear that the voluminous fabric at the bottom of her dress wouldn't allow them to easily walk side by side. Cassius took hold of her hand, sliding it off his arm and lacing their fingers together instead. Slowly, he lifted her hand until his lips dragged across her knuckles. The blacks of her eyes expanded, swallowing up that lovely color and adding just a touch of sin to her sweet. She jerked within his grip, trying to pull away. Chuckling low, he put some distance between them, but he did not release her hand.

It took entirely too long to cross the throne room in her elaborate attire. She had to kick the bottom of her dress out before she stepped so that it wasn't underfoot. Cassius was willing to bet that the dress and the headpiece weighed a third as much as she did or more, but her posture remained rigidly upright and her steps smooth.

By the time they reached the staircase at the back of the throne room, her lips were open and her breathing quick. He was beginning to hate this dress, even if it did cling to her curves rather spectacularly.

"You know," he said, "I have a knife. I'm tempted to cut off the bottom of that dress so you can walk like the rest of us."

A smile flitted across her mouth, small at first, then widening into something playful and *bright*. It called to the darkness in him. "You could try. But you'd likely find that knife at your throat with my mother on the other side of it."

"Not you?"

"If I had my way, we'd burn it once you cut it off. The headdress too."

He smiled, and for the first time in a long while it felt almost natural.

"Perhaps we'll celebrate our wedding with a bonfire."

Every time he mentioned the wedding, she tensed. It was, of course, already agreed upon and signed in ink, but he had plans that would not succeed if she remained reluctant.

They ascended the first few steps slowly, the beaded fabric of her dress pulled taut around her legs. He wanted to throw her over his shoulder and charge the rest of the way, but he distracted himself with studying his surroundings instead. The hallway they were leaving behind was filled with paintings and statues of the Pavan Stormling ancestors. At the hallway's end a massive, gold-painted statue of the current queen stood in a decorative alcove. Once upon a time, there might have been altars to the old gods—places to pray for good harvest or fertility or even luck—but those days were long past. Too many years of unbridled destruction and unanswered prayers.

No, Stormlings were the gods now. It was Cassius and the people like him who either answered prayers or ignored them.

"You said you faced a blizzard on your journey, but you did it without an affinity."

He squeezed the hand he still held. "I did."

She pulled her bottom lip between her teeth, scraping at the white paint that covered her skin. She asked, "Would you tell me about it sometime? The blizzard?"

He angled his head to smile at her again, and she looked away. *Shy.* So many pieces to her puzzle. "On one condition."

"Which is?" He had expected her to be like most of the well-born ladies of the court in Locke: sirens with claws and teeth or frightened little mice, made to be gobbled up by this world. Aurora seemed neither vicious nor weak, but she was working so carefully to show him a façade that he could not pinpoint exactly *what* she was.

He had to know. It was his curse, the reason he thirsted for the thrill of a storm. He had to know how things worked, had to know *why*. And the girl in front of him was no different. In fact, the need to unravel all her secrets was stronger than he'd ever felt because she would be *his*. And he had a feeling that conquering her would prove more exhilarating than any storm he had ever defeated.

Rather than giving her his condition, he released her hand and wrapped an arm around the slim circle of her waist. She tried to step back, but her feet tangled in her dress, and she gripped his tunic to stay upright.

There it was. A thread of fear in those eyes. He could have stopped then, but he had little self-control when it came to these things. It was not enough to see a measure of her emotions on her face. He wanted them all. So he pushed a little more. "You might be patient enough to fight with this dress, but I am not. Let me get us to the top of these stairs, and I promise to tell you whatever story you want to hear."

She jutted her soft chin out and said, "You have a deal."

The paint had begun to wear away on her lips, revealing rosy skin underneath. Was the rest of her flushed beneath all that powder? He dragged his fingers back and forth over her side, feeling hard ridges beneath the heavy, embellished fabric. "Corset?"

She sucked in a breath, and he knew he had shocked her. Innocent. He collected each morsel of her identity like a scavenger in the jungle. He saw just a sliver of panic before she hid it away and met his gaze.

Brave little bird.

"It will have to be like this." Before she could change her mind or reason could catch up to his own actions, he bent, winding his arms around her thighs, and lifted. She was tall but slight, and he held her tight against him so that her hips pressed against his chest and her stomach hovered in front of his face. She gasped and braced a hand on his shoulder, reaching up to balance her headdress with the other. He could not see her face like this, but he imagined she was scandalized. He chuckled. "I suppose I should have given you some warning."

He risked offending her or word getting back to her mother through the guards that followed them. Both of which paled in comparison to the risk of his father hearing of his actions. He was a child, poking at a fish with a stick, rather than reeling it in the way he was supposed to. But he could not seem to help himself.

With some measure of urgency, he started up the stairs. Her body swayed toward him, her beaded dress scraping against his chin. This close, he felt her breathing speed up. The hand on his shoulder migrated to her chest, doing her best to cover the cleavage that was only just above his line of sight.

His instincts said to push again, but this time he reined them in. He kept his head down and quickened his feet. Again, the movement made her sway toward him, harder this time without her hand on his shoulder as a brace. He turned his face to the side, and her belly pressed against his cheek just for a moment before her hand was back at his shoulder, righting her position.

He took the last few steps at a pace that was nearly a jog, and when he reached the top, he looked up at her face. Her mouth was open and soft; he knew by the rise and fall of her body against him that her breaths were ragged, and in her eyes was a gleam. Not fear. Not panic. Not even anger.

Want.

He could work with that.

The capital city of the Locke kingdom seems to lie at the very edge of all things. Jutting out into ravaging sea and hemmed in by wild jungles, it is the edge of the world, the edge of beauty and danger and power. It is a gleaming gem cradled in the jaw of a predator, and to touch it, to live there on the edge, is to know life and death and command them both.

—The Perilous Lands of Caelira

2

If Rora's eyes had been closed, she might have believed that a firestorm had struck indoors and that embers were scorching along every surface of her skin, burning and burning and burning until she turned to ash. Cassius's hold loosened, and Rora's body began to slide down his toward the floor.

His eyes were not black as she thought before, but a deep blue. Like the ocean in the midst of a storm. Or how she envisioned the ocean to be, since she had only ever read about it. Her favorite book was about an explorer who sailed the sea in search of a safer land; she had read it so many times that the spine was broken and the pages soft. She would like to know how it felt to stand and feel the crash of waves against her knees. Maybe Cassius would take her someday.

She felt the future rolling out in front of her, like the wind moving through the wheat fields. *Too fast.* Everything was too fast. But he looked at her mouth, and she looked at his. A spark burned up her spine, and for the first time in her life she could imagine exactly what it was like to control skyfire.

To be powerful.

Just when excitement overtook the fear, and she started to *want* things to be too fast, his hands slid away and he stepped back. Taven and Merrin had been maintaining a discreet distance until Cassius had lifted her, and now they waited only a few steps below them.

She was certain her guards could see the red flooding her cheeks, that they *all* could see, even through the layers of powder. In her mother's efforts to seclude her and protect her secret, Queen Aphra had effectively cut Rora off from almost all personal contact. She'd traded friendship for solitude, social interaction for books. At her mother's insistence, at her queen's demand, Rora alienated everyone she knew to keep a secret that weighed on her more than this gown and headdress ever would. Even the maids who assisted her rotated regularly to prevent anyone from getting close enough to learn the truth.

Rora had certainly never been pressed against a man as she had been in Cassius's arms. She was terrified that he would be able to see her nerves, that this would be one more area where she would be found lacking. But he didn't laugh or tease her. Instead, Cassius knelt at her feet. Her heart skittered up into her throat as he carefully straightened and smoothed the mass of black fabric at the bottom of her dress. When he looked up, her thoughts tangled over their imagined wedding night. About how she would have to get used to him being even closer and more intimate than this.

Her thoughts spun out of control, but below her Cassius was unhurried and unembarrassed. He offered her the softest smile, softer than she would have thought him capable. Maybe her mother was right. Cassius had his rough edges, but perhaps there was happiness to be found with him.

"There," he said, straightening in front of her again. He touched the curve of her chin, tipping it up slightly. His hand left her chin for the smooth crystal of a skyfire bolt on her necklace. His finger ran along the edge, and though it didn't touch her skin, it was close. Maybe the crystal was crooked and needed straightening too. Or maybe it wasn't. She only knew that she wanted him to do it again. He gave her a cheeky wink and said, "Your mother will never know a thing."

Before she could make sense of her flurry of emotions, a door beyond them opened. A servant asked if they were ready, and Rora nodded shakily. Moments later cheering could be heard within the great hall beyond. Cassius clasped her hand and pulled her forward.

When they stepped through the doorway, Rora's heart caught in her throat. Hundreds upon hundreds of people were crowded into the room to celebrate her betrothal to Cassius, smiling faces as far as she could see. The applause echoed around the room, filling her ears until she could not even hear herself think. Her favorite thing in the entire palace was the chandelier her great-grandfather had constructed by trapping the magic of skyfire in an elaborate glass structure, and she fixed her eyes on it. Tonight it shone brilliantly—lightning frozen behind glass as if the goddess herself had plucked it from the sky.

A squeeze of her hand pulled her attention to the side, to Cassius's too handsome face. He smiled at her, the widest one yet, and she found herself smiling back. Something trembled inside her, like the plucked string of an instrument, and it seemed to grow, thrumming through her bloodstream until her whole body buzzed with an unfamiliar sensation.

It had been a long time since Aurora had truly felt like a princess. She made few public appearances, another attempt to hold her secret as long as possible. Occasionally, she would join her mother on carriage rides through the city, but she only ever waved through the windows. She was better off without the attention. She enjoyed her time alone, reading or riding her horse, Honey, or studying. She did not want to wear fancy dresses or attend parties or experience the frivolity of court life.

At least, that was what she always told herself. Now she felt as if she had stepped into the pages of one of her books or strode out of the shadows of her own life for the first time.

The applause died down, and Cassius led her to the center of the room for their first dance. He pulled her close, his long, muscled arms wrapping her up like a butterfly in a cocoon. He smelled of leather and salt and something distinctly male. She fought the urge to lay her head upon his chest as the music began and they started to move.

She had expected to spend the whole night on edge, protecting her secret and her mother's plan to keep the throne in the Pavan family while also guaranteeing a ruler who could protect the kingdom. But between one twirl and the next, all those worries fled and thoughts of Cassius, of their potential future together filled the gaps.

Aurora's flushed skin was beginning to show through the powder in places—the hollow of her throat, the crest of her cheek, the curve of her lip. Cassius fought the urge to finish the job, to rub it all away so he could see her truly. "You're different than I expected," he murmured when the dance brought their bodies close.

Something had changed in the way she looked at him, *softened*, as if her initial distrust had all but melted away. A part of him wanted to shake her, to tell her she was being a fool for trusting anyone, let alone a man like him. But a greater part of him craved that look, yearned for her eyes on him the way a flower strained for the sun. But if he were a flower, he would no doubt be poison. He drew her closer anyway. Cassius felt the irrational urge to mark her, claim her as his; and if the only way to do that was to let some of his poison rub off on her, then so be it.

"Different in a good way?" Confusion and hope and worry warred on her face. For a girl that had tried before to be ice-cold, she was a riot of barely checked emotions now.

He let the hand on the middle of her back stray to her side, dragging his fingers along the stays of her corset again. "Very good."

"You are not what I assumed either." She offered him that sweet smile.

If she knew what that smile did to him, she would be less generous with it.

Emotion was not something with which he had much experience. His parents' marriage was one of strategy, and that same attitude extended to their parenting. As a boy, he had not known that bloodthirsty competition between siblings was not the way of every family. But he knew now; he felt the yoke of his father's control constantly tightening around his neck, and it was only recently that he had cared enough to fight it. Or perhaps, he had stopped caring altogether. Consequences meant little to him now.

So he did not react when he noticed his father glaring, eyes flicking down to the hand Cassius still rubbed scandalously along Aurora's side. He'd come here at his father's bidding, but the king would not be pulling Cassius's strings for much longer. He tucked the princess closer, until he could feel the hot puffs of her breath in the hollow of his throat. He slid his hand dangerously low on her back. This was one thing his father would not control. Aurora was his way out, *his* fresh start. And once they were married, the king would realize that his control over Cassius had died when they left Locke.

The first song ended, and the floor grew crowded with more couples. He led the princess over to where both their families gathered on a dais. Queen Aphra sat upon an elaborate throne made from the same sandstone as the palace, and it glittered gold in the light. A smaller version that was likely Aurora's remained empty, and several ornate chairs had been added to the dais for his family.

Despite the smaller chair, his father sat as if this room and the people in it were his to command. His mother surveyed the room with a scrunched nose as if already planning how she would change the palace around her. He led Aurora to her vacant throne. Before she could take her seat, he pulled her to a stop and lifted her hand to his mouth, giving the back a slow, grazing kiss. He watched the delicate column of her throat move as she swallowed. When she lowered herself into the chair, he took up sentry position beside her.

After a moment, their parents returned to their previous conversation, and he heard his father questioning Queen Aphra about Pavan's holdings. They discussed the various crops that grew in the fields surrounding the city, the river that provided water from the north, as well as borders and resources and interaction with several of the nearest Stormling strongholds.

Cassius had spent his life hemmed in by sea and jungle. Few braved the perils of any of the unclaimed wildlands territory; far fewer braved the wilds that led to Locke. Conquest was nearly unheard of in the modern era of Caelira. The challenges of protecting the land were too consuming to dream of conquering more. But even so, Locke's lethal location provided a great deal of protection and privacy, and most important, it allowed them to control the flow of information in and out of the city. The power of the Locke family was renowned across the continent because they made it so. Pavan was the centermost city of the continent, and thus had potential allies (and threats) on all sides. It would be . . . an adjustment.

The king's corresponding stories about Locke were exaggerated and embellished as always. Cassius tuned out as Queen Aphra inquired after his uncle, who was protecting Locke in their absence. He didn't care to listen to fabricated stories about a brotherly relationship that was just as poisonous as the one he had with his own brother. Bending close to Aurora's ear, Cassius murmured, "Take everything the king says with a grain of salt." He touched the pointed tip of the skyfire crystal that perched upon her shoulder. It was sharper than he had expected. "We're all putting on shows today."

"And you?" she asked. "Should I disbelieve everything you say as well?"

He didn't back off; instead he traced the crystal down to the curve of her shoulder. As he considered how to answer, he dragged his fingers toward the nape of her neck. Her head dipped forward slightly, and he curved his palm over the back of her neck. "When you're raised to be king, you're taught to choose your words carefully, to utilize them with as much precision as a sword in a fight. But I—"

"You're the second son."

He frowned, and his hand tightened on her nape for just a moment before he realized his error and released her. "Yes, I am. And I am not like my father." He knew there was too much aggression in his tone, and when she cast her eyes up, he nearly lost all his patience for this game. He wanted this girl. More than that . . . he *required* her. And he was not always the most patient hunter. He was preparing to ask her for another dance when his brother stepped into view.

"A princess as lovely as you should spend the entire night upon the dance floor. Allow me to correct my *little* brother's error."

Casimir held out a hand in offering, and Cassius's fingers itched for the blade he usually wore at his hip.

"Mir," he grumbled in warning. But that only made his brother push more. They were alike in that. When Aurora laid her hand in Mir's, he pressed a kiss to her palm. A long kiss. Fire licked up Cassius's spine, and nearly a dozen Stormhearts burned hot and cold and everything between as they filled with his energy. His brother was very, very lucky that the Stormhearts could only influence storms, not create them. He wouldn't have been able to stop himself from raining down fire and floods, brother of his blood or not.

Cassius snapped, "That's enough, Casimir."

"Come now, Brother. Surely, you would not deprive me of the chance to get to know my future sister."

Cassius bared his teeth in grim smile. "Get to know her from a distance." There was no hiding the threat in his words.

Mir winked at the princess and said, "He never has been good at sharing."

"And you never have been good at keeping your hands where they belong."

Cassius was nearly vibrating with fury now, but his brother was still as calm as could be, his thumb lazily stroking Rora's palm as he kept hold of her hand. "No. No, I have not."

Cassius gripped Aurora's shoulders and pulled her back against his chest. The headdress blocked his view for a moment before he leaned around and fixed his brother with a glare.

"Careful, Cassius." His brother smiled. "You'll frighten her away before she's truly yours."

"Boys." A tinkling, fake laugh drifted over from where their mother sat. "At least pretend to be civilized." The dais was set apart enough that no one could have heard their words, but his mother's warning cleared Cassius's head enough to remember that people *were* watching.

"A little healthy competition never did any harm," his father replied, looking at Casimir with approval. Once upon a time that might have been a painful blow to Cassius, to see his brother favored over him, but take enough of those hits, and eventually you don't even feel them.

His mother turned to the Pavanian queen and said, "You are so lucky you have no sons. They are beasts on their best days."

Queen Aphra's smile faltered only for a moment, but it was long enough. Unlike in Locke, where secrets were easy to bury, there was not a kingdom on the continent that had not heard of the death of Pavan's heir. His mother looked out at the dance floor, her lips tipped up in mimicry of pleasantness. Everything about his mother's looks should have lent her warmth—her honey skin, dark brown hair, and eyes that shone somewhere between. But there was no disguising the cold in her.

Enough. He cared not for silly dances and frivolous parties, but he would keep Aurora on the floor until morning if it kept her in his arms and his family at a distance. He took her hand and began pulling her away without explanation. To his brother he called back, "You'll have to beg a dance another time. Perhaps after our wedding. Tonight is ours."

Aurora's cheeks hurt from smiling, and her face was hot from what felt like one unending blush. She held Cassius's elbow, leaning in to him as she tottered like she had drunk her weight in wine. She hadn't had a single drop, but she felt slightly drunk all the same. He held both her hands atop his forearm, keeping her steady every time she inevitably tripped over her dress.

Yesterday she had been certain that life as she knew it was coming to an end, with her future resting on a blade's edge as thin as the half-truths they'd told for years. But now . . . all the world looked different through hope's glow.

She peeked behind Cassius's shoulder at the brooding brother who trailed them. He was playing chaperone, king's orders, as Cassius walked her back to her rooms.

Casimir was nearly as tall as his brother, but his body was leaner, his face a little softer, more pampered, perhaps. His hair was longer with a slight curl to the ends. If she did not already know which was which, she would have assumed that Cassius was the famed elder brother known as Prince Cas. Taller and broader—she assumed him the more powerful, but perhaps that misconception was part of what made

Casimir all the more dangerous. He was quicker to smile and joke, and would no doubt make a charismatic ruler, but there was a hint of cunning to him. As if every word was a strategic move on a game board that she could not see.

The three of them made their way down the main stairs onto the ground floor. "Prince Casimir," she called back, "my mother said that you were also recently engaged to be married."

Casimir's eyes flicked to his brother's back before he answered, "I'm afraid your mother's information is outdated. That betrothal was dissolved."

She wasn't sure whether to offer condolences or ask for more information or remain silent. But she'd never been one to keep her mouth in check for long. Still soaring from her unexpectedly wonderful night, her curiosity got the better of her.

"How *does* one go about dissolving betrothals?"

She was smiling widely as they entered the north residential wing, and a few moments passed before she noticed the brothers had gone rigid. Cassius's expression was dark and hard, like that of the intimidating man he'd been at first sight, and it made the air feel thick in Rora's throat.

"There's only one way a betrothal sealed by a royal contract can be broken," Casimir answered.

It wasn't the eldest brother who continued, but Cassius. "She died, Aurora."

She wanted to rip one of the skyfire crystals off her necklace and shove it down her throat.

"I'm sorry," she said, but she knew the words meant little. They couldn't change anything, couldn't unravel time. But he thanked her anyway, and dropped back as they approached the ornate archway that separated the royal chambers from the rest of the wing. Cassius touched the gold-painted, carved wooden frame, but didn't pass under it. Rora whispered, "I'm sorry I brought up the engagement. I didn't know. I never would have—"

Cassius cut her off, grasping her chin between his fingers. She went silent and very, very still. His gaze pinned her in place, making her forget her panic.

"You did not know. Besides, we Lockes don't dwell on the past. We move forward. Always forward."

"Does that come from your family creed?"

His brows lifted. "How did you know that?"

"*Eyes always to the horizon.* Is that right?"

The fingers on her chin loosened, and he dragged his thumb along the line of her jaw.

"Smart little bird."

Her nose crinkled. "I am not even remotely birdlike."

Cassius reached up and plucked one of many feathers from her headdress, trailing it over her cheek. She opened her mouth, and then closed it, scowling up at him. He laughed, the sound rumbling in his throat. It was the most carefree she had seen him yet.

"The royal chambers are through here," she said, gesturing beyond the archway.

He looked down and cleared his throat. "It's probably best if I say good night here."

His hesitant expression seemed out of place on his sharp features. For the first time, she wondered if he too had been dreading their union, if even now he only charmed her out of a sense of duty. Guilt singed through her like skyfire. What would he say when he learned the truth? When he discovered all her lies?

"Cassius, I know an arranged marriage likely wasn't something you envisioned for yourself. It's not what I saw for my future either. But—" She stopped, nerves bleeding back in for the first time in hours. "I think we could—You seem like—"

"Stop *worrying,* Aurora."

The words were punctuated by his hands cupping her jaw, fingers splaying down her neck. She did the opposite of what he said. She worried about the powder on her face that would smudge off on his hands. She worried about his closeness and the state of her breath. She worried he would kiss her and that she would be exceptionally *bad* at it.

"A treaty has nothing to do with what's between us. I fight for what's mine, Princess. Whether it's against storms or my brother or your stubbornness—I fight to win."

She eased out of his grasp, bumping into the archway behind her. For a moment, he had held her a little too tightly, the growl in his words a little too fierce. She was not sure how she felt about being *his*, of belonging to him. As a child, she had belonged to her parents, then as new heir, she had belonged to the kingdom. When her magic never manifested, her life belonged to her secrets. She had hoped that when all was said and done, she could finally belong to herself.

He cursed beneath his breath, and when he approached her again, his words and his face had grown softer. "By now I'm sure you've noticed that my family is . . . intense. The same is true for our home. We're battered on both sides—storms from the land and the sea. Our proximity to the latter makes our Slumber season so short it's barely worth calling it a season. When you live in a place so ruthless, you learn to protect the things that matter. To be ruthless in return. I know the shortness of this life, and when I make a decision, I do not look back. My decision was made the moment I laid eyes on you."

He slid his finger down one of the skyfire crystals on her necklace like he'd done after he carried her up the stairs. She sucked in a breath, and the rise of her chest caused his finger to brush her collarbone. Then he did it again. Not an accident this time. She was breathing fast, clutching at the archway behind her.

His thumb rubbed over her mouth, smearing away the last of the white on her lips. Her eyes fell to his mouth, once quickly, then again for good. He sighed, warm breath drifting over her skin. "This is where I step away and let you go to bed. Before I'm tempted to walk you directly to your door."

"And that would be a problem because?"

"I'm a thrill seeker. It's why I have these." He took her hand and lifted it over his shoulder, until together their hands surrounded the snow Stormheart at the top of his spine. The movement put their bodies even closer, and an icy draft stole over them. She should have jerked away. But instead she arched into him, seeking his warmth. His gaze appeared black again. "If I walk you to your room, if I know exactly where to find you in the middle of the night when the palace is quiet and I can't sleep . . . I might be tempted to lure you from your bed for a little adventure. And then we'd both be risking our parents' anger."

If he was trying to deter her, he was using the wrong methods. She spent every moment of every day yearning for adventure, and she would gladly take it from his hands.

"What makes you think I'd be so easy to lure from my bed?" she teased.

For the barest moment his body pressed forward against hers— muscles pulled taut, hard as stone. She melted into him, pushing back until their bodies aligned from chest to hip. Then he ripped himself away, leaving her arm hanging in the air and several steps between them.

"I like a challenge, Aurora. Do not offer yourself up as one unless you are prepared for the consequences."

He nodded his head toward the archway, his muscles tight with tension, and said, "Good night, Princess. Until tomorrow."

Rora's body followed his suggestion, slipping through the archway into a wider hallway and out of sight, but her mind was still stuck on the way it felt to be pressed against him. Rora had read of perfect kisses, prompted by perfect words and perfect settings, and she had a feeling she'd just missed a chance at having the real-life version. She moved in a daze, one foot in front of the other, but every step got a little harder, as if a rope around her middle tried to pull her back through that archway to claim that perfect moment she let pass by.

She opened the door to her bedroom, heard the squeak it made, and started to step inside, but her mind was buzzing now. When would they next have a moment this private? The days to come were a series of celebrations and dinners and meetings. There would be people every- where, always watching them. For all she knew, they wouldn't have an- other chance until they were at the altar, and then she would be having her first kiss in front of an audience.

No. She didn't want to wait. She'd spent years making the cautious choices, swallowing down her most reckless impulses, to protect her secret and the crown. Just this once, Rora wanted something that had nothing to do with storms or being royal. She wanted that kiss.

She tugged the door closed, decision made, and turned back toward the archway. As she was about to step through, she heard Casimir say, "Laying it on a bit thick, aren't you?"

Rora halted. She'd been so caught up in Cassius that she'd forgotten about his brother.

Cassius answered, his voice barely above a growl. "Let me worry about that. It's working, isn't it? She's little better than clay in my hands."

Rora's ears started ringing the way they did when a loud noise sounded too close.

"Her mother is powerful. Rumor has it that the girl might be more so. I wouldn't get too confident."

"Confidence is exactly what *she* lacks. I don't care how much power she has . . . she's tentative and unsure. She's soft. I'll have no problem bending her to my will. So you can run along and report to Father that everything is moving according to the plan."

"Where are you going?" Casimir asked, and Cassius's heavy footfalls only sped up.

"For a walk. Would you like to chaperone me for that as well, *big brother*?"

There was no reply, but after a few moments, Rora heard Casimir turn and leave too, and when his steps faded into silence she slid down the wall until her legs collapsed beneath her. The corset cut into her hips and thighs in this position, and the weight of the headdress pulled her head forward.

There was a hole in her chest, an awful, gaping hole that screamed like she wanted to. Like a cyclone, it seemed to suck up everything in its path until her knees were curled into her chest and her body hunched, and she just kept collapsing in and in and in. Suddenly unable to breathe, she clawed at the beaded fastenings that connected her headdress and necklace. One of her fingernails bent and splintered as she scrabbled for the hooks; when she could not find them, she took hold of the beaded cord and pulled until it broke, beads scattering across the stone floor around her.

The headdress tipped sideways, tugging painfully on her hair. Again and again, she pulled at the ties until her palms felt raw and beads littered the floor around her. The headdress began to sag, and she was nearly done, nearly *free* when someone stepped through the archway, and she froze.

Novaya.

Thank the skies. The dark-haired servant held an urn full of steaming water in her hands, and she stared in horror as if she had stumbled upon a monster rather than a crying girl. Nova had been Rora's closest friend before she cut herself off from everyone at her mother's command. Girls with secrets the size of Rora's could not have friends. Nova took a step forward, paused, then knelt down, her large brown eyes carefully blank.

"Should I call for your guards? The queen?" Nova asked.

"No!" Softer, Aurora said, "No. Please don't tell anyone."

Once upon a time, Nova had kept all her secrets. Now the two rarely even looked each other in the eye when their paths crossed, and it was all Aurora's fault.

"Your Highness? What *happened*?"

Rora shook her head and returned to tugging at the headdress still tangled in her hair. She couldn't say the words aloud, couldn't let anyone see how much of a fool she was. Aurora had become accustomed to her shortcomings as a Stormling, as an heir. But she'd thought she had her mother's strength, tenacity, and intelligence. But maybe that was wishful thinking. Maybe she was altogether . . . inadequate.

"Stop, Princess. You're hurting yourself." Nova put the water aside, crawled forward, and grabbed Rora's wrists. *"Aurora, stop."*

All the years spent missing their friendship came rushing back, and she froze at the sound of her name. Not *Princess.* Not *Your Highness. Aurora.* But the moment she stopped moving, it all came crashing down on her. Her naïve plan to kiss him, to experience something *real.* She should have known that her future would hold only more lies. As if she knew anything about real life, real *anything.* She lived in this palace, protected and pampered and put away like a doll on a shelf, too *fragile* for anything but appearances. And it seemed that's all she would ever be.

Cassius wanted control of the city for himself. He thought he'd have to fool her to get it, but the moment the world found out that

Rora had no magic, he'd become the ruler in truth, and she'd be the puppet at his side. He wouldn't have to feign interest in her then. He wouldn't need her *at all*.

She wound her arms about her legs and rested her forehead on her knees. Nova moved closer, and Rora sat still and silent as the girl worked to remove the headdress. Her old friend had grown into a beautiful young woman—flawless bronze skin, shiny black hair, stunning features. She'd recently begun assisting the royal seamstress in addition to her position as a maid. She probably had more friends than she could count. Aurora could not help imagining how different her life would be now if she had never become heir.

The headdress finally gave way, and Nova slipped it off and laid it on the stone floor beside them.

"Tell me what happened."

Rora leaned back against the wall. It was cool against her abused scalp, and she muttered, "Nothing happened."

At least she had that much. She hadn't kissed that beast. But what she had done felt worse. She had *hoped*. And hope broke more hearts than any man ever could.

"Should I get someone? A friend?"

Rora let out a bleak, cold laugh. As if she had any of those. Softer, she said, "I don't want to see anyone. I just need this dress off. The makeup too. I need to breathe, and I can't do it through all this mess."

"I can do that. I came to help remove the headdress and gown. Stand up and we'll go to your room. Everything will be fine, Your Highness."

She didn't tell her old friend how wrong she was, not as she peeled the dress off her and unlaced the corset. Not as she wiped away the powder that was smudged and striped on Rora's face, thanks to falling tears. Another maid came in with more steaming water for a bath and Rora let them clean her up, wishing it was as easy to wipe away the last few hours.

She sat in the bath until the water grew cold and her skin shriveled like dying fruit. She had to face the facts. The Rage season was coming, as was this sham of a wedding. And she didn't know how to fight it any more than she knew how to stop a storm.

But she would not give Cassius any more opportunities to see her vulnerable. Nor was she giving up. If there were no other way, she would marry Cassius.

But she had six days. Wars had been won, empires toppled, and cities leveled in less time. If there were a way out of this, Rora would find it.

When Slumber wakes to Rage,
The old war begins to wage.
When Slumber sleeps its last
The easy days are past.

—*A Stormling Stands: Verses of Old*

3

Aurora's knife slammed into the center of the target with a gratifying thunk. She reached both hands back, trailing her fingers over the flat sides of the knives tucked away near her shoulder blades in a worn leather holster. Pulling two knives at once, she spun, releasing first one knife, then the other as she turned. One struck directly below the blade already lodged in the center, and the other just above.

Still not enough.

A group of soldiers trickled into the training courtyard, having just returned from a run. Their faces were slick with sweat and their boots messy with grass and mud. A fine layer of dew covered the land today, another sign of the waning Slumber season.

Merrin, one of her frequent guards, said, "Need more of a challenge? We can strap one of those to Elmont and give you a moving target." He slapped a younger soldier on the back, whose face turned a blistering red.

Elmont was new to the palace guard. He was part of the regiment that manned the palace gate, and their first few encounters had been when Rora was going out for an early ride on her horse, Honey. He had been reluctant to let her leave, eager as he was to prove himself in the guard. It had taken a lot of cajoling and not a little amount of flirting for her to get her way.

She offered them a polite smile. "As interesting as that sounds, I would not risk Elmont just so I can allay my own frustrations."

Taven stepped forward, his usual serious expression in place. "Spar, Princess?"

A slow smile spread across her face, and she nodded. Taven had been the one to teach her to throw knives and use a bow. He had never laughed once when her blade spun off course or thunked handle first into the target. She'd been restless and lonely and angry, and he helped her channel that into something worthwhile by teaching her about defense. And this morning she had many emotions to channel.

Taven set the rest of his unit up doing drills, and then came back to her. They began slowly, but in half a bell, they were moving close to full speed, their bodies lunging and spinning and dodging. Taven was beyond careful with his blade, never thrusting near or hard enough to actually impale her. She understood the point was to teach her body the moves without endangering her life, but in the event she ever needed to use these skills, she doubted her attacker would be so generous. And right now, especially, she needed a bigger challenge to clear her head. She spun fast, slashing out with her blade. He ducked, and while his bigger body was still recovering from the movement, she swept out a leg, striking him below his calves and taking his legs out from under him.

The other soldiers, who were supposed to be focusing on drills, snickered and cheered. Rora immediately felt guilty as Taven rose to his feet. She should have known it would not be possible to goad a man like him into aggression. He had always been so serious and calm. The day he had been assigned to her personal guard, he had committed himself fully to her protection, as if there was no life, no purpose outside it. She had embarrassed a man that had only ever been loyal to her. She opened her mouth to apologize, but a familiar voice from the courtyard's entrance interrupted and made something twist in her belly.

"Seems the princess needs a more capable opponent."

She did not want to look at Cassius. There was such a jumble of emotions inside her that she couldn't be sure she would not burst into tears at the sight of him. Or send the knife in her hand flying. More than that, she feared he would see the distrust and betrayal written all over her face. So she answered without turning, "Taven is far more capable than I."

She offered the soldier an apologetic smile.

"Taven, is it?"

"Yes, Your Highness." The soldier inclined his head toward Cassius. He came to a stop beside her, once again dressed in black. She was dressed similarly today in an old black and gold military uniform she wore for these early-morning training sessions.

"You taught her?" Cassius asked.

"Yes, Your Highness."

He surveyed Taven for several long moments. Then Cassius turned to Aurora and their eyes met. Anger clawed up her throat, and she struggled to keep her face blank. Better for him to believe he still had the upper hand.

"You taught her well," Cassius said without looking away from Aurora, "but I'll take it from here."

Over Cassius's shoulder Taven met her gaze, eyebrow raised. She nodded; she had kept him away from his soldiers long enough, and she could not avoid the prince forever.

"You are full of surprises, Princess."

She smiled, ignoring the bile threatening to rise in her throat. "As are you, Prince Cassius. As are you."

He circled behind her, and she felt the weight of his touch against one of the knives still sheathed near her shoulder. His breath fanned over her ear as he asked, "May I?"

Without waiting for an answer, he lifted the blade from her. "Good balanced weight," he said. "I imagine it flies well."

"Like a dream."

His mouth was at her ear again—too close, too warm. "*Show me.*"

She stepped away like it burned. "I think I'm done for the day."

"Come now, Aurora." She flinched at his use of her name. Had he used it yesterday? She could not remember. But now it felt too familiar, far too intimate. "What will it take to get you to show me? How much of my pride shall I bargain away?" His hand touched the small of her back. "Or what shall I offer you in return?"

She spun, and before she realized what she was doing, she had the point of her knife beneath his chin. The courtyard went still around them, but Cassius only smiled wider in response. She was unnerved by the darkness that licked at the edge of her thoughts, of the voice inside whispering to push the knife a little harder, to show him she was not so easy to control. All she knew was that she had let fear rule her for too long, and now it was time she took the reins.

"Do you trust me?" she asked, and slowly let the knife drift along his jaw.

His eyes narrowed. "Trust . . . is not one of my skills."

"If we are to be married, if we are to someday rule, there is nothing so important as your ability to trust me, *and I you*." He watched her warily. "You want something from me," she continued, "but you'll not get it unless I trust you." She was talking about far more than knives, and from his long pause he seemed to know it.

"I'll hand over my trust in this. What would you have me do?"

She led him to the largest target, the one with an outline of a person meant to test the thrower's ability to hit a body's weak spots. She pushed against his chest until he thumped back against the target. Then she snatched the knife from his hand and said, "Stay there."

After retrieving the blades she'd left in the other target, she moved to stand a good distance away. She stowed all the knives but one and met his eyes. He was leaning on the target, his arms folded and his feet crossed at the ankles. He gave her a challenging smirk. It was possibly the most handsome she had ever seen him, and yesterday she would have been charmed. Now . . . she could only hear the words he had said last night.

Tentative. Unsure.

Soft.

Well, she had no intention of being tentative now. She gave no warning, no instructions, only pulled back her elbow and let the knife fly. It thwacked into place a finger's width to the side of his neck.

When his eyes darkened and his easy posture fell away, she smiled.

"You did promise to trust me," she said, reaching back for another knife. "Do not worry, when it comes to a blade, I am almost never *unsure*. The key is to avoid a grip that's too *soft*, while likewise not gripping too tightly."

He stood rigidly still as she carefully sent two more knives toward him. The first landed on the other side of his neck, and the second high in the open space between his thighs.

The last throw had his fists clenching so hard that she had to turn her back so she would not laugh. She pulled another knife from her harness and took a slow breath. When she was about to turn she felt hands at her hips and warmth against her back. She reacted on instinct, shoving an elbow into the body behind her, before stamping hard on his foot. She spun, her knife raised to defend. Cassius was hunched slightly behind her, his hand over his stomach. She swallowed the smile that threatened to break free.

He straightened, his head tilted as if he were surveying her through new eyes. "Was that fun for you?"

"Very."

He made a sound—a low, husky bark that might have been a laugh. Hard to tell with a man like him.

"I trusted you with my body," he said. "It's only fair you trust me with yours." His eyes roamed down her form slowly, with intent. Rora could almost swear that her heart gave out in that moment, that it refused to beat, and all the blood it held just seeped out into a puddle in her chest.

"W-what?"

It was one thing to think of kissing Cassius last night, to hope that he might be able to show her all the things she was ignorant of when it came to her body and his. But now? She knew he saw her as nothing more than a means to an end, a tool to be used and discarded when no longer necessary.

"You do not have my trust yet, Prince." And he would never have her body if it were her choice.

"Are you afraid of me?"

She scoffed in answer, mostly because she did not trust herself to lie.

He frowned. "Do you have that little faith in my skills?"

It took a moment for her to realize he meant his skills with a knife. He wished her to stand at the target as he had done. She was so relieved that she let her guard down, and he plucked the knife from her hand.

"Can you trust at least that I would not do you physical harm?"

There was a challenge in his eyes and just a hint of amusement at her fear. That set her blood boiling all over again, and she marched over to the target. He followed, retrieving the blades she had thrown earlier. He moved in close, and she tipped her chin up defiantly. His blue-black eyes roamed her face as he reached behind her back and took several more knives from her holster. He brushed his knuckles over her cheek. She fought against the urge to jerk away. "I like you better like this. No frills, no finery. Just you."

As he strode away, she saw that the soldiers had given up any pretense of training and stood lined up nearby.

"I hope your aim is as true as you believe, Prince. If not, you'll have far more than one knife coming at you." She lifted her chin in the direction of the watching soldiers.

"I told you last night, I enjoy a challenge." Cassius gave a devilish grin and commanded, "Stretch out your arms." He waited until she lifted them both and gripped the edges of the target.

Rora refused to show fear or flinch. She held her breath when his arm drew back and the knife came flying end over end toward her. It hit the edge of the target a few inches above her head, and the board vibrated with the force of the strike.

He proceeded to outline her body with blades, seeming to pay particular care to her curves. She felt pinned in by the time he had landed knives alongside her thighs, hips, and the indent of her waist. She hoped that would be the end of it, but he picked up two final knives. Her arms shook with strain, but she stayed still as he sunk another blade below her armpit, just to the right of her breast. She gave an exaggerated yawn. He grinned in response as he lined up for his final throw.

As Cassius drew back his last knife, a shrill wail pierced the air. She had only a moment to place the sound—one of the horns blown from atop the city walls that signified the imminent arrival of an approaching storm—then Cassius's arm was moving and the blade left his hand.

There was no time to think, to weigh her options. She only knew a storm was coming, and everyone—Cassius, included—would expect her to participate in the kingdom's defense with a magic she did not have.

She jerked her head up toward the sky and let her arms drop a little. Then she did her best to look shocked and horrified when the blade sunk into her left biceps.

Cassius's roar drowned out even the blare of the storm signal. When he saw Aurora's pale hand touch the hilt of the knife buried in her arm, he wanted to make the whole world bleed, starting with himself. He ran toward her, arriving moments after a few of the soldiers. He wanted to tear their hands off her, but she beat him to it, pushing away their attempts to help. Her hand was smeared with blood. She turned toward Cassius, her face nearly as pale as it had been the night before with layers of powder. The soldiers turned and looked at him like he was the enemy, Aurora too.

In some ways, he was. But not like this. He would never harm her.

"Why did you move?" he snarled.

She tilted her chin up, swaying on her feet. Her lips were beginning to lose that soft peach color. She said, "The horn. I was distracted. I'm sorry."

He growled, pacing away, tugging at his hair. He should not have been throwing knives at her in the first place. He had let himself forget for a moment what his purpose here was. Her aggression had been a surprising but welcome new morsel of her personality. He had prodded at the fire in her, treated her like a woman he truly wanted, rather than a woman he had to have at any cost. He was meant to charm her, seduce her, steal away her heart. Just another heart, he had told himself. Like all the others he was so good at collecting. Only hers would not harden into stone or glass or crystal when he claimed it.

She was now surrounded by soldiers, each fretting over her as Cassius wished he could do. "Enough," she snapped. "It is only my arm."

As if in demonstration, she pulled the blade free like it was nothing more than a needle. The spread of red was barely discernible on the black uniform she wore, but when blood started dripping onto the dirt beneath her, Cassius rushed forward.

Two soldiers stepped in his way before he could touch her, and she was swept up into the arms of the man she called Taven. As she yelled for the soldier to put her down, Cassius demanded, "Where are you taking her?"

Taven did not answer, merely kept moving away, flanked by half a dozen others.

"He is taking her to the palace physician," another soldier answered.

"I am going with her."

The remaining soldiers closed ranks. One of Aurora's guards from yesterday drew his sword, pointing it at Cassius's chest, as Taven exited the courtyard with Aurora. Cassius knocked the sword from the guard's hand with one well-placed hit and within a breath, he turned it back on its owner, pressing it harder than necessary into the vulnerable skin beneath the man's chin. He could have slaughtered the man in front of him and several others by the time they clumsily pulled their weapons.

Cassius growled, "The next time you hold a blade to me, it will end with you sliced open and your insides spilled at my feet. Now tell me where he's taking her—to a physician directly or to her room?"

The only response was the training of multiple swords on him. Cassius let out a long string of filthy curses, but not one word moved the soldiers in front of him. His mind was clear enough to see a hopeless battle. He needed to regroup and find another way to make things right with the princess.

"Very well," he seethed. "I will return to my rooms and inform my family of this accident. I expect to be kept informed of her well-being."

He threw his stolen sword into the dirt and pushed through the soldiers, unworried about their weapons. They let him go, though they followed him inside the palace until he turned down into the guest wing. As soon as he was alone, he spun and punched the nearest wall. Knuckles split and bleeding, he made his way to his room to collect what coin he had.

He should inform his father. If word reached him before Cassius had a chance to explain, his fury was likely to be unmatched by any rage his father had ever thrown. And he had thrown many. But he had to see her first. With his money purse in his pocket, he set off for the royal wing of the palace.

He did not enter the hallway that led to Aurora's room, but waited nearby in an alcove behind a statue of a Stormling ancestor for someone to leave. It felt like hours passed before a maid bustled from the hall, head down and hands full of bloodied rags.

He stepped into her path, and she yelped, several wet rags slapping against the stone floor. "Your Highness," she whispered.

"How is she?"

She hesitated, eyes darting back down the hall. He plucked a gold coin from his pocket and asked again, *"How is she?"*

The girl bit her lip. When he retrieved a second coin, she snatched them both and began in a hurried whisper. "The wound bled a great amount. But it is beginning to slow. She is awake. Coherent. But fatigued. She is pale."

"Does she have use of her arm? Can she move her fingers? Bend at the elbow?"

"It pains her, but yes."

"Who is with her?"

"Her Majesty. The physician. A few maids."

"No soldiers?"

"No. They left to evaluate the storm. To give Her Majesty as much time as possible with the princess before she must attend her duties."

"What type of storm is it?"

"Skyfire, Your Highness."

"And how long until it reaches us?"

"A bell. Maybe more, maybe less."

"Tell Her Majesty to stay with her daughter. I will see to the storm."

The girl's eyes widened and she shook her head. "Oh, I ca—"

"If the queen would like to argue, she can find me at the storm terrace. But we both know she would rather stay here." Cassius pulled out another coin and offered it to her. "Keep me informed of her condition, and I shall keep these coming. Agreed?"

"Agreed." She grabbed the coin, bent to pick up her fallen rags, and bustled away.

Cassius weighed the coins left in his purse. He had a feeling it would be quite a bit lighter by the time he had all the information he desired, starting with where exactly the storm terrace was located.

Blue-white light struck the ground in the distance like a whip forged by the gods. Cassius stood on a terrace atop the famous golden dome of the palace. He had heard that in the mornings, sunlight reflected off this dome, making it appear as if two suns hung in the sky, but now dark had fallen hours before it was due, and the clouds pulsed with light.

He sought out the skyfire crystal at the base of his spine, pulling it from the holster in his armor. The hair on his arms rose as energy crackled over his skin. He focused on his connection with the stone, drawing its magic into him, stoking it into something greater, stronger. In the distance, he felt an echo of power bounce back to him.

"There you are," he murmured. "Come and play."

As if the storm could hear him, the sky blazed with light—dozens upon dozens of skyfire bolts streaking between clouds, lighting up the expanse of the churning black that had claimed the heavens. It was a show of strength from one storm to another.

Tempests were sentient enough to seek out destruction, to chase victims, or strategize like a commander during battle. But they could not see as a man could. So when he breathed life and magic into the Stormheart in his fist, that skyfire beast could not tell the difference between Cassius and a competing storm; and with a roar of thunder it began to approach Pavan at a quicker pace.

Cassius knew how most Stormlings would fight this battle. From a distance. It was the reason for the terrace upon which he stood, and the four watchtowers facing the cardinal directions. The Queen of Pavan likely would have produced a barrier in front of the city, and waged war against the skyfire there. But casting one's energy that far took a toll. It took longer to subdue the storm, and the fields surrounding the palace would be scorched beyond use as the skyfire struck again and again in the same area.

There was no challenge, no *enjoyment* in that kind of fight. He would not stand back and watch the storm flounder and weaken against his magic from afar. He craved victory, *battle*. Those beasts of the sky—where nature and the unnatural met and merged—centuries of myths and religions and scholars had tried to understand them, to know their origins, their purpose. But the only way to truly know a storm was to flay it open, to wring out its magic, to gorge on it until all that remained was desperation and hunger and fear. That was when the moment came, when the beast stopped fighting and surrendered its proverbial neck to the greater foe.

He lived for that moment. But it could only happen if the storm came close.

He gathered his magic, pulling from the well inside himself and ripping more from the Stormheart. The magic blended together, burning beneath his skin. For a moment, Cassius simply relished the power, then he flung it out far and wide, in all directions, not just toward the storm. He envisioned his magic like a woven textile, as millions upon millions of threads—crossing and knotting until it became a flexible but durable barrier that covered the city from wall to wall.

Then he waited.

The city below was still and quiet—the people hidden away in their homes or shelters as another warning horn sounded, louder and longer than all the rest. Nearer and nearer the storm drew. A few bolts streaked down, but the storm seemed to be biding its time, saving its destruction for where it would do the most damage.

When it had almost reached the city wall, the door behind Cassius slammed open. He scowled when he saw a few of the soldiers who stood between him and Aurora before.

"Why have you not stopped it?" one demanded. "Do it now, before it hits the city."

He held up a hand, not bothering to answer, and kept his focus trained on the city wall. Every time lightning flashed, he could see the faint shimmer of his barrier. He was confident it would hold, but he would not know how much effort it would take until he felt the first bolt.

He clenched his fist around the Stormheart as the first wall of clouds touched the edge of the city. Power surged in the air moments before five bolts of skyfire rent open the sky.

They struck simultaneously, like five cobras sinking their teeth into their would-be charmer. The blue-white light fragmented against the barrier, filling the night with a bright blaze. His magic rippled under the blows, but stretched taut and whole immediately after. The soldiers behind him went silent.

And then . . . oh, then came one of his favorite parts.

A high, furious screech carried on the wind. Thunder rumbled, and the heavens rained down wrath upon the land. More skyfire bolts than a dozen men could count struck with a shattering boom, and the night exploded with light as they were repelled.

Cassius grinned despite the effort and held firm, baiting the storm to come closer.

Close enough that he could reach its heart.

Against darkened skies
And darker souls,
A Stormling stands.
Amidst thunderous cries
And raining coals,
Raise Stormling hands.

—A Stormling Stands: Verses of Old

4

Aurora had not realized an arm could bleed so much. The first few hours had been . . . alarming. Feeling woozy and fatigued, she still couldn't quite believe that she'd purposely taken a knife to the arm. When the physician treated her, Rora's tongue had been loosened by pain, and she told her mother in no uncertain terms that she loathed Cassius. Her mother made her drink a tea steeped with herbs that dulled the pain and clouded her thoughts. She slept some, but woke from a nightmare about storms and knives and blood that could not be staunched, and weddings that could not be stopped.

The world had gone dark while she slept, and her mother stood framed in the flashing light of the open window. Rora shifted in her bed, whimpering when she put too much weight on her arm. The queen turned, an expression almost like pride on her face. "Come and see," her mother said. "It is . . . astonishing."

Aurora slid from her bed, her bandaged arm hanging at her side. As she reached the window, there was an explosion of light, as if all the stars in the sky had broken open above their heads.

Rora's mouth gaped. Overhead a skyfire storm had swallowed the sky from horizon to horizon. The thunder was so constant it sounded like the growl of a predator. Normally, the queen hurried Rora into the storm shelters beneath the palace well before a storm's arrival.

A cry caught in Rora's throat when light ripped across the sky. But the streaks of cold fire never reached the city. Instead, they collided with a nearly invisible shield, then fragmented, breaking off into dozens of smaller veins that moved over the barrier as if searching for a gap, before finally disappearing in the dark sky. With so many bolts of lightning striking at the same time, the whole sky burned like a silver sun when the skyfire spread over the invisible shield.

"How? Who?" she breathed.

"Your Cassius. We chose well. He is powerful."

Rora returned her gaze to the sky. The epicenter of the storm was nearing the palace. As she watched, something dark and ugly rose inside her. It had teeth and claws, and bitterness coated its tongue. The feeling was so potent, so consuming that it took a moment for her to give it a name.

Jealousy.

For years, she had done everything her mother had asked, given up everything that made her who she was because it was safer that way. Because her queen required it. She'd thrown herself into her studies with rigor, wanting to prove that she was worth more than her magic-barren body. She had committed her mother's every instruction to memory, believing that to rule was about more than magic—it took leadership and intelligence and compassion and strength. She cultivated those qualities in herself as best she could in her relative isolation—like a plant trying to grow in the dark.

And still . . . it was Cassius Locke her mother admired. Already Aurora could picture how her future would unfold. After the wedding, after her secret was spilled . . . she would be pushed aside by Cassius and her mother both. And the queen would finally have the heir she always should have had.

The darkest part of the storm began to stretch over the palace, and Rora saw the faint shimmer of the barrier disappear. That bitter envy reared up again, clawing through her veins. Then a single light flared, so blisteringly bright that she cried out, covering her eyes. All the power of the storm pummeled a single spot high on the dome, and then like a doused flame, the world went dark and still, and the storm raged no more.

Her mother murmured more praise, but Rora spun back toward her bed. The bile of jealousy and anger was beginning to drain away, but in its place Rora felt . . . ashamed and sad. Maybe she should just accept what was coming. Marry Cassius, let him rule Pavan, and she would continue her life in the same fashion as recent years—locked away somewhere with only her books for company.

A maid came to check her bandages, and the queen stopped her before she left to make a quiet request. Then her mother sat down beside the bed, looking pleased.

Rora felt bad for her earlier bitterness, but one thing was becoming clear . . . she wanted adventure and exploration, not more isolation. She wanted to feel like she was . . . *more*, not less.

"He is more than I had hoped for," her mother said.

Aurora could not stop her derisive scoff. "As long as he refrains from throwing knives."

"You mean, as long as you do not move into the knife's path."

"I had no choice! He would have expected me to take over storm duties. I did what I must."

Her mother hushed her, brushing fingers through her hair. "I know you did. You always do. I wish that we did not have to make such hard choices. I wish that as a woman, especially an *ungifted* one, you did not have to fight for every bit of space this world gives you. But we do." She touched Rora's bandaged arm. "And the skies know my girl is a fighter. Our world is brutal, but you are brave enough to face it. I know you are."

Nothing about this situation felt brave to Rora. It felt like giving up.

"I don't trust him," she whispered.

"Good. You *shouldn't* trust him. Or anyone. But better the beast you know. At least you will retain the crown and our home. The alternatives would be far worse."

Rora knew that. While the various kingdoms in Caelira had not waged war against each other since the Time of Tempests began, conflict within the kingdoms was more common. Families disputed who was the rightful heir—who was the worthiest or the strongest. Other nobles tried to wrest control. Her mother had squashed a few such rebellions after the deaths of her husband and son. It was how Aurora knew her mother would have no pity for the hurt Cassius caused her. One did not rule in this world without learning to be ruthless.

"Did you know I fell in love once before I met your father?" the queen asked. "He was dashing and brave and handsome. I was smitten before he ever spoke to me." The queen's gaze was far away, in another time. "But he had no intention of being shackled to a crown. He was a free spirit. An adventurer. He slipped out of my life with as much ease as he came into it. I was devastated, of course. Swore that I would never love another man."

"But then you met Papa?"

Her mother smiled softly. "Your father was a safe choice to rule by my side—wellborn, highly educated, and willing to take the Pavan name and submit to a woman as his ruler and wife. I thought that was all we would ever be—a safe choice. It took a little longer, but I fell so deeply for your father that it seemed impossible I had ever felt otherwise. I'm not saying you'll grow to love your prince. Though stranger things have happened. I'm only saying that time tempers all emotions, and what feels terrifying now will not always be so."

A knock sounded at the door, and the queen looked almost guilty. She squeezed Rora's hand and said, "You, my daughter, have a will stronger than a hundred tempests, and that is something not even magic could ever give you. You can allow him a chance or fight him. I hope you will choose the former."

The queen left the room, and Rora's stomach pitched when she heard a familiar, deep voice. The door eased open with a creak. She pulled the covers up high and pretended to be asleep.

Cassius said her name from the doorway, and then a click sounded. Rora hoped he left, but the scrape of boots against the floor told her otherwise. He sat down in the chair by her bed, and she kept her expression relaxed and her breathing even.

She fought a flinch when he touched her hair. He wound a strand around his finger, tugging just enough that she might have woken if she were really asleep. Did he know she was pretending?

"You don't deserve someone like me," he said. She clenched the fist hidden beneath her pillow. "But you are mine all the same."

Long moments passed with Rora pretending to be asleep. The air tickled her exposed skin as if the energy of the skyfire storm still swirled around him. He murmured, "It's not enough. But it's a start." Then he placed something on the pillow beside her.

Another knock came, and when he went to answer the door, she peeked at the object he left behind. Her breath caught.

A skyfire Stormheart.

Had the blinding light that blasted the storm terrace been Cassius taking a Stormheart? And if so, *how?*

"Your Highness. I brought more herbs for the princess to ease her pain." Rora recognized Novaya's voice.

"Please come in. Though I'm afraid the princess is sleeping."

Footsteps followed, and then another glass of tea was set on the bedside table.

"What is your name?" Cassius asked.

"Novaya, Your Highness."

"That is a lovely name. And your accent is not Pavanian. You're from . . ."

"Taraanar, originally, but I've been here most of my life."

"Ah, is the Rani Delta as lush as they say?"

"It is, Your Highness. It is a stunning contrast to the surrounding deserts."

His voice moved closer to the bed, to Novaya.

"How fitting then that it is your origin." Rora heard Nova suck in a gasp, followed by Cassius's low murmur. "You are beautiful. I've never seen hair shine so much as yours."

A cramp formed low in Aurora's belly. He was flirting with Nova? *Here?* Bile rose in her throat, and she swallowed it down. Not long ago she'd fallen blindly for his compliments. She had wanted to believe that someone could deem her special. Even with all her flaws. She wanted it with an ache that permeated every breath, and he'd used that to manipulate her.

Was he doing the same now to Nova? Or . . . was he truly interested in her old friend? Nova *was* beautiful. Once the wedding was done and he no longer needed to woo Rora, would it be Nova he sought out instead?

"Y-your Highness." Nova's voice had climbed higher. "I should take my leave."

"Not yet. I have more questions." His earlier sultry tone faded into something firmer. "Tell me about the markets in Taraanar. I'm told they are *extraordinary*."

"I was quite young when we left for Pavan. I remember little about the markets."

Rora heard the twist of the knob and the creak of the opening door, only for it to slam closed again. "And what of the markets in Pavan? What can you tell me of those?"

All Aurora could decipher of the conversation that followed was that Cassius wanted some information and would not take no for an answer. She heard mention of the storm cellars, various street names, something about a lantern and an eye.

"You'll be glad you told me, Novaya. You want me as a friend." She heard the distinct clinking of coins. "Keep your silence, and I promise you'll be the first person I come to when I next need a favor. Don't keep it, and I'll be much less friendly when we meet again."

The door opened and closed, followed by an odd thud. Rora waited, unsure if Cassius remained in the room, then slowly peeked out from beneath her blankets. The prince was gone, and Novaya sat slumped against the door, fists clenched at her sides and her breathing ragged. Had Cassius done something to her? Rora leaped from the bed and darted toward the girl. Before she got close, Nova held out a hand and cried, "*Don't*. Please don't come any closer. Just give me a moment."

"Did he hurt you?" Rora asked. She would not put it past him. Nova had clearly been reluctant to give him whatever information he wanted. After several deep breaths, Nova's fists unclenched and her body relaxed, her face dotted with perspiration. "I'm fine. I sometimes get . . . overwhelmed. But . . . I'm well now." Nova pressed the heels of her hands against her eyes and asked, "Were you awake the whole time?"

"I was. I didn't want to see him, so I pretended to be asleep."

"Your Highness, you must know I would never encourage anything untoward—"

Rora waved off her concern. "That doesn't matter. I'd rather know what information you gave him."

Nova froze, her face twisting with fear. "Please, I did not want to tell him."

"Tell him what?"

Nova's fists clenched again, and she shook her head sharply.

Rora asked, "Do you hate me that much? That you would side with him over me?"

"Hate you? I could never hate you, Rora. And I'm siding with myself. The place he's going . . . it's illegal. I would be in a great deal of trouble if anyone knew it was I who directed him there. Or if Cassius found out I told."

Illegal? Maybe the way out of this marriage had just fallen into her lap. If she could prove Cassius was unfit to be king, perhaps her mother would consider other alternatives.

"I need to follow him." Rora spun for her wardrobe, intent on finding some kind of disguise.

"No. Absolutely not. You can't."

"I can. You mentioned the servants' storm shelter. I'm guessing that's how he's getting out of the palace." They'd used that exit so many times as children it was hardly a secret anymore.

Rora searched through her wardrobe until she found a plain brown traveling cloak at the back. It used to belong to her brother, a keepsake she had secreted away as a child. It would be too large, but it was the only thing plain enough not to draw attention. As she began pulling it over the nightgown she wore, Nova rushed over. "Your Highness, please don't do this. It's not safe."

"Neither is spending my life married to that man. I'm going no matter what you say. So you can help me or you can leave."

"I am going to regret this," Nova murmured, wringing her hands. "At least hide your hair. The color is too recognizable to risk some of it slipping out from the cloak." She braided Rora's hair and twisted it up into a bun. Then she covered it with a cream-colored scarf wrapped in a traditional Taraanese style. Rora shoved her feet into a nice pair of boots and hoped the cloak would cover them. She risked missing him if she took any longer, so she moved for the door.

"I'll go with you," Nova offered.

"No. If it truly is dangerous, I'll not risk you for my recklessness."

"It's not as though we have not done reckless things together for most of our lives."

Rora smiled and took hold of the girl's hand. "I have missed that more than you will ever know. But this is something I have to do on my own."

Rora set off for the servants' wing in the quickest walk she could manage without drawing attention. Shortcuts allowed her to avoid palace guards, and in record time Rora was standing before the entrance to the storm shelter. She scurried down the stairs into the dark.

The servants' shelter was merely a long empty room, whereas the royal shelter had elegant fixtures and furniture and even a few beds. Rora did not dare light a sconce as she walked through the shelter. Eventually, out of the darkness formed the shape of a familiar set of stairs that led to the outside. She opened the cellar door enough to slip out and then softly set it back into place. On the darkened street that ran along the palace wall, things became trickier. Cassius might have beat her here. She could head in the direction of the main road and hope she caught up to him. *Or . . .* she could assume that she changed quickly and took enough shortcuts to arrive ahead of him. She was still considering her options when the door behind her creaked open. She pulled the hood forward to hide her face as much as possible and began walking slowly toward the main road. She hunched and shuffled as if she were an old woman, then peered back briefly over her shoulder.

The newcomer wore a wide-brimmed hat angled to cover his face and a black traveling cloak. His height and build matched Cassius, and he walked with the same calm confidence. She continued her slow gait, and eventually he passed her. Rora waited until he was a decent length ahead of her, and then she dropped the act and followed as quietly and inconspicuously as possible.

As they neared the city's center, the streets became less deserted. Two people huddled in a small alley. A shadowed form darkened a doorway. A group of men stood outside a seedy tavern, their voices loud and slurred, discussing the earlier skyfire storm as if they'd fought it themselves. Even in her disguise, a few people eyed her as she passed.

She began to worry that the possibility of getting caught by Cassius wasn't her only concern. She had left the palace often; she did it regularly for her early-morning rides and for the occasional royal tour through the city. But that was along the main road that led directly from the palace gate to the city gate. It was well paved and well lit, and could be seen by guards patrolling atop both the palace and city walls. Now she was truly on her own.

When she looked away from the group of drunk men, Cassius was gone. Panicked, she launched into a jog, scanning alleyways and side streets for his silhouette. She saw what might have been a black cloak disappearing around the bend of a dark, twisting street. She hesitated. If she were wrong, the trail would go cold.

Trusting her gut, Rora darted down the street, unnerved by the darkness that lurked around her. The buildings grew more dilapidated, and up ahead a lone figure strolled down the street. Occasionally he stopped, peered into a building or down another street, and then continued on. The neighborhood grew rougher as they plunged deeper into the city—a city that was decidedly less pristine and prosperous than the one she always saw on the royal tours.

The streets smelled of some unidentifiable muck, and houses leaned together as if holding each other up. *Surely* people in Pavan didn't live like this. Rora edged closer to Cassius so that she didn't fall behind again. When he stopped again under the flickering glow of a swinging lantern, he glanced backward and she was luckily covered by the shadow of a building.

The lantern squeaked in the wind on the silent street. Too silent. It was late, but there should have been some noise . . . people moving in their houses, a crying babe, a barking dog. Something. Light shone on the familiar hard angle of Cassius's jaw, then he dipped his head and disappeared into a building. Rora gathered her cloak up in her fists, and ran. Skidding to a stop beneath the lantern, she faced a set of stairs and a boarded-up door of a deserted building. Frowning, she approached and pushed against the wood. It didn't budge. Feeling around the frame for any hidden latches, Rora came up empty. But just outside the frame on the side of the building was something carved into the wood.

She ran her fingers over the grooves and followed the way they fanned out from a circle in the center. It reminded her of the way water in a tub swirled after the plug had been pulled. A storm. She wasn't positive what kind—a hurricane, perhaps? Pavan was landlocked, so she had never seen one in real life, but she had seen illustrations of the monstrous swirling beasts.

Her fingers traced again over the carving, following it all the way to the edge. She expected to run into the next building, as it was clear when she looked up that the two were attached, but instead her fingers found open air. She leaned over the edge of the stair railing, and found a small gap that had been boarded up to make the buildings appear connected at a glance, but left enough space at the bottom for a person to duck beneath.

That must have been where he'd gone. The gap was small, and so dark she would not have seen it if she had not been looking. It must have been difficult for Cassius to fit. She felt ill with nerves as she approached the passageway. But she had to know what was on the other side. As her mother said . . . *better the beast you know.*

She squeezed through the opening. She had to shuffle sideways for about ten steps, then the tunnel widened. Twenty paces ahead, there was a faint blue glow in the darkness. Her stomach roiled like a tossing sea, but she continued forward. The eerie silence of the street at her back gave way to a dull roar that developed into voices as she neared the exit.

"Wind charms!" one cried. "Tie it on your laundry line and never lose another garment."

A gruff male voice said, "Firestorms! Rare and potent!"

She poked her head outside the tunnel, but immediately pulled it back. There were people *everywhere,* more than a hundred, walking through narrow lanes of merchant stalls. Slower this time, she poked her head out, and when she didn't see Cassius, she slipped out of the passageway.

It was a market, like the open-air one in the shopping district. But this one was far from *open*. The backs of buildings formed the border of the market, leaving a long rectangular gap hidden from the streets. A black cloth had been stretched overhead, providing further seclusion. Lanterns were strung up around the edges and down the aisles. But they didn't hold fire inside. They glowed an eerie blue and contained . . . *skyfire*—dozens of thin branches of light that split and stretched toward the glass like the roots of a tree. The lightning was frozen inside the lantern.

It was not unlike the chandelier that she loved so much in the great hall. But she had never seen storm magic like this outside the palace.

"Need a lightning lantern?" An older woman stood at Rora's elbow, her skin weathered and dark, her voice a gravely whisper. "Guaranteed to stay lit for one year. Buy two and I'll cut ye a deal."

Rora shook her head. "No, I—no, thank you."

"Ah, ye sound like a pretty young thing. A skyfire necklace then? I've got one that's exactly like what the princess wore to meet her new prince. A lil' *smaller*, of course."

The woman picked up a chain, and it had miniature crystals that fanned out just like the one Rora had worn. The center crystal had been painted ruby red to mimic a firestorm heart.

"No, thank you."

"Sumthin' a bit more extravagant, then? I've a talisman that would protect ye from all types of storms for one week. Ye could go anywhere, see anything, and never have to fear that ye might not make it home. Or perhaps ye have an enemy? Maybe a nasty husband who beats ye? Is that why ye got so much of ye face covered? I've just the thing! A powder made from the heart of a firestorm. Sprinkle it in his food, and he'll burn from the inside out."

"No need to burn people from the inside out, Etel. This one is with me."

A large, masculine form pressed into Rora's side, and a heavy arm draped over her shoulders. The old woman straightened. She scowled and spit on the ground, and when she spoke, her tone was higher, less raspy, "Ye could have told me that, Locke, before I wasted me time."

Rora froze. *Cassius.* He'd found her. She had been so distracted by the woman and her wares that she hadn't thought to keep watch. He pulled her forward, and her feet dragged like lead. She couldn't take a deep enough breath, and her eyes began to cloud with tears.

What have I done? How will I explain this? What will he do to me?

"Come on, girl. I'm doing you a favor getting you away from that fraud. You could at least play along."

Rora lurched to a stop, and jerked her head upward. That *wasn't* Cassius. Her hood began to slip backward. She tried to catch it, but her movements lagged behind her mind, and her injured arm had grown stiff and numb. Cool air hit her uncovered cheeks, her nose, then her forehead. Even with the scarf hiding her hair, she might be recognized. And she had a feeling this was a very bad place for a princess to be.

The hood's descent halted; it wasn't her fingers that had caught the fabric but his. He was so tall that Rora had to crane her head back to see him. His hair was a dark, wavy brown and hung long enough to brush against his shoulders.

"Keep that hood up. This is no place for little girls."

"I'm not a little girl!" She clamped her mouth shut, immediately wishing she could take the declaration back. Not only because it sounded exactly like what a little girl *would* say but also because she had not tempered her volume. At all. And though it wasn't Cassius who caught her, he was here somewhere. She bit her lip in worry, and the stranger's eyes tracked down to her mouth briefly before darting around her face.

He still held on to her hood, keeping it back enough that he could see her eyes. "So you're not a little girl. Still doesn't mean this is any place for you."

She could not argue with that.

"She called you Locke."

His eyes narrowed. "Yes. And?"

"As in . . . *Prince* Locke?"

He laughed so hard that he released her hood. She rushed to grab it and pull it down to cover her face. She had no doubt people were staring now. He sucked in a breath, and then as if he couldn't help himself, burst into laughter all over again.

Still chuckling, he said, "I'm about as much a prince, as you are a princess."

Rora resisted the juvenile impulse to inform him just how much of a princess she was.

"But . . . the name," she said. "Are you related?" Perhaps he was the person Cassius had come to meet. In which case, she needed to leave *now*.

"I'd rather die than be related to that poor excuse for royalty. The name is just a name, like any other. Like yours?" he prompted.

Rora's mind went blank when she tried to invent a name to give him. So instead she shook her head.

"Good. Smart girl. This is a place for secrets. Not truths." For the first time, Rora looked away from him and her eyes caught on row after row of glass jars and tubes and bottles, each of them glowing like the lanterns she saw when she entered the market. But these weren't all skyfire. A fat, round jar contained a funnel of black and gray smoke. She squinted, certain that it was moving. That it . . . *twisted*.

The man, *Locke*, picked it up, long fingers plucking the jar from the sea of others. Inside was a tiny twister like the one that had killed her brother. She stared at it, stunned into awe. There was something truly *beautiful* about the way a storm moved. The other jars swirled with different kinds of magic—blizzards and thunderstorms and skyfire and firestorms—each more wondrous than the last. All her life she'd been desperate for magic to call her own, and now it stretched out before her as far as she could see.

The stranger spoke again. "Steer clear of the vendors around the edges. Those are the frauds. Get whatever magic you're here for, and get out. Don't talk to anyone unless you must, and for sky's sake, the next time you come here try to look less . . ."

"Less what?"

He moved closer, peering down through the shadows cast by her hood to meet her eyes. "Less like the kind of pretty girl this place would chew up and spit out long before dawn."

Whether it be thunderstorm, hurricane, or some storm on which we have not yet laid eyes, one truth remains—challenge a tempest, survive it, and you become its master.

—*The Tale of Lord Finneus Wolfram*

5

Locke knew the moment he spoke that he had said the wrong thing. Her stormy blue eyes narrowed to shards of ice, and she pushed her narrow shoulders back and her chin up. He had almost certainly guaranteed she would be back, regardless of the danger.

But before she said a word, her eyes caught on something over his shoulder. The cold in her eyes melted, her lips parted on a sharp inhale, and her whole body went stiff. He had been teasing earlier with his little girl comment, but now she *did* look young. And frightened. And it roused every protective instinct he had.

Locke started to turn, but before he moved more than a step, a hand tangled in the leather straps that crisscrossed his upper body. Then another hand—soft but with a strong grip—took hold of his jaw and pulled his head forward again.

"Don't," she whispered.

For a moment, he forgot what he was doing entirely. She was close, and whatever fear had been in her before was gone, burned away by a blazing intensity. Her skin smelled fragrant, as if she had rubbed perfume or oils over the wrist that hovered by his mouth.

"Don't what?"

"Don't *look*."

Talking to Etel, she had been adorably curious but gravely out of her depth. He hadn't been in the mood to chase a girl. His temper soured the day the Locke royal procession had paraded into Pavan like a gift from the heavens. He'd planned to snag a seat at a pub and not move until dawn, but she had caught his attention anyway.

His earlier mild interest had become a fist in his chest, gripping him tighter than the fingers she tangled in his leathers. Her cloak was too big, and the sleeves had fallen back when she reached for him. Seemingly of their own volition, his fingers touched her slim wrist. She glanced behind him again, then huddled closer, and he let his fingers graze down her arm, slipping under the sleeve that had gathered around her elbow.

For one minuscule moment, she leaned into his touch, then she jerked away, snatching her hands back like he'd tried to steal them. She slammed into a table behind her. Dozens of glass vials clanked and toppled, and on the far end a solitary jar of snowstorm magic toppled over the edge.

It smashed onto the dirt path, glass flying, and Locke's hand moved to the harness strapped over his chest and abdomen that held his supplies. He braced himself for a blizzard to form only steps away, but the snow in the jar scattered harmlessly over the ground, like nothing more than spilled sugar.

Damn. Even Velarran was selling the fake stuff. The portly shop owner's face went slack, then hardened with anger and embarrassment. Locke knew supplies were low. Storm magic was fetching a higher price than ever at the moment, in part because of the Slumber season. But the roots of this shortage had begun months before the season change. In the last year, two of the major storm-hunting crews had disbanded. Though perhaps *disbanded* was not the right word, when more than half the crew had died.

Across the aisle, Badren, a thin, oily snake of a man, had begun blustering about, yelling that Velarran was a fraud. Locke didn't keep up with local politics and gossip. The crew traveled too much for him to care about any particular city, but the animosity between these two was far older than Locke's nineteen years.

Quickly, before either man could turn on the girl, Locke took her elbow and pulled. She looked at him, wide-eyed and wary, but when she noticed all the people gathering to watch the commotion, she pulled him close, practically using his body as a shield.

She peeked around him, and once again something made terror flit across her face. But this time, she turned on her heel and tried to run. He still held her elbow, so she did not get far. "Where are you—"

She looked up at him, and even in that oversize cloak, she was impossibly pretty. The ferocity in her expression had his free hand going to his weapons belt on instinct.

"You need to let me go." That sounded like the *last* thing he wanted to do. But she continued. "There's a man at a stall behind you who is going to notice me, and if he sees me . . . he *cannot* see me. It would mean bad things for me, for you, for this whole market."

This time when she yanked her arm, he was caught off guard and she got loose, stumbling back a few paces. The urge to find the man who frightened her was nearly overwhelming. Storm magic was not the only illegal trade that happened in the Eye. Gambling, drugs, prostitution, murder for hire—it was all here if you knew where to look. Whoever plagued her was likely dangerous indeed, but Locke spent his days in the belly of the world's deadliest beasts. Men were nothing in comparison.

But she wasn't just afraid for herself. She thought this man dangerous to everyone around them. So Locke swallowed down his instincts, and instead of seeking danger, he went for the girl.

Hooking an arm over her shoulders, he pulled her in tight to his side. He dragged her hood down to cover all of her face. She resisted, squirming away from him, and he spoke low against her ear. "Be still. I'm not going to harm you. Keep your head down, and I'll get you out of here."

His only answer was her hand, snaking up his chest again to grip the straps there. All she could see was their feet, so Locke kept their gait easy and relaxed. The market was nearly at capacity, so he had to maneuver her body through crowded spaces. Sometimes he would hold her hips and guide her through a gap. Other times, he would curl her close until her cheek pressed into his chest, and they would squeeze together through congested pathways.

When they reached the booths at the outer edge, he quickened their pace toward the tents that lined the back wall of the market. He had a room at a rundown inn a few streets away, but with all their wares stored either in the market booth or in the tent, at least two of his crew stayed in the market to protect or sell their goods at all times. Few people were dumb enough to try to cross them, but, as he'd seen with Velarran, these were desperate times. He pulled back the tent flap and pushed her through the opening. He followed and breathed a sigh of relief that none of the others were here.

Tentatively, the girl pushed her hood back enough that her face was visible in profile. His eyes lingered on the high arch of her cheeks, the full curve of her lips. She glanced over her shoulder at him, then her eyes strayed to the tent around them. On the left side was a table, piled high with jars and vials. Jinx must have been enchanting a batch of containers for their next expedition. To the right was a large rug with cushions, and at the back were a handful of sleeping pallets. The days spent in cities selling their wares were always an adjustment. They only traveled and hunted during daylight on the road, but here they were mostly nocturnal.

"You want to tell me what just happened?"

She crossed her arms over her chest in a gesture that was half defiant, half defensive. "It was nothing."

"Ah, yes, I frequently go ghost white and try to run away over nothing."

She lifted a hand to her cheek as if she could feel the way her skin had paled. Then her fingers touched the scarf that wound about her head beneath her hood. Her chin tilted up again, revealing the long, graceful line of her neck. "I appreciate your assistance." Her attempt at haughty composure was almost convincing, but she looked at the tent flap like she wanted to bolt. She likely only hesitated because her dangerous man was still out there.

"And I would appreciate an explanation."

She gave him a look; clearly she wasn't used to people arguing with her. "I can't give you that."

"The man you're afraid of . . . does he—"

"I'm not afraid of him," she snapped. Her tone was so fierce he nearly believed her, but he hadn't read her wrong out there. He and fear were old friends. It had taken his parents' place to raise him when they died, and he recognized the foul taint when he saw it. Even now, it lingered about her hunched shoulders and danced over her whitened fingers as they gripped her forearms.

He eased off. "Fine. The man you were avoiding, then. Who is he?"

"I can't tell you that."

"Who is he to you? Personal or business?"

She hesitated, and there were a dozen subtle shifts in her expression as she considered what to tell him. It wasn't that hard a question, so she was either crafting a lie or this man's infiltration into her life fell into both categories. His mind conjured up possibilities for dangerous men and how they might be involved in her personal life. He didn't like any of them. His voice was barely above a growl as he asked, "He's a danger to you?"

Her arms dropped to her sides, and her long lashes brushed her cheeks when she sighed. "Probably not in the way you're thinking."

His fists clenched at his sides. Even if the man wasn't going to barrel into this tent, trying to kill her at any moment, she hadn't denied that there was danger in some form. It should not matter. She was just a girl who was in over her head. Those were plentiful in dodgy places like the Eye. If he hunted down the demons of every wayward girl, he wouldn't have time to hunt a single storm. But there was something about her. Her look of wonder at Etel's booth had caught his eye. The defiant way she stood her ground and made him acknowledge her as more than a little girl . . . that was when she got her hooks in him. She might appear fragile, but there was fire in her. And he definitely knew she was no little girl. He could still remember the feel of her pressed up against his side as he led her through the market.

Even now, she swayed on her feet and eyed the cushions to her left like she might collapse under the weight of her exhaustion, but met his gaze with a calm, fortified expression that said she would never admit defeat, not to him or her fatigue.

In a way, she reminded him of his sister. He had never realized how little strength had to do with size and power until his parents had died and left only him and his sister behind. He had been six and she eleven, neither old enough to take care of the other, not that it stopped his sister from trying. She refused to fold in the face of adversity. She was brazen and brave right to the very end.

He ducked his head, then sprawled onto the rug, leaning back to prop an elbow on one of the cushions. Give him a violent tempest any day over those memories. At least the storm he could fight.

"Sit down."

She hesitated, but complied. She made sitting on the ground look graceful as she lowered herself to her knees and eased her body back onto a pillow. He crossed his legs and leaned forward to brace his elbows on his knees and stare at her.

She did not wither under his study, but instead turned the focus on him. "Is Locke your first name or your last name?"

"Listen, princess—"

That made her flinch. "*Princess?*"

"You never gave me your name. And when I said you weren't a princess before, you had this glint in your eye like you might pull out a crown and prove me wrong. So stop dragging your feet, *princess,* and tell me about that man."

"Don't call me that."

"You sure are fond of telling me what *not* to do. This is easily solved if you tell me your name."

She growled in frustration. "You told me I was smart for keeping my name secret."

He had told her that. But that was when he had intended only to save her from Etel and send her on her way. Now . . . now he didn't know what he was doing.

Before he could examine all the reasons it was a bad idea, he maneuvered himself to sit directly in front of her. He wanted to grab her hands, but he gripped his own knees instead. "You can trust me with your name. With whatever trouble you're in."

He saw her response coming before the words were even all the way off her tongue. "I'm not in any—"

He scooped up one of her hands, pressing it between both of his own. "It's just a name, princess. Give me your name."

Something happened when he took her hand; an electric, tingling sensation tickled down her spine, making her shiver. Her first instinct told her to run, far and fast, but as long as Cassius lurked in the market outside that was impossible. She had noted Locke's size earlier—his impressive height and muscled build—but he felt even bigger sitting right in front of her. He had a scar through his right brow and another on his chin, just below the corner of his mouth. His eyes were a deep brown, and his jaw was dusted with short, dark hairs. It added a rough masculinity to a face that otherwise might have been too pretty for a man decked out in leather armor.

Scorch it all, he looked good in leather. His chest was broad, and his armor had all manner of straps and loops from which tubes and vials and jars dangled just like the ones she'd seen in the market. A row of blades at his hip added a dash of menace. When her eyes lifted again to his, that scarred brow rose along with one corner of his mouth. Menace and mirth. What a bizarre combination.

A familiar heat crept over her skin the longer he stared, and it reminded her of Cassius. The two men couldn't be more different in spite of their names. Cassius's power felt cold and controlled, whereas Locke blazed with all the intensity of the sun. But the way she reacted around them both? That was alarmingly similar. All the more reason she needed to escape this tent.

"Name," he urged again. And she was so desperate for him to stop looking at her with such single-minded focus that she opened her mouth, ready to say whatever it took to gain some distance.

"It's Ror—" Her brain caught up a moment too late. She slammed her mouth closed and considered slamming her face into a pillow. One little eyebrow arch plus a half smile and a troublesome nickname, and she forgot how to use her brain. *Again.*

"What was that? Sounded like—"

"Ah . . . Roar. You wanted a name, and that's it. Just Roar."

Not a great recovery, but only a few people knew her as Rora. To most, she was only ever Princess Aurora or Your Highness. No one would expect her to be in a black market dressed in plain, ill-fitting clothes.

His eyes narrowed. "What kind of name is that?"

"What kind of name is Locke?" she shot back.

"A nickname. It's where I grew up."

"You grew up in Locke?"

What had he said before? He'd rather die than be related to Cassius, *a poor excuse for royalty*. What did he know that she didn't?

He shrugged in answer and mumbled, "Roar." He said it again, his mouth forming the word slowly, as if it was more than just four letters strung together. "You do make a lot of noise for a little thing."

She snorted. An actual, humiliating, totally un-princess-like snort . . . because she only qualified as little in comparison to his staggering height. His smile widened at the sound, and she wanted so badly to flee. But he grew up in Locke, and he clearly knew his way around this market, and she had so many questions.

He leaned forward so their faces were level.

"Roar."

"Locke," she replied.

"Who are you?"

That was her cue to bolt. She had lingered longer than she should already.

"I have to go."

She still had questions, but none were worth the risk of his curiosity bearing fruit. She stood, and he followed, his reflexes so quick that he was fully upright before she was. All his ease and charm disappeared, swallowed up in an intensity as thick as fog. He gripped her biceps, bending to peer at her beneath her hood. His thumb unknowingly pressed against the wound on her arm, and she swallowed down a whimper.

He said, "I'm sorry. But you can't leave without telling me about the man. I can't help you if you don't *tell* me."

Until now, she had been the flustered one. But the look in Locke's eyes was blind panic. She did not understand. He dropped his hands and stepped back. Turning away, he shoveled his fingers through his hair and gripped the back of his neck. He rasped, "I'm sorry, I—"

Rora never heard the rest of his apology. The tent flap flew open, and a girl ducked through. Long blue-black hair swayed in a ponytail down her back, and one side of her head was nearly shaved bare with a geometric pattern near her temple.

"Locke, get your ass—oh."

Rora was the *oh*.

Clothed in black leather, the girl looked ready to do battle, and her short stature made her no less intimidating. She crossed her arms and studied Rora, her wide-set eyes narrowing beneath dark, thick brows.

"Picking up strays now?" she asked.

"Knock it off, Jinx."

The girl, *Jinx* apparently, stared for a long moment, and Rora had to order her back not to curve under the attention. Then Jinx dropped her arms and shrugged, sauntering over toward a table covered in glass containers. "Duke is asking for you," she said to Locke.

"It has to be me? Where's Bait? Ransom? Sly?"

"Bait attempted to woo the adjacent stall owner's daughter and failed spectacularly, as per usual. Duke sent him off to prevent any potential trouble. Ransom is playing bully to make sure no one's fingers get too sticky. And Sly disappeared. Like she does. The question is . . . what are *you* doing?"

As if her words weren't blatant enough, she followed them with a suggestive bounce of her eyebrows. Locke shifted uncomfortably. Uneasiness was such an odd look on his imposing figure that Rora wanted to spare him the scrutiny.

"It's my fault he disappeared," she said.

Jinx raised an eyebrow and snorted. "Clearly."

The insinuation made something flip low in Rora's belly.

"I've never been here before. I caused a bit of a scene, and Locke came to my rescue."

"He does that." Jinx smiled—white teeth against almond skin. "A regular old prince charming."

"Jinx . . ." A look passed between them, and it held far more meaning than just his annoyed growl of her name.

Jinx's accent was similar to those Rora had heard from Odilar, but not quite the same. Visitors from across Caelira were rare because of the dangers of traveling through the wilds, so her interactions with foreigners were limited. The contingent from Locke traveled the farthest of any in her lifetime.

"First timer, huh? I'm Jinx. In case you didn't catch that from all his huffing and puffing." She leaned back against the worktable, jars clinking behind her.

"I'm . . . Roar."

"I like it. Strong. Bold." She winked and continued: "Next time try saying it without looking like you want to disappear into the nearest wall."

That was exactly what Rora wished she *could* do. It was crazy that she was even still here. She needed to look for Cassius. If she didn't learn what he was doing, this whole risky situation would be for naught.

"I should go."

"Nonsense," Jinx said. "If this is your first time at the Eye, you've got to get the full experience. If you can handle the chaos, it's really quite beautiful."

The Eye. At least now Rora had *something* to go on. And *beautiful* didn't even begin to describe this place. She couldn't forget that first sight. Lightning frozen in a lantern. Blizzards in bottles. Storms that had terrified and fascinated her for her entire life shrunk down and small enough to hold in her hand. That alone would have been stunning, but the hidden location and the bustle of shoppers and haggling stall owners made her feel like she had entered a new world. And it was right here in her city. For years, she'd been a failure with her hand on the knob of a door that would forever be locked. She forced herself to accept it because she had no choice. There were two kinds of people in this world—Stormlings and everyone else. But this place . . . it changed *everything*. Those were regular people out there, the ungifted, buying up magic like loaves of bread.

"And you all . . . you work here?"

Jinx scoffed. "We're what keeps places like this running."

Rora looked over to Locke, not following. He answered, "We're hunters."

"Hunters?"

Jinx cut in, "Who do you think conquers those storms so the wealthy and the wicked can have their dose of power? Scorch me, Locke. You've gotten really bad at flirting if you hadn't even played the storm-hunter card yet. It's pure gold."

"Jinx," he warned again.

"Wait . . . all that"—it was hard for Rora to even spit out the word— "that *magic* out there . . . you did that?"

"Not *all* of it. But all the best stuff out there came from us."

"So you're both Stormlings? But you're not in the military?" All Stormlings not of noble blood were conscripted into the military. No exceptions. She turned to Locke. "Or did you forget to mention that you're nobility?" Maybe he was related to Cassius after all.

"Where did you find this girl?" Jinx asked. "Under a rock? If we relied on the precious Stormlings for magic, none of this would exist. We'd all be trapped in our grimy cities, bursting at the seams with overcrowding and poverty, too afraid to leave and face the storms outside."

Suddenly, Rora's stomach dropped and her head spun. Sweat slicked over her skin. If she didn't get some air, she was going to be sick. She listed to the side and stumbled slightly.

"Roar?" Hands gripped her arms, and her feet took that as permission to be even less cooperative.

"You can do storm magic?" The words came out in a slurred mess, barely more than a whisper. Dizziness swarmed her, and black spots filled her vision.

"Roar, can you hear me? Tell me what's wrong."

Her mouth watered, and her throat felt thick as she tried to swallow. "You—you can do storm magic, and you weren't born with it?"

Locke's face filled her vision. "Did you eat anything? Touch anything strange in the market?" Rora couldn't remember if she ate at all today beyond the tea she was given for the pain.

"Can you—"

"Yes," he snapped, giving a slight shake of her shoulders. "I can, and I wasn't. Now quit dodging every question and tell me what's wrong!"

Maybe everything. Or nothing. Maybe none of this was real, and she was back in her bed having an herb-induced dream. Or maybe everything she'd been taught, everything she thought she knew, was absolutely wrong.

"Locke, your hand," Jinx said.

Rora struggled to focus her eyes as the world began to spin. Locke's hand was large and rough, and something red was smeared across his palm. Now that she thought about it, a sharp ache had swallowed her injured arm.

Rora closed her eyes to fight off the dizziness, and when she tried to open them again, the dark whispered for her to stay. So she did.

The first tribes of Caelira lived where the desert met the sea in a land called Vyhodi. Blessed by the goddess with the ability to borrow magic from the natural world, they were her favored children. Over time, they desired more and more magic, nearly stripping the land entirely. Greed was their first sin. Pride would be their second.

—*The Origin Myths of Caelira*

6

Locke caught Roar as she began to slump toward the floor. She was lighter than he had expected, her frame small beneath the billowing mass of the cloak she wore. Everything went silent as he looked at her slack face. He touched her cheek in an attempt to wake her, and blood smeared from his hand to her skin. For a few moments, he'd forgotten the blood.

"Find Duke," he barked at Jinx, before carrying Roar to the rug. He shoved up her oversize sleeves and found a bandage on her upper arm that had been soaked through. Skies, had she been bleeding this whole time? He thought back to when he'd grabbed her arm before Jinx's arrival. She had flinched, but he assumed that was because of his over-reaction to her attempts to leave. Had he reopened her wound? The man she was afraid of in the market . . . had he done this? Fury flashed hot and then cold in his gut.

He leaned over her, listening for her breathing. The soft caress of warm air touched his ear, and he jerked back, swallowing. Bandages. He needed to stanch the bleeding. He searched for the pack of medical supplies they took on hunts. Duke had the most medical knowledge of anyone in the group, but Locke was more than capable himself. He returned to Roar's side with a pile of supplies—bandages, a salve made from some of Jinx's magically enhanced herbs, and a full canteen of water. He peeled back the bloodied strips of cloth, and his stomach turned. The wound was deep. One of her stitches was torn. ·

He pressed a new bandage down, and in a few moments dots of red began to show through. He cursed. Digging through the supplies again he found a plant called battle moss that soaked up blood like a sponge. According to legend, it grew on the site of ancient battlefields where the blood of the old gods soaked into the soil. But this particular batch had been grown by Jinx in under an hour. The benefits of having an earth witch on the crew.

He pressed the moss against the wound, and then wrapped a new bandage around it to hold the plant in place. He began checking the rest of her for injuries. He pulled up her cloak, intending to remove it, but hesitated when he found her legs bare and the lacy hem of what appeared to be a nightgown. His heartbeat thundered in his ears. He couldn't think about why she might be wearing only that beneath her cloak. Instead, he focused on the most pressing task. Pulling her cloak back down into place, he settled for a slow inventory of her body over her clothes. Starting at her feet, he patted his hands up her legs, searching for any more spots that might be wet with blood. He pushed up the sleeve on her other arm and found her skin pale and unmarked. She felt a little clammy, but otherwise he could find no other injuries.

He stood to wait for Duke, and paced the small area of the tent.

There was no keeping the memories of his sister at bay now. It was always harder when he was stressed, and seeing Roar lying there, pale and unconscious, had him more than a little on edge. They didn't look alike. The girl lying on the rug was fair and lean and willowy, while his sister had been much younger and looked like him: dark olive skin, brown hair, brown eyes. It was not appearances that made him connect the two but . . . their spirits.

He had precious few memories of his sister. The day she died remained fuzzy in his mind, and he was all too happy to let it stay that way. The grief had stolen bad and good memories alike. But he remembered the feel of his sister, the timbre of her soul, the bravado with which she had lived. Roar had that same strange mix of vulnerability and strength.

He had not been able to help his sister. He had been too young, too weak. But he *could* help Roar. Whatever she was into, he would help her get out of it. And maybe helping Roar would let him find some measure of peace that he had been missing all these years.

The flap of the tent opened, letting in the dull noise from the market. He saw gray hair and sighed in relief. Duke was his mentor. Locke might have considered Duke like a father if he let himself grow that attached to anyone. But he didn't, never could. Life taught him early that to love something was to tempt fate to take it away. The old man moved closer and knelt with a grace that belied his age. His long gray hair was braided and tossed over his shoulder, and his hand tangled in his beard for a moment before he touched the bandage work Locke had done.

"How's the wound?" Duke asked. "Any sign of infection?"

"No. It looked fresh. Had to use battle moss to soak up the blood."

The old man frowned. "Did it happen in the market?"

He shook his head. "Doubtful. She bled through a previous bandage, so I think the wound reopened." The old man's knowing green eyes fixed on Locke now, and even though he kept his expression blank, he knew his mentor saw much more than Locke wanted.

"You all right, son?"

Locke had been eleven when Duke had taken him in. He had hit a growth spurt, and could no longer depend on childhood cuteness to gain him sympathy and coins when he begged in the markets. Instead of looking at him with compassion, people saw a gangly boy—dark skinned and dirty and undoubtedly trouble. When you live on the streets for five years without parents or authority figures, you're bound to end up with some rough edges. But Duke saw past the attitude to a potential beneath that not even Locke had believed existed.

"I'm fine," Locke said. "Just make sure she's okay."

"Tell me what happened before she fainted. Was she agitated? Did she seem ill?"

Quickly, Locke recounted the last hour. "It was strange," he said. "She was in the market, so she had to know of the storm trade, but she was shocked to find out that Jinx and I had magic."

Duke hummed and smoothed a hand over her forehead. "There is something familiar about her, but I can't place it. She might have stumbled upon the market by accident. It does happen." He touched both

sides of her neck, then her wrist. "Clammy. But her pulse is normal."
He peeked beneath the bandage to study the skin around the wound. "I
don't see any swelling or bruising or rashes, nothing that could indicate
an infection or poisoning. She likely fainted from the blood loss. And
exhaustion by the looks of it. Some rest and food, and she'll be fine."

"You think she's hungry?" The thought sent another riot of agitation
through him. "Is she on her own?"

"I doubt it. She's too well groomed and clean. She's fatigued, to be
certain. But there are no signs of prolonged malnourishment. Whoever
she is, she takes decent care of herself. Or someone else does."

Duke meant his words to be reassuring, but it was not enough. It
worried Locke that she hadn't woken, and it bothered him more that
he was torn up over a girl he did not know. He had not survived this
long by being softhearted.

She would wake. He would find her somewhere safe to stay. His
status as a hunter meant plenty of people would jump at the chance
to do him a favor. He could find her a job. Something that would pay
well. There wasn't much time to do it in, but he couldn't leave Pavan
with this still weighing on him.

The crew came and went, bringing in merchandise from the booth
as the market closed up. Each time they ducked into the tent, their
eyes tracked to him, and then Roar.

Bait, a sixteen-year-old novice hunter, was the first to do more than
look. He squatted down beside Roar and reached out for the scarf
wrapped around her head.

"Bait, if you put a finger on her, I'm going to break it off."

A chuckle sounded behind him, and his friend Ransom clapped a
hand on his shoulder. Ran had joined the crew two years after Locke.
He had been sixteen to Locke's thirteen, and they hated each other at
first, both vying for Duke's approval. Now he was the closest friend
Locke had. And Ran was giving Locke a knowing look that only made
him more agitated.

"She's pretty," Ran said.

Locke only grunted in response, and his crew rumbled with laughter around him, which only gave him the urge to pace again.

"You're awfully touchy about this one. What exactly were you doing with her before I came in?" That was Jinx, who sat at the table enchanting jars for their next hunt. She winked, and he scowled.

"It's not like that. She reminds me of my sister."

The tent fell silent. He didn't talk about his sister, ever. But it was a poorly kept secret among the group. Everyone knew he had watched her die. He'd had nightmares when he was young that had given away that secret. Luckily these days, he didn't dream at all.

Ran was the first to speak, squeezing Locke's shoulder. "Well, in that case, I look forward to meeting this girl."

Maybe it was disingenuous to let his team think that's all it was. Locke would be lying if he said he looked at her like he might a sister. Ran was right . . . she *was* pretty. He'd have to be scorching blind not to think so. But he didn't want them harping on this, not when he still hadn't puzzled it out himself.

His foul mood kept most of the others away as they waited for Roar to wake. Jinx was the only one brave enough to broach the territory he had staked out. She didn't say anything — she just sat with him and waited. Jinx was more how he imagined a sister would be. She was loud and opinionated, and she made hurricanes look tame when she didn't get her way. But she understood that being there was more important than saying the right words. He imagined that was the earth witch in her. She knew the importance of balance.

Eventually, he started to doze and decided to catch a quick nap. He was a light sleeper, a necessity on the road, and he knew he'd wake as soon as Roar made a noise. So he pulled a pillow beneath his head, sprawled out on the ground beside her, and slept.

Rora's head throbbed as she woke, and her neck and back joined the chorus. She had woken midroll when her face slid off a pillow onto a thick, rough carpet. Next to her was a mountain of a man stretched out on his stomach. He had both hands shoved beneath a pillow, and his shoulder-length hair was in wild disarray around his face, but the name came back to her quickly.

Locke.

She sat up sharply, her head spinning. Locke jerked awake next to her. He pushed up onto his side, eyes wild and body tense. Then his eyes fell on her, and he softened.

"How do you feel?" he said, his voice gravelly with sleep.

She heard shuffling from somewhere beyond him and noticed a group seated at the back of the tent, quietly playing cards. Jinx stood and made her way over.

"Princess?" Locke asked, yanking all her attention back to him. Her hand flew to the scarf around her head, and she sighed when she found it still in place.

Jinx knelt beside her. "Need some help with that? You'll probably feel better without it."

Rora scrambled back. In an instant, Locke was up with a hand in front of Jinx to stop her approach.

"Easy," he said to Rora. "Calm down. You were bleeding and you fainted. Do you remember?"

Rora nodded. She hadn't known that was what fainting felt like—that awful, nauseating disorientation, like someone had stuck his hand in her head and stirred around.

"When was the last time you ate something?" Locke said.

She said, "This morning? Maybe. Or yesterday. I'm not sure."

Locke cursed and called out, "Ransom?" A beast of a man put down his cards and stood. His head was bare, but he wore a sizable beard and had shoulders wider than two normal people put together. Locke continued: "Can you get her something to eat?"

The man nodded and strode out of the tent.

Rora began crawling to her feet. "I have to go. I have to go *right now*." How long could she stay here without them realizing who she was? It seemed they were nomads of a sort, so they might not recognize her, but she was tired and risked giving herself away if she wasn't careful.

A firm hand settled over her shoulder, wrenching her back onto the carpet. "No, you don't," Locke said. "Eat first."

Locke's large hand stayed on her shoulder as his hard gaze raked over her face. He didn't pin her down with any real force, but she felt too tired to put up much of a fight. And her empty belly did squeeze near to the point of pain.

"Fine," she whispered.

"What was that?" he asked.

Scowling, she shoved his hand off her shoulder and said, "You heard me. No need to humiliate me any further. My current situation covers that sufficiently, I think."

A tall, skinny boy with startling red hair and a charming grin popped up beside them. He was all freckles and long limbs, probably near to her age. He held out a waterskin to Locke and said beneath his breath, "She might remind you of your sister, but I don't think those fond feelings go both ways."

His sister? Locke growled, "Bait, enough."

Bait. The boy's name was *Bait*. It appeared her haphazardly decided nickname was a good fit for this group after all.

Locke jerked the waterskin out of the boy's hand and held it out to Rora. "Drink. Unless you're too humiliated by us helping you."

Jinx slapped the back of his head, but he barely budged, the waterskin still dangling in his outstretched hand. She took the water, mumbling a sorry and a thank-you. She hated feeling helpless. When her magic hadn't manifested, she tried to make up for the shortcoming in every other possible way—whether it was through her studies or the physical training she did with the guards.

All eyes were on her as she took her first sip. The cool liquid was such a relief that she took a bigger gulp.

"Go easy," Locke said. "Little sips or you might get sick."

She wanted to gulp the whole thing down and pour a second container over her face, but she did as he said. He was trying to be kind, apparently because she reminded him of his sister. There was a sinking in her belly, and she returned to her water.

When she had nearly emptied the waterskin, the bearded man returned with food. Bread and berries and some kind of cooked brown meat on a stick. The bread was stale on the outside but soft and warm on the inside. The berries were familiar, and she picked at those next. As she lifted up the meat for her first bite, she lost the battle with the blush spreading over her cheeks. Everyone was watching, as if they didn't trust her to feed herself. Gingerly, she took some of the meat between her teeth and pulled. It was a little greasy, but a strong savory flavor burst over her tongue, and before she could help it, she moaned in satisfaction.

Locke grinned, and she nearly moaned again in mortification.

"Ran is a good cook. The best," Locke said, and the blush on her face burned hotter. Even though she immediately wanted to take another bite, she paused and said, "Thank you." That was to Locke. Then she found Ransom. Despite his hulking size, he still looked relatively young. Somewhere north of twenty but shy of thirty. "It's delicious. Thank you."

He smiled, teeth appearing amid the reddish-brown mass of facial hair, but didn't say anything back.

"So . . . are you all hunters?" she asked.

Locke nodded. "More or less. We've all got different skills, but it takes all of us to make it happen. You've met Jinx, but this is Duke." An old man she hadn't noticed before stepped out of the corner. Her thoughts were scattered, but he seemed familiar. But certainly she would have remembered an old man with a long beard, braided hair, and leather armor. The extensive webbing of scars on his arms added to that image. This man had lived a warrior's life. Locke continued: "Duke's the one in charge. He brought us together and taught us to hunt. You met Ransom and Bait and Sly is—"

"Over here." The voice came from the far corner of the tent, and Rora craned her head to see a slim girl with dark skin and curly hair cut close to her scalp. Quiet and unassuming, Sly had light, intense eyes that stood out starkly against her dark complexion.

"Everyone," Locke said, "this is Roar."

She watched his face for any hint that he knew her true identity but saw none. She cleared every bit of the food on her plate, and only then realized how cold she was. She laid the plate to the side, and shoved her fingers beneath her thighs to stop them from trembling.

"Here," Locke said, reaching into one of the leather pouches that hung off his person. "Cold front settled in while we were sleeping."

He handed her a small glass sphere and inside was a glowing red ember from a firestorm. Between her palms, the glass was deliciously warm. "It's called an eternal ember. If you keep it away from the elements, a firestorm ember will burn forever."

It was *incredible*. How had she missed so much of her own world? All of her life, she had been taught that there were the Stormlings and the ungifted. No in between. And now here were these people who hunted storms and somehow had gained magic of their own. She had thought that only the most extraordinary Stormlings could brave the danger of an unknown storm. People like Cassius who, with all those Stormhearts he wore along his spine, probably had more affinities than almost anyone else in the world. But before she fainted, Locke had said he was born without any magic at all.

She had come here for answers to Cassius's secrets, and had uncovered far more than she had hoped. Rora stayed lost in thought for so long that when she looked up, all the hunters had moved away except Locke.

"You know," he said, his voice low enough for only her to hear, "I was an orphan when Duke took me in. I was alone, getting by on the streets of Locke by doing whatever I could to survive. Duke changed that. Gave me a purpose, a way to build a life. If you need help, there are people who could help you. *I* could help you."

"I'm fine," she insisted.

His mouth settled in a tight line, but his eyes were kind.

"I mean it, Roar. We leave at sunrise tomorrow for our next hunt on the way to Taraanar. I don't know when we'll be back here. Could be months or a year. If there's something I can do—money or food or protection—if there's something you need, *please ask*."

Rora slipped her hand over the tightly curled fist resting on his knee. She wanted to tell him that she was more than fine. She was better than she'd ever been because for the first time since she was twelve, she knew the taste of hope. If these people and this place existed, maybe she didn't have to marry Cassius to keep her kingdom. Maybe there was another way. She opened her mouth to assure him, but a long, deep horn call cut through the peace of the tent before she could utter a word.

She knew that sound, and her skin prickled with dread. It was not the same signal as yesterday but a different horn they blew when they hung new warning flags on the turrets of the four storm towers, signaling a change of season. They had been yellow for the duration of the Slumber season—a color that told citizens that while storms were possible, they were unlikely. A red flag meant that storms were probable and people should be on alert for the emergency signals. A black flag meant that the Rage season had come, and large storms were both imminent and likely to be frequent.

Locke's mouth formed a curse, but she could not hear it over the second sounding of the horn. She jumped to her feet and ran outside. Her jaw dropped. The Eye was empty. All the magic of the night before was gone, only the booths left behind like the skeleton of some majestic, mythical creature. The dark tarp still covered most of the opening overhead, but she could see bits of pink and purple sky peeking in at the corners and along the sides. *Dawn.*

Rora let out a string of curse words that would have gotten her disowned if her mother heard, and began to run. Locke yelled after her, but she could not wait. She had stayed out all night, and it would be a miracle if her absence had not been discovered.

Rora skidded to a stop in front of what she hoped was the entrance she'd used the night before. With the stalls empty, it was hard to be certain.

"One more day!" Locke yelled after her. "You know where to find me before we leave if you change your mind!"

She looked back a final time at the hunter who had changed everything. He looked tall and menacing from afar, but he had been kind to her. And his mere existence shattered everything she thought she knew about the world. She lifted her hand in a wave and then ducked into the tunnel.

As soon as she stepped out into the dilapidated neighborhood that hid the market, her eyes sought out the turrets. Her throat pinched when she saw the new flag. *Black.*

Slumber had officially ended, and the Rage season had arrived.

It was not enough to punish her children. Rezna had given them a gift, and they betrayed her. And with the Time of Tempests, she purged the first tribes of their magic, stripping them the way they stripped the land. But death was not enough to soothe her rage. So the storms still come to this day.

—The Origin Myths of Caelira

7

Novaya glanced at the sun through the window. It was well past sunrise, and Aurora had not returned. She had known it was a mistake—all of it. She should not have let the princess go. And before that, she should have refused the prince and his coins. But the two gold coins he gave was more than she made in a week, and as someone who lived life ready to flee at a moment's notice, having gold saved was imperative.

Wracked with guilt and worry, Nova had stayed hidden in an alcove of the servants' wing all night, waiting for Aurora to return. Her eyelids were heavy, and her heart hadn't stopped racing since the sun came up.

The prince had returned an hour past midnight, his full coin purse clinking with each heavy step. Nova had watched the door to the shelters at the end of the hall, waiting for Rora to follow once the prince disappeared from sight. But she never came. Something terrible must have happened.

Nova's anxiety was hard to control on the best days. She would lie awake at night, consumed by thoughts of all the things that could go wrong the next day—little things like sewing a stitch wrong and losing her chance to become a full-time seamstress rather than a servant or massive things like accidentally burning the palace to the ground. Her mind would begin to unfurl elaborate disastrous scenarios in which one small mistake led to a dozen more, and her carefully constructed world would crumble around her. And when her emotions raged out of control, something inside her, something even harder to leash, raged too.

Night had gone, and the halls filled with the bustle of servants heading to their posts for the morning. Nova should go and admit her crime to the queen, so that soldiers could be sent out to search for Aurora. Already, she could be lying somewhere dead or dying, and it was all Nova's fault.

She would almost certainly face banishment for her admission, and far worse if something had truly happened to the kingdom's heir. A tingle of heat stroked up her spine, and Nova immediately doused her emotions, locking them away behind the imagined door she'd fashioned as a child. Most days, that door was all that stood between her and arrest, so she guessed in that respect, today was no different from any other day.

She had spent hours upon hours agonizing over the control of her magic, knowing one slip and the military would make sure she disappeared, and now she'd been felled by something akin to gossip. She did not know whether *disappearing* would mean death or imprisonment; it was not as if she could ask questions about the others who had disappeared without raising suspicions about herself.

She sighed, knowing that she could wait no longer. Perhaps she would only face banishment. The thought was still terrifying but easier to accept than death. She had no influence over storms, but her . . . *gift* gave her a better chance to survive the wilds than most. As she turned to go, a commotion down the hall drew her attention. Amid a group of women leaving their rooms was someone tall, completely covered by a large brown cloak.

Thank the skies. The women surrounding the princess had begun to whisper; a few brave ones voiced their suspicions louder. Nova saw a plump older woman, who worked as a laundress, square her shoulders and head Aurora's way.

Bolting down the hall, Nova called out, "There you are! I've been looking for you everywhere! Late on the first day. Mistress Carrovain is furious."

The crowd of women parted for Nova, and no one interfered when she began to lead Aurora away. Nova might have been just a servant, but her mother was one of the queen's favored cooks. And her father, though too ill to work now, had been Prince Alaric's valet. Her own newly acquired position as an assistant to the royal seamstress came with a touch of respect too.

Aurora did not fight her pull. This too had always been easier with Aurora. Nova avoided touch as much as possible, afraid that she would slip and hurt someone again. But she would never hurt Rora. She trusted herself that much at least.

The two did not speak until they were in the royal wing. The princess slowed to a stop, slipping back the hood of her cloak. She pulled at the scarf around her head, freeing that famous skyfire-bright hair, and said, "Skies, Nova. You saved me."

Anger, swift and potent, kicked wide the door she tried to keep closed. And Nova's fisted palms grew painfully hot. She hissed, "The prince returned hours ago. Where have you been? I was about to hand myself over to the authorities for getting the Stormling heir *killed*."

Aurora's eyes widened, and Nova clenched her teeth, knowing her outburst was not only inappropriate but out of character. Nova had always been the calm and cautious one when they'd been friends as children, while Rora had been as wild as a storm in a little girl's dress. Nova had been all too aware of the consequences of revealing herself. She might have been born with magic same as Aurora, but long ago, her kind of magic had been deemed *dirty*, evil even. After all, it was people like her that caused the Time of Tempests.

"I did not mean to stay out so long. I lost the prince last night," Aurora answered. "But I met someone who *hunts* storms. A whole crew of them in fact. That place was . . . spectacular."

Nova knew the crown's stance on the forbidden magics—they pretended they no longer existed, that the first tempests had wiped out all who wielded elemental magic in the first tribes, and only the Stormling ancestors had been blessed by the goddess to carry magic now. When proof arose to the contrary, it disappeared. They applied the same logic and solutions to the mercenary crews who harvested raw storm magic in the wildlands. But everyone *knew* other magics existed, even if they pretended otherwise. Nova had assumed that type of information would have been discussed between the queen and her daughter.

"I don't understand why you were so afraid," Rora said. "I'm going back. Tonight. There's so much more I want to know."

Nova swallowed the aggravated curse that threatened at the tip of her tongue. As Aurora pushed opened the door to her rooms, Nova followed and insisted, "You can't! It's too dangerous."

The princess eyed Nova over her shoulder, and Nova knew an inquisition was coming. Even as a child, Princess Aurora had never asked a question without five more following the first.

"What is too dangerous?"

The question did not come from Aurora; the voice was decidedly deeper. On the far side of the room, lounging casually on a settee, was the Prince of Locke. His suspicious gaze roamed over the princess first and then wandered to Nova, his eyes narrowing. Rora, impetuous as always, did not even attempt a diplomatic response. She squared her shoulders, as Nova had seen her do when she threw knives with the soldiers, and asked, "What are you doing in my rooms?"

Prince Cassius reminded Nova of the poisonous snakes that would lie in wait in her desert homeland—deceptively calm but ready to strike at a moment's notice. Even his movements were slow and deliberate, as if trying not to alert prey to his presence.

"I have news." He let those words settle for a moment, and Aurora stiffened. "I asked your mother's permission to be the one to give it to you. But when I knocked on your door, no one answered."

"So you decided to enter my rooms without permission?"

The prince didn't appear at all fazed by the venom clinging to Aurora's words. In fact, he grinned. "One of your maids let me in when she came to start a fire. I assure you, I intended no harm."

"Good intentions do not negate harm."

His smile faded then, and Nova's mind filled in the hiss of a poisonous snake about to attack.

He asked, "What's wrong? Where were you? And *what* is dangerous?" The last question was said in a demanding growl. The words weren't even directed at Nova, but even so nerves jumped in her belly and a flare of blazing heat followed before she tamped it down. It had been a difficult morning, and already her skin was dotted with perspiration from the flashes of fire that she'd been unable to rein in.

Aurora turned away from the prince, brows flat with agitation. "Nova, can you help me?"

The last place Nova wanted to be was between two angry royals, both of whom knew enough to turn her over to the authorities. But she stepped farther into the room and closed the door behind her anyway.

"Wait outside," Aurora told Cassius. "We can talk after I change." Her tone was curt and cold, and Nova kept her eyes fixed on the ground as the prince grudgingly went out into the hallway. When the door was closed, Aurora stomped into her bedroom, and Nova followed.

"I'm so sorry," Nova whispered. "I had no idea he was here, or I would have warned you."

Aurora pinched the bridge of her nose and stayed standing that way for several long moments, her eyes shut tight. Then all at once, she jumped into action. She dragged the brown cloak up and over her head, followed by her nightgown. Nova rushed to help her change into a blue linen dress. It was plain by royal standards, but Aurora had never been the type to care about fashion, and she was beautiful enough for it not to matter.

"Tell me you won't go back there," Nova whispered as she fastened a final hook at the back of Rora's neck.

Aurora hesitated. "I can't do that." She spun to Nova and waited expectantly. "Tell me what you know."

Nova pressed her lips together. She'd come this far. There was little harm in telling her more. She sighed and whispered, "The people who go there? They're either desperate or . . ."

"Or what?"

"Or they're not bothered by the prospect of being arrested and tried for treason."

Aurora's brow furrowed. "Treason? For buying little baubles and jars of magic that might not even be real?"

"It's real, though far more is bought and sold on the black market than just storm magic. One bauble is more than enough to ruin your life if you're caught by the wrong person. I was shocked the prince would visit such a place. His family is rumored to be ruthless with law-breakers in Locke. At least here, the worst people face is banishment."

Perhaps she'd been trying to scare the princess just a little, enough for her to grasp the gravity of the situation. But Aurora shook her head. "No. That can't be. These must be exaggerations to scare people off."

Nova tangled her fingers, curling and uncurling them in agitation. "The only reason you can't believe it is because you live in a different reality from the rest of us." Aurora started to protest, but Nova continued: "You are a Stormling. You never knew of the market's existence because you do not need it. When the storms hit, you have a spacious shelter. You know that the palace where you live will be protected at all costs. You needn't fear the cold or heat or hunger. You don't have to worry about the finite number of jobs in the kingdom or take lower and lower pay to keep from losing your position to someone willing to do the work for less, only to then worry you won't have enough to pay the taxes required to remain a citizen. The rest of us are always keenly aware that we could not survive outside these city walls, and must do everything to maintain our livelihoods within them. So *treason* might seem absurd to you, but for the rest of us, it's a fact of life."

The princess stood still and silent, and Nova feared she had gone too far, been too blunt. Aurora began to shake her head slowly, and her muttered words were soft. "You are right. I thought I *understood* what it was like to be ungifted, but I realize now it's about more than lacking magic."

Nova shifted uncomfortably. It was true . . . the majority of people lacked magic altogether. But there were some, like her, who were neither Stormling nor ungifted, born with the gifts of the old tribes. She did not know why. Neither of her parents had magic, nor had any ancestors as far as she knew. Nova was unlucky in that her elemental connection was the hardest to control and hide. She knew that other witches even studied magic beyond their element, using incantations for spells outside their natural ability, but most days it was all Nova could do to keep her volatile fire from spilling out.

Aurora continued: "If there's one thing I know it's that freedom shouldn't feel like a noose around your neck. Nor should the gift of magic be wielded as a weapon. Forgive me for my ignorance, Nova. I have lived too long isolated in my own private world, and there is much I do not know."

Nova winced. "No. It's I who should ask forgiveness. I should never have spoken to you in such a manner. It was—"

Aurora scooped up Nova's hands in her own and squeezed tightly. Nova waited for the fire to rush to where their skin touched, but it stayed caged. She never realized how little human contact she had these days until she experienced it again.

"Never apologize for being honest with me," Rora said. "No matter the differences between us, I will always count you a friend. I would rather you offend me a thousand times than hold the truth from your tongue."

Nova blinked in shock. Kindness from the princess did not surprise her, but a promise of friendship did. Nova thought that possibility had ended long ago.

"I should see what he wants," Aurora said, gesturing in the direction they'd left Cassius.

The princess moved to the door, hesitating with her hand on the knob. Her back was rigid, and her head tipped up to the ceiling as if she might find some answer there.

Nova did not know what had happened the night she found the princess crying outside her room, but she knew from watching Aurora that such a display of emotion was rare for her now. Whatever had happened . . . it was the prince's fault. Nova had been on the receiving end of his intimidation, and it had taken all of her concentration to keep her fire from slipping free in the face of that man. She did not envy Aurora's fate as his bride.

Rora took a few moments to gather her composure before stepping out into the sitting room, leaving Nova behind. A small part of her felt better knowing that she was there. Not that she thought Cassius would purposely hurt her. But having him here in her rooms was akin to turning her back on one of those big cats that stalked the grasslands southwest of Pavan. In fact, he was pacing like one when she opened the door to the hallway. He did not immediately sit after he entered, walking instead along the bookshelf that spanned the entire length of one wall, occasionally stopping to peruse the spines of the books.

"What was it that you wanted?"

Rora sounded weary to her own ears, and he studied her carefully before replying, "Why don't we sit down? We have a lot to discuss."

She sank onto the corner of a settee, and exhaustion swept over her. Even though she slept after fainting at the market, she still wanted to crawl into bed and sleep for another day. Perhaps two.

My apologies, Pavan. I cannot do my sacred duty and help fight the first storm of the Rage season. I will be too busy with my nap.

Cassius sank onto the settee beside her. The piece was built for two, but she imagined the maker envisioned her and another girl sitting here, talking away about whatever it was that normal princesses were supposed to talk about. Cassius was very much a man, and to fit, he sat close enough that their sides pressed together.

He reached over and plucked one of her hands from her lap. Lacing their fingers together, he rested the back of her hand on his hard thigh. A lump formed in Rora's throat, and she casually leaned her upper body away from him.

"You said you spoke to my mother."

"Yes, she came to see my father early this morning."

That made Rora sit up straighter. "About?"

He pushed her hand flat against his thigh, circling his callused thumb over her sensitive palm. "Are you well? Your injury?" His thumb dragged from her palm up the length of her middle finger. She considered making him feel guilty for the knife incident but knew it was smarter to put him at ease. "I worried when you weren't in your rooms."

"The wound was minor." He certainly did not need to know she had fainted from blood loss after following him to an illegal market.

"I cannot . . . I am not certain I have ever even made an apology. It's not something my father believes in. But I am sorry. I promise I will never risk you again."

She studied him. If she did not know better, she would think he was truly upset. "What is life without risk?"

"Indeed." He pulled her hand to his mouth and placed a long but chaste kiss on the center of her palm. He closed his eyes as if savoring the moment. Rora's heart thumped uncomfortably. The sooner she found a way to end their betrothal, the better. She was not sure how long she could keep pretending like this. It did strange things to her heart and head.

"You did not tell me where you were this morning." That quickly he shed the softness, his tone turning demanding.

She fought the urge to pull her hand away from his grasp, and said, "I wanted some fresh air after being confined to my bed for a day. Is that acceptable to you?"

Well, she'd contained most of her anger. She would count that successful enough.

One side of his mouth curled up. "Quite acceptable. I like that you enjoy the outdoors. My . . . brother's fiancée, before she passed . . . well, the ocean whispered just outside the gates of our castle, but I don't think she ever set a toe in the sand."

"I've always wanted to see the ocean." She'd been fascinated since she first read *The Tale of Lord Finneus Wolfram*, and it had become her favorite. And every time she'd read it since, the hunger to experience it for herself increased. "I've read about it. About ships sailing out into the deep, searching for other lands, safer ones. But the closest I've ever gotten is rivers and lakes."

"It's not the same. Someday, I'll take you. There's this lagoon a little way up the coast from home toward the ruins of Calibah. It's like a little private paradise, and the water is a gorgeous crystal blue, and you can see all the way down to the smooth pebbles at the bottom. I think you'd love it there."

She probably would. Perhaps the only thing that fascinated her more than the ocean was the fall of the city of Calibah. That plus the ocean would captivate her completely. And she hated that he seemed to know this. That he could read her so easily. But she didn't trust him, and she wasn't sure she trusted herself either. "What did my mother discuss with your father?"

His brows furrowed, and his hand tightened on hers. "We're moving up the wedding date."

"What?"

"Your mother said that you've always wanted a wedding outdoors, and she was worried that the season change could ruin that possibility. A patrol spotted a storm coming in off the western coast, near Calibah, and set the signal fires. It might be a few days before it reaches this far inland, but it's heading this way, and it's massive. So we're getting married tomorrow before it arrives."

Funny. Rora felt like it already had. Like a twister had dropped from the sky, ripping through the roof and throwing her world into a maelstrom. Tomorrow.

Tomorrow.

She struggled to stay calm, to keep her expression neutral. But her body revolted, and tears pressed at the corners of her eyes, nausea roiling in her belly. She stood quickly, fleeing to the window. It was easier when she could see the sky in front of her, could see a way out.

But her reprieve was short-lived. Rora felt Cassius step up behind her before he spoke. "Maybe it's better this way. No more ceremonies. No more dresses you hate. We'll get married, and then we'll get on with our lives."

Get on with their lives? The future was always scary. Rora knew that. But she couldn't fight the sinking feeling in her stomach, like she was drowning. Like she'd lost her way in the water and didn't know up from down, and her limbs were filled with lead, and she would never find the surface again.

"Why do you want to marry me?" The question was out of her mouth before she knew exactly what she was doing. But once it was, she could not stop. "Why leave behind your home and everyone you know to be the king behind the queen? You'll have to answer to me, give up the Locke name and take mine. You don't strike me as the kind of man who would enjoy playing politics while his wife rules a kingdom."

Part of her thought that if he admitted to his hunger for power now, if he told the truth, then perhaps she could salvage it all.

His eyes narrowed, and his mouth tightened. "You don't trust me."

"I don't trust *anyone*."

"And I destroyed the trust you gave me with your knives."

She did not answer him. Just kept her cold gaze fixed on that handsome face.

"I'll earn it back, Aurora," he said fiercely. "I promise you that. And I do not make promises I don't intend to keep. As for why I wanted to marry you? I never felt that I quite fit in my family. Maybe the king behind the queen isn't the most ideal position, but it's a far sight better than second heir." He took her hand, surrounding it with both of his. "Truthfully, Aurora. I am very much looking forward to a life here in Pavan. A life with you."

He was spinning his webs of charm as always, but that last sentence almost rang true to her ears.

Cassius continued: "We will be embarking on our life together not just as man and woman, but as king and queen. Ours is the first wedding of two royal Stormling families in over a century. We represent a historic alliance. Since the storm is due to arrive soon after our wedding . . . what if we fought it? *Together*? Between the two of us, we cover most storm affinities known to man. Our children will be the most powerful Stormlings the world has ever seen, and it would be good for people to see us working together, *fighting* together. It would send a strong message as our first act as husband and wife."

Rora played along, saying the right words, smiling the right smile, and nodding, but her mind wasn't in it. Not really. She was outside herself. Her heart grew calm and steady and quiet—the kind of quiet that came before the Rage season. As if the whole land was bracing itself for the battle to come. All the nerves and the confusing emotions melted away, and she was nothing more than a series of actions cobbled together by instinct alone.

That was what happened to an animal when it was cornered. When the danger was high and adrenaline took over. Reason disappeared then, and the only thing left was an instinct older than blood and bones. And her instinct? It told her two things.

To lie.

And to run.

A door snapped closed, and her concentration sharpened; the world no longer blurred around the edges. Cassius had left, and Rora could barely recall the end of their conversation. She leaped into action and threw open the door to her bedroom. Nova straightened from where she'd been absentmindedly dusting around the room. Rora strode toward her bed where Nova had folded the traveling cloak. Picking up the worn fabric, she asked, "Can you get me more clothes like this? Nondescript. Pants, no dresses?"

"What do you need them for?" Nova asked.

Rora looked at her. At the girl who used to be her best friend, and might still be. And even though everything else was chaos and confusion, she felt undeniably sure about something for the first time in years. "I'm making my own future."

Citizenship—whether by birth or petition—guarantees the right to live and work in Pavan under the protection of the Stormling crown. Rights may be revoked in the event that a citizen is found guilty of a criminal action or fails to surrender the required taxation.

—The Governing Tenets of Pavan,
Article 2: Pavanian Citizenship

8

Rora spent the day pretending, which was not that different from her usual day, except this time there was hope beyond the lies. As she made preparations, she couldn't quite admit to herself aloud what she was planning.

She was a princess without the power to keep her kingdom, a girl whose future had been decided for her. That was the cold hard truth. But it didn't have to be. If she had learned anything last night, it was that the world wasn't as clear-cut as she had always believed. And between the bad choices and the worse choices, perhaps there was another road that she had never known existed until last night.

She expected to change her mind as the day went on, that she might come to her senses. Instead the world seemed to be affirming her reckless decision.

She overheard a conversation between the queen and one of her advisers: "It's the Rage season, Lord Delrick. If he wants a Stormling guard to take him to Finlagh again, it will cost him. He agrees to my price, or he takes his chances on his own in the wildlands."

Rora spied a pile of tax documents on the queen's desk, the top one of which read OVERDUE in big, bold letters. When she flipped through the stack, a few papers had a large red *x* covering the entirety of the page. Did her mother really banish defenseless people to the mercy of the wildlands if they could not pay?

Rora found a massive pile of petitions for citizenship—those who currently lived outside Pavan but wished to make it their home. There were too many people for too little space and too few jobs. What had her mother said to her only days ago? *I wish that we did not have to make such hard choices.*

The royal seamstress Mistress Carrovain and her assistants, including Nova, were being worked furiously to finish alterations to her wedding gown. And when the seamstress accidentally pricked Rora with a needle, she noticed the way the older woman's face went taut with fear and her hands trembled. Even the queen's longtime seamstress appeared to live as if on a blade's edge. As if banishment waited for her over a meaningless drop of blood.

Queen Aphra had always been stern—she had to be as a woman in her position—but Rora had never seen her be cruel. But she had been kept in the dark about so much, perhaps Rora did not know her mother as she thought.

Aurora had seen enough. She donned her disguise again. On a whim, she collected her brother's twister ring from the Stormheart box that remained in her rooms and threaded it on a long necklace that she wore hidden beneath her cloak. And then, using the storm shelter exit, she left.

The dark night pulsed with silence, and Rora heard echoes that were not there as she navigated her way down the streets toward the Eye. She was afraid she had forgotten the way, but a familiar swinging lantern affirmed her path. Her blood rushed fast beneath her skin as she squeezed through the hidden entrance and down the long tunnel that separated the dark street from the market on the other side. This time Rora felt no apprehension. No fear. Only wonder and want.

Quietly she drifted along the path between stalls, taking it all in, enjoying the sound of people haggling over price and stall owners' sales pitches to wandering buyers. And then she saw whom she was looking for.

"Duke?"

The old man's hair was long and loose tonight, and some of it fell over his wrinkled forehead when he spun to face her. She had gone over and over her memories of the Eye throughout the day, and finally she'd realized why she found Duke so familiar the night before. When she'd been talking to Locke, she'd seen Cassius at a vendor behind him. Through the commotion that followed and her fainting ordeal, she hadn't immediately remembered that the vendor Cassius had been speaking to was a thin old man with long, braided hair. Seeing the hunter again now, she was certain it was him.

"Well, I'll be damned. You came back after all. Locke is around here somewhere."

Rora stepped up to the table he was tinkering over, refusing to let herself get distracted by all the interesting baubles and artifacts before her.

"Actually, I wanted to speak with you."

His eyebrows lifted, stark lines of white on a weathered, tanned face. "And what can I do for you, Roar?"

Her heart thrilled at the sound of that nickname. It was blank. Unfinished. Filled with so much possibility. *Aurora* had kingdom-sized baggage attached, but *Roar* was whomever she wanted her to be.

"Last night. Before we met, I saw you talking to a young man at your stall. Nearly as tall as Locke. Broad shoulders. He wore a wide-brimmed black hat that shadowed most of his face."

Duke's brow furrowed. "I remember him."

"You do?" Her question came out too loud, too excited.

"It's not every day that an unknown walks into my stall with Stormhearts to sell."

"He . . . *what*?"

"Three of them. I can count on one hand the number of times someone has had even one to sell. Three? Let's say I won't be forgetting that lad for a while."

Stormhearts were sacred. She had been shocked when Cassius had left the skyfire Stormheart for her as a gift. But to sell three more? Why would he give those up? It didn't make any sense.

"Did he say why?"

Duke shrugged. "Gold, as far as I could tell. I didn't have enough on hand to pay the heavy sum that three Stormhearts are worth, but he took my offer anyway. Seemed eager to get the money and get gone. I thought maybe he was trying to con me with fakes, but two out of the three came to life as soon as I touched them."

Why would Cassius need money? If the rumors were true, the Locke family's riches were vast. "And the third?"

"Firestorm. Not one of my affinities. But I took the chance since he was selling cheap, and Locke confirmed this morning that the Stormheart was real."

Rora gasped. "Locke has an affinity for firestorms?"

Duke nodded, scratching at the white and gray stubble along his jaw. "He does. He has the most affinities out of anyone on the crew."

"So, you use the Stormhearts you buy to help you?"

Duke shook his head. "There's no shortcut unfortunately. Hunters have to earn their hearts the old way. But Stormhearts are valuable for more than just the magic they can channel for Stormlings." He moved aside his long coat to reveal a complex leather belt with pockets and loops, all filled to the brim with various bottles and tubes and capsules. Duke flicked open a snap with scarred fingers and withdrew a small cylindrical tube, smaller than her pinky finger, with a fine scarlet powder inside. There was so little that it barely covered the rounded bottom of the tube.

"This is powder from a firestorm heart," he said. "Ingesting it can make your skin temporarily fire resistant. The embers still hurt like hell when they hit you, but bruises are better than burned flesh. This small amount would sell for ten gold pieces."

Thinking of Etel trying to sell Rora firestorm powder, she asked, "So it won't burn you from the inside out if you ingest it?"

He laughed. "Oh, it can. But you'd need an entire Stormheart's worth to do it. There are cheaper ways to do violence."

"Do the other hunters have firestorm affinities?"

He shook his head. "Only Locke. Some don't have any interest in the more dangerous stuff. Sly, for instance, only has a few affinities. Doesn't want more. Bait's our novie, sorry, *novice*. He's still apprenticing under Jinx, and a little too eager. Eager hunters make for dead hunters. So I've got him capped at thunderstorms for now."

There was no point trying to hide her emotions—they were bursting out of every pore of her skin. "I want to know *everything*."

"Remember what I said about eager hunters?" Duke said with an arched brow.

"Eager for information is not the same as reckless behavior." She should know—she was prone to both.

"True. But in this place, we trade. For everything. Even information."

Her face fell. She had not thought to bring coin with her. All she had were the clothes on her back, and . . . the Stormheart ring. But she couldn't. Not even for the answers she so desperately desired.

"I have nothing of value I can trade."

"Nothing of value to you, perhaps." He looked at her for a moment, then said, "The man you asked about. What can you tell me about him?"

She blanched. "Nothing. I know nothing about him." She frowned. "I don't have any coin on me, but I could get some and come back. Would you tell me then?"

Already, she was calculating whether she could make it back to the palace and return without getting caught. She turned to go, knowing the sooner she did it, the better. Servants would wake to prepare for tomorrow's wedding before dawn.

"Wait," Duke called before she had gone more than a few steps. "What do you want to know?"

She turned. "What about the trade? I did not give you information or goods."

His intense green eyes fixed on her. "You gave me information, just not with words. A man comes to me with Stormhearts to sell, and Locke tells me you were afraid of someone in the market last night. And here you are today asking about my customer. That tells me enough." Those intense eyes fixed on her again. "For now. Ask your questions."

For now? Rora swallowed her discomfort and peppered him with questions, starting with the items for sale in his stall. Some were familiar. Lightning lanterns and the eternal embers she'd been introduced to the night before, but she listened with rapt attention as he explained the rest.

Duke held up a bottle with a twister inside and explained that some people bought the raw storm magic for nefarious purposes. Someone might throw a bottle like the one he held through a window so the short-lived twister created when the bottle smashed would destroy the building from the inside out. But the hunters used raw magic for defensive reasons. Duke said, "Most storms are about momentum. Disrupt one storm by throwing another in a mix, and they'll both dissipate."

"What if they don't? What if they join together and become twice as dangerous as before?"

"It can happen. Has happened. But I've been hunting these beasts for decades, so there's not much I haven't come across. I know what works and what doesn't."

Rora wished she could open up his mind, his memories, and read them like a book. But she couldn't; all she could do was ask every question that popped into her head. "What about the rest?" Rora asked, waving a hand at all the merchandise. "The stuff that's not raw magic in a bottle."

"You met Jinx. She's the witch of the crew," Duke answered. "Earth witch by nature. But with the right incantation, she can do just about anything. She's the one who makes all our imbued pieces. And she enchants our hunting equipment to aid us. You can't have a hunting crew without a witch."

Rora's tutors had always taught that witches had been wiped out with the first tempests. Those who claimed to practice witchcraft now were more masters of deceit than anything. Stormlings held the only true magic.

Or so she had been told.

Duke handed her a necklace, and its white crystal pendant was warm against her skin. "That's our bestseller. It will burn hot when storm magic is in the immediate vicinity. It gives those who can't afford more complex magic a shot at finding shelter before it's too late. It's popular among those who work the fields outside the safety of the palace walls."

Rora returned the necklace and glanced at the other jewelry and baubles laid on the same table. "And those?"

"More storm alerts. A few are imbued with elemental energy. They give the wearer a minor ability to manipulate either earth, wind, water, or fire. They're typically only good for one use, but in a pinch they can be the difference between life and death."

The more she dug, the more lies she uncovered. Her mother had said there was no other choice. That marriage to Cassius was the only option. That *Stormlings* were the only option. But here she was, surrounded by more options than she could even fathom. Rora's eyes grew watery, and she turned away under the guise of studying a few more trinkets. Grief and anger warred in her, the latter gaining control.

"Why must this be done in secret? Surely all this could be used in bigger ways to make the world better, *safer*. I've seen the lightning lanterns and the eternal embers, but what about Stormling inventions like the palace gate that can only be opened with skyfire magic? Has anyone thought of doing something that big? You could create warning systems in villages without a resident Stormling. You could install the eternal embers in homes to provide warmth in the winter rather than burning wood that's in short supply. We could change the way the world works with this."

Duke smiled, something sparking in his eyes that she couldn't quite define. "We've not done much in the way of combining magic and machinery the way the Stormlings have, not more than necessary anyway. Hunters spend most of their time out chasing the weather. There's no time to tinker with inventions when the raw stuff is in such high demand. And inventions are big, flashy. Which means they're risky. There would be a fair few in this city who would see an invention along those lines as a threat to be neutralized."

"A *threat*? Making people safer is somehow dangerous?"

"Not in the sense you're thinking. The danger is to a way of life, rather than a life itself. Our existence here is tolerated only so long as we stay quiet and small. When markets grow and gain more power, that's when the military comes in and wipes it all clean. It has happened before, and it will happen again."

"But none of these things are a threat to Stormlings. We still need them to protect the city. It's not as if we're trying to take away their magic. There is room for both in this world."

The old man smoothed down his beard and surveyed her. "Maybe you'll be the one to change the way the world works."

"Me? But *I can't* . . ."

"Locke couldn't once upon a time. Now he can bring down firestorms and hurricanes."

Her mouth went dry, and her skin buzzed with a restless *something*. There had been several scenarios in the back of her mind when she made the decision to come back here. She hoped she might discover more about Cassius's plans or that the market sold some perfect magic object that would allow her to take the crown without Stormling powers. But one scenario had beat at her mind all day, even when she tried to pretend it was not an option. She could join these hunters and come back home having *earned* the magic in her blood.

Aurora thought about Nova, afraid to even discuss the Eye's existence. She thought about the crammed, ramshackle homes she'd passed that people had no choice but to live in if they wanted the safety that Pavan provided. She thought about every time she'd ever heard of some traveling party that disappeared, lost to the dangers of the wildlands. Maybe she *could* do something. With magic of her own, *she* would gain the crown. Not Cassius. Not a husband. And then maybe she could change everything for the better.

No more treason or banishment. No need to sell the magic in secret. She thought of her favorite book again. She had no boat to brave the sea, no skills as a sailor, but perhaps she *could* have a similar voyage of her own. If they could not sail away to some better land, then the only choice was to make *this land* better.

A hand slipped over her shoulder, large and rough, and a low voice stole past the covering of her hood. "You came back."

Rora's body tightened. She slipped his hold and faced Locke head-on. His long hair was tied back from his face. He wore dark leather pants and a linen shirt that left his neck bare. He was strapped into the same leather harness as before, vials hanging off the straps. There were powders in various colors. Some of the larger vessels held raw magic—a thunderstorm, a thick fog, and a swirling, white-gray magic that she guessed was wind. He cleared his throat, and she dragged her gaze away.

He was even more criminally handsome than she remembered. Masculine and rugged. It wasn't hard to picture him right in the middle of a firestorm, expression fierce and unafraid. Everything she desperately wanted to be. And if her imagination happened to paint him shirtless in that vision . . . well, who could blame her?

"Wait here a moment," he said, "then we can go to the tent and discuss what I can do to help."

Rora shifted her gaze away from him. "Actually, I'm not here for your help."

She had made her decision. It wasn't just about her distrust of Cassius or her yearning for freedom anymore. All her life she had been raised to believe that the kingdom came first. And what was a kingdom if not its people? She wanted to rule, wanted to help and change things, not just for herself but for them all.

Locke's eyebrows flattened to a straight line. "Oh? Then why are you here?"

She turned to Duke. One side of the old man's mouth tipped up, and she said, "I want to join your crew."

"No. Absolutely not."

Roar spun to glare at Locke, and it was a fierce and glorious glare indeed. If he were a different kind of man, he might have backed down. But that was not something he did. Ever. Call it a lesson of surviving childhood on the streets. He had not known much about dignity then, but he fought for what little he had at every turn. Even when his back was against the wall, even when the odds were impossible, even when he knew the reprieve would be far too short until he had to do it all again. He stood his ground. Always.

"Why not?" Roar demanded.

He had thought about her more today than he cared to admit, wondering what kind of home, if any, she had gone back to. But anything in this city would be safer for her than life in the wildlands.

"People die doing what we do. Do you want to die, little girl?"

Her fists balled at her hips, and she raised her chin defiantly.

"So now I'm a little girl again?"

Scorch it. Wrong thing to say. But he was too furious to do anything but double down.

"Yes. A naïve little girl."

"I'm *not naïve*. I know exactly what I'm asking."

She lifted a hand to her chest, grasping something beneath the fabric of her cloak. "I know very well what can happen. That's why I want to learn from Duke. After all, he's been hunting storms for decades. Maybe he should decide whether or not I have the potential."

Duke brushed a strand of white-gray hair off his forehead, and leveled them both with a serious expression. His eyes lingered on Locke longer, and it was plain Duke was considering it. For a man hardened by a lifetime of destruction and peril, he had a dangerously soft heart.

Locke said, "We have enough people on the team. She'll just be a liability."

Roar winced, and Locke felt it like a blade slicing across his gut.

"What happened to wanting to help me?" she asked. "Did you decide insulting me was more fun?"

The last thing he wanted to do was insult her, but the girl wouldn't listen. She appeared determined to make exactly the wrong choices, and he wanted to take her by the shoulders and shake her until she saw sense. This was why he never associated with anyone but other hunters. They, at least, understood the dangers; and if they got themselves killed, it wasn't Locke's problem. But this girl, she would be *his* problem. He could not do what he did while tied to other people. One death on his conscience was enough.

He said, "I meant I would help you find a job or a place to stay. If you want to be involved so badly, Duke can teach you to run the booth here in our absence."

She and Duke replied at the same time.

"I don't want to run the booth."

"That won't do."

Locke ran a hand through his hair, messing up the way he'd tied it back. "Why the blazes not?"

His responding growl had been for both of them, but it was Duke who answered. "The inventory we have now would last a fortnight at most. We won't be back in this area for months. A job won't be much help to her if it's only temporary."

Roar was looking at Locke with smug rebellion, and even as he wanted to shake her, he envisioned ways that he could wipe that pretty smirk from her mouth.

"So we introduce her to one of the permanent vendors. One of them has to need help."

Roar shook her head. "No. I can't stay here. I need to leave with you all. As soon as possible."

There she was, spinning him right around her finger again, turning all his ire into concern. "Why do you need to leave? What's wrong?" He stepped closer, and she crossed her arms over her chest.

"That's my business. I wouldn't want to make myself any more of a *liability* by involving you."

He ground his teeth together, before throwing his head back with an aggravated growl.

"This life is not glamorous," Duke told her. "We travel constantly. We sleep on the ground most nights. When we're not in danger from storms, we're in danger in cities where we are considered criminals. This life is not for the faint of heart."

"There are things I do not know, things I will have to learn. But I am capable. I am familiar with sacrifice. I know what it is to make hard choices."

"Tell me you're not considering this," Locke said to Duke.

The old man was silent for a long moment, both Locke and Roar looking to him for support. Duke rubbed at his mustache, a habit of his when he was thinking deeply. "Let's think about this, Locke. She's smart. And determined."

"She's a *child*."

Roar's shoulders hunched in Locke's peripheral vision, and he swallowed back the guilt. He could apologize later. For now, it was imperative that he won this argument.

"*You* were a child when I brought you into the fold," Duke said. "She's a young woman with a good head on her shoulders. And if this is what she wants, I'm inclined to at least hear her out."

Just like that, Roar's shoulders straightened, and Locke turned to watch a devastating smile bloom across her mouth. His weakness when it came to her only made him more cross.

"What skills do you have?" he snapped at Roar.

"Skills?"

"Yes, skills. What can you *do*? Or do you just plan to tag along for the ride?"

A flush spread over her cheeks, and her voice was tentative when she answered, "I'm good on a horse. Very good."

Where in the world would she have learned to ride? He quickly hardened his expression. "Horses are fine for travel, but they don't do well in storms. They, unlike you, have good survival instincts."

As soon as the words were out of his mouth, Locke could have sworn he felt an updraft—the first sign that bad weather could occur—and he knew that this time he had pushed too far.

Roar marched toward him, spearing a finger into his chest, and said, "I can read and write. I can speak Taraanese, Finlaghi, and Odilarian. I can read maps. I know enough about grassland vegetation and wildlife to survive without a market to buy food and drink. I'm good with knives and a bow. I learn quickly, and I'm not afraid of hard work. And I've spent my entire life reading as much about storms as I could get my hands on." For a moment, her voice cracked under the weight of her anger, but she took a huffing breath and continued: "I'm good with numbers. It's been a while, but I think I can probably still draw the constellations from memory, which should make me decent at navigation. I can—"

"Enough." Locke's voice came out in a deep rasp. He captured her long, delicate finger in his fist before she could continue poking him. He felt short of breath at the sight of her—livid and lovely. "Enough."

The old Locke might have kept arguing, and Roar would have met him toe-to-toe. But if becoming a storm hunter had taught him anything, it was that fighting head-on wasn't always the way to win. Sometimes strategy was required. He met Duke's eyes over her shoulder, and if he had thought Roar looked smug before, she had nothing on his mentor. The man raised his eyebrows in a challenge and asked, "You?"

He hated the idea of bringing someone into this dangerous life, but if it was going to happen regardless, he sure as hell wouldn't hand her safety over to anyone else, not even Ransom. And at the very least, it would give him the opportunity to change her mind. He gritted his teeth and nodded his acceptance.

"Good." Duke smiled. "Roar, Locke will follow you home and help you get everything you'll need for the journey."

Roar had been about to celebrate her victory, but she stopped short. "I don't need his help."

He smirked in response. "Then you're going to be sorely disappointed, princess. Because I'm in charge of your training."

Her eyes widened. "But . . . why? You didn't even want me to come." She asked Duke, "Can't I learn from you?"

"It's me or nothing," Locke cut in. "Duke is just the mastermind these days. So if he teaches you, you'll do nothing but pore over maps and measurements."

She twisted her fingers together, clenching and unclenching them. After a moment, she sighed. "Fine. But I don't need your help to get my things."

"Well, you're getting it anyway." He stalked toward her and grabbed her elbow. She dug her heels in, and tried to break free.

"I can go without you. I'm not a child in need of a nursemaid."

"What a coincidence. I'm no nursemaid."

He gave another tug, and this one got her feet moving. She stopped fighting and said, "Fine. Let go of me."

He released her as they approached one of the exits that led out of the market. "Don't bother trying to run. I'll catch you."

She gave him a tight smile, her blue eyes blazing. "Why would I do a thing like that?"

She ducked into the dark passageway between the buildings that hid the market, and he followed her into the cramped space.

"Because you can't help yourself. You have to fight everything."

He couldn't see more than her silhouette, but he heard her clearly as she spit back, "Or maybe I just have to fight men who try to bully me into doing as they say."

He sucked in a breath through his gritted teeth.

"And another thing—" She stepped out of the darkness, and the rest of her words were muffled. He turned sideways and worked to squeeze himself through the narrow opening of the passageway.

He knew something was wrong the moment he emerged. He spun, pulling one of the blades from his hip, but ground to a halt when he saw Roar. She was panting with exertion, and her glare was a dare to say something. Sprawled at her feet was a man groaning in pain. Blood streamed down his face from a broken nose, but his hands were too busy cupping his groin to stem the flow.

"What?" Roar barked. "He tried to rob me."

Locke lifted his hands, holding back a smile. "You'll get no complaints from me." He narrowed his eyes toward the man. He was about as tall as Roar but near double her weight. An impressive takedown. Though in Locke's opinion, the thief wasn't in nearly enough pain. "Want to kick him again before I turn him over to the market's enforcers?" he asked.

Roar's lips pressed into a line, the edges trembling upward like she fought a laugh. "No. The first kick was hard enough."

He lugged the man up from the ground, jerking him up to his tiptoes. The thief wailed at the movement, but one good shake shut him up. "She might be forgiving," he growled, "but the enforcers won't be. They don't take kindly to thieves preying on their clientele."

He dragged the man toward the tunnel, but stopped first to meet Roar's gaze. "I'll be right back." She smiled innocently in response, and he knew. "You're not going to wait for me, are you?" Her smile grew. "Fine. Clearly, you can take care of yourself. Meet us at dawn on the eastern road just outside the city gates. *Don't be late* or I'll leave you."

"I'll be there," she promised. "Tell Duke I said thank you."

The thief started groaning again, and Locke shoved him into the passageway. "I don't get a thank-you?"

"Maybe you'll get it when I'm no longer angry that you called me a liability."

Do not fear the thunder, nor the fire in the skies.
Rest little darling, and close your tired eyes,
For up above us now in that great, golden dome
A Stormling stands against it all to protect our sacred home.

—Pavanian lullaby

9

Novaya was wide-awake in her bed when a low tap sounded on her door. She was lying on top of the covers, still in her day clothes. She eased the door open enough to peek outside, and when she saw a familiar cloak, she took hold of Aurora's wrist and tugged her inside.

"You went out again?" Nova shook her head, glancing at the pitch-black window behind her bed. "You're getting married in a few hours!"

Rora looked around the room, eyes falling on the still made bed. "Why weren't you sleeping?"

"Couldn't." It had been a long day, and even though Nova was exhausted, her mind would not quiet. Mistress Carrovain had driven Nova and her two other assistants at a punishing pace, on top of the few duties she still had as a maid. Nova had been irritable all day after her previous night without sleep, and when one of the other assistants snidely insulted her work, she'd only narrowly avoided setting the dress in her hands on fire.

"Nova . . ." Rora began, her tone uncertain. "I came to ask something of you, a good deal more than what one might consider a favor from one friend to another. If you must say no, I will understand. But I promise, it will be the last thing I ask of you."

Nova sighed. "What do you need? I have the clothes you wanted."

"That is . . . wonderful. Thank you," Rora said. "But this is considerably bigger than that."

Nova gestured for Rora to take a seat on her roommate's narrow bed. "Should I worry that the owner of this bed will be returning soon?" Rora asked as she sat.

"Lenia is seeing one of the stable hands. She's already been here to grab clothes for tomorrow and snuck off to his room." Nova knelt by her bed and reached beneath it for the bag she'd hidden earlier in the day. "Speaking of stable hands, *here*." Out of the bag she lifted a pile of plain clothing. Trousers from Lenia's stable hand. Two linen tunics. An old skirt from Nova's mother with the hem let out. Even a worn pair of boots that appeared only slightly too large. She slid the articles of clothing back in the bag and handed it to Rora.

The princess reached into her pocket, fiddling with something inside it. She said, "I have something for you also." She lifted her hand and opened her palm to reveal a smooth, pearlescent stone. Nova's breath caught in her throat. *A Stormheart.* With a sharp shake of her head, she said, "No. I cannot accept this."

"You can. It's not one of the royal ones. And you've been a tremendous help to me. I'm told they fetch quite a price at the Eye."

"That's not why I helped you . . . for money."

"I know. And I want you to have it for far more reasons than just your help of late. Keep it. Sell it. I don't care, but please take it."

"I cannot. It's too much. What if you need it?"

Aurora gave a watery laugh. "I won't."

Now that Nova looked, the princess was indeed blinking away tears. With the Stormheart clutched tightly in her hand, Rora took a deep breath and whispered, "I don't have any magic."

Nova paused. A few nights of little to no sleep had made her delirious. "What do you mean?"

Rora's voice was firmer this time, though still quiet. "Storm magic. I have none. When I touch the Stormhearts"—she lifted the skyfire stone she held—"I feel nothing at all."

"But—but I heard—"

"Rumors. Lies. I pulled away from you, from everyone, when we found out. Mother was afraid that I would lose the crown. Everything we've done the last few years has been to protect that secret."

Nova slumped back on her bed, her thoughts racing, plucking out old memories and seeing them in a new light. Then it dawned on her. "The wedding. That's why you're marrying another Stormling."

Rora nodded. "We held off as long as we could, but now the Rage season . . ." She trailed off because she did not need to explain the rest.

"And now with the wedding tomorrow—" Nova winced as soon as the words were out of her mouth.

"I'm not marrying him. I leave at dawn."

With awe and horror, Nova listened as the Princess of Pavan told her about Cassius's betrayal and cruel manipulation of her feelings and laid out her plans to run away with a group of storm hunters.

Heat simmered beneath Nova's skin. Rora couldn't be serious. She would not leave and risk her life this way. Nova understood Rora's desperation for control. Nova lived it every day. But there had to be another way besides fleeing. Nova had done that too, but not by choice.

"What happens when the Lockes find out you've broken a royal contract?" Nova asked. "The treaty your mother has been fighting so hard for—it will end."

Rora braced her hands on her knees, took a slow breath, and lifted her eyes to Nova's. "Which is why I have to make it look like I did not willingly break the marriage contract."

"Rora," Nova warned. "Whatever you're thinking—"

"Is possibly brilliant. Or terrible. But hopefully mostly brilliant."

Rora gave a shaky smile, and Nova couldn't help but return it. She remembered all the grand, outrageous ideas they'd had as children. Nova had always said yes then, and though it led to a fair amount of trouble, she could not remember another time when she had been so happy. When her gift or curse or whatever it was had been so easy to control.

Rora laid out her plan and the part that Nova would have to play. It was bold, as the princess always tended to be.

"I know what I'm asking of you," Rora said. "If you cannot help, I will understand." Nova wanted to say yes, to be so fearless, but she had been ruled by her anxiety for so long. Rora pushed the skyfire Stormheart into Nova's palm, clasping both her hands around Nova's fist.

"Either way, please take this. It is my thank-you for your help, my apology for all the years I kept us apart, and my promise that things are going to be different when I return."

Nova was the one fighting tears now. They gathered in her throat, and made it hard to speak. She almost told Rora then about her own secret. She wanted to so badly, but years of conditioning bound the words on her tongue. Instead, she took the Stormheart and said, "What happens when the soldiers begin scouring the countryside searching for you? How will you stay safe then?"

Rora reached a hand up to touch the scarf covering her hair.

"Maybe I need another favor."

When the sky was still a deep purple, Rora found her horse, Honey, in the stable and presented her with an apple as a preemptive apology for everything that was about to change. The brown horse nuzzled into Rora's hand, and then sniffed at the scarf wrapped around her head. She could probably smell the paste Nova had mixed to dye Rora's hair a dark brown.

"Ssh, girl. We're going on a little adventure. You like adventure, don't you?"

Honey nipped at Rora's fingers in a gesture she liked to think was a yes. She'd been too busy to ride this week, and she missed it. When Rora's fingers were tangled in Honey's coarse white mane, her body tucked low against the horse's back, nothing could catch her. Not a castle guard, not her mother, not a storm in the sky, or the tempest of thoughts in her head. Now they would be escaping for far more than a few hours of peace.

She tacked up the horse with the oldest saddle and bridle she could find and set off for the palace gate. There she found one of the usual guards.

"Elmont, it's me," Rora said when she drew near.

She should have been exhausted from lack of sleep, but the quick beat of her heart was pumping adrenaline through her body. He didn't release the hilt of the sword at his hip as he peered through the darkness.

"Princess?" She cringed at the title and the reminder it brought of everything she was about to leave behind. "Where are you going?"

"Just a ride to calm my nerves."

Rora didn't let her smile falter as she moved closer, within the glow of the lantern by his post. She couldn't very well go prancing about with her newly changed hair. Not without everyone discovering the truth of what was about to happen. He looked at the scarf she wore, but did not comment.

He gave her a cheery smile. "Nervous? I wouldn't worry too much. I've not seen anything yet that you can't do. A wedding should be a piece of cake."

His face had taken on its usual red hue at her arrival. She felt a sting of guilt over the share of the blame he would take for letting her out on this particular morning.

"Elmont, you always start my days off well."

The crimson of his cheeks deepened, and he stood a little taller. "I am proud to be of service, Your Highness."

Everything had a sense of finality to it this morning. Rora's eyes lingered over every detail as Elmont opened the palace gates with his skyfire affinity. She wasn't sure when she would return to Pavan, but she knew everything would be different when she did. *She* would be different. And in many ways, she already was.

Tears teased at the corners of Rora's vision as she made her way through the quiet, sleepy city, and then in too short a time, she was past the outer walls. It was early enough that she didn't yet see the hunters anywhere in the vicinity, so she took off in her usual direction, pushing Honey into a gallop. It didn't take long to put her out of sight of the guards atop the city walls. She kept going, enjoying one last ride through the familiar wheat fields that would soon glisten gold in the sunlight. On any other morning ride, she and Honey might have meandered through the fields; Rora would have lain on her back, letting the stalks sway in the breeze around her. But this was not a normal morning.

Rora soon doubled back toward Pavan and stopped at an open field where wildflowers grew in colorful patches. She and Nova had agreed that this spot was the best setting for a fake kidnapping. She slid off Honey's back and quickly changed out of her dress and into a pair of trousers and tunic. She tore a few strips off the hem of the dress before tucking it away into a saddlebag. Then she retrieved one of her knives and took a deep breath.

She hadn't wanted to worry anyone more than necessary, but it was imperative that Nova's story was believed. Otherwise Rora would put her friend and Queen Aphra in a great deal of trouble. So with a strange sense of calm, she sliced the knife along her palm, sprinkling some blood on the torn fabric and the road. She rode along the southern road, letting blood drip as she went. Every so often, she dropped a bloodied piece of cloth, as if she were trying to leave clues about the direction her kidnappers were taking her. If all went according to plan, she would be on her way east with the hunters by the time they started searching for her. Stormling kidnappings were not uncommon, and all the rumors of Rora's incredible skill made her a more valuable target.

Finally, she bandaged her hand and doubled back the way she came. When she could see the palace dome in the gradually lightening sky, she unwound the scarf from her head. Her new hair was dark and shorter, cut to her shoulders. She kept reaching back for the rest, only to come up empty. Nova would leave the village for the wildflower field at dawn, and an hour later she would run back to the palace with the tale they had devised. It was too late to turn back, even if Rora wanted to.

Her stomach turned with nerves, but she knew she had prepared as best as she could. She'd filled her packs with everything she thought might prove useful: A bow and arrows to go with her cherished knives, books on languages and herbs and wildlife, coin enough to buy whatever she might need, her favorite book for comfort, and her brother's twister ring. It was a selfish addition, a reminder of home and of the grief she would leave behind if she did not manage to return.

Rora waited within a copse of trees until the sun breathed gold and pink across the heavens, then she pushed Honey into a trot toward a caravan on the eastern road she assumed belonged to the hunters. There were half a dozen horses, two of which were harnessed to a carriage unlike any she had ever seen. The front curved out like a globe and was made of glass. The back was boxy, and atop the glinting metal roof were unfamiliar contraptions that spun in the wind.

When her eyes found Locke, he was standing near the coach, facing the city. His arms were crossed over his chest, and his body tight with tension. She called out, "Hoping I wouldn't show?"

He turned, and his hair blew over his face in the breeze. He frowned and glanced behind Rora. "Where did you come from?"

She gestured to the road behind her. "I was too excited to sleep, so I went for a ride."

His frown deepened. "Where did you get the horse?"

"I didn't steal her, if that's what you're accusing me of." At least . . . not really. She *was* Rora's.

His jaw clenched. "I didn't say that."

"Then why ask?"

"I thought you were—"

"A helpless girl who needed you to rescue her? Did you expect me to show up with nothing but the clothes on my back, needing you for every little thing? While you might have helped me the other night, generally I can take care of myself just fine."

He ground his teeth so hard, Rora wouldn't have been surprised to see them crumble into dust in his mouth. "I didn't say that *either*."

"Good. Because I would have been tempted to have Honey here trample you if you did."

With a loud, metallic scrape, a hatch slid open on top of the strange coach, and a loud laugh poured out from it, followed shortly by Bait's fiery red-orange hair.

"Marry me. Please. Anyone who threatens Locke without batting an eye is my ideal woman."

Locke turned on the other hunter, his face set in a menacing scowl, and the young teen gave an inelegant squeak before disappearing into the carriage. Rora laughed, and Locke's scowl was turned on her. But rather than the angry retort she expected, he barked, "Your hair is dark."

Her stomach flipped in momentary fear before she said, "So?"

He shrugged, grumbling something she couldn't hear before gesturing for her to get down from her horse. He reintroduced her to each member of the crew. Most of them were enthusiastic at the prospect of her joining the team. Jinx had practically tackled her in excitement. Ransom was more subdued, but she had the feeling that he rarely showed much emotion. Sly, on the other hand, had not even tried to disguise her glare. Rora remembered only a brief glimpse of the girl that first night in the market, and that made more sense when Locke said, "Sly is our stealth specialist. You won't hear her sneaking up on you unless she wants you to hear her." The smile Sly gave Rora after that declaration made the hair on her neck rise.

"You can ride in the Rock," Locke said, gesturing toward the odd carriage. Through the glass dome at the front, she could see all manner of knobs and dials and cranks, and though she was curious, her pull toward Honey was stronger.

"I'd prefer to be on my horse."

He sighed. "This isn't going to work if you argue with every thing I say."

"I wasn't arguing. My horse has never left this area. I'd prefer to be with her, so she stays calm. Do I *need* to argue?"

"Fine," he said, but he didn't look happy about it. "Get on your horse. We're leaving now." He followed that declaration with a shrill whistle that was apparently the signal for everyone else to pack up and prepare to leave. Duke and Bait both climbed into the Rock, and the redheaded teen blew her a playful kiss before he closed the top hatch. Everyone else took a horse, leaving a few more horses to carry supplies.

Rora crossed to Honey and ran a hand along her flank before hoisting herself up into the saddle. She leaned against Honey's neck, patting the horse's jaw, and asked, "Ready, girl?"

Honey stamped her hooves restlessly as if to say *get on with it*. Rora knew it was a risk taking Honey with her, but she needed her as a reminder of home, as a companion in an adventure that was either brave or insane.

"Sly, you take lead. We're not expecting to run into any storms today, but you have the best eyes. Ran, you bring up the tail. Bait—you ready?"

From inside the carriage, Rora heard Bait call out, "Ready!"

She frowned. There had been two horses hooked to the carriage when she arrived, but now those horses were saddled with supplies, and the carriage sat alone. How did they expect it to move without horses? She heard another scrape of metal, a loud whooshing noise that morphed into a whir, and the clank of turning gears. The sound sped up, and she saw Dukc pull a lever inside the Rock. The wheels of the carriage began to roll despite the utter lack of incline on the land. The wheels spun faster, until the carriage was a dozen horse lengths ahead.

With another whistle from Locke, the remaining crew took off on horseback. Rora tapped her heels against Honey's sides, and they darted forward. Honey must have been excited or anxious, because the horse took off faster than Rora expected. With a pull on the reins and a few soft whispers, Rora convinced Honey to ease her hurried pace, and they moved into position on the left of the carriage near Locke.

"How does the Rock move?" she asked. "I have never seen anything like it."

"That's because it's the only one of its kind as far as I know. And it works on storm magic. There's an enclosed space in the back, a chamber that we throw torque magic into, and the rotation turns a ratchet system that turns other gears that turn the wheels and allow the carriage to move unassisted."

"Torque magic?"

"It's what hunters call storms that rotate around a center point. The eye."

She frowned. "I've never heard it called that. Not in all the books I've read about—"

"Ah, but your books are written by Stormlings, aren't they? They inherit their power. They rely on their magic to fight at a distance. Any idiot with an affinity can dispel a storm, but to get close and stay close long enough to steal magic—that takes skill."

"And just a dash of a death wish," Jinx called back.

"Maybe a little more than a dash." Locke smiled at his friend, and it was the first time Rora had seen him do so since she arrived.

He turned back to her and continued: "No one has ever gotten as good a look at the inner workings of a storm as us. To defeat a storm without an affinity, you have to know how it behaves, which is why we divided storms by movement. Besides torque, there's torrent—rain, snow, sleet, lightning."

"Storms that move from sky to ground?"

"Exactly. Third type is tide. Anything that sweeps over the land like an ocean tide. Sandstorms are one. Though it can happen with dust here in the grasslands too."

"Fog," she supplied quietly. Though unassuming, fog had always featured prominently in her nightmares. Perhaps it was the parallel to her real life—that slow, agonizing creep toward the inevitable. Fog had not the strength of a twister or the power of a firestorm, but fog was greedy with its victims. Once it had them trapped in the mists, it liked to keep them, wandering till madness or death or both.

"Depending on which of us you talk to, tsunamis or forest fires could be considered tide storms too."

"Those have Stormhearts?" Rora had thought it only the religious sects that worshiped storms who believed that way.

Locke shrugged. "Your guess is as good as mine. Sly believes they do because that's how she grew up. Her tribe believe all extreme acts of nature to be storms. They believe that storms come from the souls of the dead who lived exemplary lives. They're birthed again as part of the elements. But as far as I know, no one has ever successfully captured a Stormheart from one."

"Sly belongs to the Church of the Sacred Souls?" Rora had read about the cult that worshiped storms, but she never considered it more than superstition and foolishness.

Locke laughed. "Don't let her hear you say that. The Church of the Sacred Souls is a new group that borrowed some old ideals. Sly was raised by a much older tradition. In Vyhodi."

Rora's jaw dropped. Those that remained of the first tribes after the Time of Tempests were said to be extremely devoted to the old ways, the old gods. They did not even associate with the rest of Caelira. They had no royalty or palaces but lived simple lives in the near wilderness. How had Sly come to join a crew that hunted storms if she was from a tribe that revered them?

"And what do you believe?" she asked Locke.

He adjusted his grip on the reins and tossed his head to move some unruly hair out of his face. "I think this world is an incredibly complex place and we've barely scratched the surface of knowing it. But I'd rather stay dead and buried than come back as a storm."

"Then I guess we don't disagree on *everything*."

He looked at her, but did not smile like he did for Jinx. "I suppose not."

"When do you think we'll meet our first storm?" Rora asked. Her heart thumped as something occurred to her. "Will we wait for the storm approaching Pavan?"

"You are not ready to be anywhere near a storm, princess." She opened her mouth to argue, but he added, "And we only hunt in the wilds. Unclaimed territories are fair game, but near cities, the risk of getting tangled up with Stormling militaries is high. They'd sooner throw people like us to the storms than save us."

She wanted to object to his insult to the military, many members of whom had offered up their time and patience over the years to help her. She hated to think ill of them, but if Locke was wary and Nova too, she would have to learn from the experiences of others instead of just her own.

Locke picked up speed, pulling away from her and focusing his gaze ahead of them. Rora knew that was her dismissal, and she saved the rest of her questions for later.

They were moving past the wheat fields now. She loosened her grip on the reins, and twisted her torso for one last long look at home. The palace glittered in the early-morning light, the black rolling clouds of an incoming storm unfurled behind it. Pavan was not a particularly religious land. They held no monuments to the old gods, only to Stormlings. Her homeland had stopped looking up for answers centuries ago. Only one thing came from the heavens here, and it wasn't hope.

But even so, Rora said a prayer to whoever would listen. Whether it was the old gods or nature or simply the open air that surrounded her. She prayed for safety on this journey, and that Nova would not suffer any consequences from their actions today. She prayed that her mother would understand and forgive her. And selfishly, she prayed that when she returned, Cassius would be long gone, and she would never have to face him again.

With that done, she took a deep breath and said her final good-bye. To Pavan. And to Aurora.

From this point on, she could only be Roar.

Encompassing over sixty percent of Caelira's land mass, the wildlands are the unprotected territories that remain unclaimed by any Stormling kingdom. Like the boundaries of Stormling strongholds, the geography of the wildlands has changed over time as kingdoms have risen to power and fallen from grace.

—*The Perilous Lands of Caelira*

10

They rode for hours in near silence, with only the whirring sound of the Rock's mechanisms to war with the thoughts in Locke's head. He tried to stay busy, riding back and forth through the group on occasion to check with Sly at the front, then Ransom at the back. But he always found himself settling in the middle of the group, near Roar.

She rode well, he begrudgingly admitted. In the beginning, he had watched her for any sign that she might change her mind. There had been a moment when Roar turned back to gaze at the shrinking city that had made him hope she would reconsider. But after a long, lingering look, she'd faced forward, leaned into the wind, and picked up her pace. And from that point on, the only times she had looked back had been with caution, as though she expected a storm to come barreling after them at any moment.

He almost wished it would. He could use the distraction.

Little by little, her nervous glances backward lessened, so that by the time they stopped to eat and rest at a spot known as Death's Spine, she appeared completely at ease. Almost . . . giddy.

It only soured his mood more.

Jinx used her gift to light a small fire, and Ran began reheating a soup he'd made the night before. Soon they would begin hunting for the majority of their food, supplementing whatever meat they killed with supplies they brought along or things Jinx could grow. The witch had already wandered off, looking for a good patch of soil to grow some berries for dessert. He focused on Jinx, staring hard while she dug her hands into the soil, pushing a single seed as deep as she could. She kept her hands buried in the dirt, closed her eyes, and began to use her magic. It should have been enough to hold his attention—his friend coaxing a fully grown plant into existence from almost nothing.

But his eyes kept wandering to where Roar walked along the rocky line of sandstone that gave this area its name. Death's Spine was the unofficial end of Pavan territory, and from this point on it was them versus the wildlands. There was something captivating about Roar, standing upon that dividing line—framed by civilization on one side and wild terrain on the other. She stared out at the surrounding land, hair blowing in the breeze, taking it all in like she was tasting joy for the first time. He blamed Jinx's earth magic; when she worked it always seemed to affect more than just whatever plant she was focused on. The sun shone a little brighter, the grass appeared greener, even the breeze seemed to luxuriate in the presence of magic, curling indulgently around them. That had to be why the sight of Roar drew his eye.

"Think she can cut it?" Ransom asked between stirs of the soup.

"I'll make sure of it."

His friend knew him too well. "You sound less than pleased about that."

"Yes, well, I was not given much of a choice."

"Don't act like you're not happy she's here. We've all seen the way you look at her."

Locke scowled. "She was a pretty girl I never expected to see again. I certainly didn't expect her to become a permanent fixture in my life." Locke would do his duty and train her, but that had to be it. There was no room in him to care about her. Once you let those kinds of emotions in, it was a lot harder to hurl yourself into death's path on a daily basis. "Besides . . . if I did look at her in a way that actually meant something, I would hardly want to introduce her to a life like ours."

Locke left Ransom to cook and busied himself checking their supplies, far from where Roar wandered. When they sat down to eat, he listened to Jinx tell Roar about Taraanar. "If you thought the Eye was impressive, just wait until you see the Taraanese markets. They go on for what seems like forever, and even the nonmagic markets are a sight to behold. Rich tapestries and spices and pottery—"

Locke interrupted to ask Roar, "You speak Taraanese, right? That's what you said before."

Roar sipped soup from her spoon before answering, "I do."

"But you've never been?"

She shook her head. "A childhood friend was Taraanese. I picked up most of it from her and practiced by reading books in the language."

She was puzzling to be sure. There were ranking nobles that didn't speak any other languages, and yet this girl from the streets spoke several.

"Well, go on," Bait said. "Speak Taraanese to me."

She laughed. "What do you want me to say?"

"Say I'm the most handsome man you've ever met, and you're falling madly in love with me."

"Does anyone else speak Taraanese?" she asked. No one answered, but Locke knew Duke understood it fairly well.

She turned to Bait with a small smile, and she spoke. Locke had no idea what she said, but he watched her mouth move as the low, soft sounds poured out. He had never found Taraanese a particularly beautiful language. So many of the sounds were made in the back of the mouth and throat that he often thought it sounded garbled or disjointed. But Roar made it sound like a purr, sweet and throaty.

"What did you say?" Locke asked, unable to help himself.

She did not answer but gave him a curious look and continued speaking, and this time he got the feeling it was about him. He made a vow then and there to learn Taraanese. He saw Duke duck his head to hide a smile, and he asked, "What's she saying?"

Roar stopped midsound, her face blooming with red as she looked at Duke. Her voice shook as she asked in the common tongue, "You speak it?"

"Not nearly so well as you. But I understand enough to get by."

"What did she say?" Bait asked, practically bouncing on the rock where he sat.

Duke answered, "She said you were like a small puppy. All excited energy and overflowing with love. And she hopes that you don't drool like a puppy too."

Everyone laughed, but Bait did not seem to mind. He didn't know how to be serious. Sometimes Locke wondered if he did it on purpose, if it was easier to joke than face what was real. Everyone on this crew was here because they had left something worse behind. You did not choose this life if there was a better option waiting for you.

"I *am* overflowing with love," Bait said. "And it's all for you, Roar." He gave a suggestive arch of his eyebrows, and Locke fought the urge to shove him into the campfire.

"All right, lover boy," Jinx cut in. "Ease up before I lose my soup."

Ransom mumbled between sips, "Watch out. Puppies will also try to hump your leg if you're not careful."

Roar gasped with laughter, her whole head thrown back. The normally silent Ransom cracked a smile.

Jinx added, "It's true though. Bait *really* can't be trusted."

One corner of Roar's mouth tipped up. "With my leg?"

Jinx cackled. "With anything. The novie thinks it's funny to play pranks. He might flatter you now, but that won't stop him from torturing you in the name of fun later."

Locke added a second helping of soup to his bowl and said, "You might end up with a haircut like Jinx."

Roar's jaw dropped and she looked to the witch, whose hair was shorn on one side, a design cut into the hair just above her ear. "Bait cut your *hair?*"

Jinx laughed and smacked Locke on the arm. "Now who's torturing the girl? Bait didn't touch my hair. He's not that stupid."

"I don't know," Bait said, scratching his chin. "I might be. What do you think Ran would look like with only half a beard?"

"You would die before you found out," Ran growled, causing Bait to change seats and sit closer to Roar.

Locke was still hung up on the words she had said in Taraanese.

Unable to wait a moment longer, he asked, "What was it you said after the puppy thing?"

She froze and a flush rose on her cheeks. When she didn't answer, he turned to Duke.

The old man shrugged. "Not sure. Couldn't follow that part."

Traitor.

Roar bit her lip and smiled at the old man. Whatever she said must not have been flattering. He stayed quiet after that, not wanting his foul mood to spill out for the others to see. Roar was freer with them, Jinx and Bait especially, and he wondered if it was because those two gave him a harder time than the rest. She *would* gravitate toward them.

Roar marveled over the berries Jinx had grown. She asked a dozen questions about how it worked and what seeds Jinx kept in supply. Between each question, she popped another berry in her mouth, closing her eyes to savor the sweetness. He made himself look away and start a discussion with Ransom and Duke. Roar was a distraction, and in his life distractions led to death.

After they finished their soup, Bait took Roar's dirty bowl and offered to clean it with his. She said, "I can do it."

"Nonsense. As my future wife, I intend to pamper you." He finished the declaration with an exaggerated bow.

She laughed. "That's kind. But I feel it's only fair to warn you that marriage does not agree with me. I have already broken one betrothal. I'd hate to break you too." It took every bit of Locke's considerable control to continue looking uninterested as he cleaned his bowl.

Jinx chuckled, and Bait dropped to his knees in front of Roar. "You can break me. I think it will be worth it."

She laughed again, a glowing flush to her cheeks. And Bait had put it there, not him. It was better that way. She and Bait would have more in common. They'd only added the novie to the crew six months prior.

But after he stowed his bowl, Locke found himself marching over anyway. "Are you done making a fool of yourself, novie? We need to get back on the road."

Roar glared at him, but the rest were used to his bouts of surly behavior. Bait climbed up from his knees and gave a salute. "Yes, sir! Right away!"

Jinx rolled her eyes and sighed at Locke as she got up to leave too. When they were making their way back to their horses, he tried to think of something to say to ease the strain between him and Roar, but all that came out was, "Your hair is shorter."

She took her time untying her horse, and when she finished, she turned to face Locke, her eyebrows raised nonchalantly. "Hmm?"

"Your hair. It's shorter."

She cleared her throat, and when her eyes stayed just shy of meeting his, he knew he had made her nervous but not why. "I was wearing a scarf before."

"You were. But I could feel the mass of hair beneath it when you fainted and I caught you. It was much more than you have now."

She exhaled and shrugged. "It was too much. It would get in the way on the road." She flicked up one of the short strands and added, "This is easier."

"Practical." He liked that.

"Wouldn't want to be a liability."

He frowned. "Are you ever going to let that go?"

"Perhaps. Perhaps not." She pulled herself up into the saddle. "Are you going to teach me anything else about storms? Or shall we spend the next leg of our trip in uncomfortable silence again?"

He stayed on the ground below her horse, the early afternoon sun haloing her.

"Perhaps. Perhaps not," he shot back. "Silence doesn't bother me. Is it the quiet or me that makes you *uncomfortable*?" She stared at him, her eyes narrowed and hands fisted tightly in her horse's mane. He grinned, and she snatched up her reins.

It was plain she meant to end their conversation, but he lingered a moment longer. He smoothed a finger down her horse's muzzle, and the pretty mare leaned into his touch. He rubbed gently, just above her nostrils, and her ears flicked with approval. He leaned in and murmured low to the horse, "Run well for her." He gave the horse one of

Jinx's berries, and the mare pushed her nose into his hand searching for more. Roar was glaring when he looked up.

"Well?" she asked. "Are you going to teach me anything else?"

Once again, he found himself grinning. He was looking forward to wiping that haughty look from her face. "We'll start your first lesson tonight when we make camp."

"And what lesson would that be?" she asked.

"How not to die."

Novaya's hands shook as she told the story of Princess Aurora's kidnapping. She was panting, having run all the way from the flower fields to scream the news to the soldiers standing guard atop the city walls. Several immediately set out on horseback, while another rushed her to the palace courtyard that was being decorated for the wedding, dragging her before the queen.

Nova did not have to feign distress or tears when Queen Aphra collapsed in the courtyard where she had been happily inspecting flower arrangements for a wedding that would never come to be. Even as Rora's childhood friend, Nova had always found the queen frightening. She held too many secrets to ever be at ease with her ruler.

But now that strong, powerful woman was a broken heap of wailing mother upon the earth. The sounds that poured from the queen's mouth pierced through to the bone and dried up the lies in Nova's mouth.

The soldier next to Nova, a woman with bands on her uniform signifying thunderstorm and fog affinities, stepped forward and said, "We have a unit out searching already, Your Majesty. But we could use more eyes."

The words seemed to bring the queen back for a moment. She nodded, her voice trembling as she spoke. "Yes. Take them all. Take whatever you need." Then as if those words had stolen the last of her strength, she slumped to the ground, pressing her forehead into the dirt. Rora had written a letter to give to the queen, and it seemed to burn in Nova's pocket. She had to get the queen alone as soon as possible to end her torment.

A horrified quiet reigned until Prince Cassius charged down the palace steps.

"Is it true?" he growled.

When no one answered, he screamed the words again and Nova forced herself to say yes.

He marched to stand before her, his face a mask of fury. Her insides roiled with heat. He hissed, "Tell me everything. Quickly."

Her voice wobbled as she said, "I went out to pick wildflowers for—"

"I don't scorching care about the godsdamned flowers. How many were there? What direction did they take her? Was she hurt?"

Nova swallowed, and felt her magic begin to climb up her throat and fill her lungs. She balled her hands into fists and clenched her teeth.

"Answer me," the prince growled.

"Three. Maybe four kidnappers. It happened so fast. I don't think she was hurt. But she was screaming. They—they bound her. Took both her and her horse. They went south. That's all I saw. I ran to get help."

He snapped a finger, and a soldier in Locke blue rushed to his side. "You have command, Ortuze. Find her. Slaughter those who dared to take her. I want their heads."

The soldier turned to go, and Nova tried to put some distance between her and the prince, edging closer to the grieving queen. Before she got more than a step away, the prince's hand shot out, shackling her wrist. Flames licked beneath her skin, begging to be set free.

To his commander, he said, "Search the palace too. Starting with this one's room, in case she was in on the plot."

Her heart dropped, and she gasped, stumbling as he pulled her back to him. "I—I would never. She's my—"

"I'll be the judge of that."

Nova looked to the queen for help as two Locke soldiers surrounded her, but the woman was lost to the world, trapped by whatever horrors were trampling through her mind. Within moments, the Locke commander had dozens upon dozens of men leaping into action, including the Pavanian soldiers.

As Nova was led away to the palace, she was grateful the soldiers did not touch her. But it was only a small mercy as they kept their hands on their swords. Heart racing, she waited until they were inside the palace, and then reached into the pocket that held Aurora's letter. She crumpled the paper in her fist, then slipped her hand free. With slow, measured breaths, she pulled on her magic, letting the heat flow through her hands.

If the soldiers noticed the smell of smoke, they did not react, as bit by bit the paper burned in her fist, and she allowed the ash to sprinkle onto the stone floor in her wake.

She would find another way to get word to the queen. First, she had to survive the prince.

Rora's legs were stiff from the saddle, but she didn't complain. She was too busy soaking up everything around her. The land, while still mostly flat, had become dotted with green hills. The road they'd taken from Pavan had become much more difficult to traverse a few hours past Death's Spine. Ruined Road, the hunters called it. What once had been a long road of flat stones that led from Pavan to Taraanar was now pitted with holes or washed away altogether in places. The Rock made loud, metallic groans every time the wheels hit a patch of uneven road.

The farther they traveled, the more the wildlands lived up to their name. She'd been fascinated with every bird that flew overhead and the grazing deer that would stop and stare as they approached, and then lope off at a surprising speed. The Napatya River, which flowed down from the mountains north of Pavan and curved around part of the city, appeared shortly after their stop at Death's Spine and ran nearly parallel with the road from then on, winding out of sight at times, only to come back into view a while later. An ominous feeling seemed to always hang in the air, but so far they had seen no hint of a storm.

They stopped for the evening on a flat swath of land between the Ruined Road and the river. The Napatya, named for the old goddess of rivers and lakes, was lined with trees, so Roar could not see the water, but she heard it rushing as they made camp.

Her hips and thighs twinged with pain as she slid off Honey's back and led her to the river for a drink. It was darker under the canopy of trees, and insects hissed and trilled, filling up the night with sound. Honey ambled into the water until it covered her hooves and then bent to drink. Roar was contemplating wading into the cool water herself when Locke appeared beside her. He'd not spoken to her since their stop at Death's Spine, but she'd caught him glaring more than once.

"Bait will care for your horse. It's time for your first lesson."

Bait popped up behind her and snatched Honey's reins. He gave her a wide-eyed look and muttered, "Good luck."

She sighed. "Okay. Teach me how to stay alive."

"Follow me." He started up the bank and out of the trees. When they passed the last line of branches, he began to run. She followed, but frowned when they passed the others making camp.

She held back her questions, knowing how they agitated him, and focused on keeping pace with his longer legs. She was relieved he stuck to the road. Twilight had cast their surroundings in eerie shadows. When his pace increased, she matched it. She was in decent shape from her occasional runs with Taven and his unit—her mother believed in being strong in both body and mind. An unexpected pang struck her at the thought of her guard. She knew how seriously Taven took her protection. He must have been out of his mind with worry. Perhaps she should have thought to leave him a note as well.

"What?" Locke barked, his eyes narrowed on her as he ran.

She shook her head. "Nothing."

"Tired already?" he prodded.

She was. Her thighs were screaming with the effort to move after riding all day, but she wasn't going to tell him that. She scoffed and said, "Hardly."

He sped up again as if to test her, and she shoved down her pain to keep up. He frowned when she kept his pace without faltering. His eyes flicked to her arm. "Injury giving you trouble?"

"No. It was nothing." When he kept staring at her, she rolled her eyes and answered, "I was thinking about someone I left back home."

He stopped abruptly and spun to step in front of her. She barely managed to avoid crashing into him, and he was entirely too close as she struggled to catch her breath.

He said, "Tell me now if you can't handle this."

She lifted her chin. "I can handle anything you throw at me."

"I meant all of this. Leaving your home. Leaving people you *love*." He said the last word with his nose crinkled with derision. "If we need to turn around, tell me now. Because if we spend a week on the road and then suddenly you're consumed with grief, you'll have to find your own way home."

"You would leave me to the wilds by myself?"

He ground his teeth together, breath coming in heavy pants, but did not reply.

"I won't change my mind," Rora said. Her heartbeat was a rapid drum, but she did not know how much of that was exertion and how much was anger. "Pavan was my home. Everything and everyone I know is there. But that doesn't change why I'm here with you, with Duke. I'm sure you missed home at first too."

Locke scoffed, tilting his head to stretch his neck. "No, I didn't. I don't think a hunter here did."

"There was no one you left behind?"

"They were all dead," he answered flatly, "so I would have missed them the same no matter where I was. If there's someone you love back in Pavan, maybe you should go to them before your answer is the same as mine."

He turned and took off into the night. This time he didn't bother to gradually increase his pace but quickly climbed to top speed. She growled and charged after him. Unlike stubborn, controlling men, running was at least something she understood. It was simple, quiet, *peaceful*.

But by the time she caught up to Locke a few moments later, she was beginning to realize that there was no peace the way Locke ran. He ran as if a pack of wolves was nipping at his heels. Like the earth was crumbling behind as they went and to slow down even a little, to look back, would mean their end.

Every muscle in Rora's body burned, but she didn't fight it. She gave herself over to the hurt because it had never been more stunningly clear that she was alive and *free*. And as long as she met Locke's expectations, as long as she exceeded them, she had the chance to become exactly who she had always wanted to be.

Eventually her mind went blissfully blank—no anger, no pain, no sadness. It was too dark to see farther than a few paces, so she forgot her surroundings completely. She did not even realize Locke had stopped until he called out her name, shattering her focus. Her knees felt wooden as she slowed and turned.

"If you're going to pressure me to return home again," she said, "I'd rather not hear it."

His frown deepened. "Fair enough."

"I know you didn't want me here." He interrupted with a mocking bark of laughter, and Rora's stomach jerked painfully. "But this is all I want. It means . . . everything. So even if it's hard, even if it's dangerous, even if everyone I left in Pavan ends up hating me for it—I will not change my mind."

After a moment, Locke turned and began walking back the way they came. Roar had stood still too long, and now her legs felt like they might shatter if she stepped wrong. But even so she asked, "What? We're not going to run back?"

"Save your legs. We'll be doing this all again in the morning."

She stared after his retreating figure. "Running? That's it? That's my lesson?"

He strode back toward her. The gleam of moonlight combined with his serious expression highlighted the sharp angles of his face. His cheekbones sat high and flat, and his bristled jaw jutted out like a cliff's edge.

"There will come a day, Roar, when it's you alone against a storm. You'll have the length of a heartbeat to take in an extreme amount of information and make a strategic choice. The most important thing any hunter learns is when to fight and when to run. That instinct can only develop with time. But it's useless if you can't run fast enough and far enough to escape."

He pulled something from his pocket that she could not make out in the dark. Then he settled two long leather cords around her neck. From the first dangled a white crystal, like the ones they sold in the market that detected storm magic. He said, "Until then, I will ensure your safety in every way I can. Whoever is on duty in the Rock monitors a larger version of this crystal and will sound a horn should they detect magic nearby. But in case you're alone, you'll have this. If it grows hot, you find shelter as fast as you can."

He still held the crystal between them when she reached down for the item on the other necklace. Her hand bumped against Locke's as she brought the small tube closer to her eyes. "Firestorm powder," she breathed.

"Yes, and you'll take it if we ever get near one. Even if the rest of us are there, you take no chances. The embers are too dangerous. Do you understand?"

She nodded, and their hands brushed once more before he dropped the crystal and stepped away. She tucked the two trinkets beneath her tunic, and they fell alongside the Stormheart ring that dangled between her breasts.

They began walking back toward camp in the dark. "Roar?" Locke said. She hummed in response. It was dark enough that she could barely see him a pace away. "I don't think your loved ones will hate you for chasing what you want. But if they don't support you, they're the fools. Not you."

Roar smothered a smile. "I seem to remember a certain hunter who wasn't all that supportive of my decision."

His low chuckle carried in the dark. "Maybe he's a fool too."

Storms are the greatest predators in existence because they can destroy you with their savage strength or enthrall you with their terrible beauty. Like a poison flower with the stealth of a snake and the ferocity of a lion and the force of all the world's armies combined.

—*The Tale of Lord Finneus Wolfram*

11

Locke hadn't been sleeping well. The first night on the road, he blamed it on his adjusting schedule. On the second night, he did the same. But now after three nights of restless sleep, broken by nightmares about a girl in danger who was somehow both his sister and Roar simultaneously, he had run out of excuses. It had been ages since he'd last had a nightmare. He knew having Roar here would throw him off balance, but it was even worse than he anticipated. It was still a while yet before dawn, and he nicked several jars of skyfire magic to give him light enough to work. Across his lap, he laid out several maps of the wilds between here and Taraanar. Normally, it was Duke's job to do the navigating, but the old man hadn't complained when Locke kept bringing him suggestions for safer routes that would hopefully postpone any run-ins with storms until he felt Roar was ready.

She would be furious if she knew, but he didn't care. It wasn't just about her. He trusted his gut, and something wasn't right. And in the wilds, all it took was one mistake to wipe out an entire crew. He *had* to get his head straight.

They'd left the Ruined Road behind two days prior, opting to follow the river as it curved northeast, but yesterday in the late afternoon the river turned south again, bringing them back to Ruined Road.

As Locke studied the maps, it was glaringly obvious that there were no more *safe* routes for the next part of the journey. Hunters understood the wildlands and storms better than most. Duke was brilliant, and he could talk for hours about how nature and magic merged to make such beasts. The old hunter hypothesized that storms could form one of two ways: as a result of what he called colliding weather systems that changed the pressure of the air or from colliding natural magics. So like explorers traveling new lands, they kept notes and drew maps for everything they saw and experienced. In the Rock, Duke monitored the levels of magic in the air and kept lists upon lists of readings. They kept a separate map that marked locations of any storms they crossed or damage they saw from presumed storms. Over time, all that information allowed them to mark spots where magic was consistently more prevalent and the types of conditions or geographical features that made storms more likely.

He'd used those maps and figures to create their route so far, but they were approaching a valley called Sorrow's Maw to the south, where storms formed with frightening regularity. The land there teemed with so much raw magic that it would be a miracle if they did not encounter a storm sometime soon. Normally, they might have spent a few days camped out north of the valley, using the storms that rolled out of the Maw to bulk up their supplies. But it was too risky to camp near a hotbed when they had a newcomer like Roar and a novice like Bait.

For the last three days, he'd made Roar run morning and night, and though he hated to admit it, she was more than capable of surviving that way if necessary. Already she was probably faster than anyone else on the crew save him. And skies knew she was stubborn. He'd pushed and pushed, and never once had she asked for a break or for him to slow down. Not even last night when he'd run her until she doubled over, heaving her supper into the grass. He'd gone too far then—even his own lungs had felt on the verge of collapse—but she'd simply wiped her mouth with the hem of her shirt, then kept going.

He sighed. It was well past time to start training her for real. Clearly, she would not be scared off by a little hard work as he had hoped.

He stowed the maps back in the Rock, and then set off toward Roar's shoddily constructed tent. The thing stood haphazardly, leaning with the wind, but true to her stubbornness, she had refused to let anyone help her set it up.

He lifted the tent flap carefully, and called into the dark space, "Rise and shine, princess."

Locke heard the shuffling of blankets, and a grumbled, "I will murder you."

He fought a smile and crooned, "Come on, princess. Don't make me drag you out of there. I guarantee I'll enjoy it entirely too much."

He narrowly dodged a waterskin she tossed through the open flap of her tent, but he heard her moving around. She was always a little grumpy in the mornings, and it entertained him to no end.

"You know storms wait for no one. They come when you're sleeping or sore or tired, and those not strong enough to outrun them are those that don't survive."

"I'm coming. Calm your skies, hunter."

He dropped the tent flap and walked several paces away to wait. When she climbed out of the tent, he lost his train of thought completely. Her hair was mussed and wild, and her mouth open in a yawn. She wore a large linen tunic that swallowed her slim form, hanging down to midthigh. Beneath it her legs were bare, the light of the moon casting them in a soft glow. The sight burned into his brain, never to be forgotten.

He really did push her too hard last night. Normally, she was already awake (albeit irritable) by the time he came to collect her.

"I'll . . . leave you to get ready. Meet me at the campfire."

He forced his feet to move away before he did something stupid. He grabbed an apple from his pack and sat down near the fire they had made the night before. A few orange embers still glowed, though they provided little heat. A moment later she came up behind him, catching him off guard. "Remind me again why no one else runs before dawn."

She was dressed again in her usual attire. Her legs were covered by a pair of slim, brown trousers, and over her large tunic she had fastened on a leather harness that ran below her breasts and strapped over her shoulders. He could see the handles of several knives sticking up against her back. He stood, tossing the core that remained of his apple breakfast into the woods. He offered her one as well, but she shook her head.

"I'll pass. I've decided to wait to eat until *after* we're done running."

He bit his lip to keep from laughing and said, "The others are sleeping because they paid their dues. They've all fought storms and survived. They know what it takes. I trust them to take this seriously and prepare themselves in whatever way they see fit. But you—if you're not ready the first time I put you in front of a twister, that's on me."

Her voice shook slightly as she asked, "You're starting me with a twister?"

Good. It was about time the girl showed a healthy dose of fear.

"Don't sound so excited now, do you?"

Roar shoved hard at his chest, but he was used to holding his footing against winds far stronger than her. His lack of reaction only angered her more. "You're an ass," she hissed, whirling to leave him.

But he was quicker, and he snatched a wrist, tugging until she fell into him, one hand on his chest, two fingers' width from the accelerating beat of his heart.

"And *you* are scared," he said softly.

"*Of course,* I'm scared. Do you think I'm stupid?"

"I think you're reckless. You get an idea, and you commit to it fully. But you don't think through all the options. Instincts are important, but not when they're untested and ill informed. You've done your best to show no fear since you left Pavan. I want to know what it was about what I just said that shook up your façade."

Roar ducked her head, tucking a dark strand behind her ear. She had tied it back at the base of her neck, but already strands were escaping to frame her face. She replied halfheartedly, "Forgive me if I'm not ready for verbal sparring first thing in the morning."

He tracked back through their conversation, pinpointing the moment she'd first let her walls slip. "It was my mention of a twister, wasn't it? You've been in one before?"

"Would you stop reading into everything I say?"

He shook his head. He would never stop. If she wouldn't give up her secrets, he would discover them on his own. "No. Can't be that. If you'd been in one and survived, you would have used it as a selling point while trying to convince me and Duke to let you on the crew."

"Duke. I was trying to convince *Duke*. He's the one in charge."

"Of strategy, yes. Of this team, unequivocally. But in the field, when we're in the belly of a storm and Duke is in the Rock reading measurements? I'm in charge. He might be king, but I'm the general that keeps everyone alive. And I need to know what you can and cannot handle. So why is it a twister that scares you?"

He still held one of her wrists, and she tugged, trying to break free. His grip was secure; but, never one to give up easily, Roar twisted her body nearly all the way around, trying to worm out of his grasp. He loosened his hold, worried she'd hurt herself. But the moment she broke free, he seized her again, wrapping his arms around her middle, arms trapped at her sides, her back to his chest.

He should let her go. He knew her well enough now to know that manhandling her would only make her fight harder. But he was too distracted by the way her body fit against his own. Her soft hair tickled his neck. Even more startling, she had stopped fighting him completely. Her body sank against his, her back pressed against his chest and abdomen. He became acutely aware of where his arms wrapped around her shoulders and her midsection. She sucked in a breath, and the rise and fall of her chest moved through both of them.

He knew he should step away, but it was like he'd been mesmerized. He stood there, stock-still, his mind filled with nothing but her. If she were a storm, she could destroy him, and he would never lift a finger to protect himself.

If he did not learn to block out the instincts she roused in him, destruction could be exactly where they both were headed.

Heat from Locke's breath tickled over Roar's ear, then her cheek, and if the thought of a twister shook her up, his closeness threatened to send her heart into convulsions. She wanted to scream and shove free from his grasp, to fall back on another argument that would give her the precious distance she needed. But it felt better than she would ever admit to lean back and let the hunter behind her be the thing that held her up for a while.

She had thought *Roar* would be a fresh start, a chance to be free of all the things that stifled her in Pavan, but even after days of travel in the wildlands, her life was still not rid of secrets. And those manacles had always been the tightest of all. It wasn't just the physical toll of the torturous runs with Locke that had her drained but the stranglehold on her tongue when it came to sharing about herself.

But this . . . this was one secret she could shed.

"My brother," she rasped, out of breath for reasons she could not discern.

"What was that?" Locke's arms uncoiled, and he bent his face closer to hers. His breath touched her cheek as she answered, "I haven't been in a twister, but my brother was."

His grip went slack, and she decided she had leaned on him long enough. She lurched forward and out of his grasp.

"*Was*? Did he—?"

She did not look up as she nodded. There was no harm in admitting this. The Prince of Pavan was hardly the only person to die in a twister.

"It's a terrible thing to lose someone you love," Locke said. "And to lose them to a storm makes you feel all the more helpless than if you could put a name or a face to your enemy." He moved in closer, his voice nearing a whisper in the dark. "But that's why you've got to *trust me* with your training." She was not sure she even knew how to do that. To *trust*. Especially not when lies from her mother and Cassius still shadowed her thoughts. "Trust me not to put you into that kind of situation until you're ready. Until you're able to do what your brother could not. You are not going to die on my watch, princess. I promise you that."

On his last words, he flicked a strand of hair near her jaw. It flew up, then down again, settling onto a cheek that felt so deeply flushed, it ached like a bruise. She pushed her hair behind her ears. "I told you not to call me that."

He stepped back, giving them both plenty of space. "Live up to your other name, and I will."

She threw up her hands on a growl and stalked off into the darkness.

"I suppose that was a little closer to a roar, but it still needs work," he said, before passing her by at a brisk jog. "Come on. We're doing things a little differently today. We'll see if you can keep up."

"I will." She just hoped she could do it without spilling the contents of her stomach in the grass. One time was enough.

She fell into pace beside him and he asked, "First, tell me which direction we're running."

She rolled her eyes up toward the dark sky, dotted with pinpricks of light. She saw the familiar constellation of Rezna's Gate. That collection of stars was the closest thing they had to mark true north. There were other clusters of stars surrounding the goddess's constellation, many of them named for types of storms.

"North," she answered. "Was that supposed to be difficult?"

"No. But this is. Follow me. Do everything I do."

He set off, but this time he wasn't simply running. He picked up speed, dodging left around a boulder. She planted a foot, pivoting, and followed. He hiked up a knee and leaped on top of the boulder before jumping off the other side and setting off at a run once more. She gritted her teeth and did the same, only she had to use her hands to pull herself onto the rock, and she didn't so much jump off the other side as roll. Her still-healing arm ached from the strain, but there was no time to think about that. He took her up hills and between trees, hurtling over an obstacle course of raised roots and fallen limbs. Her legs started to burn with each leap, but she kept as close to his heels as possible. They crawled beneath raised tree roots and rolled down a sloping hill. She scraped her knees and elbows nearly raw.

Locke disappeared into the line of trees that surrounded the river. She burst through the outer layer of branches, only to find him gone. The stream was below her, trees all around her, but no movement that she could see. She tried to contain her breathing and listen, but she could not hear the fall of his feet or the quiet huff of his breath.

The skin on the back of her neck prickled with awareness a moment before she heard his voice behind her.

"You're running from a storm. You've just found these trees for shelter. What do you do?"

She ignored the anxiety of having him at her back and said, "Depends. What kind of storm?"

"Good." The word came out so close to her neck that she felt his breath crash into her skin. "Let's say skyfire."

She snorted. "I would turn around and leave. Being near a body of water is a bad idea." She made the mistake of following her own directions; that left her eye to eye with Locke, their bodies so close that her shoulder brushed his chest when she turned.

"And where would you go?" His voice was low and deep in the darkness, and he leaned closer as if she might not hear him, as if she wasn't all too aware of every sound and movement he made.

"I would . . . look for shelter."

"There is no shelter." His eyes dropped to her mouth. She swallowed, but it went down like sand. He wasn't interested in her *that* way, so she had to be imagining that glint in his eyes. Which was good because she was not interested either. He was attractive, certainly, but she was here for only one thing, and it wasn't to put her heart in danger again.

She broke their gaze and said, "I'd look for the lowest point on the land. A valley or depression. Then make myself as small a target as I could. Crouch into a ball and touch the ground as little as possible."

"And if the land is flat?"

She chewed at her lip. "Then as a last resort, I would come here. But stay away from the water. And I'd look for a cluster of shorter trees, since lightning is more likely to strike the taller trees. And again, make myself as small as possible."

"Excellent." Her stomach pitched with pleasure. "And if it were a firestorm?"

"The water."

"Then to the water we go." He edged past her and sprinted down the bank. "Then what?" he yelled as she followed.

"If I'm in immediate danger, beneath the water."

"You're currently ahead of the storm."

Heart hammering, she plunged into the stream, water lapping at her legs. It wasn't freezing, but it was cold enough to make her muscles tighten with stress.

"Then I run. Through the stream in case the storm catches up or the trees catch fire, and I need to dive under the surface."

"Which direction?"

"Umm . . . umm . . ." She looked one way down the river, then the other. She spun around, reminding herself which direction she'd seen Rezna's Gate. "Firestorms usually form over dry climates and don't move into areas with more moisture in the air. But this stream might not be big enough to make that much of a difference."

"Good. But remember we're not hiding in the stream, we're using it as a means of escape. So which direction do you run?"

Her legs began to shake in the knee-deep water. "Most rivers run toward larger bodies of water. So I'd run the same way as the river." She pointed to where the Napatya turned around a bend and headed southeast.

"Then run."

She did, picking up her knees as much as she could, so that she wasn't bogged down by the water. But even with all that effort, the water made her slow and tired. Already fatigued muscles grew heavy and numb, and it became more and more difficult to lift her knees. She decided that it would be better to run on the bank, close enough to the water that she could dive beneath it with one jump, but with firm enough ground that she didn't have to work so hard for traction. When she moved to do that, her boot connected with a flat, mossy rock, and her foot slipped. Tumbling forward, her knee hit the riverbed just before her face plunged beneath the surface.

She broke into the air, coughing and sputtering. She was still struggling to catch her breath when Locke came to a stop beside her. She was already embarrassed, and she *knew* he would make it worse.

"Did the imaginary firestorm catch up to you? Or did you just fall?"

And there it was.

Without answering, she looped her hands around the back of one of his knees and jerked forward as hard as she could. He made a satisfying splash as his back hit the water. Roar was soaked and freezing, but soaked and freezing with a smile. When he surfaced, it was with none of the hacking and flailing that she had done, just water streaming down his cold, calculating face.

He wiped one eye, then the other. His movements were slow, economical, as if not a muscle in his body ever moved without a purpose, and her heart thrummed with something like terror, but lighter, like the feel of climbing a tall tree for the first time as a child or her first successful attempt at sneaking out of the palace. An anxiety that was both awful and wonderful in equal measure. Then his hands darted forward, clasping her arms, and he pulled until her back hit the water. The last thing she saw before the river swallowed her was Locke hovering above her, the smuggest grin set on his face. She screamed, bubbles streaming up from her mouth, and hooked her legs around whatever part of him she could reach. She jerked and twisted, propelling herself upward until she successfully rolled him beneath her.

Dark hair was plastered to her face and her teeth clacked together from the cold, but that didn't dampen the victory she felt with his whole body pushed beneath the surface. When he rose out of the water, deadly calm, that victorious feeling disappeared and laughter died in her throat. She cringed, waiting for his attack.

Instead his long fingers brushed away the hair stuck to her forehead and cheek, and she flinched when skin met skin. He stilled and looked at her like hunters looked at prey, as if he were trying to make himself appear as nonthreatening as possible. Then his wet palm slid over her cheek. The slip of his skin over hers was unlike anything she had ever felt. It didn't *feel* like that when she touched her own face in the bath or wiped her cheek in the rain. It didn't feel hot and cold and every temperature in between and all at once. His thumb caught on her chin, the rest of his fingers tickling across the slick skin of her neck, and her mouth fell open from the weight. Or from how hard it was to breathe. Or from the way her heart thought it was a good idea to force its way into her throat. All of them. Or none of them. She didn't know. She could barely hang on to a thought for more than a heartbeat before it scattered under the intensity of his gaze.

His fingers curved and with the barest pressure on the back of her neck, her body tilted toward his. And it was only then that she realized she still had a leg on either side of him, and the wet fabric of his clothes pressed against the wet fabric of hers. She should have been cold. *Freezing.* But instead she had a firestorm raging beneath her skin.

Another hand, the one that wasn't on her neck, touched her hip, trailed up to the dip of her waist, and over to the small of her back. He pulled her closer, all the vials and other supplies hanging from his chest trapped tightly between them. His head angled and bent, and his breath breezed over her open mouth.

She was uncharted territory, and mountains formed where he touched her and a river of sensation flowed down her spine. She watched his mouth, watched it form her name on a barely audible whisper. The hand around her neck tightened, his thumb sliding forward to brace at the edge of her jaw.

When he spoke, his voice vibrated through them both. "Fog is rolling in. What do you do?"

"What?" Her own reply came out breathy and small.

"Fog? Low clouds that cause disorientation, even madness if that magic is potent enough."

"I know what fog is," she snapped. The hand at the small of her back sneaked lower, grazing the upper curve of her bottom and making something tighten low in her belly. "Why?" she breathed, unable to form the rest of her question. Unsure even what question she had meant to ask.

"When you're distracted or feeling strong emotions, the natural barriers of your mind are weaker and more susceptible to being mesmerized by a storm's magic. Which means something as simple as a thick fog could do much worse than make you forget where you are or what you were doing. It could keep you in the fog, even as it moves, dragging you along with it. Your mental barriers must be without weakness."

"They are." It was part of every child's lessons when they were young, and as princess her training had been more rigorous than most. His thumb smoothed along her jaw, sliding up to tease at the corner of her mouth. She did not know how to react; her brain said to pull away, but her body said something different.

"So tell me, if fog has moved in and it's too late to run, *what do you do?*"

That's what this was about? He was . . . was *seducing* her to make a point about distraction? She grabbed his wrist, digging in her nails a little harder than necessary, and ripped his hand from her face. She shoved at his chest, and he had to let go of her hip to keep from plunging into the water again.

Scrambling backward, she put as much distance between them as possible. Because right now, she was *definitely* feeling strong emotions. The old betrayal and rage she felt with Cassius mixed with the anger she felt now, until a black fury permeated every part of her.

Her words were close to a snarl when she answered, "If I were trapped in a fog and I could not run, I would tie myself to a tree before I lost my senses, so that I wouldn't wander. I would divest myself of any weapons, should the fog cause me to be a danger to myself. Then I would try to clear my mind and wait it out. And hope my mind was still mine when it passed."

She did not wait for him to pronounce her answer satisfactory; she knew it was. She whirled around, climbed up onto the bank, and set off at a hard run once again.

When he fell into stride beside her, she sped up so she didn't have to see him in her peripheral vision, anger still thick and potent in her blood. And even though he was faster than her, even though he could have easily passed her, this time he didn't. He stayed behind and out of sight. She seethed, unsure whether she was more upset with him or herself. Because she *had* hesitated. She'd gotten the right answer in the end, but it had taken too long. Long enough that had the threat been real, she likely could have been mesmerized, just like he said.

Once again a man had manipulated her, and she'd fallen right into his trap.

In facing death, the first Stormlings found life.
In risking their souls, they gained dominion over the souls
of tempests.

—The History of Stormlings

12

On the way back to camp, her exhausted legs were the only thing distracting her from the riot of emotions inside her. Roar heard a shrill whistle break through the trees, followed by the low, vibrating sound of a horn. Locke cursed loudly behind her, and she could no longer pretend he wasn't there. She spun around, and his eyes met hers.

He reached out to grab her, and she swung her arm away before he could make contact.

"Storm coming. We have to get back."

They ran through the trees, gnarled branches scraping at her arms. When she emerged into open air, her head whipped backward so fast she would likely be sore tomorrow. But the sky was . . . *fine*. A little dull for this soon after sunrise, and a smattering of clouds hung above them, but they didn't appear dark, nor did Roar see any sign of rotation or skyfire. She spun around, searching for what the hunters called storms of tide. There was none of the fog Locke had quizzed her on. No dust storm or strong winds that she could detect. There was nothing at all.

Locke skidded to a stop behind her, and she turned to see the same confusion cross his face. But when the horn blew a second time, he took off toward camp again. They'd run far enough down the bending river that the crew was nowhere in sight. And it became clear within moments that the relentless, punishing pace Locke set in their workouts wasn't even him at full speed. He'd been taking it easy on her, and now he was pushing himself so hard that Roar couldn't keep up, not even when she urged her limbs to their limits. She chased after him, her lungs threatening to rebel and collapse.

When they rounded a bend and the camp came into sight, everyone was in motion. They'd already packed up. Ransom and Sly worked to calm the panicking horses. Duke and Bait were in the Rock, the top of the carriage still open as they fiddled with different instruments. Jinx was pacing, apparently waiting for them, and she ran to meet them halfway. Roar knew she should be afraid. She was about to face a storm for the very first time, but her earlier anger blocked out the fear.

The crystal tucked beneath Roar's tunic went from warm to blisteringly hot. She sucked in a breath and tugged it up by the leather strap to keep it off her skin.

"What is it?" Locke asked Jinx as they covered the last of the distance to camp.

"No clue," Jinx said. "We were all eating breakfast when the instruments went haywire. Temperature dropped so fast Bait thought the gauge was broken. Pressure is all over the place, rising and falling like nothing I've ever seen. The storm crystal is measuring at the hottest level. Whatever is coming, it's packed with magic."

They pulled to a halt and Locke nodded, his expression blank as the sky. "Roar, in the Rock. Now."

"What? But there's nothing even happening. I can—"

"I said *now*."

She fisted her hands until her nails bit painfully into her palms.

"I can handle this. I know—"

He gripped both of her arms, pulling until Roar was on her tiptoes. "This is not a discussion. You get in there, or we drop you off the next time we're near a town. Your choice."

She batted his hands away, rage bubbling up so fast in her chest that she nearly attacked him. She wanted to . . . with a ferocity she had never felt, not even back in the water. Roar was not a violent person. Or perhaps she hadn't been *before*. Before she'd left her whole life behind, abandoned her mother, and thrown herself on the mercy of this brutal world for the slimmest chance that *something* might change.

She looked at Locke, felt his fingers pinching her arms, and rage replaced her lungs. She screamed something halfway between words and a wail. Locke's face went slack with surprise, and only his quick reflexes saved him from the claw of her fingernails. He cursed, and his arms banded around her middle, locking her elbows against her waist. Roar kicked and yelled and dug her fingers into his forearms. He picked her up, burying his head in her neck to protect his face. She wrenched her body in different directions as he barked out commands.

"RANSOM! JINX! SLY! It's on you. Spread out. I don't know what's coming, but be ready! Be quick! Be smart!"

Then he hauled her, hissing like a wildcat, toward the Rock. She clawed and punched and kicked, and when her foot connected hard with his knee, he went down. She broke free, and for a moment her mind was filled only with thoughts of destruction—of crushing and dismantling Locke and everything that surrounded her. This rage . . . it was bottomless. A vast, empty nothing that would suck up every shred of happiness in her, bleed her dry until nothing was left but hurt and the desire to hurt in return. *Punish*, it whispered. *Punish them all.*

Locke stood to challenge her once more, and over his shoulder Roar saw the sky yawn night into the day, black pouring from blue like blood from a wound. A slim, spinning funnel reached for the ground, and she swore the dust from the earth leaped up to meet it. It punched downward, fast and fierce, and touched down less than two hundred paces in the direction Locke and she had come from. It landed near the tree line, ripping up roots that had probably spent centuries burrowing into the earth, as if they were little better than the weak, worn stitching on her clothes.

Roar's heart was beating so fast, and between the rage and fear, she felt like she might split in two. Her body jerked and twisted with a desperation that she didn't understand.

Locke cursed. "Everyone—anchors now!"

One by one, the storm hunters lifted what looked like small cross-bows attached to their hips, shooting iron arrows into the earth with long ropes uncoiling from a leather pouch on their harnesses. Something thunked next to her, and she saw similar arrows being shot from each corner of the Rock, securing it to the earth.

Distracted, she didn't notice Locke coming until he picked her up and hurled her over his shoulder. The fury pushed back to the forefront of her mind, swallowing up her panic, and she beat at his back as he climbed the ladder on the side of the Rock. He pitched her none too gently inside. Jumping in after her, he slammed the hatch at the top shut. For a moment, Roar was disoriented by the chaos inside the vehicle. Dials spun and something else rang with a shrill squeal. There were maps piled precariously on a small table in the center, and Duke sat in a chair bolted to the floor near the front, where most of the tools and apparatuses appeared to be. Another seat was placed near the back by a huge metal basin like the cauldron of some fairytale witch. Beneath her was a glass floor that revealed metal pipes and gears that sat motionless. The space felt too small, and she readied herself to fight harder, scream louder; but before she managed, a hard body slammed into hers, forcing her down on the floor. That set her screaming again, and the sound echoed painfully in her ears.

Roar fought, but Locke's body lay fully atop hers, taller and broader and heavier. Her teeth found the round, muscled mass of Locke's shoulder, and she bit down, screaming into the thick leather vest he wore. He grunted at the attack, but made no other sound.

"Calm your mind," Locke growled.

Over Locke's shoulder, her eyes fixed on the twister through the domed glass at the front of the Rock. She thought it had been terrifying before, but now it was as dark as she imagined death to be, filled to the brim with debris, like a gaping maw, shoveling itself full enough to burst. And the more that thing ate, the blacker her anger became, until she snapped her teeth at Locke like she was an animal instead of the Princess of Pavan.

This was . . . not right. This was not her. And even though she told herself to stop, even though she could feel tears tracking down her face and shame filling her belly, nothing changed.

She was a monster. And monsters had to be contained.

Roar took one last look at the looming twister, saw Ransom's bulky body and bald head moving toward it, and she knew that she was endangering everyone by distracting Locke.

"Knock me out," she said through gritted teeth.

"What?" Locke panted, winded by the sheer force it took to keep her in check.

"They need you," she growled. "Knock. Me. *Out*."

He stared at her, brown eyes wide and intense. His long hair had escaped its tie and hung in chunks between them. He hesitated, and without any conscious thought, Roar reared upward, trying to head butt him. He was quick, but she still caught him in the chin. Pain reverberated from her forehead, and his chin split, dripping blood between them. She cried out, even as she took advantage of his momentary distraction to work one hand free. She reached for his hair, the long waves that she'd admired more often than she cared to admit. She gripped it without care and yanked hard. He hissed, but his only retaliation was to try and capture her hand once more. Then after another particularly hard pull on his hair, Duke came into sight over them.

Roar had a brief moment to sigh in relief before he swung a long, skinny glass bottle down and smashed it against her head.

Then she surrendered to the black. Where there was no rage. No fear. No twister.

There was nothing at all, but peace.

Blood ran from a cut near Roar's hairline, and her fierce expression went blank with unconsciousness. Locke swung around, gripping the front of Duke's shirt and dragging the old man up onto his toes.

"Why did you do that?" he growled.

"Because someone had to. I've never seen someone react to a storm like that, but I know she would have only hurt herself trying to hurt you." Even in the face of Locke's wrath, the old man was stoic and calm. "And you're the torque specialist. They need you out there."

Locke wanted to argue, but the winds howled like bloodthirsty hounds, and the Rock shook forcefully even with the anchors down.

"Fine," he growled. "Help me move her." Together they carried Roar to the back of the Rock, and Locke found a towel to cushion her head. He hesitated a moment longer, but one glance outside the glass told him there was no time to wait. Duke pulled the lever that lowered a metal shade over the glass dome at the front of the Rock, blocking their view. Locke opened the sliding door at the bottom of the Rock, grabbed a bag of the enchanted jars they used to capture magic, and dropped into the narrow space between the Rock and the earth. He plucked the horn he carried from the pouch on his left hip and blew it hard to signal the hunters to retreat.

He knew his crew well enough to know that they had been focused on weakening the twister, not dissipating it. They would have been using opposing winds to slow the rotation. Jinx would be using her abilities as an earth witch to strengthen the surrounding trees so that the twister did not gain any more deadly debris.

They could have dismantled that twister fairly quickly, but they could not siphon off raw magic unless they got to the storm's heart.

Jinx rolled into the space beneath the Rock, panting heavily, and Ransom squeezed under a moment after her. Sly was so silent that he didn't realize she was already there, her short form tucked beneath the Rock horizontally above his head, until she said, "One minute out. I tried to slow the winds, but the moment I broke away to come here, they flared back to top speed."

"It's brutal, this one," Ransom said. "Not that big, but the magic is potent. Even mesmerized me for half a second at the beginning."

Locke cursed. Ransom had some of the strongest mental guards of any of them. It didn't bode well that the twister had gotten through his defenses.

He opened the bag he'd brought with him and handed a jar to each of the three hunters. Then he rapped on the metal shell of the Rock above him and the sliding door opened, revealing a grinning Bait.

"We ready?" the teen asked, the Stormheart from his thunderstorm affinity already in his hand.

Locke nodded and said, "Good luck. Fast feet, novie. If you get killed, I'm going to be unhappy."

"Sir, yes, sir." Bait gave a quick salute, then slid the door closed. A moment later, they heard the top hatch open, and Bait hit the ground running, on the far side of the Rock. There was a crescendo of noise in the cyclone's scream, and the wind picked up, the earth trembling in response. It had taken the bait all right.

Storms were fierce, and while they displayed intelligent behavior on occasion—lashing out when threatened, zeroing in on threats, even chasing prey—they didn't have the senses that humans had. Locke had always imagined they were more like bats, who used sound to map the world around them, only storms used wind or rain or whatever tools they had at their disposal. And when Bait took off, Stormheart in hand, filling it with his magic, the twister could not tell the difference between Bait and an actual thunderstorm, but it rushed toward him to investigate.

Locke looked at his team, finding three clear and focused sets of eyes. They were ready. He waited until the first wall of the twister was close enough that the ground buckled and jerked beneath their backs. "Ready," he said, tensing his muscles in preparation to move. The Rock lurched when the wall hit, and debris battered at the sides. They covered their eyes to keep them free of dirt. After a few agonizing moments of deafening sound, the wall passed, settling them into temporary stillness.

"Now," he barked, and each hunter had rolled out from beneath the Rock into the relative safety of the eye.

Hovering just above their heads was the heart of the twister. Rotating in a miniature version of the real thing, a funnel pulsed with glowing black light—like dense smoke lit from within. Because there was no wind in the eye, it couldn't sense them, at least not if they were careful. And at the moment, he knew it was focused on the other storm it sensed in the vicinity—whether it thought the other storm was friend or foe, he didn't know or care as long it stayed distracted. Jinx stepped up first, lifting the jar she had enchanted to draw in magic. As an earth witch, her enchantments were the strongest he'd ever seen, thanks to her natural connection to nature, of which storms were a part. When he had first joined Duke's crew, they'd had a fire witch. Hers had been good enough to keep the magic in the jar once they'd skimmed some of the excess energy swirling around the storm's heart. But with Jinx's enchantment, all she had to do was get the jar close and a smoky tendril of magic peeled away from the small spinning funnel and floated down into the jar, creating an even smaller funnel of its own. A cork formed from nowhere, stoppering the jar and sealing it shut. That was another added bonus of Jinx's earth magic. Jinx blew them a cocky kiss and rolled beneath the Rock and out of sight. As Sly stepped up toward the heart, the eye began to move past the Rock, cutting off their simplest escape route. But it was no matter. They hadn't all planned to get out that way. And Jinx could continue her efforts to weaken the storm on the outside.

The enchantment on the jar called forth another tendril for Sly's jar, and once more a cork appeared, completing the job. But when Ransom stepped up to fill the third jar, the sound from outside the eye pitched higher, and the twister dug in harder to the earth, turning up mounds of soil below them. The storm stilled and the funnel narrowed around them. Sly narrowly missed getting caught up in the enclosing wall of wind and debris.

"Out of time," Locke yelled. They would have to settle for only two jars.

Almost as if in response to Locke's call, the storm began moving again, but this time the winds shifted and it began tracking back toward the Rock. He cursed and gestured a hand at Ransom and Sly for them to attack. Sly didn't have a twister affinity, but her wind Stormheart lent her some influence over the wind rotating around them, and she tried to slow it down.

Ransom and Locke fixated on the storm itself, each simultaneously pulling their twister Stormhearts from their belts. The magic flared to life, filling up Locke's chest with energy; it sharpened his eyesight, allowing him to see and feel the entirety of the rotating column around him. The twister glowed a sickly greenish black, and he focused on the wall of wind next to him, shifting quickly on his feet to remain inside the eye even as the storm moved. His feet sped to a run as the twister picked up speed, and he knew they had to take this thing down now. He took a deep breath and, with a scream, he threw out his hands, sending out every bit of magic in him, amplified by the Stormheart he held. It slammed into the wall ahead of him, slicing it open and forming another wall of translucent light. The howling winds slammed into that wall, and the shape of the tornado warped, trying to continue spinning despite the disturbance.

Locke heard Ransom bellow behind him, and the walls of the twister shuddered again. Wind breached the eye as the circular rotation broke apart. For a moment, there was no rhyme or reason to the movement of the wind around them. It was everywhere, moving in every direction, and dust filled his vision. Something hard lanced his shoulder, and he was thrown sideways. He fell to one knee and planted a hand on the earth to keep himself from sprawling completely. Before he could force himself to stand again, the terrible roaring noise faded away and the winds dissipated, curling back to the gray sky above them.

To die at the hands of a storm gives one the chance to live again in the skies.

—*The Church of the Sacred Souls: Salvation and Second Life*

13

Roar came awake gradually to the sound of the hunters shuffling around her. She recognized their voices, the tight, worried whispers that carried despite their stealth.

"And I thought I had a temper," Jinx said. "My emotional outbursts are mild compared to that."

"Your last *emotional outburst* ended with a blade entirely too close to my special bits," Ransom answered. "I wouldn't call that mild by any means."

"Funny. I wouldn't call your bits *special*."

Ransom huffed in annoyance while Jinx laughed with glee. But the friendly teasing was cut through by a quiet, stern voice that Roar barely recognized she had heard it so little.

Sly. The quiet, stealthy girl who spent more time watching than participating in the group's conversations. "She is not to be trusted. She lies."

"About what? How do you know?" Locke barked, joining the conversation for the first time. The voice came from right above Roar, and she realized that the warmth cradling her head was not a pillow but Locke's lap.

"I—" Sly began, and then stopped. "I cannot pinpoint exactly what—"

"So you don't know at all. Yet you would call her a liar."

"I'm saying that maybe you should be resting rather than guarding the girl who attacked you. Rabid as a diseased dog."

It took Roar effort to fight off a flinch at those words. She kept her lids low and her breath even, and tried not to feel the crush against her heart as Sly spoke truths that she wished were lies.

Sly continued: "She says little of her life in Pavan. Little about her life period. She flits around like a brave little butterfly with a broken wing, and you all rushed to accept her. She's supposed to be a poor girl from the streets, but she came with her own horse. Her own supplies. She knew the man who sold three Stormhearts to Duke as if they were nothing more than trinkets. And yet, she pretends she knows nothing about our world. Had never seen eternal embers or storm charms or *anything*. I can tell you nothing more than that and the feeling in my gut. This girl is not who she seems."

"Her reaction was . . . *extreme*," Bait said, his voice tentative. "What if it happens again? Should we tie her up to be safe?"

"We're not tying her up," Locke growled.

Duke's calm but stern voice cut in. "Be still, Locke, or you'll damage yourself worse than you already are."

"I'll be still when you promise not to treat her like a prisoner."

There was a tense silence before Duke spoke in a measured tone. "Locke, I know you are fond of her, but we must be cautious—"

"Did you see her face? Before you smashed a bottle into her head? Did you see the way she cried between screams? I guarantee you, whatever was happening was causing far more pain to her than it was to me. For skies sake, *she* was the one to suggest knocking her out. And yet you all think her, what? A military spy? She could have called for a raid on the market, and we would all be rotting our lives away in the dungeons of Pavan. A thief? There are easier ways to make coin than out here, unprotected and in constant danger. Perhaps she does not tell us about herself because she trusts as easily as you do, Sly."

Roar wondered if he would defend her so fiercely if he knew exactly what secrets she was hiding. The hunters had made plain their disdain for Stormlings and the oppression inherent in their way of life. Locke, in particular, seemed to grow especially tense when talk turned to them.

A long silence followed. Too long for Roar to keep calm, and finally she gave up the pretense of sleep and opened her eyes. She looked in the direction Sly's voice had come from, planning to gauge if she knew Roar was awake, but all she saw was the small girl's back as she walked away toward the horses.

That pulled Roar abruptly into awareness, and she tried to sit up. "Honey!" Pain shattered through her head, as if she'd been hit all over again. Then Locke pulled her back into the cradle of his lap and laid a newly wetted rag against her head. The water was cool and helped clear her mind.

"Your horse is fine. Bait rounded them all up," he said above her, and she tilted her head back to find him shirtless and bloodied as Duke worked to wrap a wound in his shoulder.

"What happened back there, Roar?" Locke asked.

She blanched and her mouth went dry. Of course, the only reason he would be here, taking care of her, was because he wanted answers. Well, she had none.

She shot up, ignoring the stinging pain in her head, and turned the attention back to him. "What happened *to you*?" Her voice was a barely there rasp.

Locke answered, "Nothing," as Ransom said, "The fool got skewered by a tree branch."

Locke glared at his friend. "I did not get *skewered*."

"Pierced, impaled, punctured, spiked, stabbed—should I go on?" Jinx asked.

"Penetrated," Bait said. "You forgot penetrated."

They all laughed, and even Locke rolled his eyes. As if there weren't a *hole* in the man's shoulder that was already beginning to bleed through the bandages Duke wound over it.

All the hunters were covered in dirt, and some had darker stains that were likely blood. But everyone was alive and uninjured, at least in comparison to Locke. The land, though . . . it looked as if it had been gutted and all its entrails poured out.

"How are you all so calm?" Her heart was thundering as hard now as it had been when the twister manifested.

"This is what we do," Locke answered grimly. "If only one of us gets hurt, it's a good day." He lightly touched her forehead. "Though I suppose two of us got hurt today."

She jerked away, unable to hold back the rush of violent memories any longer. She closed her eyes as she thought about how she'd felt, what she'd *done*. "What—what happened to me?"

"We need *you* to explain that to us," Duke said, his old eyes alight with suspicion that cut like a razor's edge. She had been so grateful when he kept her Taraanese words secret. If she had known he understood, she never would have been so candid about Locke, about how she was glad he was being so irritable with her because it made it easier to ignore how handsome he was and the way her lungs didn't seem to work right whenever he drew too near. Now Duke looked at her like she was dangerous, like he regretted having her here.

Roar shrank away, and her eyes found Locke. His hair had been tied back again, safely out of reach of her hands. Bruises littered his chest and shoulders, and she wasn't sure if they were from the storm or her. She flushed hot with shame and squeezed her eyes shut.

"I don't know," she whispered. "I'm not without a temper and my mouth has gotten me into more trouble than I care to admit, but never . . . I've never felt anything like that. Earlier, before we arrived at camp, I had been *upset*. But then out of nowhere there was so much rage, and it pushed out every other thought and feeling. It was like . . . I wasn't me."

Locke looked up at Duke, then back down at Roar. "And are you *you* now?"

"I don't feel . . . *wrong*. Not like I did then. Do you think the storm mesmerized me?"

Duke frowned, running a hand down his beard. "I've never heard of anybody experiencing added emotions while mesmerized. Usually, it's the opposite. The storm's thrall drains away fear and all other emotions. One feels almost blank. But I suppose it's a possibility this came from the storm's magic. An evolution of their ability to attack. We likely know more about storms than anyone else in all of Caelira, but even we have barely scratched the surface of all there is to know."

She thought back to the night Cassius had faced the skyfire storm in Pavan, the only other time she'd been near a storm instead of locked away in the shelters. It hadn't been as strong then, but she'd felt a surge of emotion then too. Not rage, but . . . "I might have felt something like this with another storm. I had thought it was just the situation I was in, that my own emotions were high because of stress. But during the skyfire storm that hit Pavan before we left, I felt overcome with jealousy, not quite as all consuming as the twister but . . . similarly out of control."

Locke asked Duke, "Is she a sensitive?"

Sensitive was code for those who could feel storms when they approached. Which was every Stormling with abilities, and a few without who had traces of diluted Stormling blood in their ancestry. But most sensitives described the sensation as a tingle of unease or dread. A restlessness that pricked at their sense of self-preservation. This had been far more than a tingle.

Duke shrugged, rubbing at his mustache. "Maybe. But the manifestation is still highly unusual."

The group fell quiet. Her head felt like it was about to cleave open, but she forced her eyes to meet Locke's. "I'm sorry," she said. "So very sorry."

"Don't worry about it, princess."

She *would* worry about it. Knowing her, she would worry herself sick over it. "I attacked you. Attacked, assaulted, mauled, beat—whatever word you want to use."

"Mauled," Bait murmured to Jinx behind them. "Good word choice."

Roar continued: "If I had had the chance, I think I would have hurt you much worse. Whether I wanted to or not." She buried her head in her hands.

"But you didn't hurt me. I'm tough enough to take a little brawling with a girl half my size."

His hand smoothed over her shoulder, and she recoiled. He was the *last* person who should be comforting her. The soft, concerned sound of his voice grated over her nerves, and she wished he would yell. That he would be angry and aggressive like always. "I *bit* you," she hissed.

Locke held out a hand to Ransom, who helped him to his feet now that Duke had finished binding his wound. He used his uninjured arm to brush off dirt and dust from his bare torso while he casually tossed out, "Not the first time I've been bitten by a pretty girl."

Jinx snorted, and Ransom groaned and rolled his eyes.

"Really?" the big man said. "That's what you're going with here?"

Locke bent at the knee, squatting in Roar's line of vision. "You didn't hurt me. Besides, you're in much worse shape than me."

"You were *speared* through the shoulder."

He shrugged, unsettling his bandages for the moment. "I wasn't the unconscious one."

"What if it happens again? What if I am filled with rage when you all are sleeping or focused on something else?"

"We'll be cautious. If you feel any emotion that isn't your own, let one of us know. And—" He looked at Duke again, frowning. "Perhaps we hunt only smaller storms until we know more."

"No!" Roar leaped to her feet, head still spinning. "Please. Don't shut me out. I'm here. I *want* to do this. I *need* to do it."

"Why?"

"Because I *do*. Because I left behind everything to do this, and if I fail . . . *I cannot fail*."

His expression softened, and again she wanted to shake him until he was as angry as he should be. As angry as she was with herself.

"You won't fail. But hunters who want to stay alive must be as prepared as they can possibly be. And for that, we need time to figure this out."

Duke added, "The first rule of hunting is knowing your limits—when to fight, when to run, and when to be cautious. We'll camp here for a few more days so that the two of you can recover. Perhaps the rest of us can make hunting runs nearer to Sorrow's Maw and begin bulking up our supplies."

Locke began to protest, but a firm look from Duke cut him off.

"You're no good to us if you don't heal properly. Ransom, set up his tent. If he won't lie down, *make him.*"

The others did have to force Locke to rest. In fact, they had to force him back into his tent several times that day while remaking the camp. Roar thought her tent looked a little sturdier this time, though still somewhat jumbled. She would get better. She had to.

Hour by hour, the others began to unwind from their adrenaline-filled morning, but she could not seem to do the same. Roar was consumed with doubt and shame, but these feelings she knew were all her own.

She thought physical activity might calm her mind, so she busied herself with clearing the debris left by the twister, piling up broken tree branches on the sides of the road to clear a path. There were gouges in the earth where the storm had torn up the soil, and even with the debris removed, the road would be rocky.

When there was no more she could do, she made her way back to the Rock, studying the outside for damage, of which there was remarkably little. Dents and dings certainly, but with the way that twister had looked she would have thought it could tear anything apart. As she stood marveling, Duke ambled over to stand behind her.

"How are you feeling?" the old man asked. His voice was not as soft as it used to be, and his lanky frame was stiff.

She almost said *fine.* But there were precious few things she could tell the truth about, and this was one of them.

"Confused," she answered. "Sore. Worried." *Guilty.*

"Confusion leads to knowledge for those brave enough to seek it."

"And if there are no answers to my questions? You've been doing this work for decades, and my problems are unfamiliar even to you."

"And is that where you want to draw your line? When you give up? At things that are unfamiliar?"

"No. Of course not. But—"

"All things were unfamiliar once upon a time. If we all gave up when there were no answers to be found, there would not be hunters like us. Sometimes you must make answers when there are none."

Her lip wobbled at the familiar saying. "How did you know I loved that book? Did you see it in my things?"

"What book?"

"*The Tale of Lord Finneus Wolfram.* Those were his last words to his uncle the king before he left on his doomed search for a new world. All my life I've dreamed of an adventure like that."

"Ah. It's a popular saying in our line of work. I did not know that was its origin."

"Perhaps it wasn't. But those words were my greatest hope when I was young. To find answers for the unanswerable, a path through the impossible."

"Then lean on them now. But let us avoid ending up like Lord Wolfram, yes? No tragedies here, Roar. This world will make you a victim every chance it gets. Don't let it."

She nodded, feeling those words sear straight to her gut.

"I'm sorry I put you all in danger," she whispered. "If you want me to leave, I would understand."

"And what would you go home to if you did?"

She hesitated, but then decided to give him more of her truth. "My mother. And a life that is stifling on the best days, suffocating on the worst."

He hummed low in his throat. "No one expects you to leave," he finally said. "I do not know what lies ahead for you. Sometimes the paths of our lives wander far from what we expect; they twist and turn and branch into dead ends. I have lost count of the number of dead ends I've encountered in my long life. Each time, when I could see no future beyond a certain point, the future always came anyway. Yours will too, Roar. All you can do is be ready to meet it when it comes."

Duke nodded his head and wandered back to the group. She considered following, wanted to, even. But then she saw Sly watching her with suspicion. Even Bait wasn't his usual silly self around her. She did not blame them. They *should* be wary of her.

She tried to do some resting of her own and retired to her tent for a nap, but she could not turn her mind off. The hunters gathered round the campfire got more raucous as the day passed, celebrating their victory and survival. She had the feeling this was a ritual, a cleansing of sorts. Each laugh hit her with the force of a punch, bearing down on an already impossible weight that sat upon her chest. Soon she was crawling out of her shoddy tent and seeking out Locke's. Maybe she would be able to sleep if she saw that he was well.

There was a faint blue glow behind the canvas of his tent, and when she opened the flap, she saw a lightning lantern in the corner, casting light on Locke's sleeping form. His chest was still bare except for the bandage, and his blankets were pushed down around his waist.

His tent was large enough that she could fit with just a slight hunch of her head and shoulders. She had to practically crawl in and out of her own tent by comparison. She crossed toward Locke on tiptoe and knelt beside his sleeping pallet.

His body was a master study in strength—all hard muscles and scarred skin. The waves of his long hair were spread out on his pillow. He had lashes that rested on cheeks that looked as if they had been cut from stone. She wanted to trace the slightly crooked line of his nose, rasp the pads of her fingers over the thickening stubble along his jaw.

She was still angry over the way he had treated her in the river, and she did not know where to put that anger when what she had done was far worse.

The bandage at his shoulder was clean, so at least the wound seemed to have stopped bleeding. She was glad she had been unconscious when he was injured. Her stomach rolled just imagining what he must have looked like with a branch piercing his skin. So like what had happened to her brother.

The bruising on his chest had darkened, and even in the areas where his skin was undamaged, she could see the faint white lines and marks of dozens upon dozens of scars. Hesitantly, she reached out and lightly traced her finger over a raised mark near his lower ribs. His skin was warm, and the muscles firm beneath it. Her pale skin contrasted against his darker coloring, and she had the sudden urge to splay both hands over his chest, touching as much as she could with the spread of her fingers, but she settled for skimming that scar once more.

"Bandits," he murmured, making her jerk backward. His eyes were still closed, and she wondered if she had imagined it, but then he kept speaking. "Not just storms and military that are a danger to us. We move a valuable commodity, and some people are not content to buy it in a market."

"You were stabbed?" She wanted to touch the scar again, but she shoved her hand beneath her thigh to keep it away.

"Between the ribs. It was a close call."

"That's terrible."

"Would have fit with the rest of my life. Survive hurricanes and fire-storms, only to be brought down by a small blade."

"I'm glad you weren't," she murmured, her eyes cast down toward her lap.

"Me too."

Those words settled into the quiet between them, and her heart kicked up speed as she searched for the right words to say.

"I'm sorry I woke you."

"I don't mind. I've been sleeping all day."

She swallowed. "I only wanted to be sure you were well. I feel . . . I feel so terrible about . . ." She trailed off, and let her hand hover over a set of scratch marks on his arm. At the last moment, she thought better of it and pulled back, but Locke caught her hand before she could go too far, pressing it down over the damage she had done to him and holding her palm against it.

"It's nothing, Roar. Doesn't hurt at all."

Her gaze traveled to the bandage on his shoulder.

"Don't you dare take that on you. Things like this happen."

"I distracted you. Delayed you. If you hadn't had to deal with me, maybe this never *would* have happened."

"If your goal is to not distract me, I regret to inform you that it's a lost cause."

She didn't know what that meant, couldn't tell if she was just reading into his words because of his deep, gravelly voice and his bare chest and the skyfire glow inside the tent that cast them both in shadows.

"I'm sorry," he said. "About the river. I did not mean to—well, I did, but my intention was not to hurt you."

"What was your intention?" she whispered.

"To teach you."

She froze and tried to tug her hand free, but his reflexes were too fast and he closed his grip around her hand before she could.

"To teach me what? That I'm soft? Easy to manipulate? Someone already beat you to that lesson. Though I guess I did not learn it as well as I should. But I have now."

"Roar. That wasn't . . . I—"

She ripped her hand from his grip and stood, her head glancing off the canvas before she remembered to hunch.

"I should let you rest."

She scrambled out of his tent and fled toward her own. She was almost there when Sly stepped out from the darkness to block her path. Roar jerked to a stop. "Sly, I didn't see you."

"Most people don't."

The female hunter had an eerie stillness to her . . . like a predator that could be on you before you even took a breath to scream.

"I think I'm going to sleep. Long day."

The girl let Roar pass, but before she made it to her tent, Sly called after her, "Just remember. When you don't see me, it's because I see you. I see the things that other people miss. The things that they don't want to see. And I'll be watching you."

Roar threw herself into the shaky refuge of her tent, pulled a blanket over her head to block out the world, and tried not to think of all she was missing back home.

Nova held herself entirely still, trying to will her body calm. When she moved, heat surged in every joint like her bones were flint and steel, sparking as they shifted against each other. She had lost track of time in her cell, but she knew days had passed since Roar left. And with each hour, the room seemed smaller, her mattress thinner.

A tray of food sat by the door, but it had long since grown cold. She did not trust herself to move toward it. Stillness was the only friend she had right now.

It was the not knowing that plagued her most. They'd thrown her in this cell, and she had seen no one since except the array of arms that reached inside occasionally to drop a tray of food. Her mind, duplicitous as ever, provided an unending stream of dire possibilities for why she was being kept in here and what was happening outside these four walls.

Even now, she wondered if this had nothing to do with Aurora. If perhaps they had somehow learned her secret, and this room, this *nothingness*, was what she had always feared.

She'd been living on borrowed time since her magic manifested as a child. A Stormling amir, the Taraanese equivalent of an admiral, had visited the house for dinner. Nova had been young, and she accidentally knocked over her drink, sending the liquid into the man's lap. He'd grabbed her wrist and snarled, and out of nowhere, the fancy tie about his neck had caught fire. The burns to the man's neck, face, and hands had been extensive. And her family had left in the middle of the night with only what they could carry, using all the money they had saved up to pay for an escort from a hunter, like the ones Rora was with now.

At the memory, the fire climbed so high up her throat that she could swear she tasted soot on her tongue. She tried to push it down, to lock it behind that door deep inside, but it would not budge. She broke her stillness to tear a strip of fabric from the bottom of her skirts. She cupped it in her hands, and then let free just a little of the power churning inside her. The flame caught quickly, easing some of the pressure in her chest. The scent of smoke calmed her somehow, reminding her that she was not helpless.

The fabric burned down to ash too fast, leaving behind an aching hunger to do it again, to burn and burn until all the heat was outside instead of inside.

A loud clank sounded at the door, and her head jerked to the small barred window above her head. It was not yet time for another meal to be delivered. She barely had time to dump the ash from her hands before the heavy wooden door swung open, revealing the Prince of Locke on the other side.

She remembered the way he had looked at her when he wanted information about the markets. His eyes had been hooded, suggestive, *alluring*. She had not been deceived in the slightest, but she preferred those eyes to the flat black coals she faced now. He made eye contact with someone out of sight and nodded, then he strode into the cell and locked the door once more behind him.

He leaned against the stone wall, crossing his arms over his chest. With a clenched jaw, he breathed in slowly through his nose, and her stomach dropped, fearing he would smell the smoke.

He reached into his pocket and pulled out something that gleamed in the dim room. He rotated it between his fingers, and Nova finally placed what she was seeing.

A skyfire Stormheart. The one Rora had gifted her.

"Anyone with storm magic can use any Stormheart that matches their affinities," he began. "We pass them down to our children and their children. But when you destroy a storm yourself, its heart is forever tied to you. It is a dangerous feat. There's no skill to it that can be learned. No magic spell. It is simply your will to live versus the storm's, and the strongest one wins. That kind of battle leaves a mark." He tossed the Stormheart into the air, light reflecting off the pearlescent surface, then caught it once more in his fist. "Imagine my surprise when I found one of my Stormhearts, a heart marked by my soul, by my sacrifice and given to my betrothed . . . in the room of a servant."

For the first time since she had been tossed in this cell, Nova went cold. Bumps rose along her skin, and the air felt charged with fury and magic. She reached for her fire, found it flickering low inside her, but could not call it out. The air was too thick, too smothered with the prince's power.

"Explain to me, *Novaya*"—he dragged out the syllables of her name as if they belonged to him—"how this came to be in your room."

She hesitated, heart thundering in her ears, fire sparking inside her, trying and failing to catch. "The princess gave it to me."

He flew across the room, and caught her by the throat. "*You lie.*" The touch of his hand spread a shock wave of residual storm magic over her skin. Her own magic leaped up to meet it, pushing at the barrier of her skin. She leaned back, splaying her hands on the mattress, and he loomed over her.

The fire made her brave, made her *stupid*, and she hissed back, "She loathed you."

He sneered, "Because of the knife wound? She's not so weak as to be bothered by that. I apologized, and she accepted."

Nova smiled, past caring about the consequences. Maybe he would kill her. Maybe she would burst into flame and kill them both. At least then, she would never waste another second worrying herself into misery. She choked out the words, "She knew. Knew you were . . . using her. Just . . . wanted throne."

All at once his constricting grip was gone, and he stood back glaring at her. His chest jerked with the rise and fall of his breath, and he spun back toward the door without a word. He rapped hard against the heavy wood until the guard outside answered. When the door clanged shut once more, locking out the world, Nova lifted her hands to find she had left behind a charred imprint of two hands on her mattress. She laughed, a high desperate sound, because she did not know what else to do.

She knew this was not over. He would be back. But she was just as capable of inflicting damage as he.

Perhaps death is all that waits for me across the great waters, but better to know death than to choose fear of the unknown.

—*The Tale of Lord Finneus Wolfram*

14

Locke's whole upper body was stiff when he woke, as if the branch had stayed inside him and grew around him while he slept. He pulled a shirt on, and his muscles burned when he lifted his injured arm to shove it through the sleeve. Sweat clung to his forehead, and he decided he was too tired to bother with buttons. He lugged himself to his feet, ungainly and awkward, two things he rarely was. He shoved out of his tent to face the gradually lightening sky, and was shocked to see Roar seated by last night's campfire, a bow and arrow at her feet and two rabbits roasting over a newly stoked flame.

His stomach twisted at the sight of her, and he wrote it off as hunger.

"What are you doing?"

She startled at the interruption, a heavy book sliding from her lap to land in the dirt.

"I was not sure if we were still to train this morning. When you did not come, I decided to be useful." She gestured toward the rabbits.

"You killed them?"

Her lips thinned. "No. They fell from the sky and landed above the flames on their own. Some strange new type of storm, I guess."

He snorted. "Calm your skies. I meant nothing by it."

She lifted her chin. "What might seem a careless phrase for one can cut deep as a blade for another."

"Now you sound like Duke."

He bent gingerly to pick up the book that had fallen. *The Tale of Lord Finneus Wolfram.* He'd known this tale as a boy, though only from stories whispered on cold nights among homeless children looking to think about anything else but their actual lives.

He returned the book and sat down on a log, leaving one between them. "Have I done that to you?" he asked, already knowing and dreading the answer. "*Cut* you with my careless words?" Somehow what began as the intent to protect and teach had become a way to scorch any connection between them, like burning back an encroaching forest before the roots could dig too deep.

Before she answered, a yawning Jinx plopped down on the log between them, stretching dramatically in an attempt to wake up.

"Don't tell me you two are arguing again," she said. "Even I'm exhausted by it, and I've just been watching. Often. It's hard to look away really. What am I saying? Don't stop. You are my only entertainment besides Ran's terrible jokes."

"I have the best jokes," Ransom said gruffly, stopping by the fire to examine the rabbits, and nodding approvingly.

Jinx clucked consolingly. "Ran, if you have to sing your own praises, you probably don't deserve them."

The morning continued with the rest of the crew ambling their way out of their tents, fatigued and groggy from the celebrations the night before.

Bit by bit, Locke was putting together the puzzle of Roar. She was so fiercely stubborn because somewhere along the way, someone had used her, had made her feel inferior, and now she protected the border of herself at all costs. What he did not understand was how a girl with all her skills and her drive could question her worth.

"Roar," he said after they had divided up the meat between them along with bread from their stores. "You have questions." She looked bewildered by the turn in conversation. "We've got plenty of time on our hands. Now is the time to ask them."

She picked at a piece of bread and said, "I'm not sure where to begin."

"Come now. I am sure there are a thousand things you want to know. Open your mouth and ask."

She bristled at the command, regaining some of that fire that blazed so brightly when they argued. "Fine. I want to know about you." Locke stiffened. "All of you. How did you come to be here? Where are you from? How did you all meet?"

He had expected her to ask about storms, but he was learning that she rarely behaved as he expected.

Bait answered first. "I grew up in a village in the forest north of Finlagh and west of Falmast." The novice's accent thickened as he talked about his home. "Our homes were built up in the trees to avoid runoff from the rains. The trees provided good cover from the storms, and being between the two Stormling cities meant that we rarely had to worry about storms from the south or east. Mostly it was the snows that came down from Durgra that gave us problems." Locke had never been as far as Durgra, the city built atop the icy tundra in the north. His southern skin was too thin for that kind of cold. "It was as good a place as any to try to survive while we petitioned for citizenship in Finlagh and Falmast."

"Neither had room?" Roar asked, and Bait shook his head. She continued: "How then do you all go into cities now to sell your wares?"

Duke answered, "Often we pay our way in. We know guards willing to look the other way for the right price. Other times we must sneak in."

She worried her bottom lip between her teeth, a habit Locke had noticed far too much. She turned back to Bait and asked, "How did you come to be a hunter?"

"Two Rage seasons past there was a thunderstorm that steered perfectly between the protection zones of Finlagh and Falmast, as if it knew the borders and snuck between them. Once it reached the forests, it seemed to stall right over us. It rained for days. Until the earth turned to muddy soup, and I forgot what it was to be dry. The mountain became a riverbed, water rushing down the land in never-ending streams. And then it was more than water coming down the slopes . . . it was mud and rocks and uprooted trees. The mountain itself came down on us."

Roar's hands were curled into fists atop her knees, food forgotten. "I heard about that. The mudslides took out the northernmost section of Finlagh."

With a light shrug that belied the heavy expression on his face, Bait replied, "That it did. After it took my home first." Locke had not even heard the entirety of this story; usually Bait stuck to the wild and outlandish tales of what came after the loss of his home. Roar, it seemed, had a way of pulling emotions out of more than just him. Bait continued: "I waited outside Finlagh for days, covered in muck and soaked through to my bones. I'd been separated from my parents when the mountain came down, and I just kept waiting for them to climb from the muck as I had. They never did. I met a group of pickpockets, and they snuck me into Finlagh, taught me the trade. One day, I was working with a partner. I'd distract, while he made the grab. Only I tried to distract the wrong girl."

Jinx snorted. "Yes, you did."

"Jinx caught my partner before he ever even got close, and he took off. I tried to do the same, but somehow tree roots had grown up from nowhere over my feet, trapping me in place."

Slowly Roar's sad expression transformed to one of delight and she finished for him, "That's why they call you Bait."

The novie grinned. "I still cover the distractions, but it's much more fun to steal magic than coins."

All of Roar's earlier reticence had disappeared, and this time she turned to Jinx. "And you?"

Before the witch could answer, Duke cut in, "Another time."

Duke gestured toward the sky to the southwest. Locke turned, and in the distance, he saw dark clouds building. If he were a more superstitious man, he might have thought Bait's story conjured the thunderstorm.

Duke said, "While we're here, we might as well do some hunting."

Locke stood to go pack up his tent, but Duke raised a hand. "Not you, Locke. You need to heal."

"It's a thunderstorm," he countered. "A little torrential rain won't hurt me."

Duke's bushy gray eyebrows drew down into a flat line. And the old man continued: "We'll take the horses. You and Roar stay with the Rock. If a storm strikes in our absence, you batten down the Rock and ride it out."

Both Roar and Locke began to argue at the same time, but stopped when Duke growled, "*Enough.*" Duke fixed his eyes on Locke and said, "Don't be reckless. She's learning not just from what you say but what you do. If you want her to make safe decisions, you must make them too."

Locke's mouth snapped shut, teeth clacking together. Scorch it all. He hated when Duke was right.

The stench of death blanketed the craggy mountainside. Blood flowed down the slope like a river from the mass of bodies that had fallen under his attack. The stench of burning flesh stung his nostrils as he studied the bodies that had been scorched by his skyfire.

He heard a rattling breath, a low moan, and charged down the rocky land and found one body set apart from the rest. A soldier was sprawled facedown, short and slim, probably little better than a boy knowing the Lockes' coldhearted ways, but he saw the sharp rise of the body as the soldier struggled to breathe. With his foot, he kicked the boy over onto his back. Blood speckled his mouth as he gasped for breath. There was a scorch mark at his shoulder, and he guessed the boy had not taken a direct hit. At least not there. A festering, charred wound marred the boy's belly, and bloodied hands clutched at the seeping sore.

"St-St—" the boy stuttered, unable to get out the name.

"Yes. You are correct, boy. It is the Stormlord you face now."

The soldier began to shake, his body seizing either from fear or the approaching hand of death. The Stormlord slid his foot forward until it rested against the boy's side. Then he pushed down, and the boy screamed.

"Tell me. Why have there been so many Locke soldiers roaming the wilds? Are the Lockes foolish enough to search for me?"

The soldier choked, useless sounds bubbling from his mouth. Pressing down again with his foot, the Stormlord said, "Tell me."

"N-not you. B-bride kid-n-napped."

A slow smile unfurled over the Stormlord's mouth. "The prince's Pavanian bride? Could it be?"

The soldier nodded, coughing up more blood in the process. The Stormlord cackled with glee, throwing himself down to sit beside the dying soldier. Leaning back on his hands, he crossed his legs at the ankles and rested his boots against the boy's bleeding stomach.

"This is more proof that the gods are on my side, boy. They were too impatient to even wait for me to bring punishment. They had to inflict some of their own. Cassius's perfect chance to seize a new throne— foiled before it even began. Of course, it's not enough." He smiled down at the boy as if talking to an old friend. He leaned in close, his heels digging into the boy's wound, and whispered conspiratorially, "The gods will not be satisfied until I've burned them from this earth and smeared their ashes upon my skin."

He flopped back, his head coming to rest on what he guessed was another body. He stared at the clear sky that only moments ago had been filled with skyfire on his command. "But still . . . it is interesting. He cares enough to send you all out here to die. Perhaps I should search for this girl myself."

He looked back to the boy, annoyed with his lack of reply, only to find glassy eyes and a gaping mouth. Dead. But at least he'd provided some service before he went. The Stormlord removed his boots from the boy's body and studied him. He would remember his face, remember this sign sent by the gods to affirm his calling.

Moving to his knees, he jerked the body up and began peeling away the scorched and bloody jacket of the soldier's uniform. When he tugged it free, the body fell away, twisted obscenely on the ground.

The Stormlord donned the coat, running his fingers over the familiar crest on his chest.

He smiled and murmured, "Time to send a message for the Lockes."

Locke helped the others pack up for the hunt, quizzing them on tactics and backup plans as he went. A hard knot formed in his stomach as they rode off, leaving him alone with Roar. They were his team, and leading them was *his* responsibility. It chaffed to be left behind. Locke shut himself inside the Rock, knowing that between the pain in his shoulder and his foul mood, he would make abysmal company for Roar. But that didn't stop her from climbing in a while later, seeking a cure for her boredom.

He'd been poring over the maps once more, looking for the impossible—a route that would keep Roar from too much danger until they knew more about her reaction to that twister, yet would allow them to stock up on magic and lead them to a place where they could sell it.

She wandered around the Rock as he worked, asking questions about the various instruments or staring over his shoulder at the different maps. Finally, he shoved a sheaf of parchment at her. They were maps from other areas of Caelira, not useful in the least for their current course, but at least they would stop her from looming over him, the scent of her hair and the sound of her breath filling up the space around him.

Eventually, he lost himself to the silence and almost forgot she was there. *Almost.*

She stood a while later, abandoning the maps to walk to the front of the Rock.

"Locke?"

Her unceasing questions were going to be the death of him. *"What now?"*

"There's something coming."

It took a beat too long for his mind to process her words, but then he was up, throwing aside the maps to take hold of her shoulders. He spun her, searching her face for some sign that her emotions were being taken over again. Those striking eyes were wide and surprised, and the breath fled her mouth in a hushed gasp. He'd pulled her in close, and now she swallowed, pink tongue darting out to wet her lips.

"What are you doing?" she asked, her words barely above a whisper.

His brows furrowed. "You said . . . I thought . . . You're not feeling strange? From another storm?"

He glanced behind her at the crystal they used to detect storm magic. Atop it sat a copper bowl filled with water and the thermascope that helped them assign numerical values to the changes in the crystal's heat. It currently measured a six. Not insignificant, but fairly normal for a period of nonactivity in this area, this close to Sorrow's Maw.

"No, not a storm," she said, shrugging off his grasp. "*People.*"

She pointed through the glass at the front of the Rock, and sure enough there were about a dozen people lumbering down Ruined Road on foot. They were moving slowly, carrying bags of belongings, and one look at their ragged appearances told him all he needed to know.

"Remnants," he said, full of pity.

"Remnants of what?"

He peered down at her. How could she know so much—languages and constellations and the best ways to survive a storm—and yet she did not know this?

"They're what Bait was before he found us, before he snuck his way into Finlagh. In the wilds, most towns don't last long. A few years, maybe a decade if they're exceptionally lucky. The towns patch themselves up as best they can after every storm, but sometimes, there's not enough left to patch up. People of the wilds are superstitious. They won't rebuild on the bones of a town the storms saw fit to wipe away. So instead, they pick up and leave, looking for somewhere new." He thought for a moment, his lips twisting. "You might have heard them called the Scourge." He hated that word, as if people in need of help were a plague to fear. He would have expected reasonable people to understand that in the wilds, they all stood an equal chance of their homes being destroyed. Storms were not selective. They did not search the inhabitants of the town before striking. They raged, uncontrolled and indiscriminate, and they destroyed anything in their path.

Roar shook her head. "I've not heard that name either."

He climbed out of the Rock and dropped to the ground, Roar on his heels. He pulled down the metal shade over the glass dome of the Rock, blocking the contraptions inside from curious eyes.

They walked out to meet the group as they approached. From what he could tell, it was mostly women, children, and a few older teens. An old woman spoke for them, her hair nearly white and her skin like parchment that had been folded too many times. Her knowledge of the common tongue was shaky, but eventually he understood that their town had been leveled two weeks past by a twister. Those who survived left together, but the dozen or so before him now were all that remained of those survivors after two weeks wandering the wildlands.

Locke led the woman to the row of plants that Jinx had grown near the camp. Bushes of berries and herbs and a few root vegetables. He told her to take whatever they'd like. Jinx could grow more in a moment. If the old woman thought the small garden on the side of a broken road was odd, she did not comment, too grateful for the additional food. As he spoke with the old woman, Roar wandered among the people, checking to see if anyone needed medical attention. For the next hour, the remnants stayed at the camp, some washing up in the river, others just resting their feet, and too many searching out Roar for her help bandaging cuts and scrapes, including several young men who did not look injured to Locke at all.

He was relieved when she retreated back into the Rock.

The matriarch began gathering her people, readying to set off once more, and Roar came darting out of the Rock, a piece of parchment in her hands. When she came to a stop next to Locke and the old woman, she thrust out the parchment. "Here," she said, offering what appeared to be a crudely drawn map of central Caelira. She had marked Pavan, Finlagh, Falmast, and Odilar to the south. She'd roughly sketched various rivers and forests and other identifiable features, and then she'd drawn large x's over a few regions and circled others. It took him a moment of looking to realize what she'd done. "In case you cannot find a town to take you in. The areas I've crossed out are known for frequent storms, but the places I've circled are less active. I cannot guarantee safety, of course, but maybe this will give you a better chance."

The woman's hands shook as she took the map, and she took Roar by the nape of her neck and kissed each of her cheeks. She whispered something Locke couldn't understand, and Roar answered in that same purr as when she'd spoken Taraanese. When Roar reached beneath the collar of her tunic, tugging off the crystal he'd given her, he stepped in.

"No," he snapped. "That is yours. You keep it."

She lifted her chin and narrowed her eyes. "If it's mine, then it's *mine* to give away."

Sighing in exasperation, he pulled her aside, crystal still swinging from her fist. "I know you want to help, but if we gave away our wares to every person who needed something, we'd never have them to sell."

"I'm not trying to give one to *every* person. Just to her."

"And then what will you do without a crystal? Contrary to what you seem to believe, Jinx does not have unlimited magic. It takes time and a great deal of energy to make those, and then she must rest between, all while still doing her other duties as a hunter."

"I'll pay for another for me."

He scoffed. "I'm not going to let you pay. You're one of us."

"Then I'll buy one for her," she said, jerking her chin toward the matriarch.

He opened his mouth to argue, but could find no more words. He would get her another crystal. Roar still saw good in this world, and he wished he could do the same. He pitied the remnants, but he knew the wilds too well to think they could walk this land on foot for long and survive.

But maybe Roar was right, maybe this would give them a fighting chance. He waved a hand for her to proceed, and then tried not to hear that worn and weary old woman weep between words of gratitude.

The matriarch hugged and kissed Roar upon the cheek several more times before the group continued on, dust rising around their feet as they searched for safety where there was none.

They stayed two more days camped in that spot, and Roar watched the others with envy as they went off to hunt. She spent her days training. Locke watched as she ran and swam, shouting orders and questions as she climbed up and down trees until her hands were scraped raw. He made her leap from branch to branch as if there were a flood below her and her only means of escape was to scurry like an animal through the canopy. She gritted her teeth through it all and imagined dunking him in the river again to give herself an added boost of determination.

She was relieved the next day when they finally packed up to move out. She knew the ride would be brutal on her tired body, but she was desperate to feel like they were getting somewhere, like *she* was getting somewhere.

Jinx and Locke found her as everyone was loading the last few supplies on the horses. Locke hung back, his arms crossed over his chest as Jinx stepped forward with some kind of vine-like plant in her hands. "I have something for you," the witch said. "A temporary precaution until we learn more about your reactions to storms. Hold out your arm."

Roar's eyes flicked to Locke, but his expression told her nothing. Tentatively, she did as Jinx asked. The vine was coiled into a small wreath, and Jinx slipped it on Roar's wrist. A tingle passed over her skin as the branches twisted, tightening to fit better. The leaves rustled and then lay flat against her skin.

"This plant is called Rezna's rest. It's a natural sedative that I have preserved with magic so that it does not die even though it has been cut. The next time you are in the presence of a storm, try to pinpoint how it's getting past your defenses. Do your best to shut it out. But if you are unable, if you're in pain or become a danger to yourself or others, tear a few leaves from this bracelet and chew them up. One leaf should relax you. Chew three or four and you'll fall unconscious within moments. The bracelet will replenish itself, so don't worry about running out."

Roar eyed the plant warily. "I guess this is preferable to being knocked out anytime a storm appears."

Locke finally spoke behind Jinx, growling, "That's not happening again. Not even if you ask. So don't."

Roar ran her fingers over the leaves, her mouth dry. Maybe the twister was a bizarre fluke. But she knew deep in her gut that it wasn't. She had always known she was different, she just hadn't understood how much.

She tried not to look at Locke as they set out again, but she was often unsuccessful. He wore a linen shirt with more than half the buttons undone so that he could easily check his bandages. He had forgone his full leather vest to wear only a supply belt around his hips, no doubt to ease the strain on his shoulder. On his orders, they spent most of the first day at a gallop until they passed out of range of Sorrow's Maw. And Locke galloping on horseback with his half-open shirt billowing in the breeze was a sight that tested her resolve not to look again and again.

He still pushed her relentlessly in training, and he began running with her again on their second morning back on the road. They still argued, often over trivial things, but she could tell he was at least trying to be more careful with his words.

Roar was beginning to find a pattern in this new life. Each day, more of the world was revealed to her—plants she had never seen, animals she had read about only in books. The crew had all laughed at her when she thought she saw a dust storm to the south, only to learn it was a distant mountain range, the first she had ever seen with her own eyes. Her life in Pavan had always felt stifling and constricting, but she had come to realize that the world was so much bigger even than her imaginings.

But each time she began to feel comfortable or confident, the wildlands seemed to rise to crush her hopes. She had to use the leaves three times over five days, and each incident stole a little more of her determination to see this through. Not only was she not any nearer to having magic, she had not even had the chance to see the other hunters work since she always ended up unconscious a few moments after a storm manifested.

A little over a week after the twister, Roar noticed something peculiar as they stopped for the night. Taraanar was due east of Pavan. Based on the constellations she saw as the sun set and the stars came out, they had begun turning south, having left the road behind several days prior.

She abandoned the tent with which she'd been wrestling. How after all these days did that thing still vex her beyond the limit of her patience? Glad to focus on something else, she marched her way up to Duke and Locke, hands on her hips, and declared, "We're moving south."

The old man did not look up from the spoonful of stew he lifted to his mouth. She caught a glimpse of what appeared to be an old tattoo on his forearm. It was faded and made even more illegible by his extensive scars, but was shaped vaguely like an anchor. Perhaps Duke had been a sailor in his early life; maybe the seas had called to him before the skies.

"We are," he answered, lowering the bowl to his lap.

"I thought we were heading to Taraanar."

Locke cut in. "Not for two days, we haven't been."

Bristling, she fixed her eyes on Locke, rather than the old man. He was a much easier target for her anger. "Why did no one tell me?"

Locke said, "I wasn't aware you cared about the destination so much as the journey."

She wouldn't have normally. Roar didn't particularly care where they went as long as there were storms involved. But there was a chance Pavan soldiers would still be searching for her and her abductors in the south.

"Are you trying to avoid storms because of me? I *told* you not to do that."

"Yes, but the last time we encountered a storm, you looked like you wanted to rip my jugular out with your teeth. And I'm rather partial to it."

She sucked her bottom lip into her mouth, as if that could pull back in the words, undo this entire conversation. She made herself meet his eyes. "Whatever is happening to me, I will find a way to control it. I'm lasting longer every time before I have to take Rezna's rest. You don't need to coddle me."

"I'm not exactly up to full speed yet either," he said, but his shoulder had not stopped him from participating in any of the recent storms. "You must learn to trust my judgment, Roar. There is nothing wrong with being strategic."

"That would imply you were actually teaching me how to take magic, how to defeat a storm, teaching me *anything* besides how much torture my body can endure before my legs commit mutiny."

His eyes dipped down, raking her from head to toe. "Your legs look fine to me." She drew in a sharp breath and fisted her hands against the urge to hit him. Insufferable man.

"As for our training," Locke continued, "setting aside the fact that you are not ready to face a storm until you can keep control of your mind, I am teaching you the only things I can." She knew it was stupid to pick this fight, knew that she could not possibly win this argument and it only hurt to have it, but she was so frustrated; she needed some way to release all this built-up tension. Locke continued: "I'm teaching your body to fight past pain, past fatigue. I'm teaching your mind how to make choices under pressure and react to any circumstance." He moved in close and pushed a blunt finger against her chest above where her heart was beating rapidly. "And here . . . right here, I'm teaching you to trust yourself, to believe in your own strength. Skimming magic is the easy part. As long as you are near the heart of the storm, Jinx's enchantments will do the work for you. But you have to live long enough to get close and get away." His finger was still jabbed into her chest, his expression fierce. "The one thing I cannot teach you is how to defeat a storm. That you have to learn yourself."

"Learn how?" she asked.

He tapped his finger above her heart twice more, and then pulled away. "You simply must have the stronger heart. You must have no doubts, no fear. You must want to survive more than the storm does. When you drive your hand into the heart of a storm, it in turn drives into you. It will search out every weakness, every insecurity. If you are afraid to die, it will know. I've seen hunters with tremendous skill—fast and strong and calm under pressure—crumble under the intensity of facing a storm heart to heart. The battle is different for every person, for every storm, but one thing always holds true—only one heart gets to live on. So tell me, Roar, do you think you are ready? Look into yourself and decide—are you willing to bet your life on it?"

Blood rushed in Roar's ears, and her stomach writhed with nausea. *Of course*, she was not ready. She might have believed in herself when this journey began, but no more. It was torture not being able to trust her own mind, to trust that she would not hurt those around her.

The rest of the hunters had gathered throughout Locke's speech, and mortification burned across her cheeks. With a hard, smug look Sly added, "It's about honesty. A storm cuts through to the truth of who you are. If it finds darkness and deceit in you, it will win. It is only the purest hearts that come out unscathed."

There was no question that Sly's tone implied Roar would be found wanting. Jinx snorted, breaking the tension, and said, "Oh yes. I'm sure we've got the purest hearts around." Ransom's deep chuckle followed, and Jinx said to Roar, "Don't let them frighten you too much. It is dangerous, to be sure, but in the end magic is simply an extension of a person's will. If you want it badly enough, you can make it yours."

She nodded, and one by one the other hunters scattered. Some sat to eat; others returned to their tents. Before he left, Ransom stepped up behind her and folded one of his huge hands over her shoulder. "I was impatient too. So much so that I refused to cook until they gave me my shot. But not even holding my cooking ransom worked." He winked, blue eyes sparkling. "They made do with gruel and refused to let me risk myself before I was ready. And they were right in the end. Trust is a muscle, same as any other. It gets stronger the more you use it. Trust Locke. Trust us. And trusting yourself will come far easier, I promise you."

She put aside thoughts of storms for the moment. Loath as she was to admit it, Locke was right. There was no point in him teaching her anything more until she proved she could stand in the presence of a storm without losing herself. The more immediate problem was their route, but she could not exactly tell them why she did not want to head south, not without revealing her secret.

If they encountered Pavanian soldiers, would her disguise hold? Was she selfish enough to risk her companions' lives? For if she were found in their company, the soldiers would assume them her kidnappers. She had known her plan was reckless, but she had thought only of the potential danger to herself, not to them.

More and more, it seemed as if she had more reasons to leave than stay with the hunters.

"Don't look so glum, child. Feeling sorry for yourself won't help."

She looked at Duke through the flickering tendrils of fire. He looked older in the low light, the lines on his face accented by shadow. "I am more angry at myself than sorry. I know I am impatient. And reckless and tempestuous and stubborn. I want to be different, I do. But all my life, I've felt like something was left out when I was made, like a recipe with a missing ingredient. And it didn't matter how hard I tried to be better because something in me was inherently . . . wrong. As if I'd been put into the wrong life by mistake."

"Sounds to me like the only wrong thing was trying to force yourself to be something you are not. Locke is stubborn, Jinx is beyond tempestuous, and I—" He looked down at the multitude of scars that crisscrossed his arms and hands. "I have been known to be reckless a time or two. People are not recipes to be carefully measured and mixed together. Life is imprecise and messy."

"But do I have what it takes to be a hunter?"

Duke tangled his fingers in his beard, his green eyes soft with knowing. "No one can decide that but you. Think about that book you love so much. Many called that expedition insane, impossible. But you can never know if something is, in fact, impossible until you have tried. And perhaps, not even then. Not until you've tried for an entire lifetime."

"You were a sailor too, weren't you?"

He looked at her, gray eyebrows raised high. She gestured to the tattoo, or what was still visible beneath his scars. He nodded. "Once upon a time. But I've not set foot on a boat in what feels like several lifetimes."

"Navy? Or a trade ship? Or . . ." she trailed off, not wanting to accuse the man of piracy.

"I've done a bit of it all. Sometimes it feels like I've lived enough lives for ten men."

He stared into the darkening night. His eyes went unfocused, and for a long while she sat there as Duke seemed wrapped up in something she could not see. Eventually, his eyes closed and he shook himself slightly before returning his gaze to her.

There was something invariably sad about the old man, and she wanted to fling her arms around him and hug him close. The only men she had ever had in her life were no-nonsense guards and stuffy officials. He was comforting but stern. It was how she imagined her father might have been, if he had lived. Though perhaps without the long beard and braided hair.

"Do you know how many apprentices I've taken on to teach about hunting?" he asked.

She shook her head, and he continued: "Somewhere around twenty-five."

"Twenty-five!"

"Some couldn't cut it or decided the life wasn't for them. Some took to it well and were smart and talented. But even when you're good at what you do, nature can catch you off guard. Ransom has had half a dozen. Sly was one of his originally. You already know Bait was brought on by Jinx. Even if they're not ready to teach anyone themselves, they have brought people to me for help. Locke has been with me longer than any of them, and do you know how many times he's brought in someone?"

She had a feeling where this was going. "No one?"

Duke nodded. "Not once. Don't get me wrong: he gets it in his head that he needs to help people all the time, but he's never once showed any interest in teaching anyone how to hunt."

She snorted. "He didn't want to teach me either."

"Trust me, Roar. If he didn't want to teach you, he would have pushed you on to Ransom or Jinx. Or more likely, found some way to leave you home in Pavan. I know how hard he's pushing you in your training, and from what I've heard you've met every challenge he's thrown at you. If you cannot hold on to confidence in yourself, be confident in him."

She weighed his words. Could she do that? Trust Locke that much?

"And what you said earlier," Duke continued, "about feeling like you were in the wrong life? I've felt that too. Felt it right up until the moment I decided to stop trying to run from storms and hunt them instead. I know what it looks like when someone finds the life they were meant to have."

He clasped a firm hand on her shoulder and then left her alone with the campfire and her thoughts. She lost track of how long she sat there, but the night was deep when she finally left for bed. Weary, she trudged back to where she'd planned to make camp for the night, only to find that her tent had been mysteriously erected and all her belongings placed inside. She glanced around, wondering whom she had to thank for the kindness, but the camp was dark and quiet, and the call of her bed was stronger than her curiosity.

Embers do not fall
And fire does not burn
In the eye.

Rain does not pour,
Wind does not howl
In the eye.

Fear does not reign.
Death holds no pain.
In the eye.

—A Stormling Stands: Verses of Old

15

Cassius paced the length of Aurora's sitting room, waiting for the guard who was supposed to bring him an update. He spent entirely too much time in Aurora's rooms. He knew that. It was bad enough he had taken up residence in the empty rooms across from hers in the royal wing, but he could never seem to stop himself from wandering in here.

Nor had he been able to stop himself from searching through all her things. He had thumbed through every book on her shelves and read the ones that looked the most worn with use. They were books about daring adventures and dangerous storms. They weren't particularly realistic, but he could admit they were entertaining. Others were filled to the brim with mushy romance that always made him want to throw the book across the room. He knew she was sweet, but if that was what she wanted . . . perhaps it was better that she had been taken before they wed.

He cursed himself for that thought, turning to pace the length of the room again. It seemed that she had been extremely sheltered by her mother, mostly because not a single person seemed to be able to tell him anything personal about Rora. He knew because he'd tried. He had questioned everyone who ever claimed to have come in contact with her. The queen had replaced her handmaidens constantly, so none of them knew anything except what herbs she liked to put in her bath and which hairstyles she hated the most, which was all of them to some degree.

The stable hands seemed to have a better sense of her, but they couldn't tell him much that he did not already know. The soldiers he had combing the wilds were supposed to be on the lookout for the horse as well, in case the kidnappers had sold it off. That would at least give him some hint as to where she had been taken. But so far they had not one clue about her whereabouts beyond the blood and clothing scraps they found that first day of searching. She had tried to leave clues, but they stopped so abruptly that he could not keep himself from imagining what had been done to her to end that rebellion. And because he was all too familiar with how the criminal element thought and behaved, his imagination was disturbingly hard to ignore.

It had been weeks. He hated thinking about how much could happen in that amount of time. He had sent out as many soldiers as he could afford, issued a reward, and even expanded their search beyond the southern region they believed her to be taken to originally. The wilds were easy enough to search. There were no authorities that could stand up to a full company of soldiers, but searching Stormling cities proved much more challenging. None was eager to let unfamiliar soldiers into their midst.

And then there were the rumors. They could not hold them off forever, of course. But he was supposed to be married by now, rendering them unimportant. Everything had gone so incredibly wrong.

While his intentions had never been entirely aboveboard, he had a plan to keep things in check, to minimize the damage as much as possible. But now . . . without Aurora here everything had turned to chaos. And he knew even if they managed to find her and bring her back, she would hate him. That thought troubled him more than it should. He could not stop hearing the Taraanese girl's words.

She loathed you.

A knock came at the door, and he barked, "Enter."

The commander of the guard came through the doorway, followed by a few soldiers that Cassius recognized as runners. They'd been tasked with gathering updates from the searching troops and bringing that information back to Pavan.

"What news, Ortuze?" he asked, his tone clipped and to the point.

The commander said, "No sightings of her, sir. And Odilar sent out troops to stop the soldiers you sent to search the city. The king has refused them entry and threatened combat if they don't leave."

Cassius cursed and fisted his hands at his sides. "And in the wilds?"

"I'm afraid the losses are quite high. Two companies were wiped out completely, two are missing, and another three suffered devastating losses. And there have been confirmed reported sightings of *him*, sir. The second company sent word four days ago about rumors among the villages of his presence. The entire company was lost to storms the next day."

"If they were lost, how do you know his presence is confirmed?"

"Another company found the bodies, sir. It took several days for their messenger to reach us. The bodies were laid out to form a message, Your Highness."

Cassius hesitated. "Well? What was the message?"

"*Soon*, sir."

Cassius pulled at his hair, pacing and biting down the need to scream.

"How many companies are still out searching?"

"Three companies remain, but with the Rage season in full swing, their odds are not good. Their numbers have already dwindled. May I suggest, sir, that we bring our men home, and prepare for his arrival? Even you cannot face him alone."

Cassius's fury boiled past his control. He picked up something from the table beside him, some trinket of sorts, and sent it sailing toward the wall. It smashed with an utterly unsatisfying crash, glass scattering over the floor.

"Those soldiers do not come home until they find her, do you hear me?" Cassius growled. "I don't care what you have to do. Raise the reward. Force conscription into the military to boost our ranks. Whatever it takes, you do it. None of this will end well unless she's found."

It might not end well regardless. But he had to bring Aurora back to Pavan. He would search her out himself if he had to, and kill anyone who obstructed his path.

"What shall I tell the king, Your Highness?"

Cassius scowled. "Nothing. I will deal with him. Go," he growled. "And bring me the girl again. The witness."

Cassius had been back several times since that first encounter, but Novaya had stuck to her story, repeating it by rote. She knew more than she was letting on, he was certain. This time, he had left her in for nearly a week and ordered the guards to cut back her meals to one a day. He would have his answers one way or another.

He was well past patience now.

Locke fought a smile as Roar's head dipped and jerked as she tried desperately not to fall asleep while in the saddle. He had thought he'd pushed her as far as she could handle before, but she had somehow dug even deeper, dredged up even more strength. He'd been left scrambling to find new ways to challenge her.

He had given up trying not to watch her. It seemed the more will-power she showed, the less he did. And when he wasn't consumed with thoughts of her, he was battered by an anxiety that had never plagued him before. For a long time, he had lived for the hunt, for the moments of uncertainty when death came close enough to brush up against him. Now he spent most days rigid in his saddle, dreading their next encounter with a storm.

After three more days of traveling south, they were between Sangsorra desert to the east and craggy mountains and cliffs of the Sahrain range to the south. The earth had grown dusty and dry, dotted with scrubby trees and patches of long brown grass. He was on edge. They had not seen a storm in several days, which had been the goal of their new route. But he did not like when the wilds were quiet. At times it felt almost as if they were being stalked, the prey of a predator lurking just out of sight.

"What's your plan?" Ransom asked from atop his mount. "Make her so exhausted that she can't ride her own horse and will be forced to share one with you?"

Locke whipped his head around to face his friend. "What are you on about?"

"It's not a bad plan. If you have to spend days on horseback, doing it with a pretty girl pressed against you is definitely the way to go."

"You're mad. I'm trying to make sure she stays alive."

"Right. Then why don't you train her to pitch her own tent instead of doing it for her like you have the last few nights? Tell me, friend, just how many times have you pitched a tent for the wild one?" Locke plucked an apple from his saddlebag and flung it at Ransom. The bald man caught it and bit into the fruit with a cheeky wink. He added, his mouth full of fruit, "Your shoulder is never going to finish healing if you keep trying to woo her via tent."

"Enough of your theories. There's nothing—" Before he could finish his denial, a terrible wail filled the air, followed by an ominous crack. He swung his head back toward the Rock, where the sound had originated, but before he could discover the cause, a scream rent the air.

Roar's scream.

He forgot about the first sound in favor of the second, and turned to see her horse reared on its hind legs. The noise must have scared it, and now the mare was bucking hard. Roar slid backward, out of the dip of the saddle, but she held tight to the pommel.

The horse's hooves crashed back to the ground, and Roar was flung forward. She winced in pain, but managed to secure her place once more. Then a strong wind gusted behind him, followed by vicious pops and crackling and the acrid scent of smoke.

Once more, Roar's horse reared in fright, and when Locke finally looked back toward the Rock he knew why. There was fire everywhere—the patchy brown-green grass went up like tinder, the scrubby trees that lined the road exhaled flame up into the sky, *the sky* . . . well that appeared to be burning too. Overhead, too low to be a naturally occurring firestorm, the sky rotated with heavy winds and spit burning embers onto the earth below.

Another scream sounded, and he whipped his head back just in time to see Roar fly from the back of her horse. She landed in a roll, coming up on her feet only a few steps away from the rapidly expanding blaze.

He cursed and flung himself down from his horse. A hard slap on its rear sent his stallion running safely away from the flames. He wanted to run toward Roar, but while other members of the team had some experience with torque storms, they were his specialty. Low against his spine, he felt the warmth of the firestorm Stormheart hidden inside the leather of his belt, and he plucked it out to hold in his palm. He drew power from within himself and from the stone, and flung a hand toward the swirling clouds. The air was stiflingly hot around him, and every breath raked down his throat and stung his lungs. The harsh smell singed his nostrils, and sweat slicked over his skin.

He stood outside the range of the falling embers, but he saw them battering at the top of the Rock, leaving black spots before rolling down the frame and landing amid the burning grass with the others. Jinx and Sly stood in the eye where no embers fell. He focused, the magic flying out from his fingers to collide with the storm. It surrounded it, searching out the edges, feeling the mass. There was no heart to this storm that he could sense, which meant it was magicborn.

There was another scream to his right, and the urge to look for Roar burned in his gut as hot as the flames that lay ahead of him. From his hip, he snatched one of the jars that held thunderstorm, pulled the cork, and threw it in the direction he'd seen Roar before. His shoulder protested, but there was no time to feel pain. The jar shattered, followed by a gust of wind and the crack of thunder. He hoped the rain would drown the burning land while he focused on the firestorm.

Once his magic had flowed all the way around it, and he knew its size, he concentrated on the right side of the storm. He raised both hands and, with a growl, used all his strength to yank the right side of the storm down and toward him. This broke up the rotation, and as he'd hoped, the storm crumbled against the resistance he provided. Without a living heart at the center, the storm was no match for his magic. The clouds folded and thinned, and the embers stopped falling, and it only took a few moments more before the dark clouds of the thunderstorm overtook the space where the firestorm had been.

"Jinx!" he yelled into the pouring rain.

He didn't know exactly where she was, but he heard her yell back, "Got it!"

Jinx was their torrent specialist. She would stoke the thunderstorm until the rain had put out the last of the flames, then do away with it as he had done with the firestorm.

Finally, he gave in to the overwhelming urge to search out Roar, and his stomach dropped when he saw her. She was soaked, and stood still and silent, staring up at the sky as if mesmerized.

The drab traveling cloak she wore had been ripped down the middle, and its torn neck now sat around the curve of her hips. The bottom of it was charred and still smoking lightly, and the white shirt she wore beneath it stuck to her skin in places and had been singed to ash in others.

He trudged through the mud and ash to reach her, but even when he stood directly in front of her, she only had eyes for the storm overhead. And it was then that he realized . . . she wasn't screaming. Or attacking anyone. Or unconscious. Whatever had happened when that twister had struck wasn't a problem now.

Large hands grasped Roar's shoulders, and it was only then she realized how badly she was shaking. Locke peered down at her, his hands squeezing, as if he could make her body still through force alone. Over his shoulder, Roar watched Jinx lift her hands. The witch glanced around one more time, and when she found no lingering flames, she curled her fingers and pulled as though she had a lasso around the middle of the storm. And, sure enough, the center of the storm jerked downward, breaking the mass of dark clouds apart. The outer edges of the storm dissolved like steam, and, after another motion of Jinx's hands, the core of the storm followed, giving way to a sky that was gray, rather than the blue it had been before. But it was calm. Quiet.

Roar watched, frozen and fascinated, long after it was over. It was the first time she'd gotten to see magic at work. She only snapped to when she felt Locke's hands dragging unabashedly over her body, over her arms first, then smoothing over her waist and hips, tugging at the cloak that tangled there.

"Excuse me." She shoved him backward, heat rising into her cheeks. "Perhaps ask before you put your hands all over a person."

He snapped right back, "I thought you were in shock. Your cloak is scorched, and you wouldn't answer when I asked if you'd been burned."

"I'm fine."

Then, to make sure she wasn't lying, she took a moment to look over her body. She finished pushing the cloak down over her hips and stepped out of it. It had caught fire when an ember bounced off the Rock and hit the bottom of her cloak, and she felt a pang at the loss of something that belonged to her brother, even if it was plain and ill fitting. She had been struggling to get it off when the skies broke open and it began to rain. The trousers she wore were soaked and burned through at the knee and below. Between what remained of the fabric and her calf-high boots, the skin on her legs was red and raw and stung in the open air.

"Fine, huh?" He grabbed the leather around her neck and pulled up the magical items he'd given her. The crystal had gone hot, but not painfully so as it had with the twister. And the firestorm powder he'd given her remained in the tiny bottle. "You did not take it?" he hissed. "I told you that we take no chances with firestorms."

Locke's voice was a fierce, angry growl, and she bowed up, ready to growl right back. She was getting tired of his moods—suffocatingly protective one second and a beast the next. Before she could lay into him, they were interrupted by Ran asking, "Who did these?"

He pointed to a small pile of jars that held still-burning embers. Locke paused long enough in his anger to glance over, and then his brows puckered in confusion.

"Sly?" he called out.

From the other side of the Rock, they heard, "Not mine."

Locke marched away, heading for the pile.

Roar sucked in a breath and said, "I did it."

He froze, twisting to look back at her. "You *what*?"

Her stomach rolled. Had she done it wrong? "I captured the embers. A bag of jars fell off one of the horses' packs, and I thought I might as well do something useful. I caught the embers as they rolled off the Rock, before they hit the grass."

He stalked back toward her. "And you did it without taking the powder. Scorch it all, Roar. You could have been hurt. All it would have taken was one ember to bounce off the Rock when you weren't expecting it and hit your skin directly. Have you seen the kind of burns they can cause?"

"Yes, I've seen them. And I'm well aware of the danger I was in. It was the same danger as every other person here, and I saw no one take any powder. So why don't you yell at someone else!"

The others wandered away out of sight to the other side of the Rock, where most of the damage was, likely saving her the embarrassment of being witnesses once again to Locke lecturing her. With a growl, she spun before he could say anything more and began marching away. He did not get to make her feel bad about this. She had seen a storm and stayed herself. She had done something useful after so long feeling useless. She thought at first that he was going to let her be, but eventually she heard him jogging up behind her.

"Roar, wait."

"No," she snapped, picking up her pace.

"Would you listen—"

"Can you just leave me alone?"

His hand seized her elbow, and he spun her around forcefully. He growled, "No. I can't."

And then his mouth collided with hers.

For a moment, Roar did not understand what was happening. She knew his lips were on hers, pushing hard enough to be punishment, and his fingers threaded through her hair, and an arm wrapped tight around her waist. But even knowing those things, she could not quite comprehend that Locke was *kissing* her.

She froze, unsure whether she wanted to allow it or shove him away. She had been so *angry*, but now that blazing heat had melted into something different, like molten glass being shaped into something new. He tilted her head back, his hand gripping tighter in her hair, and when he opened his mouth against hers, she followed. He kissed his own fury into her, melting and reshaping her again and again with each stroke of his tongue over hers.

When he broke the kiss, his mouth stayed close, his breath like fire on her tender lips. She opened her eyes and found him staring, brows furrowed halfway between confusion and anger. Slowly, the world came back into focus—the lingering scent of smoke, the wet cling of her clothes, the sound of voices not too far away.

She planted her hands on his chest and shoved, but he caught her wrists.

"You still did not *ask*," she hissed.

The indent in his brow deepened. "Ask what?"

She struggled against his hold, panic welling in her throat. "You can't just grab me and . . . and do *that*. You cannot *manipulate* me into letting go of my anger."

This time when she pulled, her wrists came free, and she stumbled backward. He held out a hand as if to catch her, but hesitated, letting her find her own footing.

"I should not have yelled at you. I was worried, and I overreacted. You—you did well. With the embers."

She wanted to yell some more, to push and shove and *protect* herself because fighting was not nearly as frightening as . . . as whatever this was. She was supposed to be learning how to trust herself, how to be confident in her strength. She could not risk that, not even for a kiss so intense that she was still shaking.

The raised voices of the other hunters intruded again, and she glanced behind him. Thankfully, the others were still out of sight on the other side of the Rock. Her face was flushed, and she did not know what she would have done if they had seen. Locke's voice was rough and low when he spoke again. "I need to find out what happened. Then we'll take care of your burns."

He didn't wait before turning and heading toward the Rock, the back of which was scorched and mangled, and not dissimilar from how she felt inside.

"Is everyone unhurt?" Locke called as he joined the rest of the group. Each member of the team checked in one by one, none seriously injured. Last to call out was Bait. The redhead stood next to the damaged carriage, his face streaked with soot and rain, his shoulders bowed as Locke stalked toward him.

"Bait," Locke growled, and Roar flinched, glad it was not her on the receiving end of his frustrations. "What in the bleeding skies happened?"

"I, uh, got distracted. And missed the time when I was supposed to add more magic to the chamber. I had to get something in fast or we were going to lose control, but I couldn't find another jar of hurricane. So I put in—"

"Firestorm. Damn it, Bait. The metal can't withstand that fast a temperature change. We're lucky the whole thing didn't rip apart."

It sure looked to Roar like the whole thing *had* ripped apart. The back end of the coach appeared to have burst at the seams. Blackened metal peeled backward in multiple directions, gaping open to reveal the inside of the contraption that used magic to power the entire machine.

"Can you repair it?" Duke asked, ripping away one sleeve of his shirt to reveal scalded skin on his forearm, more scars to join the rest.

"Maybe. With Ransom's help. But we'll need to find a village with a blacksmith. We'll have to change our travel plans again."

All eyes turned toward Roar then, some wary, some curious, some just weary from the day. She held still, worried that if she moved wrong, they would all be able to tell that Locke had just kissed the life out of her only moments ago.

"Did you feel anything?" Duke asked.

Heat bloomed over her skin, and her mouth went dry. Her wide eyes flicked to Locke and he said, "When the storm surfaced?" He frowned. "Any anger? Or *other* emotions that didn't feel like your own?"

She tried to think back to the firestorm, to before her world had been flipped upside down. She could not remember feeling much of anything after she'd been thrown from her horse, she had simply reacted on instinct. Finally, she shook her head.

"What does that mean?"

Duke and Locke exchanged a glance.

"It rules out sensitivity," Duke said. "If that were it, you would react to any kind of storm magic, even that which comes from a jar rather than nature."

"That's what I thought too," Locke said. "It could be only natural storms that she reacts to. I've never heard of that kind of thing, but that doesn't mean it doesn't exist. People are so bleeding scared to talk about magic that there's probably a lot we haven't heard of."

Duke sighed. "Well, at least we'll have plenty of time to find out while you and Ransom work on the Rock."

Duke spent some time looking everyone over, assessing burns and other injuries. Poor Ransom had lost half his impressive beard to an ember before he'd managed to douse it. Roar could tell Bait wanted to laugh but still felt too guilty to do anything more than try to be helpful. To even it up, Ran had to clip his beard until only thick stubble remained.

Locke put Bait in charge of readying the Rock by hooking up two of the horses so that it drove like a traditional carriage. Honey ended up being one of those horses because the others had burns. Roar watched as Bait harnessed Honey, and she ran a hand down the horse's muzzle to reassure her.

Each horse in the royal stables had been trained for every circumstance imaginable, so this was by no means outside the mare's ability. It was herself that Roar feared for. Her one constant right now was that she spent her days on the back of that horse, who was at once a comfort and a reminder of the freedom Roar had craved for so long. And she needed that reminder now more than ever.

"She'll be fine," Locke said, misreading her apprehension. He held up a bag of supplies and said, "Let me take a look at your legs."

She stiffened, wanting to ask for Duke to help instead, but her pride refused to let Locke know she was nervous. She followed him, and they sat on a lightly charred fallen tree trunk. He gestured silently for her to lift a leg onto the log between them. He began unlacing her boot, and she blushed.

"I can do that," she insisted, but he swatted her hand away as soon as it came near. She looked away as he worked, pinning her eyes on a still-smoking tree across the road while he eased off her boot. She hissed out a breath as the top of the boot peeled away from her burned skin, and he made low, soothing noises, running his hands over her legs, from her calf down to her stocking-covered heel. She tried not to notice the strength of his hands, the rough pads of his fingertips. He braced her foot in the space where his thigh met his hip and said, "This is going to hurt. Push against me if you need to."

He offered her a hand to squeeze, but she declined, leaning back and bracing her hands on the log below her. He opened a waterskin and dribbled the cool liquid down over her reddened skin. For a moment, it felt nice. But then that sensation seemed to break through her shock, bringing all the pain she'd blocked to the forefront of her mind. She gasped, and when she reached out a flailing hand, Locke took it, allowing her to squeeze his fingers until they popped.

"You have some blisters," he said, pouring more water over her damaged skin. "We'll have to bandage it well and often." He poured water over a cloth until it was soaked and then gently laid it over her shin, wrapping the cloth so that it covered the burns on the sides of her calf as well. He left it there, turning a little and lifting her other foot to prop up on his knee. Then they went through the whole ordeal again, only now she could concentrate on nothing but the pain. She squeezed her eyes shut and bit down on her bottom lip, trying to stay in control.

"You're doing well, Roar. Just a little longer."

She let out a shaky breath, and a whimper sneaked out with it.

"Tell me about Honey," he said as he wrapped a wet cloth around her leg.

Glad for something else to focus on she said, "She's my best friend."

He smiled. "Your *best* friend? Must be some horse."

Roar was too frazzled and aching to be anything but honest. "For a long time, she was my only friend."

"I doubt that. You're far too . . ."

"Far too what?" she ground out.

"Interesting," he answered. "And smart. And vivacious. I can't picture a world where people are not falling all over themselves to be your friend."

Her stomach swooped at his words, stealing the heat from her wounds for the flush rising up her neck. She did not understand him, did not know what he wanted from her. First, she had reminded him of his sister, then he could not look at her without bursting into spontaneous arguments, and now . . . now he seemed so *soft*—his words, his touch, those eyes.

She snapped her gaze back to the smoldering tree. "Yes, well, apparently we live in different worlds. I . . . I never quite fit in mine. Honey was my confidant. I told her my secrets and my sins. My hopes and my fears."

"We don't live in different worlds now."

She coughed out a bleak laugh. "Yes, and now that I go rabid in the presence of storms, I am sure to gain legions of friends."

He laughed, and the sound burrowed beneath her skin.

"Who knows? Perhaps with a little control, you'll be the best warning system we have ever had."

"Yes, when I start attacking innocent bystanders, you'll know to take cover and hit me with a heavy object. Perfect."

He had been in the middle of unwrapping the wet cloth from her first leg, and he paused, his eyes dark and serious. "I told you . . . no one is knocking you out again."

She was too tired to argue and after what happened earlier, almost afraid of what their arguing could lead to. She remained silent and tense as he began smoothing a sticky salve over the burned portion of her leg.

"How old are you?" he asked, distracting her with questions again.

"Eighteen."

"Have you always lived in Pavan?"

"Yes."

"Is there any Stormling ancestry in your family?"

She jerked, and it made his hand rub too hard against one of her blisters. She cried out, and his hands left her calves to grip her thighs, trying to hold her steady. "Easy. I didn't mean to startle you."

"You didn't startle me," she barked, furious that she had let her guard down.

It wasn't until he spoke again, his tone quiet, *private*, that she realized his hands still rested on her thighs. "I do believe you are the most confusing girl I have ever met."

"I'm not confusing," she insisted. He was the confusing one.

He dropped his chin toward his chest, laughing, and that sound—at once masculine and soft—sent shivers down her spine. Even with smudges of soot on his face and his wet hair wild and loose, he was beautiful. In part, *because* of the soot and wild hair. He looked every bit the daring adventurer, and that dangerous edge balanced the softer set of his mouth and the long lashes that framed his brown eyes.

"See?" he said. "That's exactly what I mean. Sometimes you are so painfully shy that my own words tangle on my tongue for fear of saying the wrong thing. Then, other times, you are frighteningly brave. I think if you met a bear in the woods, you might order him not to eat you. And he might just listen."

"Well, there are some books that suggest challenging a bear. To pretend as if you are the greater predator to scare it off."

"And *that*—why am I not surprised that you know what to do should you run into a bear, though you've said yourself you had never set foot outside of Pavan until now? I do not understand you, and it's maddening."

"You don't need to understand me." In fact, she would be in a great deal of trouble if he did.

"Ah, there we go disagreeing again. I think I *do* need to understand you."

"No, you *want* to. There's a difference."

He reached into his pack for fresh bandages, but kept his eyes on her. He finished wrapping her second leg, taking his time before answering. With her feet still balanced on his hard thigh, and the sun overhead glancing off his long dark hair, he said, "Maybe it's both. I need to know. And I want to."

She did not know how to answer that, so she deflected her attention to him.

"You better have Duke take a look at your shoulder. It's bleeding again."

He looked like he wanted to say something else, like maybe he wanted to talk about what had happened before, but she turned away and shoved her feet back into her boots before he could.

Locke was the leader of this crew, and regardless of what happened between them, she knew he would not let her face a storm until he trusted her. But the things he spoke of—the two sides of her—she did not know how to explain them outside the context of her life. How could she explain that she had spent her life dreaming of adventure, while simultaneously hemmed in by fear? She could not explain that she had never wanted for any material thing—not clothes or money or food—but had lacked all the things that came free. Companionship. Truth. Choice. She could not tell him that she was so very good at pretending that she no longer knew exactly who she was.

Sometimes she was Aurora. Confident. Clever. Cultured.

Sometimes she was Rora. Afraid. Alone. Ashamed.

And more and more, she was Roar—bold, brash, and increasingly baffled by the situation in which she found herself. And sometimes she was none of them, lost and adrift somewhere in between, like the wildlands between Stormling cities.

Stormlings are not our saviors. They merely keep us weak. They keep their heels upon our necks and call it protection. The heavens rule all, and it is to them we owe allegiance.

—The Book of the Sacred Souls

16

Cassius heard a commotion stirring outside the room he had claimed for himself in the royal wing—the heavy thud of boots and shouting voices. He pushed open his door to see a small contingent of soldiers barreling their way down the hall, swords drawn.

He stepped out, his hands held palms up. "Gentlemen, there is no need for weapons, I assure you. What seems to be the issue?"

He recognized the soldier in the lead as part of Aurora's guard, the one who had carried her after the knife incident. Taven, Cassius believed was his name. He fought a scowl.

"We demand to see the queen."

Cassius sighed. Honestly, he was surprised it had taken this long.

"I understand your concern, but the queen is *unwell*. I assure you a maid is looking after her. But I hardly think a group of soldiers barging into her personal rooms is going to help her recovery."

"I'll believe that when I see it," Taven growled. "Does she know your father is cavorting about the throne room as if it were his?"

Cassius gritted his teeth. The old fool. Did he not realize that caution was imperative? "My father is used to being in charge, and might occasionally step over the line. It's why my brother and I took over handling storm duty for Locke. I assure you, the king means no harm." The lie slid like a razor off his tongue.

"Then perhaps it's time for your family to return home."

Cassius narrowed his eyes at Taven. "So you've already given up on your princess?"

The man's nostrils flared, and his jaw clenched. "Never."

"And yet you would have *me* give up on her and leave? Take all my soldiers with me?" Cassius's eyes flicked to the bands on the soldier's arm, signifying his affinities. Thunderstorm and skyfire. "Taven, is it?" He did not wait for confirmation before continuing: "I'm going to be quite blunt with you. Your queen won't get out of bed. Your princess has been kidnapped. The Rage season is in full swing. The soldiers I have out searching for the princess have reported multiple destroyed villages, far more than is typical for this soon in the season. And yet you would have one of the strongest Stormling families in existence leave so that the city is protected only by . . . whom? You with your two affinities?" He glanced at the soldiers behind Taven; none had more than one band. "Them with only one? Do you know what happens to a kingdom with a power vacuum? It collapses while people fight over control like dogs. I can let that happen. Or . . . you can let us keep the ship sailing smoothly until either your queen or my wife is ready to take the helm."

The soldiers shifted uneasily, and Taven replied, "Then *you* stay. Your family must want to return home. The king has been absent from his throne for weeks now. I'm sure he would be glad to return home and relieve his . . . brother, was it? He must trust him a great deal to leave the kingdom in his hands for all this time."

Clearly, someone had been talking. The question was how much Taven knew. Cassius had a feeling the soldier was just stabbing in the dark. None of his soldiers would dare to speak any of their secrets. They were far too knowledgeable about his father's penchant for cruel and painful punishments.

"I'm sure my father would like to return home very much. My mother and brother too. But they are staying as a kindness to me. Even with my betrothal to Princess Aurora, my position here is tenuous at best. If left here alone, some might see me as a stepping-stone to taking the throne for themselves. And I'm not keen on being collateral damage in a coup. So, you see, we are simply doing what must be done to keep the kingdom stable."

Most of the soldiers looked mollified. Taven did not. Cassius sighed dramatically. "I suppose we could let *one* of you in to see the queen. But you must not upset her. She's been distraught for some time, and has only recently found any peace." Cassius was fairly sure that was because his father was paying the maid to keep her heavily sedated, but of course they did not know that. He did not even know it for sure. He just knew his father too well.

The others remained in the hallway while he took Taven inside the queen's rooms. A maid rose from her seat by the bed, the same maid Cassius had paid all those weeks ago for information. He was sure she had no qualms about taking his father's gold. She curtsied and moved aside as they came closer. The queen lay abed, her eyes open but unseeing, fixed on the open window and the land that stretched on and on until the horizon.

Taven sheathed his sword and knelt beside the bed.

"Your Highness."

Queen Aphra did not respond.

Tentatively, the soldier reached and touched her hand. It lay limp on the bed. No reaction.

"Do you see?" Cassius asked. "All is as I said."

It did not stop Taven from glaring at him. "I've never seen her like this."

"Yes, well, her only remaining family has never been kidnapped, has it?" he hissed.

Taven clenched his fists and turned away, back toward the bed. He took the queen's hands once more and bent to kiss the ring on her finger. "Do not lose hope, Your Majesty. We will return Aurora to you."

The queen blinked, her fingers tightened, and she said in a rasp, "They've killed her by now."

Cassius stiffened, then moved closer to the bed. This was new.

"No. Don't think like that," Taven said. "She's of far too much worth for them to harm her."

The queen squeezed her eyes shut tightly and shook her head against her pillow, her already tangled hair mussing further. "The goddess is punishing me for my disbelief. She took them all, one by one."

"Your Majesty, please. All hope is not lost."

But Queen Aphra was no longer listening. Her gaze returned to the window, and her grip went soft. Taven tried to rouse her again, but this time not even her daughter's name pulled her from her stupor.

Taven stood and marched across the room to Cassius. "My men are at your service for the search of Princess Aurora. Whatever you need. Just find her."

The soldier left and, before Cassius followed, looked back at Queen Aphra. Cassius hadn't meant for it to be like this. But he did not know how to fix it without Aurora.

Perhaps he too should reconsider his belief in the gods. How else could things go so incredibly wrong at every turn? After all, he had lost not just one bride now but two. He would not let the same hold true for kingdoms.

Locke thought he probably should have felt guilty, seeing the blood drain from Roar's face when he told her where she would be riding now that her horse was pulling the Rock. But Ransom had put the idea into his head, and it had stayed there, tugging at his mind. And it *did* seem like a much better idea to have her ride on his horse with him than for her to squeeze into the already packed Rock with Duke, Bait, and now Sly.

Besides, if he could not scrape up any guilt for kissing her, there was little chance he'd feel any about having her pressed up against him on a horse.

According to their maps, there had once been a town a few hours east of their current location. No one could remember any specifics about it, so they just had to hope it had a blacksmith, but the first concern was finding out if the town was even still there.

And if having Roar on his horse gave him the opportunity to wheedle a little more information out of her, then all the better. He heaved himself into the saddle, then held a hand out to help her up too. She gave him that furious glare that never failed to make his blood pump a little faster. She ignored his hand and hauled herself up behind him without any help, and her tall, lithe frame molded against his back. Almost immediately, she shifted, trying to find a way to sit comfortably in the saddle while also touching him as little as possible. The saddle was large, but not meant for two people, so she would end up pressed against him sooner or later. He only smiled, and snapped the reins.

He hadn't lied when he'd told her he didn't understand her, at least not completely. She'd kissed him back, but he honestly did not know what she would do if he kissed her again—accept him or punch him. She was a bundle of contradictions, but one thing he understood all too well was her independence.

It reminded him of his own early days with Duke. The old man, whose hair had been shorter and darker then and only streaked with gray, had given Locke more than he could possibly hope for. A purpose. A home. It was on the road and ever changing, but it was more of a home than what he'd had in Locke. But even with the delirious happiness he felt with his new life, he had chaffed under Duke's control. He'd been a scrawny child the last time anyone had ever told him what to do; and for every ounce of strength he spent holding on to his new life, he expended just as much energy rebelling against it. Hell, it wasn't that long ago that he'd slipped away in the night to go after a hurricane alone when Duke had expressly forbidden it.

He was intimately familiar with Roar's sort of reckless independence. It was one thing for him to risk his own life, but to see her risk hers uncorked emotions in him that he thought he had buried years ago.

For the first hour, Roar was stubbornly silent behind him. She had pushed herself back so far in the saddle that she sat on the upward curve at the back, and had to clench her legs tight to keep herself in place. And even then, a change in terrain or speed sent her tumbling forward, her hands grabbing his waist to keep from slamming into him. After the tenth or so time she had tried and failed to keep from falling against him, he was out of patience. Wrapping the reins once around the pommel so he didn't lose them, he reached both hands back to grip her thighs, well above her burns, and tugged her forward. She squeaked in response, her fingers tangling in the leather straps and holsters that crossed his abdomen. He would be lying if he didn't admit that he got pleasure out of both her outraged cry and the feel of her surrounding him.

"There," he said, his voice low so that only she could hear. "We're touching. I can feel you, all soft and warm against my back." He heard her sharp intake of breath behind him, and he could swear her fingers tightened on the holster around his midsection. "You can feel me, and the world has not descended into flame again." Though there was plenty of heat moving down his spine.

"You are *such an ass*!"

He smiled. "Probably."

"Definitely."

"Yes, but I'm an ass who gets what he wants."

He hadn't meant those words to sound quite so possessive. He still thought it was a bad idea to get attached to her, but since the kiss, he was having trouble getting himself to care. All the thoughts he had ignored so diligently before abraded him constantly now. Good idea or not—he wanted her. He feared she was fast becoming a chink in his armor, but with her arms still around his middle, those long, delicate fingers splayed out over his stomach, the last thing he wanted to do was pull away.

The sun was setting, but they were near the town on the map, so they pushed on. A smell hung on the breeze that singed his nose and made his eyes water—the rot of death and the smell of burned flesh. In the falling night, they could not see the town clearly, but he had a feeling he knew what was waiting. And sure enough when they got close enough to see, the town was in ruins. Stone and wood lay in heaping piles, the shape of what once was visible only in a few places where a wall or a chimney had miraculously stayed standing.

Behind the ruins of the town they found a funeral pyre, only half burned. He had a feeling this was the town the remnants fled. They likely set the pyre ablaze before they left, and the fire died before it finished the job. Roar buried her face between his shoulder blades and he heard her taking short, broken breaths. Duke lit the pyre again, and the scent of smoke and horror followed them long after they left.

When no trace of death clung to the air, they stopped to make camp for the night. No one wanted to go to sleep, nor did anyone want to light a fire after what they'd seen. So they sat for a while in the dark, talking quietly. They ate bread and berries grown by Jinx before exhaustion forced them all to sleep.

The door to Novaya's cell slammed open in the dead of night. She was curled up on her pitiful cot, and she quickly adjusted her threadbare blanket to ensure it covered the handprint-shaped burn marks on her mattress.

Prince Cassius stepped inside, a torch held high in his hand, and Nova's magic shook awake at the sight of the flame.

She had not bathed properly in weeks. A handful of times they had dropped a bucket of water into her cell. She had tried to make it go as far as possible, but even on those days, she never got fully clean. Even her body seemed changed—her arms and legs thinner, the roundness of her hips and stomach less pronounced.

Was it not enough that the prince came to question her during the day, now he had to disturb her nights as well? Before all this, night-time had been the height of her anxiety. But now it was her one solace. The air grew cooler, soothing her heated skin. The dark blocked out her surroundings so that just for a little while, she could pretend she was back in her own room.

Cassius cut straight to the point. "The queen seems to be under the impression that her daughter is dead. Do you know why that might be?"

"Rora is *not* dead," Nova hissed back.

"And you know that how? Perhaps because you were involved in the plot to take her?"

"I've told you. She is my friend. I would never harm her. Never cause her pain."

"Would you put her in danger?"

Nova hesitated. She *had* put Rora in danger, not purposely, but from her inability to tell her friend no. And she'd certainly had more than a few dark thoughts since about all the things that could go wrong in the wilds.

"You know, I had my men search your room again. And do you know what they found? Hidden beneath a loose floorboard under your bed? Quite a stockpile of coins. Perhaps, payment for services rendered?"

"I saved that money myself. Some of it even came from you, if you recall. Bribing me for information on the Eye."

His eyes narrowed. "All that tells me is you are willing to break the law for gold."

"And what were you willing to break the law for?"

"I am the law."

Nova scoffed and gestured around the cell. "Clearly."

His face was harsh in the flickering glow of the torch and he growled, "I do not wish to hurt you, but far more depends on Aurora's survival than you know. I will do what I must to get her back. I am not afraid of crossing lines. You would be smarter to cooperate before I do. Did you tell the queen something different in your account of the kidnapping? Something that would make her believe the princess to be dead?"

Nova's stomach sank. The queen thought her daughter had been kidnapped for her Stormling abilities. Only the two of them knew Rora had no magic. No wonder the queen was so brokenhearted. She assumed that when the kidnappers discovered Rora was no use to them, they would dispose of her.

Nova said, "I told her and everyone else in that courtyard the same thing I told you. I *am* cooperating. I don't know what else you want from me." Nova swallowed, her throat dry, and asked, "Can I see the queen? Maybe I can comfort her."

Cassius sneered. "What could you possibly say that hasn't already been said? If you know something, you'll tell *me*, and I'll decide if it's worth telling the queen."

Nova sat up on the bed, pushing the blanket off her legs as the fire inside her began to rise. She did not want the queen to suffer, but she had made Rora a promise. And telling Prince Cassius that the princess knowingly broke a betrothal treaty could make things far worse.

"I have told you everything there is to tell."

"You are a good liar, *Novaya*. Many would likely believe you, but I am not so easily fooled. I know the taste of a lie better than I know the truth. I don't know what secret you're keeping, but I will. Eventually. Perhaps if sleep does not come so easily, you'll find your tongue loosened."

He took hold of her wrist and dragged her up from the bed. She barely fought; she had to focus too hard to keep from burning him where he stood. And when she felt a surge of heat at her back, she thought for a moment she had failed.

But then she opened her eyes and saw that he'd tossed his torch onto the bed, and the thin mattress, filled with straw, had gone up like kindling. Her anger surged and with it the fire on her bed. Flames licked as high as the ceiling, and a dozen fiery fingers seemed to crook at her, beckoning her toward the blaze.

Instead she stumbled back, her body slamming into the stone wall behind her.

"Why are you doing this?" Nova asked through gritted teeth.

The fire cast flickering shadows over the hard angles of the prince's face. And for the first time, he did not look cold and emotionless to her. He looked . . . *desperate*.

"I'm doing what I must, doing everything I know to make this right, to bring Aurora home. While it's still hers. If you won't help me, then you are my enemy. And I have no mercy for enemies."

He opened the door and a guard in a blue Locke uniform set three buckets of water just inside the door. Then they left, and it was just her and the fire, raging inside and out.

Nova did not bother going for the water. Instead she stood and ambled closer to the bed. The smoke burned down her throat and the heat was enough to make her drip with sweat. But she closed her eyes and stuck her hands into the blaze. It did not burn. It never did. And instead of trying to douse the flame, she pulled it to her instead. She imagined it soaking past her skin, engulfing her muscles, streaming through her blood. She coaxed it up her arms and toward her chest and shoved it down, down, down toward that door barred inside her.

One thing was clear to her now. Cassius would not release her, not ever. If she wanted to be free, she would have to make the opportunity herself. So instead of denying the fire, she would save it up. And she would wait. Wait until a moment presented itself.

When there was no more fire to pull, she opened her eyes and found her bed charred black, only the smell of smoke left behind. At least she did not have to worry about the handprint burns any longer. She stumbled back, feeling like she was filled to the brim, like her very soul was stretched to its limits.

Then she went to the buckets of water in the corner, and for the first time in weeks, she scrubbed herself completely clean.

The hunters did not find another town until late afternoon on the next day. At first sight it appeared whole, if not a little worse for wear. A stone wall encircled the town, probably about as tall as Locke. It wouldn't be much good for keeping anyone out. In at least two places, Locke saw piles of rubble where the wall had been knocked down. Storm damage. They were at the westernmost edge of the Sangsorra desert. What little grass there was had been swallowed up by a sea of rusty-red sand that had given the desert its name. Sangsorra meant *blood sands* in Vyhodin. The trees were the short, brushy type that could live through long droughts. Some of those appeared to be broken or split. Skyfire.

The town looked better on the inside than the outside. The houses, though simple, were in decent shape and made from some kind of clay that was nearly the same color as the earth. People walked and talked in the streets, but they were clean and well dressed. Neighbors, not beggars. A few stared at the group as they made their way down a dusty road toward the town center, but the townsfolk appeared friendly enough.

Locke spotted a nearby building with an oversize chimney and a blacksmith sign out front. He caught Duke's eye and nodded. The town roads sprawled out like rays from the sun, everything meeting together in the center. They slowed the horses as they approached a courtyard in the middle, and already waiting for them was a well-dressed man with graying hair and a thick mustache. He stood with hands linked behind his back, strong posture, chin tilted up with confidence. At his back were a few sturdy men, not quite menacing, but with the potential to be so.

Roar's arm was wrapped around his midsection, and he laid his hand atop hers. She tensed behind him, but he kept her fingers pinned where they were, and gave a quick squeeze.

"Stay here. Stay alert. If something goes wrong, take the horse and go."

Her fingers twitched beneath his. "Well, that's stupid. I wouldn't just leave you here."

He peeled her hands away from him, holding them a moment longer than necessary. Just a moment, not enough to hurt. "Glad to know you care about my well-being."

He slid carefully off the horse, and Roar mumbled, "It's only because I'm safer with you than without you."

"You can't fool me, princess. It's too late. I know your secret." She blanched, her already light skin paling further.

Scorch it all. How could someone so bold be so skittish? He patted her knee, just above her bandages, and said, "Sometimes in small towns like this, local bullies like to throw their weight around. Never anything too bad. It usually gets sorted out with a little coin, maybe a couple fists. But I would rather not take any chances with you. If things go sour, get safe, and I'll find you when everything is over."

"How about if things go sour, you yell for my help." She touched one of the knives tucked over her shoulder to make her point.

He scowled up at her. He didn't have time for this. Duke was already out of the Rock and heading for the men, but suddenly he was thinking about kissing her again, tugging her down until their mouths crashed together. Would she yell at him or kiss him back? He shook his head and said, "If you get hurt, you won't like the training sessions I devise as punishment."

"If I'm hurt, you can hardly make me run all day."

He sighed. "*Please*. Stay on the horse."

He joined Duke in time to hear his mentor introduce himself and explain that they were looking for a place to stay while repairing their carriage. The man with the mustache was clearly the leader, and he leaned to look past Duke at the Rock. His eyes flicked over the horses and the wheels, not seeing the damaged back end, and he said, "Seems to be working fine."

This was always the hard part about staying in small towns. The bigger cities allowed them to pass unnoticed, but that was impossible in a place like this. And the decision on whether or not to reveal their status as hunters was always complex and dangerous.

"Hello. Name's Locke," he said. "We ran into trouble earlier today with a firestorm, and it did some damage. We could have her fixed up and on the road in a few days. Maybe a week."

The man scratched two fingers over his mustache, brown eyes flicking repeatedly to the carriage and the rest of their crew. "Never seen a carriage like that before. What's put you folk on the road? You scourge?"

Locke's spine straightened, and he clenched his teeth. That hateful term told him they would indeed have to tread carefully here.

"We're tradesmen. We flee no storms."

"What kind of tradesmen?" The man was suspicious already, his voice hard.

Duke cut in. "We want no trouble. Nor do we seek to sell and hamper your own businesses. We were just passing through and hit a bit of misfortune. We'll pay well for food and lodging as well as the help of your blacksmith."

Locke looked to one of the men behind the leader, a dark-skinned man whose posture seemed more relaxed than the rest. The man nodded. Mustache said, "We can accommodate you. But you will have to make an offering. Everyone in this town is a follower of the Sacred Souls. It has kept us alive while others nearby have perished. We do not require membership, only observance."

Damn. It would have to do, but a Sacred town would not be Locke's first choice for refuge.

"Locke?" Duke's voice snapped Locke back into the moment, and he focused while the town's apparent leader explained what would be required of them. Locke nodded at his mentor, who said, "I'll take care of payment with Minister Vareeth, if you'll explain to the others."

"Of course."

"Welcome to Toleme," the minister said as he led Duke away.

Locke made his way back to the group. He heard the minister reciting an invocation, and Duke repeating it. Locke glanced over his shoulder to see his friend lay something on a large circular stone altar just beyond the well in the center of the courtyard. He fought off the shiver that climbed his spine and gestured for the others to dismount or exit the Rock. They met on the road, out of earshot of the minister's men who stayed nearby to watch them. The expressions on his team varied from grim to hopeful, and in Roar's case a confused sort of eagerness.

"Did he say Sacred Souls?" she asked. "They follow the old ways?"

"They are not old ways to us all," Sly said, and her normally soft voice held a cutting edge. He would have to keep an eye on that. He trusted Sly, but whatever rankled her about Roar, he couldn't let it fester. Hunters who weren't completely focused and in tune with each other became dead hunters more often than not.

"They'll let us stay. But only if we observe their ways with offerings."

"What kinds of offerings?" Ransom asked. He, like Sly, was raised around religion, but the two had left home with vastly different perspectives on what it meant to worship storms.

"A token of sacrifice or daily blood."

Sacred Soul communities differed widely in their degree of devotion and the severity of their traditions. It certainly could have been worse. While a nuisance, it wasn't a great hardship to offer a few drops of blood every morning. And a token of sacrifice only needed to be something of importance, something used well and often that the person offering would miss. But in some places, a token was not enough, and much greater sacrifices were required. Ransom left his hometown after his childhood sweetheart was offered up as a sacrifice, and he'd met Duke less than a year later in Odilar. Locke knew his friend wouldn't take well to this town, no matter how mild their customs.

Ransom ran a hand over his mouth, scratching what was left of his beard in agitation before replying, "Fine."

Locke gave everyone a moment to decide what they would offer and fetch it if need be. All scattered except Roar. She glanced behind him at the altar with fascination and a healthy dose of fear. "I don't know what to offer," she told him. "Nothing I have is particularly valuable." She clutched at something beneath her shirt, a necklace he guessed. "Nothing that I can part with anyway."

"It's not about the value of the object, but the value of the sacrifice. To these people, the storms are gods. Not the kind you pray to or the kind who grant miracles or comfort. They are like the gods of old who were a race all their own. Immortal and proud and unpredictable . . . and prone to cruelty. Like a child crushing a bug beneath his heels because he can. Followers of the Sacred Souls believe if they willingly sacrifice to the storms, they're less likely to tempt their wrath."

Locke didn't loathe religion the way Ransom did, but he'd been a hunter long enough to see that storms cared nothing for trinkets or blood. But this town believed, and it had helped them survive without a Stormling this long. So he would do what he must.

In the end, Locke, Roar, and Bait chose blood, while Ransom, Jinx, and Sly chose tokens. He led the way over to the altar where Minister Vareeth and two others waited. The dark-skinned man was walking away with Duke, and Locke guessed he was the owner of the inn.

Sly volunteered to go first. She wasn't technically a Sacred Soul follower. Her beliefs dated further back than the customs followed here, but it was close enough. She pulled back her hood, revealing the dark curls that were cut close to her scalp. Sly favored simplicity, another inclination from her childhood, so she didn't keep much with her on the road. She walked up next to the minister, and then removed the shoes from her feet. She had others, he knew, but they were old and worn, and she had replaced them just weeks ago in Pavan.

She held her new shoes in her hands, and the minister smiled, approving her choice.

"Repeat after me," Vareeth said. "We call to the heavens, to the Sacred Skies."

Sly glanced briefly back at Roar, then at Locke, before repeating the words the minister spoke.

"We call to the souls ancient and wise. We humble ourselves before your strength. We beseech you for your mercy. We honor your power and control."

The minister gestured for her to place her shoes upon the altar where dozens of other items already lay. Like most Storm altars, it was made from a mineral. This one was a glassy black crystal, cut through with brownish-red stone and sediment. Locke guessed it was fulgurite, which formed when skyfire met sand, cut to form a raised circular altar. Sly set her shoes down carefully and repeated the last of the minister's chant.

"We offer a sacrifice to you in hopes you find it worthy and true." When she was finished, the minister ran his thumb vertically from the bridge of her nose to the top of her forehead, where the Sacred Soul followers often wore painted markings in their more formal ceremonies.

"May the Storms grant you mercy and peace. Welcome to Toleme."

Sly took the blessing in silence, and then stepped aside for the next in their group. No one immediately came forward, so Locke pulled a blade from a holster at his hip and took his turn. He repeated the same invocation, then before the last lines, pricked his thumb with the tip of his knife and let the blood drip onto the black stone as he said the final words. He pulled a kerchief from his pocket to stop the blood and stood patiently as the minister gave him the same blessing. When he backed away, his eyes shifted to meet Roar's wide-eyed gaze. He watched her observe the others, as one by one they made their offerings. Ransom gave a knife, and Jinx one of the many rings decorating her fingers. Then finally, Bait spilled his drops of blood, and it was Roar's turn.

She squared her shoulders, set her jaw, and stepped up to the altar. He saw her hand shake as she reached back to pull a knife from the harness at her back. Her pale skin had gone ashen, and she looked . . . nervous. She usually did her best to hide all her emotions but anger, but now, it was as if she couldn't.

It only took a second for him to decide, and he turned to the minister. "Father, if I may, can I stay with her? She is new to our party, and this is well beyond the scope of her experience."

It was a testament to her anxiety that Roar didn't even argue when he removed the knife from her grip. He took her shaking hand in his as the minister began to speak.

Roar felt so ashamed, so *embarrassed,* but not even those emotions could push out the one that crowded in her chest and made it hard to take a full breath. Worse, she couldn't even give the emotion a name. She only knew that as each of her companions had recited the words, calling out to the heavens, she had grown more and more uncomfortable, like a heavy weight pressed down on her shoulders. She was not afraid of a tiny prick of a knife when she had willingly taken a blade to her arm not so long ago. But some bone-deep instinct whispered of danger here.

She wished she had taken the time to find a token, but the only true belongings of worth she had were the twister ring about her neck and the *Finneus Wolfram* book that she brought along for comfort and inspiration. Both meant far too much to sacrifice, but something about the notion of dropping her blood on that altar did not sit well with her.

The minister began to speak, and Locke steadied her hands. She would worry about the vulnerability she was showing him later when her heart did not feel like it was about to burst from her chest. She squeezed his fingers, pressing them into the knife he held, and she dared not look at him. "Easy," he whispered. "There's nothing to be afraid of."

She took too long to say the first line of the invocation, so the minister repeated it again, as if she hadn't heard. Her voice came out as little more than a whisper as she said, "We call to the heavens, to the

Sacred Skies." Little bumps lifted along her skin, her hair standing on end as she continued: "We call to the souls ancient and wise."

Out of nowhere, lightning streaked overhead, splintering the quiet sky. She jumped and turned away and Locke was there, his chest wide and warm and solid against her cheek. When no more lightning appeared, she eased herself out of his arms.

The minister watched her with confusion, but it was Sly just behind her shoulder that stared with clear, unadulterated distrust.

She was being silly. It was only blood. She had sprinkled far more than a few drops of it along the southern road out of Pavan. She nodded for the minister to continue, but the moment she spoke her next words, lightning lit up the sky once more. She finished the sentence quickly, praising the strength of storms as one attempted to make itself known overhead. She glanced at Locke for the first time, and she could not help but let him see her fear. If a storm formed now, here with these strangers, and she reacted badly . . .

His hand rubbed soothingly up and down her spine. Any other time she would have shrugged off the touch. There were too many people around. But it did calm her. Just that little touch made breathing feel like less of a challenge. "Don't worry about the skyfire. It's only in the clouds for now," he said. "Finish this, and we'll go inside. And if a storm comes, the others can handle it."

That only made her more furious with herself. She didn't *want* the others to handle it. In fact, she should be jumping at the chance to face a skyfire storm. That was her family's strongest affinity, and she could not go back home without it.

You are lightning made flesh. Colder than falling snow. Unstoppable as the desert sands.

She couldn't say the rest because she was done pretending to be Stormling, but the rest was true. Her blood, like her ancestors' before her, was filled with the light of skyfire. She knew her heart could freeze out fear and doubt because she had done it all her life. And her will, her desire to obtain storm magic, had pushed her through far worse situations than a tiny drop of blood on an altar.

She kept her eyes on the sky as she said the next two phrases.

"We offer a sacrifice to you . . ."

She did not flinch as the skyfire above her bounced from cloud to cloud, lighting up the sky from horizon to horizon.

Locke peeled back the fingers of one hand she had been fisting at her side. He smoothed his palm over hers, once and then again, tracing the healed scar from when she had cut her palm to sow the tale of her kidnapping. Then he made the tiniest of pricks on the tip of her index finger. She watched a single drop of blood land, and above her head, the sky exploded with light, so bright that it burned like the sun in her peripheral vision. She snatched her hand to her chest and threw her head back, but the sky was dark and still once more. She spat out quickly, "In hopes you find it worthy and true."

Then she put several steps between her and the altar, clutching her blood-smeared finger inside her other fist. The minister didn't approach to touch her, but rather said his blessing from afar, his eyes wide and fearful.

Listen to her roar. Listen to her wail.
Listen to the grief that lives inside the gale.
        —"At the Heart," a Sacred Souls hymn

17

The outside of the inn was nearly the same color as the reddened earth it sat on. It was plain and squat. But the inside was a sunburst of color—rich woven tapestries, intricately painted pottery. The calming smell of incense hung in the air.

She could feel the others peeking at her when she was not looking, and nausea rolled through her stomach. A headache throbbed at her temples. One by one the hunters collected a key from Duke. Quickly, she reached into her pack for her coin purse, glad she had brought enough with her to last a while. When she asked Duke how much she owed, he shook his head.

"No need."

Sly, who had just received her own key, gave Roar a hard look before walking down a hallway to the right, her feet muffled by the thick, blue rug that stretched the length of the hall.

"I have money. I can pay my way."

"Keep your coin," he said. "None here have paid their own way until their training ended and they began receiving a cut of the market sales. You will be the same. It is our investment in you."

Roar had been a lousy investment so far, and would continue to be so, for she had always planned to leave once she had what she needed.

"Please," she said, "I would really prefer to take responsibility for my own needs."

"It's already done, child. I'll not argue with you. You have Locke for that," he said with a knowing grin. Her face flamed, and she took the key without another word.

"Last room on the right."

She kept her face forward as she walked down the hall. She sorely needed a bath and sleep, and everything else could wait until tomorrow.

But her mind refused to wait. Thoughts beat at her as she bathed in the cramped tub in chilly water brought by a young maid. Her feet were raw from breaking in boots that were fitted to someone else's feet, and she carefully covered her blisters and wounds with a healing salve.

But for every measure of pain the salve soothed, the more room she had to think of home. What was her mother doing now? Surely, she had received the note Nova was supposed to give her. Was the queen furious? Was she afraid?

Roar pulled her worn copy of *The Tale of Lord Finneus Wolfram* from her pack. Lord Wolfram was the nephew of the last king of Calibah. Southwest of Pavan and just north of Locke, Calibah was all dangerous swampland and ruins now, given over to the predators who lurked in the murky waters. A year before she was born, the kingdom had been beset by storms. Again and again, it was ravaged with no reprieve, until not even the royal Stormlings could hold them all off. Many died. Many times many. Wolfram volunteered to lead an expedition out to sea in the hopes of finding a land that was not afflicted by storms. That had been in the year of Aurora's birth, eighteen years prior. The ship was never heard from again.

The book was neither unrealistic fairy tale nor harsh cautionary tale. It walked a fine line between hope and despair—a land that Roar had walked most of her life. And if there was some small chance that Finneus Wolfram had lived to find a land safer than this one, perhaps she could too.

She'd read the book so often that the pages had grown thin with use. The spine was cracked and the edges worn. No matter how many times she read the story, it had never failed to enthrall her.

Until now.

For tonight, she was much closer to despair than hope, and she could not see the potential for truth on the pages, only fiction. More likely, Finneus Wolfram had gone the way of every other Stormling who had ever ventured out to sea. And she was a silly girl if she thought she would meet a different end.

"*Enough.*" She threw the book down upon her bed and stood. She could not stay here and wallow in her fears and doubts any longer. She dressed quickly, pulling her boots up over brand-new bandages. She no longer had a cloak, and a chill clung to the rocky desert outside. She still had the cream-colored scarf that she had wrapped around her hair when she left Pavan, so she draped that around her shoulders like a shawl and sneaked out of her room, down the darkened hallway and out into the night.

She kept to the shadows, darting down roads without any specific destination in mind. When she found a gap in the village wall, she climbed over the rubble and outside. Her feet sank into the sand as she walked. Overhead, the stars blazed from horizon to horizon, brighter than she had ever seen them before. She found an area without brush and cacti, where the red sand was thick enough to be soft, and she lay back, stretching her arms and legs out, until she saw nothing but sky.

She had done this more times than she could count back home in Pavan. But the earth there was soft in a different way; it did not shift and stick to her skin as the sand did here. She missed the breeze blowing through the wheat stalks. Here, the wind was either absent or blowing in great gusts that dragged the sand along with it. No in between. The stars at least were the same.

It should not have been a comfort, to feel so small in comparison to the rest of the universe. But she didn't mind feeling small. When the world loomed large above her as it did now, it was easier to have hope. Because surely somewhere out there in the far reaches of the world, there was a place without storms. A place with answers. She closed her eyes and listened to the sound of the gusting wind, the sprinkle of sand as it settled in a new place, and the call of insects as they poured their songs into the night.

"You have a real bed and a room to yourself, and you choose this?"

She startled, jumping up into a sitting position, and twisting to find Locke behind her, his hands shoved into the pockets at his hips.

"What are you doing here?"

It wasn't enough that he kept intruding on her thoughts, now he interrupted her solitude as well.

"I could ask the same of you."

"I couldn't sleep," she snapped.

"Sometimes that happens after a while on the road. You teach your body to only sleep when exhausted, and it is confused when the routine changes. We could go for a run if you would like."

She snorted. "I'll pass."

He settled into the sand beside her, his long legs bent at the knee with his elbows braced on top. "I'm not that bad, am I?"

"You are relentless and demanding and unwavering."

"I only hear good things coming out of your mouth."

She laughed, and he lay back like she had been before, his hands pillowed behind his head, completely at ease. Curse him.

He smiled and said, "That sounds good too."

"What?"

"The way you laugh."

She frowned, wanting to lie down again, but too afraid of how it would feel to be that close to him. So instead, she folded her legs and sat with her hands in her lap and her head tilted up toward the sky.

"I went by your room to see if you needed help changing the bandages on your legs. And . . . if you wanted to talk."

Oh heavens. She imagined what would have happened if she had been in her room, if he had come inside and sat on her bed and touched her legs. It was enough to make her shiver and pull the shawl tighter around her shoulders. She was a fool. A stupid, stupid fool.

"I changed the bandages myself."

He said, "Earlier . . . at the altar—"

Roar sucked in a breath. Could this man do nothing but poke at the things that she was trying desperately to ignore?

"It was nothing," she said quickly. "There is very little religion in Pavan. The old myths are but fairy tales there. I suppose I let myself get spooked by the idea that the storms could hear us, could listen and choose and act as a human might."

That was a good enough reason, and might have even been the truth.

"I don't know that they listen. But choose? Yes, they do that. You will learn quickly in the field that you can never depend upon a storm doing what it ought. The more potent a storm's magic, the more . . . *sentient* . . . it seems."

More things for her to fear, to fill the swirling mass of information in her brain that just wouldn't *stop*.

"Are you superstitious?" he asked.

"Not particularly." Though fear was its own kind of superstition.

"Then why worry so much over a bit of blood on a stone?"

"Because clearly I know scorch all about the world. About this life. Even about myself. Perhaps I *should* be superstitious."

After all, hadn't lightning flashed overhead as she spoke the invocation? Maybe it knew what she was after, that she meant to steal its heart and return home.

"Blind belief is a comfort; it is the frame that puts the rest of the world into context. It allows us to block out the things that don't make sense, that which frightens us. It narrows our vision so that the world does not feel so large. Would it comfort you to have the frame of superstition? To believe that if you say the right words and sacrifice the right things, then your world will stay exactly as it is? Or do you wish to choose what you believe, what you trust and understand?"

"I do not wish the world to stay as it is. I do not wish to narrow anything. I spent my entire life confined in Pavan, confined in my thoughts and my actions. No. I would not wish the world small, not even to be less afraid."

"I do not think you could be small if you tried."

"What is that supposed to mean?" She had been poked fun at for her height before, most often by petty boys who had to look up to meet her eyes and did not know she heard their whispers. She hadn't expected it from him, even with all the friction between them.

"I did not mean it as an offense," he said, sitting up, his body suddenly much closer than it had been. She abandoned looking at the stars to stare at her hands, the lines on her palms and the curve of her nails. "I only meant that you are . . . rather impossible to ignore."

She scoffed. "If you're not meaning to give offense, you are spectacularly bad at giving compliments."

"I never seem to say the right thing to you."

"It's just as well," she said. "I have lost all appreciation for compliments. They're little truths and half lies that say more about the person offering them than they do about me."

"I don't think I have ever met a woman who hated compliments."

"Not hate. I just don't trust them."

"I'm sensing a pattern when it comes to you and trust."

"And I'm sensing a pattern when it comes to you and saying the wrong thing."

He laughed and held up his hands in mock surrender. "Very well. I am done pushing."

He didn't continue, and she didn't know how to reply, so the night grew quiet between them. A gust of wind picked up her hair and blew it across her face. She turned to dislodge it and found him staring at her, his body leaned back and propped casually on his hands. She faced forward again, and let her hair blow as it would. She asked, "What do you believe? What frame do you choose for your world? Or do you believe in anything at all?"

"I believe in survival, which means my frame is flexible, ever changing. I believe what I must, do what I must."

"Is that why you became a hunter?"

He asked, "Is it why *you* became a hunter?"

"You cannot answer a question with a question."

"I believe I just did."

Infuriating man. "You were young, when you met Duke. Weren't you afraid?"

His legs moved in the corner of her vision, the heel of his boot scraping at the red sand. "By the time Duke found me, my choices were few. The number of us children on the streets had grown, and the crown saw us as a nuisance. Children began to disappear. Some likely snatched and conscripted into the military. Others were too young. There were guesses about what happened to them, most of them horrible. I would not put anything past the Lockes. By that point, I saw death as an inevitability, so if there was a way to do it outside that miserable city, that was enough for me. But, as it happens, being unafraid to die makes for a very good storm hunter."

She glanced at him over her shoulder, not turning completely but enough to see the way the moonlight reflected off the bridge of his nose and the sharp angles of his cheekbones. "How old *were* you?"

"Old enough."

And *he* thought *her* frustrating.

"I am not the only one with trust issues. You were more honest with me when I was a stranger in the market than you are now when our lives depend upon one another."

He sat up, dusting the sand off his hands and turning sideways to face her. He folded his legs to sit like her, but there was no making his tall, muscular frame any smaller. He loomed in the edge of her vision, impossible to ignore. "What do you want to know? Ask and I will tell you."

This was dangerous territory. If she asked, he might expect her to reciprocate. And there were some things that she could not tell him, regardless of whether she wanted to or not.

"I don't wish to take any secrets you don't wish to tell."

"Ask, Roar. I have nothing to hide."

She could have asked him about his childhood, about growing up in Locke, but other words poured from her mouth before she could help herself.

"Do you still think I made a mistake? Coming here?"

"Do *you*?"

"No answering questions with a question. And this isn't about me. I want to know what you think, if you regret saying yes to me."

His hand touched her back, long fingers spread wide, pressing against her. She suddenly could concentrate on little but the shape of his hand and the pressure his fingers exerted. Finally, he said, "No, I don't think you made a mistake."

"Even after the twister? And the thunderstorm and all the others? How am I supposed to hunt storms when . . . when . . . I don't even know what to call it! I cannot even trust myself, which means I cannot trust anyone."

She had been so sure, so certain when she left Pavan. But now she could not depend upon herself. She was drawn to Locke when she shouldn't be. She wanted to run back home when she should be brave. And when the storms came, she lost herself.

"You can trust me," he said, his hand trailing down her spine and then up again in a movement that was probably meant to be comforting. But she felt it too intensely for it to cause anything but fear and frustration.

"No, Locke. I really can't."

It was a blow, to be sure. But like any wall, Roar's would not fall without effort, and Locke was more determined than ever to see that happen.

"Why?" he asked. "Do you think I mean you harm?"

"No, I don't—"

"Do you think I would judge you? I don't care what your life was before, Roar."

She scoffed. "You would. You all would."

"There is not a person on this crew who does not have a past, myself included. You know I was an orphan. I have already told you that my only directive in life is survival. Can you not imagine that I have done things in my life I am not proud of? But I'm here. I am alive. That is more than could be said for many. Whatever it is that haunts you . . . you're here now. That is what matters."

He had lost control over his own hand, and it trailed up and down her back now, tracing the delicate line of her spine again and again. And with each pass, he claimed a little more of her, until his fingers swept up her neck into the fall of her dark wavy hair.

She shivered, and her voice was softer as she spoke. "If it were just the guilt, I would tell you. But it is more complicated than that."

"When was the last time you tried letting someone else in? Have you ever?"

Her spine stiffened beneath his caress, and he knew he was losing her. There was heat enough to burn in her next words. "I *did* try. Not that long ago. I was afraid and worried, and I trusted that someone else could help me. That we could be partners. But he was a liar, and he only ever meant to break my will beneath his own."

Locke couldn't stop the fierce protectiveness that rose in him, and before he knew what he was doing, he had caught her face in his hands, turning it toward him. "Who was he? The man from the market?"

"Locke, *please*—"

"If a man needs to hurt a woman to feel good about himself, he is not much of a man."

"It wasn't like that."

"Then how was it? Say the word, princess, and I will hunt him down. It's what I do, and I am *very* good at it."

She paled. "No, no, not that. It was only my pride and my heart that he hurt. Nothing more."

It should not have made him jealous, to know someone broke her heart. He should only have been mad for her, sad too perhaps. But he could not help the part of him that envied the man she had allowed near her heart in the first place.

Two paths diverged before him in his mind. Since the kiss, he had been content to chase her without thinking of the consequences. But now he knew that he either had to be certain or he had to let her go. He looked at her—at the curve of her cheek and arch of her neck and the bow of her lips—and he knew he could not do the latter.

"I will make you a promise," he said. "You don't have to tell me anything unless you want to. I will do my best to stop pushing you. But know that you have my trust."

"But—"

"*You have it.* You were strong enough during that twister to know that something wasn't right. And we will work until you're stronger still. Until we find out how to get past this. You asked me if I thought you had made a mistake by coming with us, and my answer is no. You are exactly where you are supposed to be. And I am here with you. If you have questions, ask them. If you have fears, shed them. If you have doubts, give them to me and I will crush them beneath my heel. If you need help, I will provide it. Even if you only need someone to yell at, I can be that too. And when the time comes that you need someone to trust, I will be that person. I promise."

The words had rushed out of him, like a current he could not fight, and he had been so concentrated on the words, on saying exactly what he meant, that he did not notice her tears until he was silent. Wet droplets brimmed along her lashes, and with each blink, more tears streaked across her cheeks like shooting stars. He had seen her upset, seen her furious, but never had he seen her look so sad, so *broken*.

"Ah, princess. Don't cry."

She shook her head, her lips trembling, and he touched her again, unable to resist. He wiped away the moisture on her cheeks, cupping her face in his hands.

"I—I can't—" She choked on the words and clutched a hand to her chest like her heart physically hurt in her chest.

He acted on instinct alone, pulling until she sat in his lap, her side pressed against his stomach and her shuddering body cradled against him. He kissed away a tear at the corner of her eye, and she inhaled sharply before choking out another cry. The wind blustered around them, and he pulled her closer, knowing the shawl she wore provided little warmth. His lips moved over her cheek, less of a kiss and more of a caress.

"What can I do?" he asked, desperate. "Tell me how to help. Tell me."

She didn't speak, but she did pull him closer, her willowy arms winding about his neck, until her chest pressed against his own and their foreheads met. He could feel her gasping breaths on his mouth, and he felt the ghost of that touch all the way down his spine. His hands roamed over her back, partly in an attempt to keep her warm and partly out of loss for what else to do. He wanted to understand her, wanted to help, but he had just finished telling her he would not push.

So he rocked her and said whatever words he thought might soothe her. And when he could not help himself, he pressed his lips to her cheek, her temple, her jaw. And with each one, her grip on him tightened until her fingers slid up his neck and tangled in his hair.

She let out a low, keening sound that threatened to shred his heart and he begged again, "Tell me how to help. Tell me what to do."

He did not understand what it was that caused her so much pain. Her past must have been even more complicated than he thought, because it was agony written on her face now, undiluted and overwhelming.

She pressed her lips together and tears darted over them, falling in quick succession. With her hands in his hair, she pulled him closer until his mouth rested against the crest of her cheekbone. "This helps," she whispered, the words broken.

She turned, and when her mouth met his, the sky broke open and it began to rain.

The falling rain was a shock to their senses, and Locke tried to pull away, but Roar held him fast and pushed her lips harder against his. Grief drenched her, filled up her lungs, until she was drowning with every breath. It pressed at her, from outside and within, until she felt like she might be crushed or torn apart at any moment. She could barely breathe, let alone speak.

She knew it wasn't her sorrow. She had known sadness, but nothing like this, nothing so oppressive that she felt shattered. *Irreparable*. It was coming from the storm, that much she knew, but she did not understand *why*. All the other times had been anger, *fury*, and now this? She was baffled, but in this at least, she posed no danger to anyone else. If she were ever going to find a way to break through the storm's hold, this was it.

The one thing that helped was the man whose arms were wrapped around her now. The pain didn't go away, but the closer he was and the more he captivated her thoughts, the more she felt like herself. When his lips met hers, the grief faded to a dull roar in the back of her mind. When his tongue traced at the seam of her lips, begging for entrance, she gave it without another thought.

Even in the soaking rain, heat licked over her skin at the first slide of his tongue against hers. It was different from their last kiss. That had been hard, furious. Now she did not feel so much burned by his touch as that they were burning together. The kiss began slow, seeking, but built as they reacted to each other. He groaned when she buried her fingers deeper in his hair, so she gripped the strands a little tighter. His teeth scraped over her bottom lip, and her whole body shuddered; so he did it again, soothing the sting with his tongue.

Something between desperation and hunger ignited in her, and it made her press back harder, move faster, push closer. His hair was wet in her hands, and the skin of his neck was slick against her forearms. She sat sideways in his lap with her upper body turned to him, and he had been holding her in carefully innocuous places as she cried. But now one hand was dragging from her knee up her thigh, and she ached for him to keep going, to hurry. Toward what, she wasn't exactly sure.

When he reached the top of her thigh, his hand skated innocently over her hip and fisted the wet fabric of her tunic at the small of her back. He held it there, pressing in against her spine, as if he were trying to imprison his hand so it could not wander.

She wanted to tell him it was unnecessary, but she was afraid that as soon as they separated, the grief would overwhelm her again. So instead she let her own hands wander. She explored his shoulder, but her fingers only slipped over soaked leather that was probably being ruined the longer they sat here. She tugged at the straps on his chest, wishing he were closer, wishing she could feel his skin. She reached for his cheek, the only place she knew she could really touch him, and the stubble along his jaw tickled her palm. He loosed one hand from behind her back to mirror her touch, only his hand was so big that it touched her cheek and her neck, and his fingertips nestled into her wet hair.

She shifted her hips, twisting until her knees touched his side and she could lean her chest completely against his. He groaned, breaking their kiss, and her whole body tensed, waiting for the onslaught to come. His mouth slid to her jaw, tasting the rain against her skin, and though she could still feel the foreign emotion, and tears still mixed with rain on her cheeks, it remained muted.

His ragged breaths crashed against the sensitive skin of her neck between kisses, and she shivered as an intense shock zipped down her spine. She leaned back, tilting her head, and *finally* the hand at her back loosened its hold on her shirt and slid beneath the wet fabric to curve around her ribs. The tips of his fingers were burning embers against her bare skin, and she pushed up against his touch, encouraging him the only way she could. Her hands tangled again in his hair, and she was shaking under the barrage of sensations.

"Roar," he murmured, his lips grazing over her pulse point.

Oh skies, that was good. Such a little touch, but she felt it *everywhere*.

"We should go inside."

She only tightened her hold, and arched her body into his touch, wanting more. She could lose herself in this man. She could shed more than just the sorrow that tried to smother her. In his arms, she could let go of everything. He even outdid the pull she felt to her home and the responsibilities that waited for her there. For this man . . . she could let go of Aurora and be only Roar.

"You'll catch your death of cold out here," he said, resisting her pull and leaning back to look at her face. "Roar?" His brows furrowed, and those perfect, tempting lips dipped down in a frown.

She sat up, trying to drag him back, trying to reclaim that intensity that had pushed everything out of her mind. But his hands found her cheeks, and she knew the moment he saw the tears still gathering. His jaw went slack, and he reared back in horror.

"P-please," she stuttered, trying not to choke on the false emotion that was flooding back in. She was shaking still, but now it was tremors of agony. "Hurts," she whimpered.

He cursed, a long string of insults for both himself and the storm. Gently, he eased her off his lap and onto the wet sand. She hurt too badly to do anything more than lie back and struggle to breathe. The rain bombarded her face, so she rolled to her side and squeezed her eyes shut. She heard Locke yell, a savage sound that was much more like her nickname than anything she had ever done.

She didn't know how long she lay there, shaking and soaked to the bone. But she could hear Locke panting just outside the reach of her vision. His labored breaths and grunts told her that he was fighting to take the storm down.

And after a while, she heard no more thunder. Skyfire did not light up the dark behind her eyelids. And the pound of rain on her body had ceased.

She opened her eyes, and though the skies were still black, she knew the storm was gone. Locke stood a few paces away, his shoulders rising and falling with his heavy breaths, his back curved ever so slightly. She could not see his face, only the wilted shape of his normally strong form.

The grief had drained away, but every part of her body ached as if something really had been crushing her. She felt hollowed out, like the sorrow of an entire lifetime had passed through her in moments. She stayed there, curled up in a ball, shaking from the cold. The longer Locke kept his back to her, the more doubt crept in.

When he did approach, he didn't say anything. He just scooped her up into his arms, and began carrying her back toward the town. She swallowed down the instinct to snap that she could walk on her own, because she wasn't sure she actually could. She leaned her head against his shoulder and squeezed her eyes shut. She wanted to curl her hands around his neck, but she didn't have the courage, didn't even know if she *should* want that.

This wasn't her life. Not really. It was only a detour before she went back to her world, no matter what she had thought in the throes of his kiss. Even if she could trust him, *he* couldn't trust *her*. And that gutted her.

Bitterness lined her tongue because she saw plainly now that she had done to him what Cassius had done to her. She'd manipulated and lied and used him to get what she needed. She curled her head into her hands and pushed her palms against her forehead, trying to block that line of thought. At least until she was alone.

"Almost there," he said, his voice deep and gruff. He was taking care of her, even after what she had just done.

"I can walk." Her own voice rasped, barely above a whisper.

"*Don't.* Just . . . please don't, Roar."

She wasn't sure if he meant don't walk or don't talk or don't look up at the hard set of his jaw and the grim line of his mouth. So she assumed it was all of them and returned her head to his shoulder and shut her eyes against the world.

The first people of Caelira lived where the desert met the sea. They were proud like their makers and thrived in a savage land where there were far more ways to die than to live. But over time, they began to believe they needed no masters. And they took what they wanted and behaved in whatever way they wished.

—*The Origin Myths of Caelira*

18

He would never forgive himself. She was soaked to the bone, her skin too pale, her body curled up with her hands against her chest as if to protect her heart. He should have known the moment that it had begun to rain. She wasn't the type to cry easily, and certainly not in front of him. Scorch it all, he should have *realized*. She had pushed him away after their last kiss. Why would she have suddenly thrown herself at him now?

But when her mouth touched his, every other thought fled his mind. She had clung to him so hard, which he now realized was probably because of the pain the storm had fed into her. She was not herself, probably terrified, and he let his attraction to her overrule his better instincts. It had taken more control than he wanted to admit to even keep his kiss gentle, his desires in check. He wanted to devour her, touch and taste every bit of her he could reach. The cling of wet fabric to her skin had only enflamed him more.

He swallowed back the bile that rose in his throat and quickened his pace as they approached the inn. It was late, and there did not appear to be another soul awake in the entire building. When he reached her door, he asked if she had the key. Her tired hands searched her pockets, her movements slow and jerky, and he wondered if she was still in pain. He had to set her down to unlock the door, and she leaned into him for support. He still wanted her, even though he clearly did not deserve her. And the instinct to protect and care for her was stronger than ever, even though it was him she needed protecting from.

He kicked the door open and wasted no time scooping her up into his arms once more. He didn't want to get her bed wet, knowing that she would need to rest, so he carried her toward the wooden chair in the corner of the room. Her hands trailed over his forearms as he situated her, then dropped into her lap. Her head drooped, and his heart cracked.

He had been such a beast to her. He had lived so long thinking only of himself. Survive. Thrive. His every action had been focused on those goals, and anything that threatened them he pushed away. To lead a life like his, you had to be a little selfish. He swallowed a dark laugh, because for the first time in a while Roar reminded him of his sister again. His selfishness had harmed her too, had led directly to her death.

"I can try to wake a maid," he said. "A bath might take away some of the chill. Or food, maybe? Something warm to drink? Or I can leave. You probably want to be alone."

She caught his arm when he began to turn away. "Don't. Don't leave." She took a shuddering breath and tilted her chin up to face him. "We need to talk."

Of course. She deserved the right to rail at him for what he had done. But first, he wanted her resting. He moved to her bed and turned down the blankets, and then he cursed prolifically.

"Bait," he growled, when he saw that her bed had been filled with sand. He swore. Not only were the novie's pranks rarely funny, he always had the worst timing. It would take too long to clean, and Roar was practically falling asleep in the chair behind him.

Resigned, he gathered Roar's bags and her tired form and took her to his room instead, and made a mental note to make the novie pay tomorrow. Once again, he sat her in a chair, then laid her bags at her feet. He checked his bed, relieved to find that Bait was not stupid enough to prank him as well.

"You change into dry clothes," he told Roar. "I am going to get you something to eat and drink. Then . . . we'll talk."

He left her there, both relieved to escape and aching to stay. He could apologize. Maybe he had not completely ruined the chance for trust between them, but there had been too little to begin with. Someone had hurt her, and now he had as well. So much for the promises he had made her only a little while ago.

But he was still her mentor. It was her survival he needed to focus on now. He needed to discover whatever was happening to her and find a way to fix it. Or temper it at least. Otherwise, he would *have* to take her back to Pavan, whether he wanted to or not. He would not let her suffer every time a storm came near.

He searched the main part of the inn and found a night maid on duty. She looked at him with wide, nervous eyes that only made him feel guiltier. He was tall and broad and not just a little intimidating. Most of the time, he leaned into that image, but tonight he wished he could be different. Softer, somehow. With a hot cup of tea and a plate of toast, he ventured back to his room.

He knocked, but Roar didn't answer, so he carefully eased open the door, keeping his eyes low in case she was not finished changing. When he heard no scandalized scream, he looked around to find Roar fast asleep. She had changed clothes as he suggested. But she lay sideways on his bed, not even under the covers. How bad must the pain have been to leave her in such a state?

He gritted his teeth against his frustration and laid the tea and toast on a rickety table beside the bed, in case she woke later and wanted it. Then as carefully as he could, he lifted her sleeping form into his arms. She groaned and mumbled something unintelligible, pressing her face into his chest. He dipped down, wrenching back the covers and laying her gently on the sheets. She curled up on her side once more in the same way she had during the storm. The sight sent a twinge of pain through his chest, and he rushed to pull the covers up to hide the reminder.

He'd made the choice to care about her, and he could not undo that now. In fact, he was sure it had been inevitable from the moment they met. He took a seat in his desk chair, resigning himself to a night sleeping upright.

"I'll figure this out," he vowed in a whisper.

He had to. It was the only way he stood any chance of keeping her.

A cold smile spread over his lips at the sight before him.

It was rare to see this many people gathered in the open air in a wildlands town. Normally the people tended to spend their days indoors, and when they did venture outside, they walked with a hurried pace as if their presence might tempt the skies to unleash their rage over the mere sight of a human. Like scurrying, insignificant insects hiding in their holes.

But the one thing that could always lure them out into the open was gossip, and he brought plenty of that. Still dressed in the dead Locke soldier's uniform, he had stumbled into the town this morning, gasping and crying out for help. The people were wary at first—so superstitious the wildlanders were. But when they saw his uniform, they surged forward to help. After all, their town sat only a few days' ride from Pavan, and everyone knew that the Locke prince had soldiers scouring the countryside searching for his bride.

With his voice shaking and blood smeared on his clothes, he told everyone who would listen of the fearsome Stormlord who was picking off companies of Locke soldiers one by one. He sowed tales of the Stormlord's ability to call a storm from the sky with whim alone. He spoke the storms' language; they followed his command. He even bore the image of one upon his chest, as if his very heart were a storm and it beat only for destruction, for carnage, for death.

No one is safe, he told them, feeding little morsels of gossip to different groups here and there. *You must tell everyone to beware. Beware the Stormlord. The rumors say he was sent by the gods to cull the prideful plague of Stormlings. And he can do it. After all, he had already laid waste to Locke.*

He had feigned distress. *Oh no. I'm not supposed to say that. No one was supposed to know. You cannot tell.*

Each time he *accidentally* let the truth spill to a new group, the villagers clamored for more, squealing like pigs before the slaughter. But he told them no more.

The King of Locke himself swore me to secrecy. I cannot. But . . . beware. He's coming this way, demolishing every town he lays his eyes upon. He will not rest until he destroys Pavan, destroys the Lockes, and every Stormling thereafter.

He created the spark, and then sat back and watched the flames rise. He had done this in every town he passed since he walked from the wreckage of Locke, and every time it played out the same. The people were not stupid. They put together quickly enough why one of the Locke heirs wanted to wed into the royal family of Pavan, and the king had forbidden soldiers to talk of the destruction of Locke. Then, oh then, the fury came. These poor people, forsaken by the Stormlings, barred from their cities and protections, pushed to the very fringes of civilization and then forgotten—they were already disillusioned. The perfect kindling for his blaze.

He slipped into the shadows, content to watch the havoc he had created. The stories were told and retold with more anger and fear each time. And when the whole village was aflame with the news, he left, the soldier's uniform tucked beneath his arm.

Then he called down a friend to play, a firestorm that seethed with hatred and hungered for slaughter. "Punish," he whispered to the storm. "We'll punish them all."

And he let the town burn in truth.

Not all of it at first. He kept leashed his friend's thirst for blood until a few dozen insects had escaped. Then he rained down fire and fury until nothing was left but a smoldering pile of ash and the remnants who would walk the wilds before him, carrying on his words.

Roar woke to a pounding on her door, and she jerked upright, her heart flying into her throat. She looked around, disoriented, trying to piece together why her body felt like she had taken a beating and her eyes were swollen. Even more confusing . . . the bed was on the opposite side of the room from what she remembered.

She spotted a cup of tea and toast on the table, both long cold, and then the night before came back to her. Locke had gone to get her something to eat, and she had stayed back to change. He had brought her to his room, and she had been working up the nerve to ask him to stay with her, *really* stay. She wanted to sink into his arms and let him hold her together through the night. But apparently she had fallen asleep before he returned. If she was in here, where had he slept?

The insistent knock came again, and she bolted out of bed, both afraid and eager to see him on the other side. She wore her second pair of trousers, the ones that fit a little too snugly across her hips. But her favored pair had been burned in the firestorm and now sat wet and wrinkled in a heap on the floor. Her hair was a wavy, wild mess upon her head, but there was nothing to be done about it now. She calmed it as best she could with her fingers. What did it matter what she looked like anyway? Locke had seen her look far worse. With a deep breath, she pulled open the door and narrowly missed getting knocked in the face by the fist of an impatient Jinx. Laughing, the witch said, "Sorry about that. We're having a meeting over breakfast. Locke said to let you sleep, but I figured you wouldn't want to miss out."

Even through the chaos of her other emotions, she snagged on to the familiar feel of annoyance. He was always trying to leave her out, but maybe this morning it had more to do with not wanting to see her at all.

"Let me clean up, and I'll be right down," Roar said.

Jinx nodded, but made no move to leave. In fact, the girl looked her up and down and said, "We really do need to get you some new clothes while we're in civilization." Then Jinx pushed inside, plopping down on the unmade bed. "I hear we were both the victim of one of Bait's abysmal pranks."

Roar vaguely remembered something about there being sand in her bed.

"I like the kid, but sometimes I want to bury him alive. I could do it too. He could not let us have one night's sleep in a real bed before he tried to ruin it? I threatened to start an earthquake beneath his bed if he didn't switch rooms with me. I didn't even have to use my scary witch expression."

"And what does your scary witch expression look like?"

Jinx shook her head. "No can do. It loses its potency if I use it too liberally. Special occasions only."

Roar laughed, feeling a little better than when she woke. Quickly, Roar washed her face at the water basin in the corner and used paste to clean her teeth.

"You know," Jinx said behind her, "I love the color of your hair. That dark is so striking against your pale skin."

Roar nervously smoothed her strands, worried somehow that Jinx would be able to tell it was not her natural color. Nova had given her an extra jar of the dye so that she could touch it up when it faded, but what would she do when that ran out? "Thanks," she said simply. "I like your . . ." In lieu of the words, Roar gestured toward the side of Jinx's head, where her hair had been shorn short, cut with a jagged pattern. "It really makes you stand out."

Jinx snorted. "That's me. Always standing out."

"No, I mean it. I've liked it from the first night we met. It's clear that you know who you are and you own it completely."

"You're not too bad either." Jinx smiled. "You ready?"

"Sure." She had to see Locke sooner or later, might as well do it now.

Jinx bounded for the door, and Roar followed. Roar heard the other hunters in the taproom before she saw them—Ransom's booming laugh followed by Bait's "Come on! It was funny."

There were four long tables with bench seats. The hunters were the only ones in the room. Roar was fairly certain they were the only guests in the inn at all, likely the only guests this town had had in a long while. Locke scowled at a grinning Jinx. Somehow, Roar had the feeling that Locke hadn't just suggested they let Roar sleep. He had probably demanded it, and Jinx clearly didn't care to take his orders.

The witch sat down on the left side of the bench across from Ransom and patted the seat beside her for Roar to take, which would put her directly across from Locke. She took a deep breath and slipped into her seat. "What did we miss?"

She and Jinx both began loading up their empty plates from the breakfast laid out on the table. Glazed pastries and jams and eggs and even meat. After weeks on the road eating only things that could be cooked over a fire, Roar's stomach rumbled with eagerness.

"We were just about to discuss our plans for the next few days," Duke said, and then gestured for Locke to take over.

He glanced briefly at Roar, and then got right down to business. "I spoke with the blacksmith last night after we arrived and arranged a deal for the use of his forge and equipment. It could take a few days to over a week to fix the Rock. I'll know more after I get a good look at the damage today." Roar didn't relish the idea of spending an entire week in this town. She was already dreading the blood she would have to offer again this morning. Locke continued: "Since Ransom and I will be spending most of our time working on the Rock, Jinx will be taking over Roar's training."

Roar froze with a bite of food halfway to her mouth. "*What?*"

Locke did not meet her eyes as he explained, "With her earth magic, she can challenge you in ways that I can't. And now that we know you don't react negatively to magicborn storms, she can use those too."

The food in her mouth tasted like ash as she swallowed it down.

"And"—Locke shot Roar a pained, apologetic look, and she suddenly wished she were back in bed—"you all might have heard a thunderstorm last night. Before I dismantled it, the storm had a *similar* effect on Roar as the twister."

"She attacked you again?" Sly sat diagonally across from Roar, and her glare was furious. "And you said nothing?"

Roar's stomach sank and an uncomfortably hot flush spread up her neck.

"She did not *attack* me. And I'm saying something now," Locke answered. "As with the twister, Roar was overcome by an emotion that was not her own." He didn't elaborate, and Roar was grateful. She felt clammy and queasy just thinking about revealing what happened last night. "My guess is that Roar *is* sensitive, but not to storm magic. I think she's sensitive to the hearts of the storms, which would explain why she was not affected by the firestorm magic or the thunderstorm I released to manage the flames."

That *couldn't* be true. Roar had held Stormhearts in her hands. She wore one even now beneath the fabric of her shirt. None of them had *ever* reacted to her. She began to shake her head, but Locke cut her off. He said, "I know that we all have different beliefs about storms. I'll be the first to admit that while we've always acknowledged that storms have hearts, I had never really thought of them like human ones. With the capacity to feel and want and hurt. But I don't see any other explanation. Roar was overcome with violent rage moments before and during the twister. And again . . . last night . . ." He hesitated, and Roar braced herself for him to spill everything. "Last night you grieved when that thunderstorm rose. I could tell just by watching that you felt intense emotional pain."

Jinx cut in to say, "We could ask around town. Sacredites worship storms. If it's possible for someone to feel an emotional connection with a storm, they might know."

Sly cut in, "I've never heard of any such thing."

"Still, it is worth exploring," Duke said. "Perhaps I can subtly ask around so that Jinx can focus on training Roar."

"Is this your nice way of telling me you don't think I can be subtle?" Jinx asked.

Ransom mumbled, "I think you have answered your own question."

"I heard that."

"You were supposed to."

"All right, then," Locke cut them off. "Sly and Bait, you'll be with Duke the next few days. He wants to flesh out our maps of this area while we're here. See if there are any hotspots within hunting range. Now all of you finish your breakfasts so we can get to work. Bait and Roar, don't forget we need to go to the altar for our daily blood offering."

Roar *really* wished she had just stayed in bed.

They ate quickly, and Roar only listened while the rest settled into their usual easy banter. They all teased each other like brothers and sisters, and she imagined that this *was* a family for them. She knew Locke had no blood family left. He had implied the rest were all the same. And look at the damage that she had already done to their unorthodox family. Sly barely spoke, which wasn't unusual except that there was a palpable air of anger emanating from her. Locke didn't join in the conversation with the rest of them either. He sat stiff and silent, and Roar knew it was her fault.

A while later, a quiet maid cleared away their plates, and everyone set off in different directions. She followed Locke and Bait outside toward the altar. In the morning light, it glittered like black glass, but she saw clumps of rocky sediment in it too. She guessed that whatever it was, it had been dug up from the red sands that surrounded the village.

The minister was not there with them, so she whispered to Locke, "Do we have to say the words? Or can we just drip and be done?"

He glanced around. The courtyard was not empty. There were people at the well, waiting in line for water. Others walked through the streets, presumably on their way to jobs or home. When no one seemed to pay them any mind, he shrugged. "Just the blood is probably fine."

Bait stepped up first, let a few drops fall, and then called out, "I'm off to help Duke. See you both later."

He ran off, his bright hair flopping in the early-morning wind. And then it was just Roar and Locke. He unsheathed a knife from his hip and stepped up to the altar. He let his offering fall, cleaned the blade of his knife, and held it out to her, still not quite meeting her eyes.

She took it, weighing the heft of the weapon in her palm. "This is a good knife," she said. "Well balanced."

His head tipped back toward the sky and she thought she saw the corners of his mouth lift up. "Where did you learn how to handle a knife?" he asked.

She hesitated. "I knew a soldier, back in Pavan. He taught me."

Locke's jaw tightened, and he stepped back, leaving nothing between her and the altar. She spun the blade in her hand. That same uneasiness rose in her again as it had for her last sacrifice. What if she wasn't born without power as she always thought? What if her powers had just been *warped* somehow? She could not control storms, but could . . . read them? But that supposed they were like people with desires and fears and everything in between. She didn't like to think that storms had that much life in them, not with what she was about to do. But she could not deny that the emotions she had experienced with each storm had been frightfully potent. If those belonged to the storms, then they felt even more alive than she herself did.

"Roar?"

She looked up at Locke. He had one large hand curved around the back of his neck, and his hair swung free from its usual tie. She flashed back briefly to the night before, to what he had looked like with the rain falling all around them. She felt an alarmingly strong ache low in her belly and she cleared her throat. "Yes?"

"Do you want me to help again?"

The only thing that came to her mind was the night before. She had pulled him so close that his mouth rested against the curve of her cheek, and she had asked him to help. She *did* want that again with a surprising ferocity. But then she saw that he was gesturing toward his knife that she still held. He meant help her with the blood offering. Skies, she was an idiot.

"No. Sorry. I have a lot on my mind."

"Listen, last night was . . ." He trailed off, his hands going to the vials and weapons that hung off his harness. His fingers ran over each strap, as if checking that everything was in its rightful place. He looked almost . . . *nervous*. "Last night was my fault, and—"

"No, it wasn't."

"It was. It was a mistake, and I'm sorry."

That was that, then. She squeezed the handle of the knife in an attempt to calm herself. For a moment, she might have believed it was stuck in her belly rather than held safely in her hand. But this was . . . better, surely. What future could there possibly be here? Eventually, she would have to leave. He was saving them both from getting any more attached.

She stepped up to the altar and quickly pricked the tip of her finger again. Three or four heavy drops fell as soon as she turned her finger over, and once again the sky overhead flashed with lightning.

Before any more drops could fall, Locke's hand shot out, pulling her hand away from the altar and pushing her back. With one hand around hers and the other at her waist, he tipped his head back, surveying the sky. The lightning had only flashed the once, but little bumps rose along the skin of her arms. Whether that was from the skyfire or Locke's proximity, she wasn't sure.

"I knew it," she said. "There *is* something wrong with me. That's not normal."

"Roar." Locke's voice was soft, and she could still feel the heat of his big hand at her waist when he looked down at her. "There is nothing wrong with you." But he offered no elaboration because there was none to give.

Locke cleared his throat, and she could have sworn that before he removed his hands, his thumb grazed over the dip in her waist. But then he stepped back. "Ransom is waiting for me."

She nodded, her throat dry as she tried to swallow.

"Jinx is waiting for you back inside."

She nodded again, but still he didn't leave. Even though they no longer touched, she had the feeling that they were both holding on. And that after this moment, nothing would quite be the same.

He cleared his throat once more and in a low, rumbling whisper said, "I'll see you around. If . . . if you need me at all, just ask a local where to find the blacksmith."

He walked away, not in the direction of the inn but toward the road they had come in on the day before. When he was fifteen paces away, he stopped and turned. She blushed to be found still watching him, and he called, "Maybe think about a token you could offer tomorrow instead." His eyes flicked up to the calm sky before he turned and left for good.

"You two seem . . . off," Jinx said when Roar approached the front of the inn.

"How so?"

"You haven't argued all morning."

Roar released a slow, relieved breath. "We don't argue all the time."

Jinx raised her eyebrows. "Yes. You do."

Roar ignored that. "So you're my new trainer."

"I am."

"What do we do first?"

A wide grin spread over Jinx's mouth. "If you're going to train like a hunter, it's time you looked like one."

Half a bell later, Jinx had filled Roar's arms with things she said were absolutely necessary, piling on more as they went through the row of stores near the center of the village. When they left around noon, Roar's coin purse was considerably lighter, and Jinx's infectious enthusiasm had begun to take over. Roar wore knit trousers that fit snuggly, but stretched and gave with her movement, along with a new pair of boots. And rather than the billowing shirts she had been wearing before, Jinx insisted she buy a sleeveless top that fit as well as her pants. Over that, she now had a leather harness to match the ones worn by the rest of the hunters. Hers even had detachable shoulder guards that were thick and sturdy but with a somewhat feminine design burned into the leather. She'd also bought a cropped jacket that would keep her arms warm, but left all the various holsters and loops around her middle uncovered so that she could easily get to supplies in an emergency. On a whim, to guard her forearms, they'd added vambraces that each had three small loops where she could store vials of magic.

Of course, at the moment, all of the loops and hooks on her harness and vambraces were empty. But Jinx promised to take care of that soon. For the first time since the twister, Roar did not feel like this life was hopeless. She felt almost like she belonged.

They broke for lunch at the inn. Then in no time at all, she and Jinx had saddled up their horses and were heading out of the town into the dusty red landscape.

"We don't want to upset the Sacredites," Jinx had told her. "If they think we're bringing storms near the town, even magicborn ones, I doubt they'll be so keen to grant us shelter."

They rode for over an hour, dust rising in their wake. In the distance large rock formations could be seen, the same red hue as the sand. But when Jinx pulled her horse up to a stop, it was in a flat area with mostly dry, dusty earth, a few swaths of red sand, and one lone tree—its branches bare and the bark bleached nearly white by the sun. They tied their horses to the tree, and Jinx told Roar to wait while she walked over the land. She stopped here and there, placing her hand upon the earth as if listening to it in some way. When she was about a hundred paces away, she stopped and knelt. This time when she pressed her hand into the dirt, she did more than listen. The ground rose under her command, creating a long line of earth that became a knee-high barrier or marker.

She dusted the sand from her hands and jogged back to Roar, grinning.

"Before we get to the fun stuff," she said, "there's a few more things to take care of. You have your crystal and your firestorm powder?" Roar nodded. "Good. A certain someone was very insistent that we take all precautions. And you have plenty of leaves of Rezna's rest in case a storm comes while we're out here?"

Roar looked down at the vine coiled around her wrist and the bitter leaves that grew there. She was so tired of having to use them. Each time, they left a foul taste in her mouth and the weight of hopelessness on her chest.

"I know this is a lot," Jinx said, "but it's temporary. Just until we learn what we're dealing with here."

Roar dragged her bottom lip through her teeth and asked, "What if it's not? What if I'm never able to do what you do?"

"Very few people can do what I do. I'm special that way. You don't think my magic was awful in the beginning?" Jinx touched the side of her head where her hair was cut short. "I keep my hair like this as a reminder to myself that I am in control, because for a long time I wasn't. When I was six, a little boy in my town cut my hair to be cruel. Right there in front of everyone, it grew back. In fact, it kept growing, fast and out of control. Then that boy and a few other children started throwing rocks at me. And even though it hurt, I couldn't get my magic to stop them. I could not get it to do anything useful. It only made my hair grow down to my ankles. For weeks afterward, my mother had to cut my hair ten times a day. I think it was because deep down I was scared to leave my house and face the other children. And as long as my hair kept growing, I did not have to."

"Children can be so cruel."

"They're afraid of anything that's different. And I was too. But eventually, I stopped fearing my magic, stopped fearing what made me different, and my abilities became less volatile. I still had the occasional incident, but I was able to harness my magic to make my life better instead of worse."

"I can imagine earth magic is very useful."

"It is. But it took time to realize the full scope of my abilities. I thought at first that I could only do small things—making plants grow faster, fruit grow larger. It was not until later, until I *needed* my magic to be bigger, that I did anything more advanced. That's how Duke found me actually. My mother died when I was in my teens, and it wasn't safe to stay behind in the home we shared. So I set out on my own. My connection to the earth made it so that I could always find food. Or grow it if I needed it. And when storms came, I could coax the trees to provide shelter. But one day I happened to be traveling along the same road as Duke's crew when a firestorm hit. There were no trees, not that they would have done me any good. We were all more than a little shocked when the earth opened up to swallow me and the hunters both until the storm passed."

"That's *amazing.*"

Jinx's smile was so genuine and content. "It took me a while. But I know myself now. I know my worth. My mother always said that every kind of magic requires balance. You might see only the bad things now, but the good exists. You just have to be willing to find it."

Jinx went to the saddlebags on her horse and began rummaging for something. She pulled out a small crossbow with a long rope attached. Roar recognized it as the tool the hunters called their anchor. Jinx tied one end of the rope to Roar's harness, then attached both the crossbow and the small pouch that held excess rope to a metal loop on her hip.

The witch stood back and grinned. "*Now* you look like a hunter."

Roar's heartbeat picked up, excitement thrumming through her, and she smiled back.

"We'll start with something simple," Jinx said. "A thunderstorm. Your goal is to get to that line of earth I made. My goal is to stop you."

The hunter raised her eyebrow in a challenge, and Roar answered, "You're on."

She lined up and set her sights on the finish line as Jinx pulled a jar filled with dark clouds and swirling rain from her holster. "I'll keep the storm contained so it doesn't spread too far. You just be ready for whatever comes," Jinx told her.

Jinx pulled the cork and threw the bottle. Dark clouds began to rise from the jar like smoke as it flew through the air. When it hit the hard earth, the jar shattered and a gust of wind blew out in all directions. It picked up the sand, carrying it on the wind like a frothing, bloody wave. Roar covered her eyes, but she was too slow to close her mouth and she choked on the dust. Thunder cracked, so loud and close that the ground rumbled beneath Roar's feet. And then it began to rain, the clouds reaching out like groping hands to snatch up more of the sky. It took a few moments to remember that she was supposed to be running, and by the time she did the rain had reached her, pummeling her skin and making the sand clump to her boots.

She set off at a hard run, her eyes fixed on that line of earth that was her goal. So she did not see when the ground bulged up only a few strides ahead of her. She tripped and went sprawling, mud spattering across her face. She looked behind her, and beyond the newly formed mound of earth was a smiling Jinx, standing still in the pouring rain.

Roar shoved herself up off the ground, and her hands sunk into the sticky mud. She slid back on her knees, her entire front covered in muck. Her boots were caked and heavy when she stood and began to run again. This time she saw the next trap coming, and she hurdled over the rising barrier.

Wind and rain lashed at her face, and she had to squint to protect her eyes. Another test came at her only moments later, but this time it was no small bit of earth made to trip her. It was much bigger, and the ground actually did quake as a wall of dirt sprang up in front of her. She tried to stop, but her feet slid in the mud, and she turned just in time for her side to collide with the blockade. It was tall, but narrow, so she used her momentum to spin, letting her back roll against the wall, until she met open air again. The downpour had only gotten heavier, and clods of dirt had plopped onto her head and shoulders from the impact. She brushed off the bigger clumps and ran again.

She was not even halfway to the end of the course, and what had looked like a simple distance to cross now loomed out in front of her as an endless muddy sea. Her eyes stung, but she did not dare try to wipe them. The rest of her was far less clean.

She leaped and dodged and spun over a few more obstacles, and her breath ripped from her lungs in heaving gasps. She just had to get to the end. She could do that. She was three-fourths of the way there now.

When the earth shook again, she readied herself for another wall, but instead the ground began to split in front of her, a chasm opening that stretched all the way across the magic-made obstacle course. Roar jumped. But the rift kept widening while she was in the air, and soon the ledge was out of her reach. Her feet landed on the slope of the crevasse. She clawed at the ledge above her, trying to pull herself up, but the wet earth kept coming loose in her fingers. Her feet slid until she came to stop in a trench that had to be at least ten feet deep.

The water was already up to her ankles, and more was pouring in, sliding down the walls of the pit like a waterfall. She could try to find the end, but she imagined Jinx could just keep lengthening the trench forever if she wished. And it would not take long for the water to rise. She could wait until the water was high enough to carry her to the surface, but there were too many things that could go wrong. Better to attempt to climb out before all the walls turned to mud around her.

She looked around, but could find no footholds. So she decided to make her own. She pulled one of her knives from the holster on her back, and cut into the wall of the trench. She scraped until she got past the wet surface to the dry earth behind it. She made a notch just large and deep enough to put half her foot inside. She knew she would only have a limited amount of time to dig the next one before the first foothold became too saturated by the rain and crumbled beneath the pressure of her boot. So she grabbed a second blade with her left hand and took a steady breath.

Quickly she used her blades to scoop out the dirt that she had cut loose, then she lifted her leg and shoved the toe of her boot inside. She sunk the knife in her left hand into the wall high above her, and pulled herself up. She held her breath, hopeful, and when the wall did not collapse beneath her, she quickly carved out another notch in the dirt. She shoved her next foot in, and did it all over again. Two more notches put her high enough that she could see over the ledge.

The end of the course, that final low-lying earth wall that Jinx had made at the beginning, was ten, maybe fifteen paces ahead of her. The rain stopped just shy of that line, so unlike the rest of the land around them, that barrier stood dry and firm. Roar pulled the crossbow anchor from her hip and aimed it at that wall. She pulled the trigger just as the footholds that held her up gave way. She slid down the wall in a splash of water and mud, the rope attached to the arrow uncoiling fast from the pouch at her hip. When the flight of the rope halted, she gave it a tentative tug. It held.

She had no idea if she'd hit the wall; she fell before she could see if it made contact, but she hoped that whatever it hit was strong enough to hold her weight. She sheathed one of her knives, keeping the other to sink in the wall and give her added leverage if she needed it, then she used the rope and began to climb.

When she made it back to the ledge again, she heaved herself up by the rope one final time. Her belly scraped over the edge of the trench as she pulled herself free. She crawled first on her hands and knees, then scrambled to stand and began to sprint as hard as she could for that ending line. She expected another obstacle, another test, but nothing came. And when she cleared that final hurdle of the wall with a jump, she landed in a patch of dry, red sand, untouched by Jinx's storm. She collapsed onto her knees, rolled onto her back, and laughed.

The sand stuck to her muddy clothes and skin, but she did not care. That was . . . *amazing*. She laughed again, louder, the sound echoing out across the land.

Jinx appeared over her a few moments later, the sun haloing around her head, and Roar realized the storm was already gone—dark clouds had disappeared to reveal blue once more.

The witch crossed her arms over her chest and nodded. "That was pretty impressive . . . *novie*."

Treat others with kindness. For you do not know which souls will visit you again as storms rather than men.

—*The Book of the Sacred Souls*

19

The inside of the blacksmith's shop was sweltering. Locke and Ransom had both stripped off all their gear except their Stormheart belts. They were both damp with sweat. The forge roared, the blacksmith's thin apprentice pumping the bellows as sparks mounted their daring escapes from the flame. Inside the blaze was the half-finished tank for the back of the Rock. They didn't tell the blacksmith that the tank would hold storm magic, and luckily the man did not ask.

The metal glowed bright as the blacksmith set it on the anvil, and all three of them set about shaping the thing with small hammers while the young apprentice kept at the bellows. They had worked on the tank with huge sledges this morning, battering a large piece of iron until it slowly began to take shape. They were finishing up one rounded side today, and tomorrow would do the other and fit them together, and then they'd need one or two more days to install it in the Rock and repair the surrounding frame.

They'd worked straight through lunch, so by the time the blacksmith called it a day and locked up his shop, Locke and Ransom were ready to get back to the inn. Locke needed to know that Roar and Jinx made it home safely.

"Thinking about her again?" Ransom asked, as they turned on to the road where their inn was located. Locke shot his friend an annoyed look. He *was* technically thinking about Roar, but not in the way Ransom's smug grin implied.

"I was thinking that I'll feel better when the Rock is fixed, and we can get back to normal."

"I don't think *normal* is what you are ready to get back to."

Locke rolled his eyes. "Ease off, would you?"

"Why would I do that? I never realized how much fun it would be to see you twisted into knots over a girl."

"Oh? I imagine it's about as enjoyable as seeing you pine over Jinx forever."

Ransom shrugged, reaching up to wipe sweat from his brow with his forearm. "I'm numb to that particular prod now. So have at it."

"Numb. Really?"

"I have had two years to get used to it."

"Some might say you have had two years to grow a spine and say something."

"It's better this way. She is too young to settle down, and the moment she was mine, I would want to lock her away in some Stormling city and never let her set foot in the wilds again."

"Which would make her insane. I'd give it a month before she started an earthquake in the middle of your house."

"Exactly. I don't know why you're laughing. Your girl might not be able to start earthquakes, but she won't let you keep her out of the action either."

Locke cringed. "You didn't see her when that thunderstorm hit. I felt like my heart had been ripped out of my chest and dropped in the dirt just *watching* her. There is nothing worse than seeing her cry, but *that* . . . that was a great deal more than crying." Belatedly, he tacked on, "And she's not *my* girl."

The clop of horses' hooves drew their attention to the road ahead. Locke recognized Jinx first as she climbed from her horse and tied it up outside the inn. Beside her he guessed was Roar, but she was covered in drying mud—it was plastered on her clothes and smeared across her cheeks and forehead.

When they were within hearing distance, Locke called, "What did Jinx do—throw you into a mudslide?"

Roar looked up from the post where she'd been tying her horse with the widest smile he had ever seen her give. The sight of her, even when filthy, made him feel like she'd punched a hole through his chest and then decided to stay and stake her claim, vital organs pushed aside to make room. She called out his name and then began running toward him at full speed.

"Not your girl, huh?" Ransom said.

A few seconds later Roar slammed into his body, knocking him back a few steps. He chuckled, and her face pressed into his chest, arms winding about his middle. She smeared mud everywhere she touched. He pretended to complain, but she laughed and wiped more muck on him on purpose.

"I take it today went well?"

She stepped back to grin up at him, and he beat back the urge to drag her into his arms for just a few more moments.

"It was wonderful. I mean . . . exhausting and a little messy." She looked down at her dirty clothes and laughed. "But just . . . perfect. Exactly what I needed."

He looked over her head at an approaching Jinx and said, "She's never this happy after any of our training sessions. You must not be pushing her hard enough."

Roar just collected a little more mud from her clothes and smeared it on his cheek. When he lunged like he was going to retaliate, she squeaked and bolted toward Jinx.

"Quick. Do one of those wall things," she said to Jinx, and the witch laughed.

Locke lifted his brows in question and Jinx said, "I put her through an earth-magic obstacle course during a thunderstorm. She went through it twice as fast as Bait."

The corners of Locke's mouth twitched up. "Of course she did." Roar smiled widely, and their eyes met. Hers were soft, and he could die a happy man if she kept looking at him like that. So of course his stupid mouth had to tack on, "Because I trained her."

She rolled her eyes, and said, "I think I learned more from Jinx in one day than I have from you in several weeks."

"Is that so?"

"I think it might be."

He stalked a little closer, passing by Jinx, and said to Roar, "How long did it take you to go through the obstacle course?"

"No more than a quarter of a bell."

He whistled. "That's good. But if you're caught in a storm you might need to last longer than a quarter of a bell."

"I can."

"You sure?"

"Of course. Jinx is an excellent teacher."

A laugh rumbled up in his chest. He had forgotten how much fun it was to play with her. Since that day they'd wrestled in the river, he had done his best to avoid it, but no more. "We'll see just how much you can handle when *I'm* training you again."

Roar hesitated, the playful spell breaking as her head tilted to the side. "You are not passing me off to Jinx permanently?"

He felt like that question knocked the air out of him. "Would you *rather* stay with her?" Her eyes flicked behind him, and he turned to look for Jinx, but both she and Ransom were no longer there. They must have gone inside, leaving Locke and Roar in the street as twilight fell. "Would you?" he asked again. "I would not hold it against you. Jinx is good. She would be good for you."

"If you don't *mind* working with me, I like the way you . . . push me." He knew she was talking about training, but that did not stop the heavy thump of his heart against his rib cage. She continued: "I mean, it would be nice to still work with Jinx on occasion. Her earth magic makes for a really interesting challenge. But . . . I don't want to have any doubts the first time I stand in front of a storm's heart. And I think my best chance to do that is with you."

"Even though we argue?"

Her mouth twitched. "Even though we argue."

Nova smelled the sweet scent of wildflowers, and a breeze tickled through her hair. The earth was warm beneath her bare feet and the sun baked her skin until sweat beaded along the back of her neck. She should go inside or her skin would burn. She swallowed, and sweat tracked from her forehead over her cheeks.

Can't burn.

Cool. Think cool thoughts.

A breeze. The shower of rain upon her skin. Dark shadows.

No, not shadows either. Light. Think of light.

Sweat burned in her eyes, and her hands shook with the effort of pretending.

Can't burn, Nova. Don't. Burn.

Metal clanged, pulling her out of her reverie and into the stifling hot cell. The door opened just enough for a tray of food to be slid inside, then it was locked once more. She turned back to the window, too hot to care about the hunger gnawing in her belly. It had turned cold outside. She knew that. But in this tiny stone cell with one door and one window, she felt like she was cellmates with the sun. There was too much magic inside her. It wanted out.

"Don't burn," she mumbled under her breath. Flame had never harmed her skin, but she did not know what would happen if her magic got loose, if it raged out of control. Could she die by fire if it consumed her?

She stood on her charred cot and grabbed hold of the window's bars. She could just barely feel the breeze from outside. She sucked down tendrils of cold air like it was water and she was dying of thirst. She had to get control. She grabbed one of the empty water buckets, turned it upside down on the bed, and used it to get closer to the window, where the air from outside could hit her whole face.

But when she looked out over her city, she gasped.

The Pavanian flags that normally flew around the palace and city walls were gone. And in there place, the blue flags of the Locke family snapped in the wind.

Tears gathered in her eyes and a cry stuck in her throat. That was it then. She knew Cassius said that the queen was despondent, but Nova had harbored a secret hope that when the queen was well again, when she realized what had been happening to Nova, she would intervene and set her free.

But if the Lockes had taken over, the queen needed an intervention of her own. If she still lived.

Roar came home from her second day of training with Jinx just as exhilarated as the first. Today she'd had to complete another obstacle course, but this time in a sandstorm. She had barely been able to see or breathe, and she resolved that as long as they were in the desert, she was going to keep a scarf around her neck for use in such emergencies.

In her room, she removed the leather harness, laying it on the floor by her bed. She moved to the water basin in the corner to wash the sand from her face and arms. She pulled off the various necklaces she wore—crystal, firestorm powder, and the twister ring—and shoved them in her pocket. After she splashed her face with water, she heard a commotion in the hallway—a crash and yelling. She groped for a towel and quickly wiped the water from her eyes. There was a startled cry toward the front of the inn, and a harsh male voice yelled, "Quiet!"

Several dozen feet stomped down the hall, breaking off into smaller groups. There was a succession of loud crashes, one after the other. She darted for the harness that held her weapons at the same time her door burst open, wood splintering and flying through the air.

Several men rushed inside, and one kicked the hand she had on her harness. The impact reverberated painfully up her wrist, and several knives clanked as they scattered over the floor. The man snatched her still-aching wrist, twisting it behind her back, and pushed her toward the center of the room. The other two began ransacking the place, tearing the mattress off her bed, emptying her bags, tipping over furniture.

"Who do we have here?"

The man who held her had black, short-cropped hair and an uneven smile that sent shivers down her spine. He reached out his other hand to finger a strand of her hair, and she jerked away. He laughed. Her hours spent sparring with Taven rushed back in a jumble of information. She jerked the hand he held up above her head, making him follow and opening him up. Then she swung fast and hard with her free hand. It was her weaker arm, so the hit wasn't as hard or as clean as she would have liked, but his head snapped to the side and he stumbled back.

That was when she looked at what he was wearing. What they were *all* wearing. Familiar blue military uniforms. These were *Locke* soldiers. She backed away toward the door, but another soldier caught her from behind, pinning her arms at her side. He was heavyset and smelled of sweat and dust.

"Look at that," he said, his mouth too close to her ear. "I think we found us our prize."

Her heartbeat screamed in her ears and her chest grew tight with fear. They knew. They'd come for her. Oh gods, had they found the other hunters? What had they done to them?

The one with the unsettling smile approached, rubbing at the reddened spot on his cheek from her fist. His hand shot forward, gripping her jaw hard and tilting her head back so that he could see her face.

"Not her," said a third man still searching the room. But the soldier who held her face did not loosen his grip.

"I know that, Hamish. But we've been searching for weeks. The prince's bride is long gone, but he won't call us back. Surely we deserve a *reward* for our dedicated service."

They did not know who she was. Thank the skies.

But they *were* searching for her. She had expected Pavanian soldiers, but apparently Cassius had the Locke military searching for her as well. If they had come from the south and the Pavanian soldiers from the north, the land was likely to be teeming with soldiers.

"What's your name, sweet?"

She couldn't tell them Roar. The hunters might not have caught on to the similarity with her real name, but these men were more likely to be suspicious. Her mouth was puckered from his grip, but she spat out "Nova" with as much force as she could.

He laughed and gestured to the weapons she had lunged for before.

"Think you're some kind of warrior, *Nova*?"

"Galren," the third man, Hamish, snapped. "We don't have time for this."

"Oh, I don't think it will take long." His hand slid from her jaw, down her neck, trailing toward the curve of her breast. "She might dress like a man. But I don't think the little woman will put up much of a fight. Will you?"

Galren was *very* wrong. She jerked her head back, slamming it against the forehead of the man who held her from behind. His arms dropped, and she spun, sweeping her foot beneath Galren's legs in front of her. He went down hard, but when she tried to go for her knives again, he snatched at her ankles, and then she was the one sprawling on the floor. She kicked out, her boot connecting with something hard.

She scrambled across the floor toward her knives and found one as the heavyset man recovered and grabbed her legs. Her hand slid over the blade first, but she gripped it tightly, uncaring about the cuts to her fingers. The soldier yanked her backward, and Roar screamed, flailing her legs. The knife was slick with her own blood, but she managed to get her hand on the hilt and swung it back at the soldier, catching him in the forearm and freeing her legs. The momentary reprieve allowed her to look backward, and she saw Galren stalking toward her, his cheek split and bleeding from what must have been her boot. She didn't think, only acted, and she sent the knife flying. It slammed into his thigh in a spot she knew would bleed a lot and quickly. As blood poured from his wound, and the other two soldiers stared in shock, the broken door to her room flew back on its hinges again.

"Don't touch her." The growl came from Locke as Ransom and Jinx entered the room behind him.

Hamish rushed to Galren as he stumbled, his hand going to the knife in his thigh. The heavyset soldier growled, "What are you going to do about it? She attacked a member of the Locke military."

Locke's eyes went ice-cold. "I don't like soldiers. Especially not from Locke. I watched my sister swing from a noose in Duvrall square thanks to pigs like you. And nothing would bring me more pleasure than gutting each and every one of you. If you even look at her again, I'll *take my time*."

Galren snorted, but his face had grown pale. His uniform was drenched with blood, and his feet slipped in the pool of it on the floor. He rasped, "We've over a hundred soldiers in this town. You would never make it out of this room alive."

"Maybe not," Ransom said, his bulky arms crossed over his broad chest. "But neither will you if you don't get that bleeding to stop. And your two friends would be dead before anyone even knew to come running."

"Easy," Hamish said, one hand outstretched. He'd been the one to halfheartedly try to rein in Galren. "We're not looking to start anything. We're here searching for a kidnapped princess."

Locke growled, "The only woman I see in trouble here was put in danger by *your* men. And considering you are not in your own territory, I don't think anyone in this town would fault me for killing you."

"We'll leave," Hamish said. "We've done what we came for. There's still more of the town to search."

Hamish grabbed Galren by the back of his collar, tugging him toward the door. He stumbled, grown weak from blood loss. Roar fought the strong impulse to find another knife and send it into the soldier's back. Just when she had started to get her confidence back, that monster had made her feel helpless all over again. And unlike a storm, he could be hurt by a knife. She *wanted* to hurt him.

But then all three soldiers pushed past the hunters and out of the room.

Locke was by her side a moment later, his hands cupping her face. She kept her eyes down because she didn't want to see the look Locke wore. It didn't matter if she saw rage or pity there—both would make her feel inadequate.

She shoved her hand in her pocket to find her brother's Stormheart ring. Usually it calmed her. She just felt so *angry* and useless. Touching the Stormheart gave her some measure of peace. Not enough, but some. It eased the desire to go after those men and unleash the rage pounding through her.

One of Locke's hands left her face to trail down her arm. "Let me see your hand," he said.

Roar left the ring in her pocket and brought up her sliced hand for him to see. Jinx was behind him, offering up a handkerchief that he quickly wrapped around her fingers, squeezing to stop the bleeding.

"Roar, look at me." She didn't. She *couldn't*.

Before he could ask again, the crystal in her pocket went hot and a horn blared. Locke cursed and Ransom said, "Storm?"

"Yes." That was Duke. She wasn't sure whether he got here before or after the soldiers left. She hoped it was after.

"Let the soldiers handle it," Locke growled.

Duke sighed. "They won't care at all for this town. Unless it directly threatens them, they're unlikely to do anything."

With her eyes still cast down, she saw Jinx's small feet move toward the door, followed by Ransom's. When they were both gone, Duke said, "I'll stay with her."

"No," Locke growled. "I will."

Duke sighed. "Locke—"

"Go," Roar whispered, finally meeting his eyes.

His hand squeezed around her wrapped fingers. "You want me to leave?"

"I want the others to be safe, and the best way for that to happen is if you're there with them."

"I promise I won't leave her side," Duke said.

"I'll be back," Locke whispered, his head dipping toward her ear. "And then it will be me who won't leave your side."

Roar did not watch him go, an act she immediately regretted when she realized she had no idea what kind of storm was out there waiting for him.

The hunters only had to leave the inn to see the reason for the siren. It was another twister, menacingly dark and large, and it was eating up ground at such a fast pace that it might hit the edge of the village before they could get close.

Locke cursed. He looked to Ransom, and his friend's eyes were grim.

"Sly," Locke said, "start pulling wind away from the storm. Try to dissolve the updraft powering that thing."

"Jinx—"

The witch didn't even wait for Locke to give her instructions, she spouted off her own plan. "I'll reinforce the wall in case the town gets hit. And I'll start cooling down the earth. That should weaken the base."

"Good," Locke replied. "Ransom?"

"I've got your back." Together they took off down the road after Jinx and Sly, Bait hard on their heels.

"What can I do?" the boy asked. He was still enough of a novice that he couldn't do much. His only affinity was rainstorm. Locke's gut told him to send the boy back to the inn to stay with Duke, but one look at Bait's face told Locke that was not an order with which Bait would comply. So he gave Bait the only job he could. "We might not be able to take that thing down before it hits the village. You start hitting doors near the north end and evacuating as many people as you can."

"Got it."

He took off, and Locke hoped he wouldn't regret sending him right into danger. But there wasn't time to second-guess it now.

As they neared, he got a clearer picture of the mammoth twister. Rain poured around it, swirling with the wind and debris and sand, the latter of which gave the twister an ominous bloodred color. About a hundred paces past the wall, a line of soldiers stood in the twister's way. They were completely still, not running. None of them appeared to be working any Stormling powers.

"Mesmerized," Jinx called from up ahead of him.

Locke cursed and called back, "Strengthen your mental shields. It has to be potent if it got all those soldiers. If any one of us gets mesmerized, grab whoever it is and retreat toward the inn. Better part of the town get destroyed than us." As he spoke the words, the twister's winds reached the first line of soldiers, and they were swept up like pebbles into the churning vortex.

Behind them, more soldiers were retreating; a few appeared to be trying their best to fight the storm, but whatever magic they had was not enough. Locke could feel the storm's pull. Even this far away, it was trying to ensnare his mind. But he was prepared.

He could not say the same for the next group of soldiers who were picked up and swallowed into the maelstrom. There were fewer than ten soldiers remaining outside the walls, and realistically, he imagined most of those would be taken out too.

"Stop!" The others pulled up at his yell. "We make our stand here."

They were fifty paces from the wall now. They didn't have long before they would be in danger from flying debris. The ground trembled beneath their feet, rippling until sand drew up around the village wall, adding extra bracing.

"Good girl," Ransom shouted to Jinx.

Locke felt a wave of cool air sweep up his calves. Jinx didn't look at the others as she focused on pushing that air out toward the twister. But she called back to Ransom, "Talk to me like I'm a dog again, and I might just bite!"

Locke plucked the black Stormheart from his belt. A rush of wind blew past his face, Sly sucking air away from the storm. He used his magic to search out the edges of the twister. It was huge, and it roiled with magic so fierce that it bucked his hold.

With a twister affinity, he should have been able to take hold of the storm, surrounding it with his magic and forcing it into submission. He could suffocate it, force it back into the sky, or just break it apart. He didn't have to break it apart from the inside like he did when they hunted. So it should have been easier.

But this was by far the fiercest twister he had ever faced. Each time he thought he got hold of it, a smaller funnel would push out from the larger one, challenging his grip.

He heard screams—the remaining soldiers, he guessed—but he could not spare even a flicker of concentration. The earth rumbled and a series of thunderous booms sounded. In his peripheral vision he saw roofs tearing from buildings and walls crumbling under the force of the outer winds.

Finally, he locked his magic around the lower half of the storm. The cool air coming off the earth had weakened the bottom of the storm, and it began to skip, lifting off the earth, only to touch down again a few moments later. He focused on pushing his magic up the column, surrounding it all. It had begun to narrow, no doubt due to a dwindling updraft thanks to Sly's work.

It was weakening, and in one great lunge, his magic swallowed up the rest of the storm. He could sense Ransom's magic layering over his, adding their strength together. Locke took a deep breath and pushed every bit of power he had at the storm, crushing it beneath his magic like a clod of dirt in his hands. Tension eased from his spine as he felt the storm give against his power. It thinned and wobbled, lifting off the ground and pulling back toward the sky—almost completely dissolved.

He eased off, but just before the twister disappeared completely, he felt one final lash of magic at his mind, crashing into his mental barriers. He fell to his knees, clutching his head, holding tight to his control. The assault lasted only for a moment, and then it was gone with the rest of the storm.

Calibah will not bend to tyranny, even if it comes from a storm rather than a king.

—*The Tale of Lord Finneus Wolfram*

20

Duke and Roar began righting the room in silence. They returned the mattress to the bed, and picked up overturned furniture. Roar knelt by her bags, folding her clothes and putting them back inside. She picked up her copy of *The Tale of Lord Finneus Wolfram*. The binding was loose and a few pages fluttered to the floor. She wanted to cry, but no tears came. Instead she just felt . . . tired.

And she could hardly worry about mere possessions when the winds were screaming outside, an ominous rumble shaking the walls. She was on edge, waiting for the storm to draw close enough that she felt its presence, waiting for the invasion of emotions that weren't hers.

"They'll be fine," Duke told her, after she spent too long sitting still, her eyes fixed on the window. "I'm more concerned with how you are."

"Me? I'm fine. I'm always fine."

"Roar. I want you to know that you can talk to me."

"I know I can."

"The man who sold me Stormhearts in the market in Pavan, the man you *know* . . . he's a Stormling, isn't he?"

She stilled, then fled to the water basin to clean off the blood smeared over her skin. "I don't know."

"I assure you, Roar, that I am the last person who will judge you for wanting to leave behind that kind of life. If you have Stormling ancestry, it could help us understand the way you react to storms."

"I am no Stormling," she said truthfully.

"You are no girl from the streets either."

She whirled back to face him. "What does it matter? All the hunters had lives before joining the crew. It's in the past."

"Is it truly in the past for you?"

She thought back to the soldiers. Would there be more? How many were searching for her? Could she possibly hope to go undetected by them all? "For now."

"Just know you don't have to keep carrying all those secrets alone, and the past has a way of holding on to us, even when we want to let it go."

Duke helped bandage her cuts, the two of them silent through the long process. Eventually the winds died down outside, and the nervous tossing of her stomach eased. The others were safe. They had to be.

But how long would that remain true while she stayed with them?

"Perhaps we should turn our route back toward Taraanar," she said, her voice tentative. "The Locke soldiers . . . they said they were searching the southern regions for their missing princess. It might be better to avoid them."

Duke's green eyes fixed on her, but she did not meet his gaze. She knew how perceptive the man was, and that she had just given him the key to her identity. But she did not know what else to do. She would rather risk herself than the other hunters.

He hummed and scratched at his beard and said, "I'm sure that could be arranged. We'll have to talk to your Locke."

"He's not my Locke."

She didn't know what he was. How could she possibly decide what she wanted from him when she did not even know what she wanted from herself? With him, there was no crown making her appear more than she was. There were no rumors of her magical skill to make her seem more desirable. He had seen her covered in blood, dissolved into tears, taken over by rage, and frozen by fear. He had seen each and every weakness she had, and somehow, he managed to make her feel . . . strong. If the skies made her feel small, then Locke made her feel big enough to face whatever waited for her up there.

But she was *still* Aurora, no matter how much she was Roar.

If she accomplished her goals, if she returned home with Stormhearts that answered to her touch, would her mother allow her to choose her own future? Could a princess choose a hunter as her prince?

As soon as Locke had checked on each of his teammates, he was running back for the inn. He knew the town had sustained significant damages, and there had been significant loss of life, though it was difficult to feel any sense of loss for the soldiers after what he had walked in on with Roar.

He was panting by the time he fell through the broken doorway to Roar's room. The furniture had been righted, and her belongings put away, but pools of blood still stained the floor. The water basin in the corner was a vivid red, and Roar sat silently on her bed, her hand now properly bandaged.

Her whole body was tense, and he wanted to scoop her up into his arms and hide her away from the world. Instead he grabbed a towel and began mopping up the blood. Duke got up to help, and he quietly filled Locke in on her condition. She had several cuts—one across the fatty part of her palm and the others around the first joint in her fingers.

When the room was as clean as it was going to get without scrubbing the floors, Duke left to assess the damage from the storm, and Roar finally looked at Locke. Her jaw was tight, and her nostrils flared with strong, slow breaths. He focused on keeping his expression blank. She said, "Is everyone okay?"

"Yes."

"Shouldn't you be with the other hunters? Or talking to the minister or—"

He shook his head and said, "I'm not leaving you."

"I want to be alone. Please."

"Then I'll sit outside your door."

"My door that's broken and hanging off its hinges? Yes, that will really give the illusion of solitude."

She was angry, and he didn't blame her. He still wasn't sure how he'd let those men leave the room without sinking his blade into each and every one of them. It had taken a monumental amount of control, and in the end it was only the thought that he did not want to put her in more danger that held him back.

When he did not budge, she insisted, "I'm fine." He had lost count of the number of times he had heard her utter those words. And he had never believed them less than he did now. Her fists were clenched at her sides, and her voice grated as if her throat had been stripped raw.

"Roar—"

"I mean it," she snapped. "*Please* just leave."

So quickly that he might have imagined it, her eyes dropped to his mouth and then she whirled away, sitting on the bed facing away from him. Even though it went against everything his instincts told him, he left the room and even took a few steps down the hall out of sight before he sank down against the wall. He propped his elbows on his knees and buried his head in his hands. He tried to still his thoughts and drain his anger.

Listen.

That was all he needed to do. Just exist and listen in case she needed him. He was not sure how long passed, but it felt far too long. Finally he heard her call, "Locke?"

He called back, "I'm here."

She was silent for a long time, then said, "I'm sorry about your sister."

A breath rattled in his chest and his head thudded back against the wall behind him. "Thanks, princess."

She made a noise that sounded somewhere between a laugh and a sob. Far too close to the latter for his comfort.

"Sorry. *Roar.*"

"It's fine. I don't think I care anymore."

He hated not being able to see her face. Especially when her voice sounded so hollow. He heard shuffling in her room, and she sounded closer when she spoke.

"Soldiers did that to her?"

He rubbed a hand over his mouth. He did not talk about this ever. But he'd rather split open his chest than suffer through her silence, so he answered, "On orders. But yes."

"On orders from whom?"

"The king, I suppose. She was just one of thirty that day."

He heard her gasp. "*Thirty?* Was that . . . common?"

"Common enough. Locke isn't like Pavan. The weather there is even more brutal because of the sea. And the jungles surrounding the city make it a hard place to leave. The people who live there are desperate, and desperate people don't always think about consequences. And there were consequences for almost everything in Locke."

"Your sister . . . was *that* a consequence?"

He scrubbed his fingers through his hair and tried to deaden his heart for the rest of the tale. "I told you I was young when my parents died. They died during a hurricane. It was just my sister and me left, and she was five years older than me. We weren't prepared to fend for ourselves. Begging and the few belongings we had left from our parents kept us alive for a couple of months, but that ran out fast, especially after the crown seized the house and all our belongings. I met a man who gave me a gold coin to be his lookout and alert him if I saw any guards. I don't know what he did while I kept watch. I did not ask. I wanted the coin too badly. He said I did good and if I wanted to make more I could find him at a tavern not too far from the abandoned building where my sister and I slept. That man was the first person to introduce me to the black market.

"It wasn't like the one in Pavan. There were too many guards, too much danger to keep the market in one place. So, it rotated around the city. He paid me and a few other boys to keep watch. My sister begged me to stop. She insisted we would find another way, even when the few coins I brought home were barely enough to clothe and feed us. She begged on the streets and did odd jobs for anyone who would have her, but I brought home more from one night than she could bring home from a week of working herself ragged. So I kept going back. One night, she followed me, tried to convince me to come home with her. We fought, and I sent her off. I was distracted, so I didn't notice the guards until it was too late.

"The military raided the market, and I barely got away, hiding behind a cart until I could squeeze through the crowds and run. They rounded up everyone they could get their hands on. Even innocent bystanders who just happened to be in the wrong place at the wrong time. I ran all the way back home, but at dawn when my sister still had not come home, I knew something was wrong. I got to the square just in time to see them lining everyone up. I was so small, I had to climb up the gutter of a building to see. She was eleven, and they hung her there with mercenaries and thieves and men that she would have been scared to stand beside, let alone spend her last moments with. I don't remember much. But at one point, I think she saw me in the crowd. Tears were streaking down her face, but she did not make a noise. She smiled at me. One of those, supposed to be reassuring, everything-will-be-okay kind of smiles. And that's all I remember. I lied before. I don't recall the moment it happened. Maybe I looked away or ran. Or maybe I've just blocked the memory. But she died that day. Because I dragged her into something dangerous."

Roar did not answer, and he could not blame her. It was a depressing story, not exactly the kind of thing you say to cheer someone up. When he looked up, she was standing in the doorway.

She asked, "Is that why you never took on any apprentices?" His brows lifted. "Duke told me."

Of course he did. "That's part of it, yes. I entered this life because I had no other choice. I hated that city. I hated the streets and the guards, most of whom were exactly like those men we just encountered. I hated the royals and the people who cowered in their homes rather than speaking out. I hated everything. And Duke offered me the chance to get out, so I took it and never looked back. Honestly, I think I was hoping I would die. That it would just end. I had lost my parents and my sister, and for some reason, despite ample opportunity, I could not seem to follow them. Before Duke found me, I was becoming more and more reckless with my behavior in the black market, associating with dangerous men, taking risky jobs that were bound to go wrong; but no matter what kind of peril I threw myself into, I always seemed to crawl out of it still breathing. Still do, I guess. I've grown to love this life, but I still would not recommend it to anyone who has another option."

She moved closer, and then sat beside him with her legs crossed.

She ran her hands over the smooth fabric of her pants, from her knees to her ankles and back again. With her head down she asked, "Is that why you fought to keep me from joining?"

He swallowed. And there was more emotion in his voice than he wanted there to be when he said, "I would fight it still if I thought it would work. But I find now that I am loath to part with you. I'm sorry for all the times I pushed you away, for all the times I made you angry. It's only, after I met you . . . for the first time in a very long time, I had no desire to throw myself into death's path because I could, to see if I could survive. Because death meant leaving you, and that was unthinkable. *Is* unthinkable. Feeling this way, the way I do about you, Roar, it's scarier than any storm I've ever faced."

She made a soft, hurt sound and burrowed closer to his side. She turned her face against his shoulder, and he felt the dampness on her cheeks. He let his hand fall to her uninjured hand resting on her knee. He would have been content just to touch, but she laced their fingers together, squeezing tightly.

"Why go by *Locke* if you hated it so much?"

He sighed and huffed out a halfhearted laugh. "You are determined to make me spill all my secrets, aren't you?"

She pulled away, eyes wide and head shaking, and he immediately wished he had never opened his mouth. She said, "No. Not at all. You don't have to—"

He pulled her back against him and said, "My secrets are yours. Every one of them." She swallowed, and the answer didn't please her as much as he thought it would. He continued: "When Duke took me on, I did not remember my real name. It had been so long since someone used it. Mostly I just got called kid or boy. There was a hunter on the crew then named Bear. He was tall and skinny and bald, not a speck of hair on his face. To this day, I still don't know how he got the name Bear. Anyway, he got tired of calling me boy and started calling me Locke, since that's where they picked me up. I was too young and intimidated to ask for a different name, so I let it go. It was maddening at first, but eventually . . . I did not mind it so much. It was a reminder of where I came from and the mistakes I made. A reminder to do better in the future."

"*Oh.* Poor thing."

He frowned. "You don't have to feel sorry for me. That's not why I told you any of this."

"I don't feel sorry for you. I feel sorry for that little boy who lost everything, including his name."

When she leaned her head against his shoulder, her cheek against his biceps, he did not feel like someone who had lost everything.

"Give me something else to call you," she murmured. "The name Locke doesn't deserve you."

"I would accept handsome, strong, superior male specimen—"

She pushed him hard enough to send him sprawling over onto his side. But she was laughing. And she could push him as many times as she wanted if he could hear that.

"I'm serious. You've never thought of going by something else? You could choose anything."

He levered himself back up to sit beside her, then shrugged. "I've been Locke for nearly half my life."

"And you don't think everyone who knows you would gladly call you something else if it was what you wanted?"

"There's no point. None of us use our real names."

"So choose another nickname."

"I can't choose my own nickname."

"Fine, I'll choose one."

He smiled. "Really? Let's hear it then."

"Not right now. That's too much pressure. I need time to think and choose the best option."

"My whole future is in your hands here, my very identity."

She laughed. "Thank you, that certainly reduces the responsibility," she said and leaned her head back onto his shoulder.

They were still leaning on each other, hands entwined, when the others came back in. He expected her to pull away, but instead she leaned in a little closer, held his hand a little tighter. Ransom's expression was grim as he approached, and Locke asked, "How bad?"

"It got the whole north wall and about two dozen homes. And . . . all the soldiers. Minister Vareeth has people searching the rubble to see if there were any more casualties. He was very grateful for our service. He offered to let us stay as long as we needed."

"Well, that's good at least."

Ransom said, "Did any of you think this storm was more sentient than most? At the end, when we had already broken it up, it lashed out with magic one last time, trying to mesmerize me. It might have had me if I'd been distracted or injured."

"I felt it too," Locke said. "Struck hard enough to send me to my knees." Roar leaned closer to him, her bandaged hand sneaking up to lie on his thigh. "So from now we don't let our guards down for even a moment while we hunt. I didn't like the feel of this one. It was nearly more than we could handle."

"Yes, sir," Bait said with one of his playful salutes.

Roar rested her chin on Locke's shoulder, and her breath played across his neck. He did not think she had any clue just how much power she wielded over him.

"We could call you captain," she suggested.

He turned his head slightly and it brought their foreheads close together, their mouths nearly touching. "Pass," he said.

"General? Sargeant?"

He was smiling. He couldn't help himself. He didn't even care when Jinx let out a suggestive whistle.

"I told the innkeeper we would help set this place to rights. As much as we can anyway," Duke chimed in.

Sighing, Locke climbed to his feet and held out a hand for Roar. She took it without any argument. "Let's get to it then."

"Are you mad?" Cassius yelled, storming into his father's rooms. The man was surrounded by a sea of food and women, and he smiled up at his son without a care. "You switched the flags? You understand we will have a mutiny on our hands, don't you?"

"I have men rounding up dissenters as we speak."

"What men?"

The king chuckled darkly. "*My* men. Did you think they would all remain loyal as you sent their brothers off to die in search of your whore? After the first group of malcontents are hung from the palace walls, I doubt we will have many more."

"It didn't have to be this way. With a little more time, they would have accepted us willingly. This will only foster rebellion."

"*Now* is the time to cement your position, before any of the nobles think to try it themselves. Your brother understands. He has decided to orchestrate the hangings himself. And yet my ruthless eldest son has gone soft," he spat.

Cassius ground his teeth. He supposed his father was letting go of all pretenses now, even the lie that Casimir was his firstborn. *Of course,* Mir was diving at the chance to win his father's approval. Pretending to be the eldest over the last few weeks had gone to his head. He'd gotten a taste of power and, like all his family, he craved more.

"Do you think I did not know your plan, boy? To get rid of me once you married the princess? You forget, I taught you how to lie, taught you to deceive. I know what my son looks like when he's planning a betrayal. And I'll not have another kingdom stolen from me."

A chasm opened up in Cassius's chest, a horrible thought occurring to him now. "You didn't . . . did *you* have her kidnapped?"

The king barked a laugh, and one of the girls beside him flinched. "I should have. It was a good ploy. But, no . . . the skies offered me that gift. I'm merely taking advantage."

"And when the skies turn to fire at the Stormlord's arrival? When the walls crumble under crushing winds? When twisters bombard us from every direction? What then?"

"All the more reason to do away with the farce now and enjoy ourselves while we can."

"You are *mad*. The roads are teeming with remnants, all fleeing destroyed wildlands towns. He's picking them off one by one as he comes for us, and you are making enemies of the Pavan soldiers when we should be banding together to fight him."

"That can be your job. Since you seem to care so much. Perhaps now you'll reconsider all the soldiers you're sending off to die in search of a princess we no longer need."

On the fifth day in Toleme, Locke and Ransom completed the last of the repairs to the Rock. They were sweaty and covered in soot, but it was done. They'd thanked the town's blacksmith, paid him for his help, and retrieved horses to move the Rock to the inn. Even after the town had seen them combat that twister, they did not want to draw more attention by letting them see what the Rock could do.

Back at the inn, Locke worked with Ransom to return the various supplies to the Rock that they'd taken out before the repairs. Jinx and Roar returned from another training session as they worked, and Locke was glad to see Roar looking eager and excited once more.

Roar had continued to give blood sacrifices each morning and without fail, skyfire streaked across the sky each time. It had never shown any sign of developing into a storm beyond that, and neither he nor Duke had any clue why it kept happening, but he would be relieved when it was no longer an issue.

Roar ran her hand along the newly crafted exterior of the back of the Rock. "It really is such an incredible invention."

"That's all Locke," Ransom said, pointing a thumb over his shoulder at him.

"And Duke," Locke replied. "I thought we needed something more reliable than horses to ride into a storm, but faster than our own feet. Duke was the one to design most of the mechanics, I just found a way to bring it to life."

"It's incredible," she said. "It could revolutionize travel through the wilds."

"Except that it runs on illegal magic."

She frowned. "Yes. Except that."

He and Ransom loaded the last of the supplies, and Roar lingered while Jinx went inside.

"Did you need something?" Locke asked, and Roar's eyes tracked his movements as he lifted his shirt to wipe his face.

"I've got all this excess energy after training with Jinx, and it's making me restless. Thought I might go for a run, and I was wondering if you wanted to join me." Her words were hesitant, broken up with unsure pauses.

He started to ask if he could bathe first, but he supposed that would not make much sense if they were about to run. He was sure he smelled of smoke and sweat, and a small part of him wanted to look his best for their first extended time alone in days.

"Sure. I could do with a run."

She grinned at him, and it nearly took him to his knees.

"You ready?" she asked, bouncing slightly on her feet.

He laughed. "I don't think I have ever seen you this eager for a run. I *know* I haven't."

She darted back a few steps, and when he followed at a lazy pace, she scurried a little farther. "Maybe I missed running with you."

His heart began to ease into a faster rhythm, and even though he was tired and sore from the last few days' brutal work, he felt a burst of energy.

"You missed getting beaten?" he asked with a smile.

She twined her hands behind her and walked backward, pulling him along like there was a lure stuck in his chest. "I don't know. I'm feeling good tonight. I think today might finally be the day that I leave you in the dust."

"Doubtful," he growled, picking up his pace to match hers.

"Prove it," she said with a smile, then turned and took off at a hard sprint.

Soul of fire, soul of rage
No longer bound by flesh or cage,
Soul exalted, soul made new
Reserved for those devout and true.

—"The Way of Souls," a Sacred Soul hymn

21

Roar could hear Locke hot on her heels, and her heart beat at a frenzied pace. She was in the mood to have fun. For so long, in every part of her life, she had felt like she had been cornered into one choice or another. When she hadn't been taking risky leaps of faith, she'd been trudging down lonely roads because there were no other options. She'd been miserable from the stress of it all, and after days of agonizing over the future, she realized she was falling into the same patterns here in the wilds. For once, she did not want to be ruled by the future. She wanted adventure. She wanted *fun*. And she wanted it with Locke.

No more wavering between Rora and Roar.

She was Roar for the foreseeable future, and that was all that mattered. Running hard, she blew past one of the village gates, heading out into the dusky twilight. The sun was down, but the sky was still spattered with purples and pinks and blues. Stars winked overhead, a multitude of dazzling lights that seemed to dance and swirl together in some faraway place.

Snapping out of her distraction just in time, she changed direction as Locke lunged to catch her. He missed, and Roar laughed, speeding away while he refocused.

She could not outrun him for long. She knew that. He was much faster than her, but she was counting on his fatigue and her own restlessness to give her the edge for a little while. But she had not counted on the single-minded intensity with which he pursued her. She realized very quickly, as she had to dodge him again and again, that while he might be tossing playful taunts as he trailed behind, he certainly was not playing around. Every time he came near, her body buzzed with anticipation for that moment when his hands would take hold of her. And each time she delayed the inevitable, the sensations became more intense, until she *wanted* him to catch her. Until she craved it.

She did not hold out long before his huge body plowed into her from behind. Her legs tangled together as his arms wound around her chest and shoulders, and the only thing that kept her from falling was his agility. He lifted her up, spinning to keep from falling himself, whirling her around in the process. She screamed and reached her hands up to clutch at the arms that held her. They were both laughing as her feet touched back on the ground, swaying together to recapture their equilibrium.

"You did not have to *tackle* me," she breathed.

"I didn't tackle you. I *caught* you. And it was surprisingly easy. Has Jinx been going easy on you?"

Feeling daring, she leaned back fully into him, resting her head on the curve made by the arm still wrapped around her. "If I say yes, will I be in trouble, *commander*?"

He squeezed her closer and let out a barking laugh. "*Commander*, really?"

She shrugged, but the movement was restricted by his hold. "How about *strict overlord*?"

"Rolls right off the tongue." The words were low and joking, but he said them so close to her ear that it felt like a slow burn had begun at the base of her spine. She wanted to have fun. And though she did not always let herself admit it, she was intrigued by the idea of having a different kind of fun with Locke.

With Cassius, the idea of being intimate had felt frightening and overwhelming. And after his betrayal, it had made her skin crawl. But with Locke . . . the prospect of making herself vulnerable to him was not as scary as she thought it would be. And what little fear remained was overshadowed by curiosity and desire. She thought about that kiss in the rain, and she wanted to know what it would be like to kiss him when there was no storm distracting her, no anger between them.

For now, though, she decided to continue playing hard to get. He had relaxed his grip, holding her softly as his chin rested lightly against the back of her head. She used her body to push him backward and then wiggled out of his hold and ran.

When her footing slipped and she ended up on one knee, she took the opportunity to throw a fistful of sand at an approaching Locke. He dodged easily, but the glint in his eyes was so worth it. He prowled toward her, and there was a drumming in her ears, beating too fast to be her heart, surely.

"Gonna pay for that, princess."

"Maybe I'll call you Wolf," she said as he drew nearer. "A predator that hunts in packs." He made a growly sort of grunt, but didn't protest. "Or maybe Tiger. Or Lion."

He lunged for her, and she rolled in the sand, throwing another handful as she went.

"Sneaky. I could call you Fox."

She could have run again, probably should have, but something kept her there. She lay back against the sand as she had the first night they arrived in this town. She stretched out her arms and legs, dragging them back and forth a few times to leave an impression in the sand beneath her. It was getting darker, the sun long gone. The night was a deep violet mixed with dark blue. And out of the corner of her eye, she saw Locke moving closer. Instinct flared, and she nearly ran again. Except that . . . she didn't want to. At least not all of her. She felt restless, but she knew running would not fix that. She was just nervous.

As he eased within touching distance, he asked, "You are not going to throw sand on me again, are you?"

She pretended to consider it for a moment. "Probably not. But I make no promises."

He stretched out beside her, propped up on his side, his long hair cascading over the hand he used to hold his head up. "Did I wear you out already?"

She bit her lip and shook her head. She didn't understand the way she was feeling. Her mind kept flicking from one thought to another, like a bird that would not perch in one place for more than a heartbeat. And she knew it was because something could happen between them tonight. And she wanted and feared it in equal measure. "We should get our horses and go for a ride," she said, stalling. "It's been days since I've felt the wind in my hair."

She turned her head toward him to find him smiling. "I'd like that. But it's dark, and I don't want to take any chances that we'll run into a storm with just the two of us."

She swallowed and nodded her head. He was right. But that didn't stop the longing. She wanted the cool rush of the wind and the hard pound of hooves. She wanted the kind of speed that left everything else behind and gave her the simplest, purest form of happiness there was.

"Let's go to a tavern," she said. "I've never actually been inside one."

He touched her cheek, tucking a strand of hair behind her ear. "I'll take you sometime. But tonight, I'm afraid we are both covered in sweat and sand." He rolled closer, sliding his hand from her cheek to tangle in her hair. "You're restless tonight. What's going on?"

Opposing impulses crashed inside her.

Run—wild and free.

Stay—close and warm.

She wanted both of them. She wanted safety and adventure and excitement and comfort. "I don't know," she answered honestly. "I feel like doing something wild."

One moment she was lying there in the sand, staring up at the sky, her fingers fidgeting against her thighs, and the next he'd pulled her so that she lay half on top of him, one leg strewn over his and their chests pressed together.

His voice was a low rumble as he said, "I can think of a few wild things."

She felt her heartbeat everywhere—at the bottom of her throat and the base of her spine and the hollow of her knees. One of his hands ran up her side, mapping out the curve of her waist. He brought her close, so close she could feel his breath against her mouth. She shut her eyes, hovering there so near his warmth but still separate. The anticipation made her hand tremble against his chest, and all her limbs felt hollow. She wanted him to close the distance, wanted to do it herself. But something held her back. Her distracted mind had not stopped, only now it flickered between the curve of his lips and the wall of his chest and the sand blowing over their legs and the bird that was chirping somewhere in the distance and the lone insect who was fighting valiantly to fill the whole night with sound.

A hot flush of irritation swept over the back of her neck. She rolled away from Locke, feeling frustrated and petulant, which made zero sense. He was here, and if he stared at her any harder, her skin would catch fire. When his fingers touched low on her back, she shuddered from pleasure at the same time that her fists clenched in her lap.

That was when she noticed her bandages had come undone and she had reopened the cuts on her fingers. Locke had warned her that they would not heal easily. She hadn't realized how often she used her hands until each strong flex of her fingers broke open the wounds again.

"Roar?"

Irritation seized her, and when the blood from her hands dripped onto the sand a moment later, that irritation bloomed into wild delight. The hair on her arms stood up on end, and blinding white sky-fire split the sky in two. Sound exploded in her ears; the whole world seemed to shake when the blazing light pierced the earth so close that she felt a stinging shock push through her, locking up each and every muscle in her body.

It was gone faster than it came, and a few moments later, it struck again, splintering a brush tree and leaving fire in its place.

She swore. The land was flat, not a single large tree within sight, which meant she and Locke were the biggest targets out here. She heard another jarring crack, like the snap of a whip, and light flared in her peripheral vision. Glee welled up inside her—eager and excited, and so at odds with her own terror. She moved on instinct, pulling her legs in so that she sat in a ball. She curled her hands over her head and looked beneath her arm for Locke. She expected to find him fighting the storm or readying himself to do so. But instead, he sat still, his legs sprawled out and his upper body supported by his elbows, likely the same position he had been in when she rolled off him without warning. His handsome face had gone slack, his eyes big and blank.

Mesmerized.

She swore again, louder and with trembling panic. He had one of the strongest minds she had ever known. She did not think he had ever been mesmerized by a storm, at least not that he had told her, and he loved to tell all his most frightening stories to convince her of the danger. This was her fault. She had distracted him and weakened his control. Skyfire hit the earth again. She couldn't see it, but she could feel it, like the knowledge that a blade swung and came far too close.

She didn't know what to do; she wanted desperately to go to him, but that might make them more likely to get struck. Before she could make a decision, skyfire streaked down again, and it landed only steps away from Locke. It didn't hit him, but his body jerked, spasming for a moment as his elbows gave and his body collapsed back on the sand. She knew the shock from skyfire could travel through the ground and affect people who were not directly hit. And sure enough, when she scrambled to his side, she found him unconscious.

"No." The word choked in her throat, broken and gasping.

Another flash, lighting up Locke's lifeless face in the night. She spread her hands over his chest, sliding up to cup his neck and check for a pulse. She thought she felt it, but it seemed weaker than it should be. Every other time she had touched his chest or neck, she could feel his heartbeat strong and wild and forceful, just like the man himself.

Another crack, and she screamed, senseless words scraping her throat raw, "*Stop! Please, stop!*"

Her eyes were flooded with tears, cascading over her cheeks, dripping down onto her shaking hands. And when the next bolt flashed, it did not touch the ground. It flitted from cloud to cloud several times in quick succession. Her confusion was too strong, too consuming to be only her own. Panting and at a loss for what to do next, she focused on the foreign feelings flooding her mind.

It was a mess of jumbled emotions—mirth and impatience and a playful restlessness that she now realized had been influencing her for far longer than just the length of the storm. Again the skyfire storm flashed overhead, deafening and terrible, but calmer. And inside she felt a corresponding rush of feelings. It was too fast to make sense of them separately, but together, they reminded her of a child who had been told no, gearing up to throw a tantrum, a building whine of disappointment.

That restless feeling built and built until the air grew thick with electricity, and she felt the intention of the storm a moment before a bolt of skyfire raged toward the ground. It was too bright to tell where it would land, but she threw up her arms and yelled "NO!"

She waited for the crack, for the pulse of power that radiated out every time the lightning met the land, but it never came. And when she uncovered her eyes, the storm rolled and flickered above her, but did nothing more. It . . . *waited*.

She stared, incredulous and shaking as the storm's emotions washed over her. Feeling crazy (and desperate and afraid and every emotion there was tangled and mixed together in an overwhelming chorus), she began to think that the storm *listened* to her.

This . . . *connection* . . . she felt, did it work both ways? Could it understand her?

Two bolts of skyfire speared the sand simultaneously, but far enough away that she didn't feel any overflow of energy. And somehow, she knew that answer was an unequivocal yes.

"Scorch me," she breathed, and then immediately threw up her hands in a panic. "No, don't! Don't scorch me! I didn't mean it!"

Thin, quick streaks danced overhead, and she somehow *felt* laughter, rather than heard it. It bubbled up in her chest, and she experienced the urge as if it were her own.

Breathing heavily, she stared up at the sky in wonder. And feeling like she had lost her wits, she whispered, "You don't want to hurt me?"

The sky blazed with light—bright and beautiful and as nonthreatening as a skyfire storm could possibly be.

She thought back to the way she'd felt all night. That urge to run and jump and be free and fun. She had already gone this far, so she did not see the harm in suspending her sanity a little longer to ask, "You want to play, don't you?"

More cloud-to-cloud flashes. Joy and excitement and endless energy.

Her fear was so strong that she had somehow carved out a space in her mind that was only hers, but she could feel the storm's consciousness surrounding it, and there was no doubt in her mind that the skyfire above was conscious. The constantly shifting emotions gave her a sense of its impulses, and though she couldn't hear thoughts or anything like that, she could almost *feel* them. She was stunned to realize that the skyfire heart had the feeling of a *child*.

"Can you . . . go somewhere else?"

A sizzling bolt came down twenty paces away. He—she could not say how exactly, but she knew the storm was male—had stayed far enough back not to harm her, but the displeasure at her question was clear.

"I didn't mean to hurt your feelings, it's only—my friend is hurt. We can't . . . *play* with you without being injured."

More zigzagging bands striped overhead, and Roar fell back to the ground, stunned by corresponding messages so strong that they felt almost like visions. She saw the land—flat and wide, as if from overhead. Followed by repeated images of her, a knife to her finger as she stood over the altar each morning for her offering. Then a final image of her sitting where she was now, her hands dripping blood from her reopened wounds.

Horror filled her, and she actually felt the storm recoil in response, which meant he could feel *her* exactly like she felt him. She tried to fill herself with remorse, and she felt the tentative brush of him against her mind. She looked at Locke, frighteningly still on the sand, and sent all her fear and worry to the storm.

Thunder rumbled, and though she saw no corresponding light, she felt the same emotion come back at her that she had sent before. *Remorse.*

She sat there, stunned, her body still pulsing with adrenaline. She looked to the distance, to the craggy rolling hills that she could not see against the dark sky. But she imagined them as they were in the day and pictured the storm lighting up over the rocks. She tried to infuse the image with happiness, tempting the storm to move there.

She swore she heard a whine on the air as lightning touched down again, close, but not too close. She thought of the way a dog's ears would drop and its tail would curve down when someone yelled for it to go.

She was trying to think of how to bargain with the young storm. Could she ask it to let her take Locke to safety, to the hunters who could make sure he was okay? Would he let her if she promised to return? She was contemplating how best to communicate this when a groan sounded behind her and Locke's body shifted on the ground.

"Stay," she told the storm. "Wait."

And dutifully, the skyfire remained overhead, only streaking between clouds.

Locke was awake and disoriented, but she saw him fumbling with his belt, the only piece of equipment he wore. He pulled out a skyfire Stormheart. When his skin touched the stone, she felt a flare of electric magic, and moments later, curiosity, followed by the eager image of two skyfire storms, flashing together in the night, playing over the land like friends.

"What are you doing?" Roar whispered to Locke.

He winced as he sat up, gripping the stone harder. "Calling out the heart."

All at once, Roar had a much clearer picture of how Stormhearts worked. Because as she sat there beside Locke, she could *sense* another storm. She could feel its *soul*—intense and protective and riddled with guilt—and she knew it was Locke. That somehow when he touched the dead Stormheart, his own soul brought it to life. And she could tell the storm above thought it was real. The child storm waited restlessly for a friend to form. Just as she could feel his presence before the storm manifested, he thought that was what he was feeling now—building magic in the air and a rising soul that would collide to form a playmate for him.

A brilliant light shone above her, not the blinding flash of another skyfire bolt but something both brighter and softer. A small, swirling orb of energy drifted toward them. The light was white, but as it swirled and moved, she saw a dozen other colors reflected inside the revolving sphere, flicking in scattered branches like a smaller version of skyfire. And she knew that inside that cluster of lights lay the living heart of the storm. Every emotion and desire she felt bleeding into her came from that ball of light.

"Get back," Locke said, using his free hand to physically push her away from him. The storm's heart hovered closer now, so close that tears gathered in her eyes at the brilliance of it. It seared through her—intense and beautiful. "When I move," Locke said, "you run. Hard and fast back toward town. Don't look back, princess. No matter what."

Then before she could protest, he lunged toward the soul, thrusting his free hand inside it like a blade into a heart.

Roar screamed. Locke screamed. The storm screamed.

Agony burned through her—sharp and hot—accompanied by a burning smell so strong it singed her nostrils. A dozen small spears of skyfire shot off in every direction, and Locke's body convulsed, rising off the ground as he held tight to the soul that trembled and throbbed with pain.

"Stop!" she cried out, but she did not think he could hear her. She could barely hear herself over his tortured yells and the wailing inside her head. She could feel the storm fighting back, funneling a terrifying amount of energy into Locke. He was weak and fatigued, and she could sense all too clearly the way the battle between their souls tipped back and forth. He had caught the storm off guard, giving him the advantage, but the skyfire's magic was potent and powerful. She knew Locke could win, but what damage would be done to him in the process? The storm's strength began to crumble, its light dimming, and the pain was unimaginable, as if her own soul were being ripped open.

Before she could think it through, she ran and tackled Locke, catching him by surprise. His hand pulled loose, and the storm howled in pain. Roar's body was on top of Locke's, and she saw his eyelids flutter as he struggled to stay conscious. She could feel his pain too—acute and crippling. And then the world around them became nothing more than fire and light.

"I did it," she cried. "It's my fault. I called it. Oh, gods. I called it."

The storm howled and raged, lashing out with every bit of power it had, the earth shaking as dozens of bolts struck all at once. They did not strike her or the man she covered with her body. But the waves of power reached them anyway, conducted through the earth. Locke groaned and his body shuddered. Now it was *him* that was in danger, Locke that was fading. She could feel his soul through his Stormheart, but it was faint, too faint.

"ENOUGH!" she yelled at the storm.

There was a momentary pause, long enough for her to sit up and stare at an orb so bright that her eyes burned. But the little storm was too hurt, too afraid. And she could not blame him. She sent waves of calm and healing and remorse, but fierce and frantic, he bucked her hold. And when she saw clearly his intent, electricity crackling through the air around her, she had no other choice.

She whispered, "I'm sorry." Then Roar thrust her own hand into the storm's soul. For one moment, she felt only the soul's shock and confusion and *hurt*, then its fire poured into her, burning her from the inside, tearing her apart. She screamed, and thought with every bit of strength she had, *Surrender to me.*

Locke woke in time to see Roar thrust her hand deep into the heart of the skyfire storm. Her head flew back, her mouth opened in a hoarse scream. Then the orb of power burst with a blinding flash of light. Roar remained standing, her head still back and her arms limp at her sides. It was by far the fastest he had ever seen someone take a Stormheart. And most hunters would have been blown back by the force of the dying heart. He had been knocked out for nearly a bell after he took his sky-fire heart.

She swayed on her feet, and then her knees crumpled and she sank to the ground. He rushed toward her right as she released an awful, keening wail that made Locke fall to his knees beside her. She writhed and cried—great, gusting sobs that wrenched her whole body. He tried to touch her, to hold her, but she kicked and squirmed, falling on to her back with her eyes squeezed tightly shut.

"Roar?" He took hold of one wrist, holding on tight to keep her from breaking loose. "Listen to me, princess. Open your eyes. Tell me where it hurts."

Her free hand tore at the harness crossing her chest. Quickly, he undid one of the straps, wondering if it felt too tight. More likely, it was her chest that hurt, reacting to lingering power from the storm she had destroyed. But when the harness slipped free, she clawed at the sleeveless shirt beneath it, pulling the neck down to bare her collarbone, followed by the curve of her breast. He froze, immediately intending to look away, but he couldn't. Not even when her shirt tore, revealing more of her body.

Because her skin . . . glowed. Her chest, the area directly over her heart, flashed as if her veins were filled with light. That light pulsed, zigzagging beneath her skin like her heart had traded places with the storm she'd just taken and skyfire now beat within the cage of her ribs.

He had never seen a reaction like this before, not when he'd taken his first skyfire storm or when the other hunters had taken theirs. They had all been weak and bruised and aching from the inside out, sensations he felt keenly at the moment, but the only lasting effect had been the desire to sleep. And of course, the connection to a Stormheart that had given them new abilities. At that thought, he checked her hands and the surrounding earth, but found no stone. He searched wider, unwilling to go more than a step or two from her still-shuddering form. But there was nothing. No Stormheart. Unless . . .

He looked back at her chest, watched her nails scrape over the skin there, clawing as if she were trying to reach inside and pull something out.

No. It couldn't be. That was impossible.

But it really *did* look like lightning streaking beneath her skin. Again and again, the light diverged from a center point, right where her heart should be, splitting into branches that stretched in every direction but faded before they traveled too far from her heart.

He had no clue what was happening. But he knew she was in terrible pain. Her beautiful face was twisted and scrunched, and her body heaved and jerked against the sand. Quickly, he bent and took hold of her squirming body. She pushed against him, but she was weak and tired. And with her in his arms, he ran. His legs ached and threatened to give out, but he wouldn't. He *couldn't*. He had to get her to Duke. Maybe his mentor had seen this before. Maybe he would recognize what was happening and be able to stop her pain before . . .

No. He couldn't think about possible outcomes. He could not comprehend the possibility of life without her, though he feared he might not be given a choice. He gritted his teeth and ran harder. She slid into unconsciousness, her trembling body going still.

"No, no, no!" He pushed his legs faster until all the pain disappeared and only desperation remained.

The other hunters were gathered just outside the village's wall; no doubt they had been on their way to fight the storm. He groaned with relief at the sight of them. His knees gave out moments before he reached their position, slamming hard into the dirt. He pitched forward, but did his best to keep Roar up until he could ease her onto the ground.

"DUKE!" he yelled, his voice swallowed by desperation. "Help her!"

The old man moved faster than Locke had seen him run in years. As soon as he was close, the whole story began rattling out of Locke's mouth. He didn't have all the pieces. He'd been unconscious for a time. But Duke didn't even appear to be listening. As he knelt on Roar's other side, the old man's gaze was riveted to the skyfire flashes in her chest. Locke reached out, folding the torn pieces of her shirt to cover all but the upper half of the streaking lights.

"I had the storm," Locke growled. "I *had it*. But she pushed me away. *Why did she push me away?*"

"To the point, boy! How did she get like this?"

"She touched the heart. She took it, faster than I've ever seen. She shoved her hand into the light, and it was so bright I had to look away. Then the storm was just gone and she was inconsolable, screaming in pain . . . like she was burning inside."

Tentatively, Duke touched her skin where the light forked below it. His hand shook, as if he expected it to be hot. But it wasn't. Locke knew. He'd touched it himself, and her skin felt normal. No cuts. No heat. No scars.

"What else?" Duke snapped, feeling for her pulse, touching her forehead, lifting her closed eyelids. Jinx held up a skyfire lantern to cast light over them. For the first time, Locke's eyes fixed on something besides Roar's anguished face and the bizarre phenomenon of her heart.

Her hair . . . it was white. Pale, bright white. Like the light in her chest.

"What else, Locke? Think. Did you see anything? Hear anything?"

Locke felt numb. His body was cold and shaking, and he was fairly certain he was going into shock. "Called it," he mumbled. "She—she said she called it."

"That's not possible," Jinx said. "Not even the strongest Stormlings can summon a storm. Only control those that already exist."

"Don't you think I know that?" Locke snapped. "But . . . but how is any of this possible? There should have been a stone. But there wasn't. There was nothing left of the storm that I could find except *that*." He punctuated his words with gesture toward Roar's chest.

Jinx didn't reply. No one did. They only stared, as baffled and terrified as he was.

"Your welcome in Toleme is revoked. You all need to leave. *Now*."

The hard voice came from the direction of the town, and the other hunters parted to reveal Minister Vareeth. His expression was curled into a sneer, and his eyes flashed with fear and loathing when they fell upon Roar.

"I want you out of my town. Now. We want nothing to do with her kind."

"Her kind?" Locke asked.

"I did not believe. I heard the whispers. The rumors from scourged who tried to seek refuge here. I thought it fearmongering from the Stormlings. Thought they were trying to lure people from the wilds to seek shelter in the cities."

"What rumors?" Locke demanded, launching to his feet and surging toward the man.

Ransom caught him, holding him back.

"The Stormlord. She is like him," the minister said. "Varatempia."

"Vara what?"

"It's Vyhodin," Sly said, stepping up to stand between Locke and the minister. "It means . . . 'with a heart of storms.' But I've only ever heard it as an exaggeration. For unruly children with bad tempers."

"Go!" the minister yelled. "If I were not a man of faith, I'd have you all hanged for the peace of mind of my people. If you do not leave now, I might reconsider."

"We can't go without our things," Bait snarled. "Our carriage. Our horses."

"Then get them and go. But she stays here. She will not taint our Sacred town again."

Locke broke free from Ransom and charged toward the minister. "Who is this Stormlord you speak of? Why do you fear him?" He took hold of the man's shirt, dragging him up onto his toes, even as Ransom appeared again, trying to haul him back. "Who is he?" Locke growled.

"He is destruction. The very soul of death. He's the worst perversion of magic, the prophesized end of days. And like her, storms beat beneath his chest."

Ransom finally succeeded in pulling Locke away, and he went, snarling. "Superstitious garbage. We saved your pathetic town. And you would put us out in the night because of old religious texts that haven't been relevant for centuries? What kind of coward are you? You would let your fear of the imaginary make you cruel to real people, flesh and blood!"

"It is not fiction. The Stormlord lives. He has already destroyed the city for which you are named."

"Wh-what?" Locke stumbled, fatigue raking down his spine. "I don't understand. Locke—"

"Swallowed up by the sea," the minister growled. "Battered and drowned until not one brick lay upon another. Total destruction. And I'll not have my home be next."

Sometimes we must make answers where there are none.
                    —*The Tale of Lord Finneus Wolfram*

22

She'll wake today, Locke told himself. She had to. He did not think he could survive another night with her unconscious. It was not abnormal for those who survived a skyfire strike to fall into an unrelenting sleep. But while Roar had not woken, she whimpered and gasped and moaned in pain, the skyfire flash in her chest speeding up when she did. He felt so helpless, so afraid—both emotions he had not felt since his childhood.

Two nights prior they had left Toleme in the dark and traveled through the night to reach Taraanar. And now as he and Jinx wove their way through a crowded market—this one selling fine silks and pottery and spices, he unconsciously reached for his supply harness for what must have been the dozenth time, only to come up empty. He had been forced to leave everything that could be considered dangerous magic back at their camp for this visit.

Stall owners shouted at them as they passed, shoving various wares in their faces, promising the best prices in the whole market. Jinx looked back at him, her normally distinctive hair covered by a scarf. "Remember," she said, "be nice. We need her to help us. Do *not* lose your temper."

Locke grunted in response. Perhaps he had been a *little* irritable over the last few days, but what was he expected to be when Roar still lay unconscious in the Rock? He'd had to leave her to come into the city. They'd not been able to bribe their way in on such short notice, and it was much easier to sneak two people inside than an entire crew and a hulking metal carriage.

They turned down the far row of the market, and took a hidden set of stairs down into an abandoned tunnel that used to be part of an aqueduct system and now was home to Taraanar's storm market. They walked for a while in the dark, their footsteps echoing in the enclosed space. Then eventually, they began to pass stalls. The tunnel was not wide enough to have more than one lane of stalls and the walkway, so they wound their way through the market tunnel for nearly a bell. They passed old acquaintances and familiar bits of magic, but they did not stop to visit. They kept walking until they finally came upon an enclosed market stall curtained by beads and silk fabrics with a sign that read DIVINER.

Jinx said the woman inside was one of the oldest and wisest witches in existence, but it looked more like they had stumbled upon a cheap soothsayer scam. The woman had lived for a time in the Sahrain mountains near where Jinx grew up, and Jinx's mother had brought her to the witch when she was young and her magic was out of control. Jinx would not say what the woman had divined, only that she could, and her ability was most definitely real.

His body tensed as Jinx rang a bell outside the curtained stall. No one answered. His heart began to sink, stinging as if it sank into acid. Jinx went to ring the bell again and the curtain parted. He could see nothing inside, but when Jinx ducked past the curtain, he did not hesitate to follow. The curtain dropped back into place, settling them all into darkness. A cold sensation ran over the back of his neck, and he shivered.

A candle lit out of nowhere in front of them, a small golden glow in the still, dark space. Then dozens more followed, blazing to life all at once. The witch sat at a table, watching them.

He had expected her to be old and decrepit. She was the former, but far from the latter. Her silvery hair hung long and straight like her posture. Her dark face was smooth, and the only wrinkles he spied were a few at her neck and across the backs of her hands. Her eyes were an eerie, washed-out blue.

"Jezamine," the woman said. "It has been some time."

Her voice crawled over his skin, and it felt as if it clung to him, *learned* him. He fought off a shiver. *Jezamine.* It had been a long time since he'd heard someone call Jinx that.

"Hello, Avira. It's good to see you."

The old woman laughed. "Is it? This one doesn't look particularly happy about it," she said, jerking a thumb in Locke's direction. He straightened his posture and cleared his expression as best he could in his unsettled state.

"My name is Locke," he said. "And I'm very pleased to meet you."

Her lips quirked, revealing a few more wrinkles. "Oh, I know. The spirits have been quite keen to tell me about you. You look as distraught as they said." He stiffened. "Jinx did not tell you I was a spirit witch?"

"I told him," Jinx said. "You've spooked him is all."

Avira surveyed him, her eyes frighteningly intense. When they weren't piercing through him, they flicked around his head, as if glancing at something he couldn't see. He had the sensation of something crawling along the back of his neck, and he had to fight not to swat at the imagined things around him.

"You must learn to find your feet even among things that unsettle you, young hunter. For far more unsettling things await you."

Cold swept through his chest. If that was prediction, he did not like it. But Avira said nothing else. She only turned toward Jinx and said, "Sit. Tell me your purpose."

Jinx sat at the table before the spirit witch, and Locke stood behind her. On the table was a sample of each of the elements—the flame from the candle, bowls of water and sand, and what he recognized as the magic of a windstorm. The latter was in a bottle that had been uncorked, but somehow the magic remained inside instead of spilling out.

He crossed his hands over his chest and listened as Jinx told Avira about Roar's peculiarities and the way she had taken down the skyfire storm. Locke watched the witch's face, searching for any sign of recognition or emotion, but the woman was unreadable. Except for the moments when her eyes flicked away from Jinx to stare at the open air, as if someone else were there, filling in gaps of the story.

When Jinx finished recounting the story in its entirety, she said, "It would take us several weeks to reach Locke to confirm the minister's story. Instead, we thought you could *see* for us. And if you're willing, we hoped you could take a look at Roar. She still has not woken and—"

"I do not need to see the girl. She will wake when she's ready."

Locke lurched forward. "She will wake, though?" There was desperation in his voice that he knew he should hide. He knew better than to show his emotions to someone he wasn't sure he could trust, someone who could easily manipulate him.

"My abilities do not work that way, hunter. I see actions, cause and effect. My ability to see and understand spirit does not extend to the living. She will wake. That's all I can say. And when she does, it will be to a different life than all the ones she led before."

Jinx asked, "Have you heard any news of Locke? Or seen anything in your visions?"

"Aye, the minister spoke the truth. The city by the sea is no more."

Locke waited to feel something. Remorse or nostalgia or anything. He knew there had likely been tremendous loss of life. But he could not make himself feel sorrow for that place. The city had been beautiful, of that there was no doubt. But like too many beautiful things, it had rotted on the inside.

A Locke prince had been in Pavan to marry their princess, so at least part of the royal line survived. He wished they'd all been destroyed. Perhaps he should have felt guilty for that, but he could not bring himself to do that either. That kingdom was tainted, and the world was better off with it gone.

"What about this Stormlord?" he asked. "Tell me it's superstitious nonsense."

"I cannot tell you that."

"But you cannot tell me if he is real?"

"I can only tell you that every spirit I send to search for him never returns. Your inferences here are as good as mine."

He met the witch's gaze again. Her eyes were a blue so light that they almost looked illuminated, and he felt that tickle on the back of his neck. This time he could not stop himself from reaching back with a hand and rubbing at the spot that felt colder than the rest of his skin.

"You should go," the woman said, settling back into the worn, cushioned chair on which she sat.

Jinx stood, crossing toward her. "Avira, please. Grant us a little more time. There's so much we don't know. About Roar's abilities, whether or not she truly did call that storm."

"She can tell you herself."

Locke lost his patience then. He had let his guard down, and his anger slipped past the tight leash he had kept it on for days. "No, she *can't*. Something is wrong with her. She's sleeping, but I can tell she's in pain. I know it. That *thing* in her chest lights up, and she whimpers, and—and—" He fisted his hands in his hair and squeezed his eyes shut tight. "*I don't know how to help her.* Tell me how to help her."

The old woman stood, unfazed by his loss of control. She drifted toward the curtains and pulled them open in a not so subtle suggestion.

"My final advice to you is this: listen. Listen when she speaks and when she doesn't. Listen when you understand and when you don't. Listen with an open heart, for a closed heart becomes a cold one if left for too long. That is how you can help her, Kiran Thorne."

He jerked back, stumbling over his feet as his heart roared within his chest. "What did you call me?"

She waved a hand in front of his eyes, as if she were clearing cobwebs from between them.

"Your head may have forgotten, but your heart has not. Remember that in the future. Now go. She will wake soon."

Roar sat on the bank of a small tributary in the Rani Delta. She looked over the unfamiliar land around her—swaying palm trees, tall grasses, and in the distance, sand as far as the eye could see. It was easier to focus on what was around her rather than within her. She was supposed to be washing up, like she had begged to do only a while ago. But her body ached, and her mind was muddled, and inside . . .

Inside she felt . . . untethered. As if the strings tying her soul to her body had been cut, and if she did not concentrate, the two might separate completely. As soon as she had woken, there had been so many faces and voices around her, but none was the one she wanted.

Carefully, she removed the only article of clothing she wore—a large tunic that went to her knees and smelled like Locke. Duke had given her a linen towel and a smaller cloth with which to wash. She pulled the larger towel around her shoulders to ward off the chilly winds that came in from the sea and edged forward to the river. She dunked the cloth into the water and scrubbed her skin clean as best she could while sitting on the bank.

She heard something crashing through the copse of palm trees behind her. Branches parted, and Locke stepped into view. His face had darkened with exertion, and the hair over his forehead stuck to his skin with sweat. He looked like he'd just run half the world to get to her, and yet from the moment he'd seen her, he hadn't taken another step. He stood frozen in the shadows of the swaying palms. His eyes dipped down, taking in the towel that covered her. Her skin warmed as his eyes traced over the length of her uncovered legs. Abruptly, he turned away.

"I should have announced myself." His voice was low, but it carried on the wind, and the familiar cadence of his speech was like an embrace that she had not realized she needed.

She smiled. "Your crashing through the trees was announcement enough."

His head lowered, and she could see the beginning of a smile. She took a moment to study him while he was turned profile. His harness was missing, but he wore his Stormheart belt. Over his linen shirt was a thick hooded leather jacket in the same style as the one she had bought in Toleme, made to allow easy access to his weapons and supplies. He looked . . . weary.

"I'll go. Let you finish, uh . . . finish."

He turned back the way he came and she said, "Wait!"

He did. She didn't know how to put into words the clawing feeling she got in her chest at the thought of him leaving. Duke hadn't told her where Locke was when she woke, only that he would be back, and that he had barely left her side the previous two days.

Two days. The thought still boggled her mind.

"Roar?" Locke asked, his voice strangled.

"Just give me a moment. I'm almost done, and then we can talk. Stay there, just as you are."

He swallowed, and then nodded his assent.

Trusting that she was strong enough to endure a moment or two in the water, she shed the towel and waded in. The water was so cold it stung her skin. She crossed her arms over her chest to block the wind, and shuffled a little farther in. The current was swift, so she bent down where she was rather than risk getting any deeper. She scooped up water in her hand, splashing it over her upper body. She gritted her teeth against the shock, and tried to move as quickly as she could.

Some of her hair fell down into her face, a tumble of snow-white strands. She jerked backward in shock and lost her footing, falling back into the water.

"Roar? Roar, what happened?"

Her body shook with cold, so the words came out in a stutter as she said, "I—I'm f-fine. I fell. That's all."

"Let me go get Jinx to help you."

"No," she said, "I can do this." He groaned and scrubbed a hand over the back of his neck, but didn't protest. "Why don't you sit down?" she asked. "You are making me nervous."

He shuffled closer without looking at her. Then he sat down facing toward the palm trees so that he couldn't see her without turning all the way around.

She focused back on what had made her fall in the first place. How was her hair blond again? Surely it could not have faded in mere days. Nova assured her that the dye would last for several months. She grabbed a chunk of hair, pulling it within her line of sight, and sure enough, all of it was once again that familiar pale blond—from the ends, to as far up as she could see.

"Locke . . ." she called out from where she still sat in the rushing river. "My hair is *different?*"

He cleared his throat. "It was like that after . . . after the skyfire."

Light flashed below her, and if she had not felt her heartbeat pick up, she would have known it by the flickering lights in her chest. She leaned her head upon her knees and focused on breathing, on staying calm, not on all the things that were wrong. She must have stayed silent too long because Locke called out her name again.

"Almost done," she said, pushing herself back into motion. She decided to dunk her head beneath the water and call that good enough. She came back up shivering, but her head felt clearer and her body less fatigued already. Carefully, she pushed up to her feet and wobbled toward the shore. Water sluiced over her skin in icy rivulets, and she snatched up the linen towel as soon as she made it to the bank, pulling it tight around her. For a moment, she stood there, trying to shake off the cold, staring at Locke's broad back. He looked tense, and he kept running a hand through his hair, a nervous habit of his.

There was something empowering about knowing she made him nervous. That it wasn't only she who came unraveled when they were together.

With her hair sopping wet, she dried her body as much as she could, and pulled the tunic back over her head.

"I'm covered." The tunic still left her legs bare, and it clung to her damp skin in places, but it was more modest than the towel. He began to turn slowly. The line of his jaw came into view first, and her eyes caught on the hair that grew there. It was thicker than usual, closer to a beard like Ransom wore. She wanted to run her fingers over his face, to learn the texture of his bristled jaw.

Then his eyes were on her—on her wet hair and her flushed face and shaking hands and bare legs. He was on his feet immediately, crossing toward her and pulling her against his hard chest.

"You're freezing."

She burrowed further into his hold, pressing her face into the hollow of his throat and breathing in the scent of him. He smelled like the woods and sweat and horses and warmth. The heat he gave off transcended touch. It filled up her lungs and her heart and the aching hollow place inside that she had been wrestling with since she woke.

For long moments, they were content to stand there wrapped up in each other. He held the tears at bay, held back all her fears and doubts. Over and over, he ran his fingers through her wet hair, and that easy, safe moment came to an end when he said, "This color suits you. I did not think anything could make you more lovely, but I was wrong."

She spun away from him, gasping, as the rest of the world came rushing back in.

"I should take you back to camp," he said. "You need to rest."

"No," she cried, her voice too loud, too desperate. Softer, she said, "I'm not ready to go back."

He looked like he wanted to disagree, but after a moment's hesitation, he peeled off the leather jacket he wore, leaving him in a linen shirt that was rolled up to his elbows. He didn't give her a choice, only picked up her hand and pushed it into one of the sleeves. She was still cold, so she didn't fight too hard as he coaxed her into his jacket.

He took her hand and pulled her farther up the bank, into a nook between a semicircle of palm trees that blocked some of the wind. He settled her between his knees, wrapping his arms around her as another layer of warmth.

"How do you feel?" The deep gravel of his voice made her turn; she found his head bowed and his face turned sideways, his eyes fixed on her beneath the fall of his dark hair. She should not have felt pleased at the distress he wore like a second skin, but she had spent her entire life feeling like she wasn't enough. To think that a man like Locke felt so strongly about her was a boost to her weary spirit.

She did not know how to answer, but then he began to speak, recounting the rise of the storm and his own attempt to diffuse it. Her throat ached when she swallowed, and she focused on breathing to fight the tears she could feel begging for release. She said, "You went for the heart when you could have just dispersed it. Why?"

"It was a powerful storm. Strong enough that it might have taken me a long while to dismantle it. And with it right over us, there was too much risk that you or I would be struck before I could get it down. Going for the heart was the fastest way to end it."

"And more dangerous for you." She couldn't stop the anger in her words. The memories were rising, and she could not forget the way it had felt to feel both his pain and the storm's.

"I've taken on skyfire before. I knew I could handle it."

She wanted to shake him, to beat her fists on his chest until he was as distraught as she. "I could *feel* it. I felt your soul struggling. You could have *died*, Locke. And then after I pushed you away, you . . . you *were* dying."

Her voice broke, and the tears came. She was too weak to hold them off. She buried her face in her hands, curling into her knees, and cried for how terrifying that night had been, for her fear of losing him and the way it had completely shattered her inside. And she cried for that storm. That frightened, *innocent* storm.

He made a noise between a groan and a growl, and pulled her tight into his body. He wrapped his arms around her, knees and all, and held her tight.

With his forehead pressed to the back of her neck, he said, "You could have died too, you know."

That only made her cry harder because it wasn't true. That storm would never have hurt her, and in return she had . . . killed it? Was that the word when you ripped a spirit out of existence? It tore at her all over again because when she had reached into that soul, she felt clearly how afraid and confused it was. And she had confirmation that the Sacred Soul believers were right about at least some things. She'd seen flashes of a small boy in a desert town not too different from Toleme. She'd seen his parents—love and adoration clear on their faces. She experienced flashes of his childhood—games played with other children, the bed he shared with his older brother, and the storm that had taken his life. Rather than passing on, he had stayed to watch over his family, too afraid that he would miss them if he went. And when they grew old and died, he simply faded into the ether until Roar unknowingly called him from the sky with her blood sacrifices.

She grieved for him, for what she'd taken from him. And when she saw the flash of her skyfire heart below her, she could not help but wonder if some part of him was with her still.

Locke's hands ran up and down her bare legs, from ankle to knee again and again—soothing away the chill that clung to her skin. He turned his head, pressing his cheek against the left side of her back, above her heart. "Shh, princess. We are alive and together. That's what matters. We're both okay."

If only that were true. But Roar had begun to think that she was very much *not* okay. She could *feel* things. Things that scared her. Things that she hoped she was imagining. She rested her chin on her knees, staring out at the swift current of the river. When the words came, they were barely above a whisper. "It's my fault."

"No, brave girl. None of this is your fault."

He always thought too highly of her, even when she did not deserve his trust, and never had. She uncurled, straightening her legs, and he wasted no time in pulling her back against his chest, winding his arms around her middle. He felt so good around her, so safe. She turned her head to the side, hiding her face against his neck. But as much as she reveled in his touch, she felt equally compelled to pull away. To make him pull away. To make him understand that she was nowhere near as good as he believed her to be.

"It is," she insisted. "Everything that happened that night was because of me. I called that storm and then I killed it."

"You didn't *kill* it. You did what you had to do to survive. That's our frame for this life, remember? We survive. Nothing else matters."

"You don't understand. You couldn't."

"Try me. Tell me why you think you called the storm."

She could tell him a great deal more than that. Even now, she felt the cold brush of hundreds of souls around her, thousands, maybe more. She could feel them in the earth, in the trees, in the rushing waters. They lingered in the air, and she had the peculiar fear that if she took too deep a breath she might breathe one in. Some were sweet, innocent, like her skyfire boy. Others bore more resemblance to the twister that had filled her with such fury. Those souls were dark and twisted and *hungry*. They wanted to be storms, pushed at her to make it so. And she knew with a bone-deep certainty that she could do it. She could call any one of them to be a storm.

The thought frightened her enough that she gripped the hands Locke had on her abdomen, pressing them in, *making* him hold her harder.

She said, "He was innocent. I called him to manifest as skyfire and then killed him when all he wanted was my attention."

"Why are you calling it a him?"

Oh gods. She didn't know if she could admit out loud what she had done, just how heinous a betrayal it had been.

"I felt his soul, Locke. Not just emotions. His *soul*. I communicated with it. It was . . . a child."

"You mean like a young storm?"

"No. I mean that the soul of that storm used to belong to a human child. The emotions I feel from storms come from real souls of human spirits that have not passed on. The soul of that twister had been consumed by violence and revenge. The thunderstorm was overwhelmed with grief. And the skyfire . . . the skyfire was a child who didn't want to leave his family. That restless feeling I had before the storm? That was him. I had been calling to him for days, and he was tired of waiting. He wanted to . . . play."

"I've never come up against a storm that wasn't bent on violence and destruction. That storm certainly didn't feel innocent when it was trying to scorch me."

"He was afraid. I know it sounds insane, but I promise you he did not mean to harm us. Not in the beginning. While you were unconscious, we . . . *spoke* in a way. Images and feelings passed back and forth. When I explained that you were hurt, he felt remorse."

"Roar, it's not poss—"

"It *is* possible. I know what I felt. That storm was more afraid of us than we were of it. And I—I killed it. I *destroyed* it. I'm the monster here."

"Don't do that."

She was crying again. She couldn't help it. She kept remembering the feel of that soul, his fear and confusion and the way he had surrendered to her without any hesitation. *He trusted her.* Locke's hands started those soothing, sweeping movements again, this time along the outside of her thighs—knee to hip and back again. "You are not a monster. You could never be."

"You don't know." He did not know anything about her. Not really. If she told him the truth—not just about the storms but about who she was—he would never forgive her.

"So, tell me. Explain it to me. I'll listen. But I promise, nothing you say could make me care for you any less."

She stiffened. All she wanted to do was turn around and tell him that she cared about him too, far more than she had let herself realize until she'd seen him unconscious and near to death in the desert. "You don't know what you're saying."

His hand found her jaw, and he turned her head, tipping it backward so that she was forced to meet his eyes. "I have had days to sit by your side, praying you would wake. Days to think of everything I wish I had said and done. I know exactly what I'm saying."

Her heart felt like it might burst from her chest, and before she could do something stupid, like tell him she loved him, she said, "I must have called the twister too. The one that killed those soldiers and destroyed all those homes. I—I have a twister Stormheart. It belonged to my brother. I keep it on a chain beneath my clothes most of the time, but on that day it was in my pocket. I cut my hand on that knife, and later I touched the Stormheart while I was thinking about those soldiers, about how a part of me wished I had hurt them. Or worse. The twister happened only a few moments later. It was me. I know it was. I took out an entire *company* of soldiers over the bad deeds of a few."

His face remained stoic, and she never saw the disgust she expected to find. He said, "I would have killed those men if I thought I could do it and still keep you safe. The rest of those soldiers were in the wildlands, they knew the risk. It's not as if you put a blade through each of their chests. You are not responsible for the actions of a storm, even if you called it."

She jerked her head out of his grasp, turning away. "If Ransom had died, would you say the same thing? Or Jinx? Or Bait? Or Sly? You blame the military for your sister, even though they were just following orders. In a way, that twister was following mine."

"Enough. I don't care. I don't care if you called that storm, if you called every storm there ever was. I would love you anyway."

She stilled, and her breath caught in her throat as an ocean rolled over her eyes, blurring everything around her until all she could do was feel—feel his heat, feel her heart rage with joy and terror, feel the desperate grip of his hands on her thighs as he waited for her to speak. And for the briefest moment—she left behind everything she was and had ever been.

No more Aurora.

No more Roar.

For a few seconds, she was only the girl that Locke loved.

And maybe she was selfish, but she wanted to remain that girl as long as possible. She wanted to pretend that there was no kingdom waiting for her and no dangerous abilities she did not understand. So she turned and kissed him, and held on to that girl with everything she had.

Sweeter than wine and softer than silk—Roar's kiss was the kind of kiss that could bring a man back to life. And in a way, that was exactly what it did. Locke had been running on instinct, on grit alone, for far longer than the few days he had waited for Roar to wake.

When Duke had offered him a way out, he *had* taken it to get out of Locke. But there had also been that blackened, broken part of him inside that thought *surely* his luck would run out in the wilds. But again, fate dealt him another hand. He was a good hunter. *Very* good. Again and again, he went after storms that no one else would touch. At sixteen, he'd thrown himself into a firestorm when men twice his age were running in the other direction. At eighteen, he ran away to face a hurricane on his own after Duke had declined to go after it with the whole crew.

He survived the flames and the waves and the winds.

Again and again and again, he survived.

But with each narrow brush with death, he felt a little less alive. Each scrape with devastation scraped off a little more of his soul.

Until this kiss. When she breathed hope through his lips, filling his lungs with joy and sowing dreams beneath his skin. Roar made him want to do more than survive. With each soft sweep of her mouth over his, she dismantled the frame of his world and built a new one.

Tentative hands crept up his arms, tracing into the dip of his elbows and curling around his shoulders. She twisted her body, bit by bit, trying to press flat against him, whimpering into his mouth when she could not make the position work. He took her by the hips, and as he lay back, he pulled until her smaller body rested on top of his. He'd had to remove all his weapons and magic when he visited the witch, so now he felt the full press of Roar's body against his own with nothing in the way.

The light brushes of her mouth were as maddening as they were euphoric. He wanted her with a desperation he had never experienced. He tried to pace himself, tried to let her hold the reins. He focused on familiarizing himself with every part of her he could reach. He dragged his hands up from her hips, learning the softness of her waist and the valley of her spine. He traced his fingers along the paths between her ribs, pushing beneath his heavy leather jacket to touch the twin wings of her shoulder blades. He thought he could touch her for years on end and never know her as well as he wanted to.

When he smoothed his hands over her sides, venturing near the curve of her breasts, she inhaled sharply against his lips. He paused, unsure if he was crossing a line. He waited for her to say something, but she remained still above him, her eyes squeezed shut and mouth still open on a gasp. Then, ever so slowly, she arched her body, turning so that his right wrist grazed her chest and the heel of his hand continued over her curves. He took that as permission, learning the shape of her there too, and when she exhaled on a moan, he lost the battle with his desperation.

He rolled, pressing her back into soft soil, and crushed his mouth against hers. Her response was equally feverish and frantic. Her fingers pulled at his hair, and her knees surrounded his hips, nestling him deeper against her. She arched up into his hand again, and he plunged his tongue into her mouth as he gave her the contact she wanted. The contact they both wanted. His other hand trailed down to one of the thighs hooked around his hips, and when he touched her bare skin, her teeth caught his bottom lip.

He groaned, sinking his hand beneath the tunic she wore, *his tunic*, until the perfect curve of her bottom filled his hand. She surged up against him, hips mashing against hips in a way that made him break their kiss and drop his head to the hollow of her throat to catch his breath. Her hands left his head to run down his back and then up again, and he covered her pulse point with his mouth, feeling the wild, rapid reminder of her vitality against his lips and teeth and tongue.

She moaned, and the sound burrowed beneath his skin, burning him up with want. Their hips began to rock—slow and subtle at first. But as he covered her neck with kisses and teasing nips of his teeth, she began to pull his hips down with her legs at the same time that she lifted her own hips up. It was torture and bliss all at the same time.

From beneath the thin fabric of the tunic, a blue-white light flickered with increasing intensity. He pulled back, watching that pulse of light with both wonder and trepidation. He slid his hand up from her chest to the neat row of buttons at the top of the tunic. Giving her plenty of time to protest, he undid the buttons gradually until the top of the tunic was loose enough that he could ease it down to reveal the light branching out over her chest. It streaked up to her collarbone and across to her sternum and over the slope of her left breast. The tempo of the flashes increased as he stared at her, and he could not help but lower his mouth to experience the marvel with more senses than just sight. He closed his eyes, and the beat of her heart lit up the black behind his eyelids.

Again and again, he followed different bolts of light with his lips, racing in an attempt to keep up. Sometimes, the action made her laugh, shivering as if the quick glide of his lips tickled. Other times she clutched his shoulders and held her breath, especially when he traversed the slope over her breast and the valley in the middle. He forgot about racing the light in those places and took his time, letting the light come to him again and again. Soon, she pulled his head up from her chest, and he went with a growl that she soothed with the softest, sweetest kiss he had ever received. Against his mouth, she whispered, "I've never—You . . . you are the first."

He loosened his hold on her body and tried not to jump to conclusions. Lifting himself up a little, he braced his weight on his elbows and asked, "First what, princess?"

Her eyes were wide, worried almost, as she answered, "First *everything*?"

He thought back to the first time he'd kissed her—hard and angry and demanding. He felt the sudden urge to worship her lips, to worship all of her to make up for his mistakes.

He covered her cheek with his hand and trailed a thumb down to her mouth, over the reddened curve of her bottom lip. He felt far too much satisfaction that these lips had never known another pair but his.

He leaned down to nip at her swollen bottom lip. "I'm the first to touch this mouth? To taste it?" Her nails dug into his shoulders, and her blue eyes flashed with heat. She nodded, her tongue darting out to soothe the skin he had tugged between his teeth. "That means it's mine. My territory. And I'm prepared to protect it, every hour of the day if I must."

Those lips that were now his tipped up in a smile. "That's very dedicated of you."

There was still so much he wanted to know about her. But he didn't want to assume that because she kissed him, she trusted him. He finally had her in his arms. The last thing he wanted to do was push her away.

Her long fingers rubbed at the corner of his jaw, down the side of his neck, and slipped along the collar of his shirt.

"I want you to show me," she murmured.

"Show you what?"

She smiled again. "Everything? Show me what you said before."

"You mean that I love you?"

She nodded, her grin widening. "Yes. Show me that."

He groaned and leaned down for another quick taste of her lips. He wanted to give her what she asked. He would love nothing more than to spend the next few hours explaining in explicit detail with his mouth and hands just how beautiful he found her.

But it wasn't long ago that she had fallen in that river, too weak to even stand. And now that he knew he had her firsts, he was determined to make each one as special as she deserved. Which meant the bank of a river, while she suffered from the cold breeze with wet hair, was definitely not the right time.

"I will show you," he promised her, "as frequently and thoroughly as you like. But not now. Not here. Let me get you back to camp where it's warm. We've got all the time in the world, princess."

A soul is a curious thing. It is all the forms of one's self—what one was, what one is, and what one could be. And the trajectory of both life and death are ruled by the self each of us clings to the most.

—personal journal of spirit witch Avira Croixell

23

"I'm telling you, she's too much of a risk. It's only a matter of time before the news about this Stormlord and Locke spreads. Then she'll put us in danger in every city we visit. One look at her chest, and they'll put us in the stocks at best, the noose at worst."

Roar's stomach sank as she and Locke approached camp and overheard the discussion happening there.

"What would you have us do, Sly?" The question came from Jinx. "Abandon her in the desert? Leave her in Taraanar? Besides, if she *can* call storms, maybe it will be useful. We would no longer have to use our own raw magic supplies while we hunt. We could save it all for the markets. Maybe she could even call a specific storm when we're running low. We could collect the magic without the risk and time it takes to search out a storm."

"People are not meant to have dominion over storms," Sly said. "It's unnatural. *She's* unnatural."

Locke wrapped his arms around Roar, spinning her behind him as if the words were arrows, and he could take the hit for her.

"It's okay," she whispered to him.

"It's not," he growled. "I should have ended her complaints about you weeks ago."

She lifted a hand to his face, the bristles along his jaw tickling her palms. "She's not wrong."

"Of course she is. Did you do anything to gain these powers? Before you felt the emotions of that first storm—were you under some enchantment? Did you utilize some magic without telling us?"

"No, but—"

"Then whatever this gift is, you were born with it. Which means while it might be rare, it *is* natural."

"Locke . . ." She should tell him about the souls she could sense around them. Maybe then he would understand that this *gift*, as he called it, was too dangerous. Too much. Born with it or not, it did not feel natural to be able to manipulate spirits in such a way.

Before she could find the words, Sly continued her complaints. "I'm not saying she is evil. But you have to admit we know very little about her. Between us, we have decades of experience with storms. We come from all over Caelira—cities and wilds alike. In all that time, there have only ever been two people with these abilities. Roar. And a man who single-handedly destroyed an entire kingdom. We would be fools to trust her blindly."

Roar pushed out of the trees and past Locke, saying, "What did you say?"

Sly spun around, her mouth open with shock, and for a moment *fear* flickered in her eyes. Roar recoiled, and Locke was there behind her, hands at her waist.

"I—I only meant—"

"There's someone else like me?"

It was Locke who answered, his voice low and soothing. "It's only rumors. We know nothing for certain."

"Tell me the rumors." When Locke did not continue, she turned to Duke. He had always been willing to answer her questions. "Duke?"

The old man cleared his throat, and Locke's grip at her waist tightened. Duke said, "The minister in Toleme, he was afraid when he saw the skyfire in you. He had heard rumors of a man who held a storm in his chest like you do now. That man could command storms and used them to wipe out a city."

Roar gasped. "Calibah? Is that why the storms there were so relentless?"

Duke drew back, shock and even a little horror in his expression. His voice shook and his eyes darted wildly as he said, "I—no, not Calibah. But . . ." The man trailed off with a quiet curse, and his scarred hands shook as he covered his mouth.

"It was Locke," Jinx finished. "Apparently, the city was demolished by storms from the sea."

"What?" Roar's head spun and that instability she felt in her soul— like it might slip outside her—flared up again. Suddenly, the souls that surrounded them were too close, and she choked on the air in her lungs. Her skin went slick with cold as all those souls reached out for her, as if they wanted *inside* her.

"ENOUGH!" The skyfire in her chest shone bright and solid, not flickering, but beaming. The badgering souls disappeared and it took all her strength to stay standing.

"Roar?" Locke yelled. "Roar, what's happening?"

"See!" Sly shouted. "This is what I meant. She is an *aberration*."

Locke snarled, "I have always considered you a friend, Sly. But say that again, and I'll not hesitate to make you my enemy."

"Quiet. All of you." Duke stepped into the middle of the group, his expression fierce and disappointed. "This is not how we behave. The battle is out there, not here between us. Sly, some would say the storms themselves are an aberration. And you've spent your life showing them respect. You will provide the same courtesy to Roar. Locke, I understand how you feel, my boy. But love's first inclination cannot be to war. Calm yourself. And we will figure this out together."

The light in Roar's chest flickered, went soft, and disappeared. Then Duke turned to her. "Roar—we need to know what you can and cannot do so that we can decide how to move forward." Locke tensed, and Duke added, "Together. Perhaps we can take her back to the witch for advice."

"We can't," Jinx cut it. "Avira told me she was leaving, and she would not tell me to where." The earth witch turned to Roar and said, "She told me to tell you—listen to the souls, but do not let them in. And whatever you do, hold tight to your own."

"What is that supposed to mean? Why didn't she tell *me* that?" Locke asked.

Jinx lifted an eyebrow. "Because you were out the door as soon as she said Roar would wake."

"I know what it means," Roar whispered. But she wasn't sure she knew how to accomplish that last piece of advice.

Her eyes strayed to Duke, who watched her with curiosity tinged by sadness. "Well?" he asked. "Can you do it? Call a storm?"

She brushed away Locke's protective hands. "I can."

"How?" he asked. "What do you have to do?"

She glanced at Sly, uneasy with revealing the information in front of the hunter, but they would have to know eventually.

"I only know how I did it before. I'm not sure if there's another way. But in Toleme, I did it unintentionally. When my blood touched something connected with a storm."

"The altar," Jinx said. "It was made of fulgurite. Formed by skyfire."

Roar nodded. "It works with Stormhearts too."

"How do you know?" Duke asked.

Rather than explaining, Roar asked, "Where are my things? The clothes I wore before?"

Jinx retrieved her pack for her, and Roar dug through the contents until she found the pants she'd worn before, and inside the pocket, her fingers closed around the twister ring. Souls brushed against her again, and she imagined her skin as armor, blocking them out and trapping her own soul inside. Her heart glowed solid again, and she heard the others shift nervously around her.

She pulled out the ring, and let it dangle by the chain.

"Twister," Ransom breathed. "That was *you*?"

"Not the first," she said. "At least not that I know of. But the second, the one in Toleme, yes, I believe that was me. I was not aware of what I was doing, I promise. I'm sorry. So very sorry."

Locke moved behind her, curling a hand around the back of her neck and whispering in her ear, "It's not your fault. You don't have to apologize."

"If it was an accident before," Ransom said, "how do you know you can do it again?"

She turned her head to look at Locke, wishing she had made time to tell him before, when they were alone, but there was nothing to be done about that now.

"Since I woke, I have been even more . . . *sensitive.*" When they continued staring at her, she sighed and explained, "There are souls around us. Everywhere. They're part of the earth, of nature. But I'm aware of them and am able to interact if I choose." And sometimes without her consent. "I believe I could consciously choose a soul to tie to a storm."

They were all silent, and she was hesitant to meet their eyes. She would rather look at the ring, spinning at the end of the chain she still held. But she could not stop herself from looking at Locke, worried even now that he would change his mind about her. "I hate it when you look at me like that," he whispered. "Like you're afraid of me."

"Only afraid you'll stop being so blind to my faults."

"Not blind, princess. Realistic. It's you who doesn't see yourself clearly."

She wanted to kiss him, wanted to crawl up his body and wrap herself around him, and let him block out the world.

But she couldn't. "You said Locke was destroyed. Do you know when?"

Did the Locke family even know? What if even now they waited in Pavan, searching for her, while their home and all their loved ones who remained behind were gone?

Duke looked to Jinx and Locke, and the former said, "Avira did not say when. She only confirmed that it happened. Considering it's the Rage season, communication between cities is understandably slow, and with Locke communication was frequently nonexistent, so the absence of it would not tell us much. Could have been recent or months ago. Who knows?"

"Surely, it was a recent development," Roar said, "or we would not have run into a company of Locke soldiers only days ago. Nor would the entire royal family be visiting Pavan."

"What do you mean the entire family?" Locke asked.

"In Pavan. For the wedding. The king, queen, and both princes were set to attend." Quickly she lied, "I saw them when the processional came through the city."

"That can't be right," Locke said. "Why would the entire family attend the wedding and leave Locke unprotected? Surely only Prince Casimir would be needed."

"You mean Cassius," Roar corrected.

"No, Cassius is the firstborn. As heir he *should* have stayed in Locke."

Roar started to argue again, but held her tongue. Locke had been destroyed. The entire royal family was in Pavan. She remembered the mocking tone of Casimir's voice when he called Cassius *little brother*. She'd overheard Cassius's plans to manipulate her; he'd even mentioned something about his father and a plan. She collapsed, retching with horror; her stomach twisted and jerked, as if trying to wring itself out, but there was nothing in it to expel.

Oh skies. Cassius did not want to marry into the throne. He wanted to seize it, to replace the one they'd lost.

"We must return to Pavan. Now. Something . . . something is very wrong."

They rode out immediately from Taraanar, despite complaints from Sly. Locke did not know what troubled Roar, nor would she tell him, but he knew she was distraught over something. And he and Duke both trusted her enough to follow her word without explanation. When they made camp the first night, she did not bother trying to set up her own tent but crawled into his. She clung to him tightly and when he tried to get her to talk, she silenced him with a kiss.

"Please," she whispered against his mouth. "Help me forget."

He did not know what he was helping her to forget, but he hated seeing the hurt and fear in her eyes, and if he could ease that . . . he would do anything.

He pushed no further than he had by the river. He did not want their first time together to be when she was upset. But he distracted her with his mouth, with his hands on her skin, with tender words spoken against the rapid flicker of the light in her chest.

And eventually, the tension in her eased, the fear fled from her eyes, and she went soft in his arms. He held her for a while, but neither of them drifted toward sleep.

Nervous, he took a deep breath and said, "I need to tell you something."

She stiffened and asked, "What?"

He almost wished he could take the words back. Already the worry was creeping back into her eyes. He smoothed his fingers over the furrow in her brow and said, "The witch I went to see with Jinx . . ."

She returned his touch, trailing her hand down his cheek to the line of his jaw. "What about her?"

"She told me something."

Roar sat up, the blankets falling to her waist. "A prediction? About me?"

"No, *about me*. She . . . she told me my name."

Roar gasped. "And you are just telling me now? After all my silly nicknames?"

He sat up and took one of her hands between his. "I like your silly names."

"What is it?"

When he hesitated, she shook off his hold and climbed into his lap. Her hands cupped his cheeks and brought their faces close together.

"Tell me," she whispered, followed by a soft kiss. "Tell me what to call the man I love."

His breath caught, and she was already calling storms to life, for there was one inside him now—fierce and proud. She had hinted that she felt the same. Had said it without saying the exact words, and he saw it constantly in her eyes. But hearing it now out of her mouth washed away the last of his doubt.

"It's Kiran," he told her. "My name was Kiran Thorne."

She said the name back to him, and he liked it a great deal more coming from her.

"It's a good name," she said. "Strong. We can ask Sly to be sure, but I think Kiran means 'ray of light' in Vyhodin. And you are very much that." She ended her pronouncement with a quick kiss and added,

"And Thorne would make an appropriately fearsome nickname for a hunter."

He laughed. "Yes, I can't wait for Jinx to call me a thorn in her side."

"I like it." She looped her arms about his neck, drawing their bodies even closer. "Thorns protect the rose. And from the moment we met, you've sought to protect me always."

"And I always will."

She smiled, but it was not as bright as the ones she usually gave him. Fear's hold on her was too tight, even now. She looked at him, her gaze flicking back and forth between his eyes.

"There are things I have not told you," she said. "About my life in Pavan."

He rested his forehead against hers. "I don't care. None of that matters now."

"It will matter again. Soon."

"So then tell me. There's nothing that you could say that would change the way I feel."

Her face scrunched up as if she was in pain, and her voice shook as she said, "I—I am—"

She broke off with a gasp as heat flared between their chests. The crystal she wore around her neck had gone fiery hot, and she scrambled from the tent, barefoot and wearing only one of his tunics. He groped around until he found his harness, and the warning horn he kept attached to it. He blew the horn as he crawled from the tent, pulling the harness over his chest.

It was the dead of night and he could not see whatever storm came for them. The other hunters began scrambling from their tents, supplies in hand, each of them spinning around, trying to find the threat.

"Fog," Roar breathed. "I can feel it. Hungry and sinister. It meant to take us as we slept."

As she spoke, Duke held up a lightning lantern, and then he saw it. They had camped in a small thicket of trees, and swallowing up the branches around them was a thick gray cloud. He spun, but it was all around them, blocking them in.

He retrieved his fog Stormheart, the other hunters that had one following suit.

"Stop!" Roar cried. "Put down your hearts. I can handle this. But it's too confusing to feel all of you."

Locke hesitated and she said, "Kiran, please."

Then he did as she asked, returning the stone to his harness and telling the other hunters to do the same. For a long moment, nothing happened. And his hands itched to take up his Stormheart again, especially when Roar stepped closer to the creeping fog.

But then . . . it began to roll back. Roar marched forward, and with each step the fog retreated farther and farther until he could not see it at all.

The storms continued to come as they made their way toward Pavan, and each time they did Roar made them surrender. As she had learned from the skyfire storm, the connection she felt went both ways. If she was not careful, their souls, their desires could bleed into her. But she could do the same to them. She had sowed fear into the fog, the certainty of its destruction, and it retreated rather than fight. She soothed the rage of a twister until its winds slowed and it broke apart in the sky. She stood in the eye of a firestorm and offered it comfort, even as burning embers rained down around her.

One by one she exerted her will over the storms, and eventually her awareness of the souls around her was so strong, stretched so far that she began to soothe the darkest spirits in the world around them before they could even become storms.

The hunters pressed on toward Pavan, moving far faster than they ever had. And the closer they got to her home, the more malevolent souls she sensed. She tried to soothe them, tried to break the hold of their rage, but they were too twisted, too cold for her to help. When she tried to find some fragment of humanity in them, some piece of who they used to be, she found only bottomless fury. And each of those irredeemable storms had one thing in common. They felt pulled to Pavan, drawn toward something there, bent on the city's destruction.

At Roar's request, the hunters rode even harder, pushing later into the night and setting out earlier in the morning. And when they were only a day's ride from the city, she became aware of huge numbers of souls, streaming toward Pavan. These, however, were still living.

Remnants. By the hundreds. They trudged on by foot, many injured or weeping. There were so many that they covered the road, and the hunters had to slow their pace to weave through the sea of bodies.

They heard whispers among the people of towns leveled, of a madman who wielded storms like swords and cut down everything in his path. They believed the Stormlings were their only hope, the only ones who could stop the carnage.

And when they reached Death's Spine, the rocky outcropping that marked the edge of Pavan territories and overlooked the grasslands that stretched all the way to the golden dome of the palace, Roar's worst fears were confirmed.

At the top of the dome and all along the city walls flew flags of blue.

"Are you all right?" Kiran asked her, wrapping his arms around her and pressing a kiss to her neck. She held tight to his arms, soaking up every bit of warmth he offered. She turned and took a real kiss, pouring every bit of her love and fear and worry into it.

Because it was time.

To say good-bye to Roar.

And become Aurora once more.

EPILOGUE

He wove between the sniveling insects that marched on toward the city, marched toward what they thought would be their salvation. He passed among them unnoticed as they wept over all that they had lost, all that he had taken from them. It suited him to be invisible. It had allowed him to infiltrate town after town, circling Pavan like a bird around its prey.

Soon. Soon they would all know who he was. The goddess's vessel, the tip of her sword, the brunt of her rage.

He wondered if the Lockes were cowering inside their new city. Did they jump at every wail of the wind? Sweat at the sound of thunder? Was their sleep plagued by nightmares of the last time he came for them? Did they remember the howl of the hurricanes closing in from every side? The way the city burned beneath firestorms even as towering waves crashed over their battlements? He would not rest until he had poured out tenfold the amount of agony and horror and despair that they had given him as a boy.

But the Lockes had taught him that fear only compounded over time, it pressed in on you like madness, swallowed you up until you could think of nothing else.

It was not enough to destroy them.

He would make them *want* it, beg for it, hope for an end to their torture.

He reached out to his friends, the tormented souls that mirrored his own, who had followed him all this time, from the jungles of Locke to the grasslands of Pavan. They gathered in the wind, lay in wait in the earth, flowed through the rivers that surrounded the city.

Suddenly, he stopped. Remnants stumbled into him; some even dared to yell in annoyance as they dodged around him. Any other time he would have slaughtered them all on the spot. But his focus was not here. Not on these pitiful souls. It was on a soul far behind him, at the very edge of his consciousness. It was not warped or cruel like the ones he usually sought. Instead, it was bright. *Too bright*. Radiant as skyfire streaking through the night.

But even so . . . this soul . . . this soul was like *his*.

ACKNOWLEDGMENTS

I'm not even sure where to begin. The journey toward this book started over a decade ago. I've written and published other books, all of which I loved immensely. But since I was a teenager it was my dream to write a YA novel. I took several amazing detours before getting here, but I am so grateful to have had the chance to fulfill this dream (and hopefully continue it).

First, I must thank my family. I could fill a whole other book with all the ways you have loved and supported me over the last decade, and yet those words would never be enough. The year 2016 especially was the most difficult year of my life, and I could not have survived it without you. To my mother: thank you for instilling in me a love for reading, writing, and great characters. To my sisters: we fell in love with YA together, and you encouraged me from the very first time I put pen to paper. For my father: thanks for killing all the spiders and, you know, all the other multitudes of ways you keep me sane, safe, and healthy.

To Lindsay, my dearest friend: No books would ever get finished without you. Mainly because I always insist they're garbage until you tell me otherwise. To Jay: Every time I thought this book would kill me, you picked me up and set me straight. I adore you. To all the other dear friends who better my life and books—Bethany, Joey, Shelly, Jennifer, Ana, Amber, Zach, Heather—a thousand times thank you.

Also thanks to Suzie Townsend, Sara Stricker, and all the other New Leaf Ninjas for all the tremendous work you do. Whitney Ross and the team at Tor Teen: You took a chance on me and this book sight unseen, and I'm still stunned and humbled by your faith in me. And I'm even more grateful for the patience and support you showed me during a difficult year.

And to everyone reading this book, thank you for making my dreams come true.

ABOUT THE AUTHOR

Cora Carmack is a *New York Times* and *USA Today* bestselling author. Since she was a teenager, her favorite genre to read has been fantasy, and now she's thrilled to bring her usual compelling characters and swoon-worthy romance into the worlds of magic and intrigue with her debut YA fantasy, *Roar*. Her previous adult romance titles include *Losing It* and the Rusk University and Muse series. Her books have been translated into more than a dozen languages around the world. Cora splits her time between Austin, Texas, and New York City, and on any given day you might find her typing away at her computer, flying to various cities around the world, or just watching Netflix with her kitty, Katniss. But she can always be found on Twitter, Facebook, Instagram, Pinterest, Tumblr, and her website www.coracarmack.com.